YA Harmon SS
Harmonious hearts

$16.99
ocn899137912
First edition.

HARMONIOUS
HEARTS

A HARMONY INK PRESS
ANTHOLOGY

DISCARDED

Harmony Ink

Published by
HARMONY INK PRESS

5032 Capital Circle SW, Suite 2, PMB# 279, Tallahassee, FL 32305-7886 USA
publisher@harmonyinkpress.com • http://harmonyinkpress.com

This is a work of fiction. Names, characters, places, and incidents either are the product of author imagination or are used fictitiously, and any resemblance to actual persons, living or dead, business establishments, events, or locales is entirely coincidental.

Harmonious Hearts
© 2014 Harmony Ink Press.
Edited by Anne Regan.

Cigar, Parasol, Star © 2014 Laura Beaird.
Counting Stars © 2014 L.A. Buchanan.
The King of Dorkdom © 2014 Avery Burrow.
Happy Endings Take Work © 2014 Morgan Cair.
Tess © 2014 Becca Ehlers.
Our First Anniversary © 2014 Trisha Harrington.
The Dragon Princess © 2014 Eleanor Hawtin.
An IRL Love Life © 2014 Rebecca Long.
On Their Own Terms © 2014 D. William Pfifer.
The Gift of Flame © 2014 Scotia Roth.
Glitterhead © 2014 Benjamin Shepherd Quiñones.
City Lights Will Carry You Home © 2014 Amanda Reed.
Waiting © 2014 Annie Schoonover.
Quiet Love © 2014 Gil Segev.
Paranormal Honor Society © 2014 Leigh Taylor.

Cover Art
© 2014 by Aaron Anderson.
aaronbydesign55@gmail.com
Cover content is for illustrative purposes only and any person depicted on the cover is a model.

ISBN: 978-1-63216-186-4
Library Edition ISBN: 978-1-63216-187-1
Digital ISBN: 978-1-63216-188-8
Library of Congress Control Number: 2014940254
First Edition July 2014
Library Edition October2014

Printed in the United States of America
∞
This paper meets the requirements of
ANSI/NISO Z39.48-1992 (Permanence of Paper).

TABLE OF CONTENTS

INTRODUCTION

Welcome to the first annual Harmony Ink Press Young Author Challenge anthology, *Harmonious Hearts*.

When the editorial staff came up with the idea of a short-story challenge aimed at young authors writing LGBTQ themes, we had no real idea what to expect. We were more than pleased with the response—over sixty entries from teens and young adults around the world. Selecting the stories to appear in this anthology was a challenge in itself, though I'm sure you'll enjoy the results.

The authors in this volume range in age from sixteen to twenty-one. Their voices are sometimes humorous, sometimes heartbreaking, but always genuine. For many, it is their first professional publication, but I suspect it will not be their last.

If you're a young writer yourself, or know someone who is, we'll be looking for you in future Young Author Challenges. Please watch for information at www.harmonyinkpress.com.

In the meantime, enjoy meeting this group of young writers.

Anne Regan
Executive Editor, Harmony Ink Press

AN IRL LOVE LIFE
REBECCA LONG

THERE WAS something fascinating about Jaime Lane.

I never did figure out what it was that sparked my obsession with him—his looks, perhaps? Maybe it was his acting—how he could immerse himself in a role so fully, so perfectly that you found yourself looking at a completely different person each time.

All I know is this: when I watched *A Danger to Discern*, I became obsessed with Jaime Lane.

First were the pictures: photographs the paparazzi had snapped the instant they caught a glimpse of him, behind-the-scenes looks, or screen shots of his different movies. I looked them all up—I combed through the Internet and printed out almost every single one I could find, and when the ink ran out, I went to the library to print the rest. Then I pored over each one, examining his chiseled face, that beautifully muscled torso, those long legs and big hands. I kept all the pictures hidden in an old shoebox that I pushed to the farthest, darkest corner under my bed.

To understand Jaime Lane, one must first understand *A Danger to Discern*. I read somewhere that Jaime's character in *ADtD*, Zane Baker, was most like Jaime's actual personality. This bit of information made me positively giddy. I did, after all, first become fascinated with Zane Baker.

The character is an ex-con—a man who just got out of prison after pulling off a multimillion-dollar heist when he was only seventeen years old. He's street smart and quick thinking and always has something witty to say. There are brief moments when he comes across as arrogant, but it's more funny than annoying, as he never uses his arrogance to insult people. I loved that. I loved everything about him. But until 1:22:17 in

ADtD, Zane Baker was just a funny character. Then he became so much more than that.

That was when I became obsessed with Jaime Lane.

I'm not really sure what was so significant about that scene. It was—well, it was a sex scene, but that didn't mean anything. I had seen other sex scenes before, in a ton of other movies. I had seen *The Terminator*, for God's sake, and I didn't blink an eye at that sex scene. It wasn't even graphic. I got a glimpse of Jaime's back and that was it. Suddenly I had the urge to see every single picture of him that existed. I had the urge to watch everything he was in.

I watched *ADtD* a few more times after that. I paid close attention to the sex scene, trying to see what I found so interesting about Jaime. But I couldn't come up with anything. It was just... the way it was.

My mother came home after a few hours to repossess the television, and so I moved to the computer and began my search for pictures. I scrolled through page after page on Google; then I tried another search engine. I printed out a few pages, cut off the white borders carefully, and put them in a careful stack on my desk.

In the hours following The Great Picture Search, I made a list of all the movies he'd been in. I wrote down the year each one came out and Jaime's age next to that, and then I stapled it to a screenshot from that movie.

Looking back now, I realize how unhealthy this all was. But at the time, it was perfectly normal. I was a fan. A fan who was a little more involved than most fans, but a fan nonetheless.

Finding the shoebox was an interesting experience. I had already printed over fifty pictures before I had the brilliant epiphany that it would not be a good idea for somebody in my family to find them, and I should probably find a good hiding place for them. I had developed a sort of possessiveness over Jaime—nobody in my family had seen *ADtD* yet, and I had no intention of letting them find him.

He was mine. All mine.

My first thought was to hide them under my mattress in a rubber-banded stack. But soon it became obvious that I had too many papers for that. The next option was to put them into the back of my closet, behind my shoes and clothes, but I ruled that out almost immediately. I was careless with the contents of my closet, and I worried the photographs would get wrinkled—they would be ruined.

I was stressing out over this. I was doing the whole crazy-person thing where I paced around the room and rubbed my face until it was red. The obvious solution—and this came suddenly into my head at three in the morning—was to put them in something. Like an envelope. Or a box.

It was sad how much my face lit up over this. I leaped out of bed—this was the middle of the night, remember; my mother was sound asleep, my sister, Katy, at a sleepover—and began searching the house for a box.

I finally found one in Katy's room—it was pink and decorated with cartoon flowers and colorful dots of printed confetti. I scribbled it all out with a big black marker, and the pictures went in.

The next few weeks were dominated by watching Jaime's movies. I went down my list several times and wrote down every description of his character with my favorite quotes and the movie dates paper clipped to it. They went in the box too.

Precisely two months after discovering the existence of Jaime Lane, I found the fan fiction.

Dear God, there was so much of it. Entire stories—entire novels, sometimes—based around a single fandom, created by fans. It was overwhelming. The most popular of these was called "Kane"—a sort of ship of Zane Baker and the villain of *ADtD*, Krazy Lars. I liked these. I printed out my favorites, and these, too, went in the box. I read a lot of these, in my free time, when I wasn't watching videos. But I avoided AU—alternate universe—fan fiction. I didn't like people changing Jaime, making him sullen or goth or arrogant to the point where he was annoying. All that made me uncomfortable. I couldn't handle it.

After three days of reading fan fiction after fan fiction, I got an account and started rating, commenting, and making suggestions.

I got an e-mail after a few weeks of this. A personal message from a member of the fan fiction site with the username "i<3zaneb@ker." It said:

Dear afra!D,

I could not help but notice your frequent commenting and ratings on AO3.

AO3 was the fan fiction website I frequented.

I have also, however, noticed your suggestions to other authors. This is, no doubt, one of the main reasons why you have such a large number of followers. People enjoy reading your ideas and insight. It is no surprise that I do, as well. Every day, I interrupt myself to check if you posted anything. I do so adore how that brain of yours works. One thing, however, puzzles me. You are obviously immersed in all Jaime Lane-related fandoms, and you always have good ideas for fan fics. Why is it, then, that you do not write any?

Here, i<3zaneb@ker inserted excerpts of some of my comments.

I beg of you to consider pursuing this. You probably get a lot of mail, and probably won't even read this. But if you do, please send a message my way containing your decision. Thank you for your time.

Sincerely, your greatest fan,

Henry

I replied to the e-mail with a fan fiction in which Zane Baker met a character from another of his movies, a man named Tyson Perry. At the end of the e-mail, I typed:

You are the spark to my revolution.

Thank you for believing in me.

—I

When I received his glowing response, I published the fan fic at the website. Then another. The ideas were pouring out constantly. Then I was drawing art I didn't know I was even capable of. I wasn't an artsy person—not because I wasn't good at it, but because I thought I was too cool to draw. These pieces included detailed profiles, charcoal-smudged nudes (I thought this was odd, but I got a ton of requests for it), and scenes from different movies.

The art I made—both the drawings and the fics—got an awesome response. People loved them. The most dislikes on any piece, I am proud to say, was ten, and that was a small percentage of the people who liked it.

As I posted more drawings and fics onto the website, I got more requests. People wanted me to draw them into the pictures. A few wanted a picture of them having sex with the guy.

For a little while I refused to do it. I didn't draw specialized pictures for people because I still felt a little possessive.

Then I got another e-mail from i<3zaneb@ker with a request to be drawn in with Jaime. He wanted to be kissing him in it.

I sent a reply asking for his picture.

When it came I stared at it for some time before picking up my pencils.

Henry—which was i<3zaneb@ker's name in real life—was very tall and had carefully sculpted muscles, narrow hips, and broad shoulders. His face was long, and he had a wide mouth and a Roman nose and deep brown eyes framed by long lashes.

Henry was, to put it simply, beautiful.

Once I had examined his face and the shape of his body, I set to work on the drawing. I drew them both in the hotel room in *ADtD*. I rumpled the floral-patterned comforter, made the painting on the wall hang crooked. Henry I drew lying flat on his back, and I drew Jaime Lane bending over him, his lips tantalizingly close to Henry's.

When I was done, I set it aside and drew another. This was set in the dark forests of another of Jaime's movies, *Dying Again*. I placed Jaime, standing, pressed up against the rough trunk of a tree, lips locked with Henry, who was wrapped around him.

It wasn't until my hands started making marks on the paper that I realized I was sweating.

Why was I sweating? Because I was a teenage boy. And I had an attraction to a certain somebody. But all I thought at the time was *What the hell is going on with me?*

The next day, I sent Henry the two pictures. The reply came almost immediately:

afra!D, I have never seen something more beautiful than this. This is so much more than what I asked for. I love it. You made this school day bearable.

School? I checked his picture. He didn't look like he would be in high school. Maybe he was talking about college.

Henry sent another message:

I think if I wasn't the gayest kid in this class, I might be in love with you.

I didn't quite know what that was supposed to mean, but before I could ask, there was:

Don't go to college. Huge mistake. Take it from a fellow obsessed.

I sent *I'll remember that* because I didn't know what else to say.

Henry and I continued speaking, trading e-mails and IMs. We became very good friends. When I wasn't reading fan fiction, I was talking to Henry, or I was doing both at the same time and discussing it with him if he had the time to pull it up too.

Almost exactly a year after I first watched *ADtD* and began my fascination with Jaime Lane, my mother decided to look for socks.

If Henry was the spark to my revolution, this occurrence was the douse of water to my flame.

When I came home from school, I could hear my mother speaking on the phone in my bedroom to somebody—a somebody I later learned was Conrad. Conrad, the bastard who kept me up every night from the moment I learned what the shouting and yelling and bruises on my mother's skin meant.

"I wasn't *snooping*," she was saying. "I was looking for *socks*. I was doing the *laundry*."

I froze in the hallway and peered through the thin crack between my door and the wall.

My heart stopped.

I couldn't breathe.

She was holding my box.

My obsession was in there—my life's purpose was in that box.

"No," my mother was saying. She pulled out one of my drawings of Jaime—a portrait—and blinked at it. "Conrad, listen. He's obsessed. You should see all of this—he's writing about this man and drawing him, and there are so many pictures…."

My fists clenched. If she didn't stop riffling through that, I might go in there. I might hit her. I had never felt this kind of violence before. And now, years later, I can't remember a moment I am more ashamed of.

"Conrad," my mother whispered. "This is why he is doing so badly in school. He needs help. Whenever he went into his room, he said he was doing homework or taking a nap. I never thought…." She stopped speaking for a moment. "Please. We need to find him a psychiatrist or a therapist or a shrink or something. He's pulling away from us, Conrad.

He's putting himself into this fantasy." Another pause. "Who's the man? I have no—"

I pushed open the door. My mom started. She looked up at me with wide eyes, and my box dropped to my bed.

"What are you doing in my room?" My voice was stony.

"Isaac, what is this?" She gestured to the box. I continued staring at her.

"What. Are you doing. In my room?"

She shrank backward. "I was looking for socks," she said. "And— and I found—"

"Why would there be socks in there?" I pointed at the box. "Who puts socks in a cardboard box? Nobody. People actually use laundry baskets every now and then. News flash."

My mother's gaze darted to my bed. "Isaac, I think you need help."

"I don't need help," I said. "I need my family to stay out of my things." I grabbed the box, shoved what had fallen out back in, and clutched it to my chest.

"Who is he? That man?"

Jaime Lane. His name was on the tip of my tongue. My chest ached. But I said instead, "A person. Just leave me alone."

My mom crossed her arms, trying to make her small form seem bigger and more threatening, even though I was, like, a foot taller than her. "This isn't healthy. I'm calling a psychiatrist for you."

"I don't need a psychiatrist."

"You've stopped hanging out with your friends, and you're doing badly in school."

"I'm doing just fine in school," I said. "I have only one D. The rest are Cs and B minuses."

"But Isaac. Your *friends*. Why don't you have *friends*?"

I had no response to this. I didn't have any friends—well, not ones she knew existed. I had Henry and a few other fans I e-mailed every now and then. They were my friends.

My mother persisted. "You need help. You're obsessed." She shook her head sadly. "I wish you would talk to me, Isaac."

"And I wish you would leave me alone. Funny how the world works, right?" My voice became low and dangerous. "Get out of my room."

She left.

After that, I thought I would be left alone. I thought she was bluffing about calling somebody. But only two days later, I was sitting in front of a curvy woman with a scarf wrapped around her neck. I sat slumped in my chair, my hands twisting in my lap. The woman—her name tag said Lacey Tan, which seemed kind of Asian, but she didn't look the part—smiled a little at me. She wrote my name on the top of her yellow pad notebook, then the date underneath.

"So, Isaac," she said, stretching out the *o* in "so." "Your mother tells me that you... have an interest. One that worries her." There were questions at the end of those statements.

I stayed silent.

"I can't help you if you don't talk to me," Lacey said.

"I don't need help," I snarled. "I told my mother this, and I told Conrad this, so it isn't my fault they didn't freaking listen."

Lacey scribbled something onto her notepad. The handwriting was too messy to read upside down. "Who is Conrad?" she asked.

"His sperm contributed to the beginning of my existence," I said. "His money occasionally supported my being raised."

"He is your father, then?"

"I wouldn't call him that. He's a crappy dad."

"Does he live with you?"

"No. He moved out four years ago."

"How is he 'a crappy dad'?"

"He drinks too much. Doesn't care about anybody but himself. Works too much. Et cetera."

"Et cetera?"

"I'm not the only one who doesn't want to see him ever again," I said, raising an eyebrow at her.

"Is he abusive?"

"Not to me. Not right now." My mother's bruises, all over her back, lining her arms like tattoos, scraped across my mind like a blade.

"But to somebody else?" When I didn't answer, she let out a soft breath and wrote a few words on her notebook. "Do you have anybody you can talk to, Isaac?"

I thought about it. I thought about all the conversations I'd had with Henry.

"I have... a friend," I said.

"A friend? Okay. What's their name?"

"Henry. We talk sometimes."

"Your mother told me that you didn't have friends. Do you never go to his house? Does he never visit?"

"Uh. No. I've never actually met him. We first started talking online." I shrugged. "We e-mail and IM now, mostly."

"Have you ever called Henry and spoken to him on the phone?"

"No."

"Do you know what he looks like?"

"Yeah. Yeah, of course. He asks me to draw him sometimes so I have tons of pictures of him."

"Draw him? Portraits or action scenes or what?"

My hands clenched.

"Or do you want to keep that between you and Henry?"

"Yeah," I said. "Can't tell you."

"That's fine," said Lacey. "I can't expect you to tell me everything on the first day." She put her notebook down, then her pen. "Listen, Isaac. I like you. I think you're a great kid. You're smart, and you have a great sense of humor—"

I stopped her. "Humor? I'm not trying to be funny."

"And I haven't laughed." Lacey tapped the side of her head. "I know these things. I know you're a great kid. I know you feel like you're misunderstood—so misunderstood that you feel you can only turn to a person you met online and Jaime Lane."

I gaped. Lacey smiled.

"Your mother took one of the pictures and showed it to me. Who couldn't recognize him?" She handed me a folded piece of paper—it was one of my earlier drawings, a portrait. "It's yours," Lacey said. "And it's very good."

I raised my eyebrows in the paper's direction, a little surprised at the gesture. "Thank you."

"You don't have to," said Lacey, "but I'd like you to come back. To talk about your feelings, or even to talk about *A Danger to Discern*. You're the kind of person I want to be friends with. Okay?"

"You aren't a regular therapist, are you?" I asked.

She smiled wryly. "I would hope not. I like to think I'm special— you know, the new age of therapists that have a normal conversation instead of the Spanish inquisition."

"Well, it's nice."

"Thank you. So what do you say? You okay with being friends?"

"I'm okay with it," I said.

The next day after school, instead of going home, I went to visit Lacey.

My box was in my backpack. Better to be caught with it than have somebody look through it while I wasn't there.

Lacey wasn't busy with anybody when I walked into her office. She had the same scarf on but a different shirt and skirt.

"Isaac." She sounded pleasantly surprised. "You came back."

"I guess so." I sat down in the cushioned chair facing her and dropped my backpack between two jean-clad legs.

"What do you want to talk about?" She hadn't even picked up her notebook yet.

I leaned toward her, resting my elbows on my knees. "What do you know about Jaime Lane?"

"Jaime? Only that he's one of the most attractive people on the face of this earth. He starred as the main character in twenty-three movies, an extra in four, and a suspect in seven television murder-mystery shows."

I stared at her. She grinned and loosened her scarf. "I had a phase a few years ago. I was completely obsessed."

"Obsessed? Really. Did you write fan fiction?"

"Of course I did," Lacey said, smiling. "I didn't really put much of it online, but I definitely wrote it. My username was seriously *save_me_jaimelane*."

I snorted. "You are such a liar. You commented on some of my fan fics the other day."

She held up her hands. "You caught me."

"I can promise you one thing, though," I said. And without even thinking about it or considering the consequences, I pulled out my box and pushed it toward her. "You weren't this obsessed."

Lacey opened the box and lifted the drawing she had just returned the day before. She set it on the table, then began looking through all the other pictures, drawings, and fan fictions I had stuffed in there.

She paused at the drawing I'd done of Henry and Jaime in the forest. She looked up at me. "Who is the other boy?"

"Henry," I said very quietly. There was something in her eyes I couldn't read.

"These are the drawings he asked you to do." It didn't sound like a question, so I didn't answer. She pulled out the hotel room scene. "These are beautiful," Lacey said. "Simply beautiful. Very passionate."

I frowned, not sure what to say. "Yeah, I guess so."

"Is Henry gay?"

I thought back to his messages. "Yes."

"I thought so." Lacey put everything back into my box carefully, like they were precious to her. "Can I speak freely, Isaac?"

"Yeah, sure."

"I believe I know why you're so fixated with Jaime Lane. It's the same reason I was. Probably the same reason Henry is." She took in a breath. "I think it's a celebrity crush, Isaac."

"What?" I opened and closed my mouth, like a fish. "What?"

"Are you gay, Isaac? It's okay to tell me."

I stared at her. "I don't know."

But what if I was?

I remembered the sweat on my hands while drawing Henry and Jaime.

It made an awful lot of sense.

Lacey let me go after that, telling me to "think about" what she'd said.

I thought about it. On the bus ride home, with the smelly octogenarian next to me, then at the dinner table, where Katy and my mother shot me concerned glances and Katy said "Isaaaac, stop looking so creeeepy," and in my room, lying on the rumpled covers my box had been thrown on a few days before.

Was I gay?

I wasn't sure anymore.

Two days later I decided I would visit Lacey again. I skipped first period and instead went straight to her office.

Somebody was there.

That somebody sat with his back to me, facing Lacey, who was scribbling something onto her yellow notepad. "Well," she said, "I'll see you next week?"

"Sure," said the guy. His voice was deep and sounded like both gravel and honey. He stood. "I think I'm going to tell you about this person I met online."

"A girl or a boy?"

"A girl. I'm pretty sure."

I smiled a little at this. Seems he had online friend problems too.

Then he turned around. And I recognized him—in fact, I knew almost every inch of his wonderful body.

"Henry," I breathed. He frowned at me.

"Do I know you?"

"Isaac!" Lacey called, her voice delighted. "Come on in. Henry, do you have another moment to spare?"

Henry was still staring at me, frowning slightly. "Sure," he said. "Maybe half an hour, at the most."

"Wonderful."

Henry and I both sat in matching cushioned chairs. I dropped my backpack.

"It seems you two know each other," said Lacey.

"I don't know any Isaac," said Henry.

"afra!D," I whispered. He stared at me.

"What did you just say?"

"That's who I am. afra!D. I drew you." I opened my box and fumbled with the papers inside, trying to reach the ones that I had done for him. "I drew these."

Henry took them. His eyes widened. *"You* are afra!D? I thought you were a chick."

I offered him a small smile. "No. I'm Isaac."

Lacey was grinning from ear to ear. "Why don't you boys go out for coffee? I'm sure you have some things to catch up on."

Henry's eyes lit up. "Sure. You wanna do that, Isaac?"

"Sure, sure." I packed up my box and looked toward Lacey. "I guess I'll see you tomorrow?"

"I don't think that'll be necessary," she said. "But if you like, we can do that."

I left with Henry, and we went to the coffee shop.

"God," said Henry after a few minutes of silence. "I'm sorry for staring at you earlier. It's just that you are so goddamn gorgeous."

My face got hot. Was I blushing? "Thanks."

"How old are you?"

"Seventeen."

"Damn. Still a minor. I'm twenty."

I nodded. Henry went to the counter. "One black," he said, "one grande quad nonfat one-pump no-whip mocha." For some reason, he had memorized what my favorite drink was from a post I once made. That made me ridiculously happy, and I couldn't help letting out a quiet laugh as we sat down at our table.

"What I said, in that e-mail," Henry said. "That I might be in love with you. I meant it."

I sipped my coffee.

Henry grinned down at his cup. "I thought I was becoming straight. Which was terrifying. I mean, not that being straight is bad, but I've known I was gay since I was seven, y'know? That's kind of a big change." He took a long, calculating drink from the mug. "Now you're a guy—well, now I know that you're a guy—and I want nothing more than to kiss that beautiful mouth of yours."

I swallowed.

"I'm sorry if I'm making you uncomfortable."

"No," I said. "I'm fine. I just… well, I thought I was straight until two days ago."

Henry laughed. "You thought you were straight? You were drawing pictures of guys making out with each other. How is that, in any way, straight?"

I shrugged and sipped my coffee more. Henry sighed.

"I'm sorry. That wasn't very nice of me. I just want to have a good life, y'know? You, Isaac... you're my dream come true. I'd like to try out a relationship with you." He gave me a shy smile. It was adorable.

I wanted to kiss it.

It was then that I realized how already in love I was with Henry.

"I think I can do that," I said.

Henry laughed and rubbed his face. "Okay, wow. I've sent, like, a ton of pictures of myself to you, and this is the first time I've seen your face. This is weird for me."

"Don't be ashamed. I think you're beautiful."

Henry smiled. "Not as beautiful as Jaime Lane, though, right? One can always hope."

I didn't answer. The truth was, I was already drawing away from my fascination with Jaime Lane. I was already out of the Jaime Lane fandom.

I was in the Henry fandom now.

I left that coffee shop with a smile on my face, Henry's cell number written on my hand, and plans for a date.

School—the three weeks left—flew by. I barely paid any attention. When I got home, the smile still hadn't left my face.

But it did when I opened the door.

My mother was crying on the living room floor, with Conrad's voice blaring through the speaker phone.

"I *told* you not to take him to the therapist!" Conrad bellowed. "Do you want him to fail in life, you miserable—"

I picked up the phone and turned down the volume, then held it to my ear. "Conrad," I said calmly.

"Isaac? What—"

"If you abuse my mother again, I swear to God I will call the cops on you. Try coming by the house, and I will have you arrested. Do you understand?"

Conrad spit a curse at me. "You think you're so tough now—"

There was something about my meeting Henry that made me feel stronger. It made me feel like I could finally stop Conrad's abuse. So I said, "I'm not joking. Try me."

And then I hung up.

My mother was staring at me and sniffling. "Isaac? Are you okay?"

I pulled out my box and stared at a year's collection of my obsession. "What I said the other night," I said, "I'm sorry about that. Completely uncalled for and rude of me." I dropped the box into the trash can. "But thanks for asking. I'm perfectly fine." Then I went to my room.

The next day at dinner, the table was deadly silent all throughout the meal. We scraped, chewed, swallowed, repeat. It wasn't until I got up and grabbed my coat that my mother said something.

"Are you going somewhere?" There was no accusatory tinge to her tone, no hint of warning. It seemed she had begun to trust me.

"Yeah," I said. "Going to the movies."

"By yourself?" She sounded worried. She had almost refused to let me go to school that day, thinking Conrad would try coming after me for what I'd said.

"No. I have a date."

Her eyes lit up, and even Katy tore her gaze from her phone to look at me. "A date? With who?"

"You haven't met him. His name is Henry." I shrugged my jacket on.

"Is Henry a nice boy?" my mother asked quietly.

"He is very nice. I think he'll be good for me." I looked meaningfully at the trash can. "He's already helped me." I had only kept two pictures—the first two I drew for Henry. They were in an envelope in my desk.

My mother's smile was wide—so wide it looked like it hurt.

"You're okay with this?" I asked.

"Isaac…." Her eyes filled with tears, but she was still smiling. "Of course I'm okay with it. Of course. I want you to be happy, and if Henry makes you happy, I'm completely okay. I love you, Isaac. Nothing can change that."

"I… ah… love you too." The words felt strange in my mouth, but they also felt right. I opened the door. "I'll be home in a few hours."

"Be careful," my mom called out. "Have fun."

Henry was as beautiful as always. Black beanie, button-up shirt, fitted jeans. We watched our movie—an action movie, which was strange for me, as I had not seen one without Jaime in over a year—then went to the park and lounged on the benches.

"I told my mom," I said finally.

"You came out to her?"

"I guess you could call it that."

Henry laughed. I love his laugh, even today—deep and rumbling and wonderful. I wanted to make him laugh more.

"It's weird, isn't it?" he asked, giving me a sideways glance. "You and me, having the same therapist? What kind of universe is that cool? I thought you would be all the way across the country. Or maybe the world. I have that kind of luck." He laughed again, and just when I was about to reply, he was suddenly serious. "Look, Isaac," he said. "I want nothing more than to kiss you. I want to touch you, and you have no idea how difficult it is to resist that. I'm in love with you, and I don't even know that much about you." He reached out, very carefully, and touched his fingertips to the knuckles of my hand. I laced my fingers with his. "I want to take it slow, okay?" he said. "I want to know you. When I say that I love you, I want to mean that I love everything about you, not just what I know about you, okay?"

"Okay," I said. "Can I kiss you anyway?"

Henry looked surprised. "You want to kiss me? I thought I was freaking you out and you wouldn't want to."

"No," I said. "No, I've wanted to kiss you since Lacey's. You don't freak me out."

"Okay." He smiled a little. "I suppose one kiss on the second date isn't too fast, is it?"

"Not at all."

He leaned forward, and his lips touched mine. So soft, moving, trembling. It was amazing. I loved it—I loved him. But then he was pulling away, far too soon. I pulled him back against me.

"I take it you're over Jaime Lane?" he murmured against my mouth. "He posted a short movie at nine. Want to go see it?"

I looked into his eyes, so deep and brown and so amazingly fantastic, so fantastically amazing that it made my breath catch and my toes curl and made me a bit woozy in my head. "I think that could wait," I said. And I pulled him in for another kiss.

REBECCA LONG started writing when she was in the first grade, and by the second grade her stories had progressed to a very, very short novel that starred a Dalmatian and a blue dragon. In the same year, she published a poem in the newsletter that she still refuses to show anybody, because she rhymed "youch" with "couch" in desperation for lack of other words.

Now she is a high school student who complains about how only upperclassmen get to have the fun classes, and is writing several novels at once and procrastinating on all of them. Sometime in the past years, she's won a few writing contests and vaguely remembers reading one of her winning pieces on television, but never really saw the recording of it.

Rebecca is the kind of person who hides inside all day, buried deep in either the internet or books, and only ventures out if her family makes her. She has a weakness for fluffy fics, cheesy romances, and YA novels that are too happy for their own good, but she is also a sucker for horror movies and tragedy.

Contact her at idreamtofreality@gmail.com.

COUNTING STARS
L.A. BUCHANAN

AMY SULLIVAN didn't hold any sort of special reverence for Tuesdays. They weren't much better than any other day, in her carefully established opinion. Amy was entirely sure that Wednesdays were the best days of the week, because they were right between the weekends. It was before the Thursday-Friday rush of teachers assigning work and just after the panic of receiving grades from the Monday submissions. Chilly Tuesday evenings—much like this one—were better than Monday classes at Birchway Academy but hardly as good as a lazy Wednesday afternoon.

Even though they weren't the best days of the week, Tuesdays did have a way of breaking the monotony. Every Tuesday without fail, Amy built herself a fort of books and binders, folders and handouts, and waited. She constructed a castle of knowledge, of information and encyclopedias, and others came. Whether it was because they desperately wanted to understand or because the headmistress had ordered it for their failing grades, other students filed in one by one for tutoring. Between Amy and the other girls who gathered, the library would be filled with hushed murmurs. Talk of exponents and electrons would overlap with the discussion of symbiosis and syntax. It was easy for Amy to allow herself to become absorbed in helping others and find a way to escape the heavy pressure that weighed on her own shoulders.

The concern was always there, of course. It wasn't as though Amy could forget her own homework. Tuesdays offered a shelter from the essays and the presentations, but the early hours of Wednesdays caused those bricks to crumble. Amy knew the time was coming soon—she would have to leave the library and face her own work after hours of the other girls' studies.

The minute hand of the grandfather clock behind the librarian's desk clunked into place at 9:16 p.m. Most of the other tutors had packed up their books and bags several minutes ago. Only Janice Howard remained, her thick glasses slipping down her nose and her dual braids beginning to fray as she patiently explained dihybrid Punnett squares to a drowsy Nicole Carter. The pair of them stayed late every week, and Amy never stayed to see them leave. She consistently clocked out at nine thirty, even though she usually spent almost forty-five minutes sitting in relative silence.

Amy began to pick at a loose thread at the hem of her skirt, and she considered leaving just a few minutes early. It was almost unheard of for someone to come in so late. If anyone was really looking for help, they would have come when more than two tutors were available. Just as Amy made a decision and reached out to dismantle her textbook citadel, the door at the front of the library creaked open. There were hundreds of girls at Birchway, but the girl who slouched past the librarian's desk was the last one Amy expected to see.

It could have been anyone who came in that evening, but in walked Leanne Terry, her tie hung loose around her neck, her sleeves rolled up, and her socks rolled down despite the brisk November breeze that made the windows rattle. Her blazer had been discarded in favor of a zippered sweatshirt, the hood pulled up to the crown of her head even though they were inside. If her uniform wasn't regulation, her hair was downright illegal. Leanne had freshly dyed her sandy locks, the ends a rich purple that probably wouldn't last very long. As she approached, Amy was reminded of summer afternoons in the backyard, the air glittering with rainbows in the cascading water from a sprinkler. Had she used grape Kool-Aid to make her hair that color? Amy didn't put it past her; it was just like the other girl to look for ways to break the rules, no matter the cost.

"I guess you're one of the tutors?" Leanne asked, tucking her hands into the pockets of her jacket and rubbing the toe of her sneaker against the carpet. Her words came in a familiar undertone. Amy had heard the other girl speak so many times; her throaty voice and irregular laugh unfailingly rang through the dining hall at supper or floated across the common room during free period. It didn't slip past Amy that Janice had looked up from her work.

"Um, yeah," Amy replied hesitantly. She could already feel an uncomfortable heat beginning to creep up from beneath her collar. Her own voice paled in comparison to Leanne's steady tone, and she wished it sounded stronger. "Do you need help with something?"

"Not really," Leanne replied, pulling out the chair across from her and sinking into the wooden seat. "Lewis said I had to show or I'd end up on probation." Headmistress Baker had retired a year ago, and her replacement—Professor Lewis—was known for giving problem students second chances.

"Uh… right," Amy mumbled, looking at the other girl with a line between her dark brows. Leanne didn't say anything in response, and an awkward silence rose between them. Amy's skin crawled, and her heart gave an uncomfortable lurch. She felt as though it was her responsibility to break the tension, to ease the uneasiness that roared through the ringing quiet of the peaceful library. "Wh-wh-what—" Amy's voice came out in a ragged stutter, and she had to clear her throat before continuing. "What did you do?" Her face flamed in a vicious blush; she could feel the heat spreading beneath her shirt, and her clothes felt itchy against her skin.

"Eh," Leanne replied with a noncommittal shrug. "Cut class too many times, I guess. Latin is boring."

"I don't know," Amy mumbled, reaching up to tug at a strand of her straight dark hair. "I think it's a pretty neat subject…."

"Neat?" Leanne repeated with a laugh, one of her eyebrows creasing her forehead as it twitched up toward her hairline. "I don't know what class you've been going to, but Gordon's isn't neat." Amy happened to think her classmate had a point, but she didn't say anything of the kind. Instead, she looked at her stack of books and then at the clock. It was ticking toward ten, and she couldn't wait to leave. She'd hardly said a word, but she felt like she'd made a fool of herself. Leanne was as smooth as silk, pretty, and popular. As much as Amy admired her, she was embarrassed to be wasting her time.

"Listen, um," she began, swallowed up in the sensation that Leanne didn't want to listen to a word she had to say. "Unless you want help with something, I should really probably get going. I have some calculus left to finish, and…." Amy trailed off there, slowly getting to her feet. Her arms were full of books when her chair caught on the carpet, nearly making her stumble.

"Yeah, cool," Leanne answered with a crooked grin that made a dimple crease her left cheek. "Whatever. I'll be back next week."

Amy was silent for a painfully awkward moment after that. "Right, okay" was the only thing she could think to say.

Leanne didn't miss her hesitation. "You thought Lewis was going to let me off with one session?" she inquired with a soft bark of a laugh. "Nah, she says I have to keep coming every week for a month."

Amy stared down at her classmate, her brain scrambling to put words together. "Maybe try to come a little earlier next time" was what finally came out. Her face flamed hot, her ears burning beneath her silky hair. Rather than apologize, Amy gathered her books up in her arms and left without another word, embarrassment welling up inside her until she thought she would burst.

The trip down the hallways was a lonely one; the other girls were mostly tucked away in their cozy common rooms, and the corridors were empty. Amy's school shoes tapped quietly on the stone tile as she walked, and her bag weighed heavy on her back. Gosh, that whole thing had been awkward. It wasn't any surprise that she found it hard to talk to Leanne—she'd always struggled with that sort of thing. Amy was quiet and shy and hardly fit in with the other girls at Birchway.

They came on their parents' money, their mothers and grandmothers alumnae of the prestigious secondary school. Amy, on the other hand, had worked her way in. Public school had been boring for her. She read too much and learned too quickly to be restricted by standardized testing and short summer reading lists. Her impressive marks on placement tests had garnered the interest of school officials, and she'd been offered a home at Birchway on full scholarship. Of course, her grades competed with the best, but that didn't mean she felt equal to the other girls. They shirked their responsibilities with iPhones, and upperclassmen proudly jangled keys to Jaguars on their sixteenth birthdays, while Amy had learned to drive in her father's ancient Subaru.

She tried to tell herself that it wasn't important, tried to tell herself that she was at school, and learning was what mattered. It worked sometimes, when she was in classes and focused on her notes or when she was tutoring. The scales were tipped when her backpack was kept company by a Coach handbag while she labored over algebra with one of her schoolmates. It was shockingly easy to forget the disparity when the playing field was leveled between money and mind. Casual conversation was a different story. It was a lot more difficult to lazily discuss this season's fashion or last weekend's horse race when one was still getting hand-me-downs from cousin Kathy.

Amy pushed open the front door of the academics building, pulling her jacket tighter around herself when a chilly gust of wind pushed her dark hair over her shoulders. Her shoes crunched through the salt sprinkled across the sidewalk, and the wind whistled in her ears.

She was a fifth year now, with only two left to go before she went to college. She'd made it through this far—it seemed silly to still find herself wrapped up in concerns about wealth or her lack thereof. Amy supposed she was liked well enough; no one was outwardly cruel to her. Of course, no one in Birchway was outwardly cruel to anyone. That was quick cause for probation. Even so, it was difficult not to compare herself to those prettier than her or better off than she was. She found herself doing it far too often.

The contrast had become more obvious as she got older, she thought as she pushed open the door to the fifth-year dormitory. Those things didn't seem to matter when she was eleven and had left public elementary school to make friends with other girls who wouldn't be held back. It hadn't bothered her when she arrived, only to find the dorms and dining hall filled with girls who hadn't studied their way in—but rather bought it. The spring semester of third year was the first time someone had snickered at her skirt, left unhemmed so it could be returned at the end of the year and traded in for a new one. That was when she'd started to worry about such things.

With a quiet sigh, Amy pushed her way into the common room she shared with several other girls. Most of them were scattered around the fireplace, giggling and gossiping over mugs of hot chocolate as they wrapped themselves in fur blankets and snuggled back into the leather furniture. The common room was the center of two large bedrooms, five girls in each. They'd been suitemates since their first year together, and they got on well enough. She hardly spent every weekend with them, but they were friendly to one another. Still, none of them spoke to her as she passed. It was a Tuesday evening—they knew she was going to be too busy to join them by the fire.

Amy didn't bother greeting her suitemates as she pushed her way into her dorm, dropped her bag and books onto her already made bed, and settled in to study. It was easy enough to shove away all thoughts of Leanne Terry and expensive things as she cracked open a physics book.

Though it had seemed quite late when Amy finally closed her books and folded herself beneath her blankets, her eyes opened immediately when her cell phone alarm went off beneath her pillow. The sound was muffled, but the vibrations were not. She was tired but managed to push herself upright and pull on her jacket, tie, and skirt and head to breakfast.

Amy walked alone through the corridors, her bag slung over one shoulder and her school shoes tapping quietly on the floors. The hallways weren't quiet; everyone was waking up, dressing, and heading for the dining hall in groups of two or three. There were a few other girls who walked by themselves, but many of them had their phones in their hands or pressed against their ears. Amy didn't mind walking alone.

The dining hall was roaring with conversation when Amy entered, and she had to weave between chairs and tables to find her place at the end of the breakfast line. It wasn't too long before she found a seat at an empty table with her eggs and french toast. Amy was entirely comfortable to eat her breakfast and read a book in silence and paid no attention as nearly all the extra chairs were pulled away and pushed in to make one more space at already crowded tables. She was finally tugged away from her book when a chair was *added* to her table, and looked up to find Janice Howard sliding down into the seat across from her, no tray in her hands.

"You talked to Leanne Terry last night," Janice muttered, her breath hissing through her braces.

"Uh, yeah," she answered. "She came in for tutoring."

"For, like, five minutes," Janice replied. "Why?"

Amy shrugged. "She said she's been cutting Latin—Lewis told her she had to come to tutoring for a month."

Janice's delicate eyebrows crinkled her forehead as they lifted away from the heavy frames of her glasses. "And she's actually going to do it?"

"Um," Amy mumbled, "yeah, I guess so. Does she really have a choice?"

"She's Leanne."

Amy couldn't help but notice the other girl's point. She had always admired Leanne Terry; it was hard not to, really. Even the people who weren't her friends liked her. She talked to everyone who was worth talking to, and everyone who was anyone talked to her. She broke the rules, and no one cared; even the Birchway administration tended to look the other way.

Before Amy could figure out what she wanted to say in response to that, the bell rang. Cacophonous noise filled the big room as chairs screeched across the tile, and voices all started saying good-bye at once.

"See you later, Amy," Janice said, standing up and joining the milling crowd of girls that slowly started to flow out into the hallway. Amy cleared her tray away from the table, arms full of books as she made her way to her class.

It was much easier for Amy to forget about Janice and Leanne while she listened to a physics lecture and took quiet notes in calculus. By the time the lunch bell rang, there were so many numbers floating around in her head that there was hardly room for anything else. However, her mathematic tranquility was interrupted almost as soon as she settled herself into a chair at an empty table at the edge of the dining hall.

She raised her head with a jerk to find Leanne Terry flopping down across from her. The other girl's tie was as loose as always, her blazer hanging open over her untucked shirt.

"Your name is Amy, right?" Leanne asked, leaning forward to rest her elbows on the table. "I'm Leanne. You probably already knew that."

"Uh, yeah," Amy replied, looking up to take in her classmate's smoky eyeliner and dip-dyed hair. "You came late to tutoring last night."

"Yeah, I wanted to talk to you about that," she said. "Lewis is going to need some proof that I showed up. She's going to want to hear that I'm doing well or whatever. Can you cover for me?"

Amy hesitated to answer. She knew she should take the side of the rules—Leanne had been given a punishment and shouldn't be trying to weasel her way out of it. At the same time, Amy didn't feel like it was really her place to tell the other girl what to do.

"D-don't you think you should just go?" Her voice stuck between her tongue and her teeth, and she had to focus to make sure the words came out. Leanne didn't seem to notice.

"I guess I could, but I'll just be wasting your time—and mine. It's not like I'm getting punished for actually having trouble. I just don't feel like going to class is all."

"Why?"

"Why?" Leanne repeated, sounding incredulous. "Because class is boring, that's why." She rocked her chair back onto two legs, crossing her arms over her abdomen.

"Yeah, but," Amy started, knowing it wasn't her place to say, "even if you don't pay attention, you could just go. That way you wouldn't get in trouble."

"You can't be good all the time," Leanne answered as her lips quirked into that lopsided, dimpled grin. She let her chair fall onto all fours, and she stood. "See you at dinner?"

Amy balked. "A-ar-aren't you going to sit with your friends?" she stammered, her voice nearly lost beneath the noise.

"Nah, they all have stuff to do. I think half of them are in detention."

"Oh, okay...."

"See you later, Amy." Leanne raised her hand, her painted-black fingernails rippling in a lazy wave.

"Uh, yeah," Amy muttered. "Bye." She stared as Leanne returned to her usual table at the center of the room. Amy noticed she was welcomed back into the group as though she hadn't even left. A few glances were cast in her direction, and Amy turned immediately back to her food. She couldn't help but lift her eyes a moment later and found Leanne's pack laughing openly. A wash of misplaced embarrassment crashed over her.

It was ridiculous, and Amy knew it. She kept her head down and told herself over and over that Leanne's friends had absolutely no reason to pay any attention to her. Certainly they had more interesting things to talk about. Still, Amy found doubt creeping in at the edge of her thoughts, staining them dark. Maybe the only reason Leanne had said anything at all to her was to find something funny to tell her friends. Amy had hardly said anything; there wasn't anything to share.

Still, as the bell rang for the girls to return to class, Amy found herself turning the encounter over and over in her mind. What was Leanne trying to do? It wasn't like the pair of them had ever been friends before. They'd barely spoken to each other let alone spent any time together. Leanne was a popular girl, always surrounded by her friends. Amy was quiet and spent most of her time making friends with books.

Leanne's family was wealthy, and Amy's definitely wasn't. The two of them were as different as sun and rain, and Amy could not understand why Leanne Terry would want to sit with her at dinnertime. It was extremely unlikely that *all* the other girl's friends were busy during dinner, and if they were, it seemed even more unlikely that Leanne would want to spend the time with Amy—at least, not without an ulterior motive.

Did Leanne think being Amy's friend would get her out of going to tutoring for the rest of the month? That actually explained a lot. Amy felt a hot wave of muted anger begin to rise in her stomach. Of course someone like Leanne Terry would only want to be friends with her for her own benefit. That hardly should have been a surprise.

Amy marched her way into her next class, heading to her usual seat in the front row. She sat down with a huff. It was usually easy for her to focus on lessons, but today her mind kept drifting back to her purple-haired classmate. Each time her thoughts lingered on Leanne, the anger became a bit weaker. Something else began to replace it, but Amy wasn't quite sure what it was. Sadness, she supposed—hurt. Why couldn't Leanne just... follow the rules like everyone else? It wasn't like the rest of them had a choice. Why did Leanne get one?

Amy allowed herself to stew all the way through her classes and was beginning to wallow in melancholy by the time evening session was over and she headed toward the dining hall. She lingered on the way, taking her time to cross the breezy campus and wind her way through the halls of the dormitory building.

For the first time in her life, she felt a bit spiteful. It had never bothered her that she didn't have many friends. Books had been the only companions she needed—until now, it seemed. Suddenly, with the whirlwind appearance of one girl who dip-dyed her hair in dollar-store juice, she felt entirely too lonely. She had realized with a shock that she was the only one who didn't seem to have a clique to settle into, and that made it even lonelier than it already was. Not to mention her only offer had come from someone who didn't seem to be interested in her at all. Not for real, anyway. Leanne was only interested in what their friendship would bring.

Amy felt a dark mood brewing and took a moment to realize what she was telling herself. Did she really have any proof for the things she was thinking? Not exactly, but that didn't mean they weren't true. And therein lay her problem. There was no way to be sure one way or the other without testing the waters, and if there was one thing Amy Sullivan hated, it was doing something without being sure how it would end. Math was easy. There was an answer to be found; you just had to look for it. There was always a way to get to the end; you just had to make sure you recognized which route to take. If only friendship could be so simple.

She struggled with herself, awkwardly lurking outside the dining hall. Even though she was hungry, Amy almost considered waiting until later to go to dinner, wondering if she could avoid Leanne. It occurred to her that life must be full of things she couldn't plan, couldn't solve. There had to be risks involved, even if she really hated them. She forced herself to hold her head up as she made her way to the dining hall.

A few minutes after she settled down with a fillet of tilapia and a baked potato, Leanne flopped into the chair across from her, a bright red apple clutched in one hand.

"Hey," Leanne greeted.

"Hi," Amy replied. The pair of them lapsed into silence—to no surprise of Amy's. They had nothing in common; conversation was hardly going to come easy. Silence built a cushion between them, the air above the table suddenly seeming heavy. Amy was crushed beneath it, the pressure filling her chest until she thought her lungs would burst. She had to break the silence, had to relieve the awkward tension.

"S-so, um," she stammered, just as Leanne opened her mouth to speak.

"Did you hear about Melissa Sanchez?" Leanne asked, polishing her apple on one sleeve and turning it over in her hands before taking a crunching bite.

"Meli—what? No. What happened?" Amy replied. She knew Melissa well enough; she'd given the other girl quite a bit of help with chemistry homework two terms ago.

"Got caught trying to sneak out," Leanne answered, her voice muffled around the bit of apple she was mulling over. "I guess she didn't realize there are alarms on the front doors."

"Where was she trying to go?" Amy couldn't help but ask, immediately enthralled in the story. Why would she have even bothered? She could have left during the weekend; it would have saved her a lot of trouble.

"Don't know," Leanne replied, leaning her chair back onto two legs and kicking her feet up onto the table. Amy realized she wasn't wearing regulation shoes. "She won't say. Probably has a boyfriend or something."

"The closest town is miles away," Amy pointed out. "She wouldn't be able to walk that far."

"Yeah, I guess you're right," Leanne muttered with a shrug, chomping into another bite of apple. "You're in advanced physics, right?"

Amy stuck on the question, turning it over in her mind a time or two before she found the ability to answer. "Uh, yeah," she muttered.

"So you're learning about space and stuff, yeah?"

Amy stared at the other girl, her brown eyes narrowing just slightly. "I mean, a little," Amy answered. "Not really. What kind of stuff do you need help with?"

"Nothing, I was just... asking," Leanne said, her voice going quiet.

"What for?" As soon as the words were out, Amy regretted them. They sounded so rude. She didn't apologize, hoping there was a chance Leanne might not notice.

"Well, I...," Leanne started, trailing off. Was that a blush darkening her pale cheeks? "I like stars."

Amy stared at the other girl, taken entirely by surprise. "Stars?" she repeated. "You mean, like, astrology?"

"No, like, astronomy," Leanne replied, shrugging. "You know, constellations and stuff."

Amy couldn't help but stare—again. "Really?" she asked. Leanne nodded and gave a small shrug. "That's neat." Amy offered a genuine, shy smile.

"Yeah, I guess," Leanne replied before crunching into her apple. "Whatever. I have to go. Talk to you later." She stood, her chair scraping loud against the tile floor of the dining hall. Amy was left blinking at the other girl's back. Just as the conversation had seemed to smooth out, Leanne had retreated. Amy didn't have much time to mull it over, though, as Janice dropped into Leanne's vacated seat.

She didn't say anything, just raised her eyebrows at Amy without a word. Amy gave a vague gesture, lifting her hands—palm up—and raising her shoulders in a dramatic shrug.

"Look, I don't know, okay?" she said. "I didn't invite her to sit with me."

"But you didn't tell her to leave."

"Why would I do that? She wasn't hurting anything. She was just talking."

Janice pressed her lips together.

"Really, she was talking about Melissa Sanchez, and then she was talking about physics."

"She doesn't even take physics," Janice argued.

"What difference does it make?" Amy tried to counter, not sure why Janice was so invested in these short conversations she was having with Leanne Terry.

"You... know how she is," Janice muttered, lowering her voice and glancing around like some terrible fate might befall them if someone overheard. "I mean... who she likes."

Of course Amy knew. Everyone knew. Leanne had no reason to hide it, and Amy had absolutely no right to judge.

"Yeah, so? Who cares?"

Janice looked like she cared very much. "What, so you like her?" she asked.

Amy felt her ears start to heat up. "No, of course not!" she protested, even though she knew her cheeks were alight with a fiery blush. Amy wasn't surprised to see Janice's left eyebrow twitch upward once more. "Come on, Janice, you know I don't...."

"Hmm." Janice huffed, and Amy had no idea what to say as her classmate stood and turned away. She frowned as Janice made her way across the dining hall, and a few minutes later, Amy stopped picking at her dinner and stood up to leave.

Amy walked slowly to her dorm upstairs, her arms wrapped tight around the books in her arms, and she gazed down at the toes of her school shoes. Did she like Leanne? Well, everyone *liked* Leanne, but that wasn't what Janice had meant. Amy was sure of that.

She'd always held an embarrassing amount of respect for the other girl; Leanne had more friends than Amy had ever had. She was pretty, she always knew what to say, and she knew how to make people laugh. Amy had never quite been sure if she'd wanted to be Leanne or be her friend. But surely Leanne wouldn't want to be her friend. Not really. Maybe she would pretend, to get out of tutoring, but not for real. Amy had to admit to herself, the thought was a bit discouraging.

With a sigh she shook the worries away, trying to smother them just enough to let them go. Up in her suite, she buried herself in books and mathematics—and didn't see or hear anything of Leanne Terry until the next morning.

In fact, she barely saw hide nor hair of Leanne for the rest of the week. The other girl seemed to be steadfastly ignoring her—not that Amy could really be surprised. They hadn't spoken at all before Tuesday; they were hardly going to be best friends on Thursday. Leanne was always in the dining hall during meals, and they passed each other in the hallway, but they seemed to return to their mutual disregard for the other. Amy wasn't quite sure what had transpired between them, but she tried not to worry about it. At least this way, she didn't have to worry about Leanne taking embarrassing stories back to her friends.

It was safe to say that the following Tuesday brought a shock. When Amy entered the library after dinner with her back bowed beneath book after book, she was stunned to find Leanne already settled in at Amy's favorite table.

"I thought you weren't going to come," Amy inquired as she approached, shifting the books in her arms as she circled around the table to stand across from her classmate. Leanne had tied her hair up today, a sloppy ponytail of blonde and fading purple.

"I didn't know if you were going to cover for me or not," Leanne replied, watching as Amy dropped her books onto the table and settled into the chair opposite. "Besides, I had to bring you this." She reached into the breast pocket of her shirt and produced a crinkled and much-folded piece of paper. She smoothed it out on one knee before handing it across to Amy.

It was a simple form from the headmistress; Amy had seen one like it before. She would have to fill it out and sign it to let Lewis know that Leanne had been attending tutoring and should be forgiven for the error of her ways.

"I probably would've," Amy admitted, her voice quiet as she laid the paper flat on the table, trying to smooth out some of the wrinkles.

"Really?" Leanne asked, sounding surprised as she rocked her chair back onto two legs. "I didn't expect that kind of thing from you."

"I-I'm not very good at it," Amy muttered, shrugging and allowing herself to inspect a tiny tear in Leanne's form—if only so she didn't have to raise her eyes to look at Leanne. "But you asked me to."

"So? You don't owe me anything," Leanne pointed out.

"I guess not," Amy replied, "but that doesn't mean I'd rat you out." A small silence lapsed between them, and Amy finally felt obligated to look up. Leanne was giving her one of those lopsided smiles.

"You know, Amy," she said, and the way she said Amy's name felt strange, "you're all right."

"Uh, thanks." Amy didn't know what else to say, and the silence enveloped them once more. It was awkward and strange, but Leanne didn't seem to mind. Amy found herself creating new lines in the form on the table, slowly folding it to create firm creases.

"What are you doing?" Leanne asked, dropping her chair back onto four legs and leaning her elbows onto the table to watch Amy work.

"Something I used to do with my sister," Amy answered, the rising panic beginning to sink away. A smile began to crease her cheek. "When I was a kid, I was really afraid of thunderstorms, so she taught me how to fold paper hearts to calm me down. I haven't made one in a long time." Still, the folding came easy, and Amy remembered every step. When she was through, she flicked the paper heart across the table. Leanne's hand came down on top of it, to stop it from falling to the floor.

"Why not?" Leanne inquired, picking up the heart and turning it over a few times between her fingers. "This is cool. Can you teach me?"

"Uh, yeah, I guess," Amy said, surprised that Leanne even cared. "It's pretty easy." She opened one of her binders and pulled out two more sheets of paper, handing one across to Leanne. Step by step, Amy walked her through folding the paper hearts, until Leanne made one, grinning as she held it up.

"Cool," she said, laying it down next to the crinkled, flimsy heart made out of the crumpled form. "Do you know how to make anything else?"

"No, not really," Amy admitted. "My sister used to fold notes like that in school and put them in her friends' lockers. I think one of the other girls taught her how to do it."

"That's cool. I wish my sisters did cool stuff."

"You have sisters?" Amy asked, for some reason finding herself surprised.

"Yeah," Leanne answered easily. "Two, and a brother, but they're all a lot older than me."

"I don't know why I thought you were an only child."

"A lot of the girls here are," Leanne said with a shrug, slowly beginning to take apart the paper heart she'd made, only to put it back together again. "I think I have the biggest family."

"What's it like?" Amy couldn't help but ask.

"I don't know, kind of annoying," Leanne said. "I always wanted to impress them and stuff, you know? But my brother was eight when I was born, and my sisters are older than him, so they didn't really want to hang out with me, you know?"

"I guess that makes sense," Amy murmured. She hesitated for what felt like a long time before speaking again. "Sounds kind of lonely, though." Silence stretched between them.

"I mean, I guess," Leanne replied. "It was kind of cool too. When he got a little older, my brother started to do stuff with me. He took me stargazing for the first time when I was eleven."

"Is that why you like astronomy?" Amy asked, honestly surprised at how candid her classmate was being.

"Yeah," Leanne said, "I just thought it was so cool, to be able to see space and stuff from our backyard, you know?"

"It's been a long time since I looked at the stars," Amy admitted. "I'd like to go sometime, but there's nowhere near my house that's any good."

"There's a hill near here that's pretty good," Leanne said, looking up at Amy. "There's going to be a meteor shower Saturday night. You could come watch it with me, if you want."

"What, really?" Amy blurted, stunned at the offer.

"I mean, you don't have to," Leanne muttered.

"No, that sounds… that sounds fun," Amy said, starting to smile.

"Okay, sure," Leanne said after a moment, giving Amy that lopsided grin in return. Amy saw Leanne pocket the paper hearts they'd made, but her head seemed to be swimming in the air of the warm library as Leanne said something about making room for people who needed help and stood. Amy said good-bye when it was her turn, but later she wasn't quite sure what had happened. All she knew was that Leanne wasn't like she'd expected. It took her a moment to gather her thoughts and invite another girl over to the table for tutoring.

She found herself taking the long way back to her dorm after she left the library, even though her shoulders were already aching from the weight of her backpack. Her steps were slow and steady, even though her thoughts were racing.

Leanne was cool. She was nice and funny and surprisingly easy to talk to. Amy wanted to spend more time with her and was looking forward to Saturday more than she'd looked forward to a weekend in a long time. Still, she wasn't sure if she really should be as excited as she was. Was this stargazing thing a date? Amy felt like it was, and that made her giddy, even though Janice had made it pretty clear that some people didn't approve. Not that Amy cared, but... she did care. A lot.

What people thought about her was important; at least, she thought it was. She didn't want to feel like no one liked her, but everyone seemed to like Leanne—and she'd had a couple of girlfriends before. Not that Leanne was even thinking of Amy like that. Amy sighed as she made her way upstairs to her dorm. She was confused and tired, and wasn't sure what to think.

She thought about Leanne as she tried to fall asleep. She stared at the ceiling above her bed, turning the conversation they'd had at the library over and over in her head. Every time it was just as nice as before. Amy rolled over and wrapped her arms around her pillow with a smile. Who cared what Janice said? She couldn't be good all the time.

The rest of the week seemed to trickle by at some points and rush past at others. Amy's classes seemed to lag for the first time in a long time, and she caught herself staring at the clock far more frequently than she was used to. It was easy to count the minutes until lunch or dinner or whenever she was going to see Leanne next. Every time she was sure she'd bridled and bound her feelings for her classmate, they returned with a vengeance, her heart leaping when she saw that purple hair or that lopsided smile that she'd grown fond of so quickly. It had only been a few days; she felt so ridiculous when she caught herself daydreaming during calculus.

She supposed it had been a long time coming. Leanne had been an unobtainable figure just a week ago, and now they ate lunch together nearly every day—even after Leanne's friends stopped being "busy." Amy worried that she was mistaking close friendship for infatuation, but she managed to reassure herself on that front. This couldn't be what normal friendships felt like. She'd read way too many silly love stories to know that much.

At 10:00 p.m. on Saturday, Amy made her way down the nearly deserted halls, wrapped up in every warm piece of clothing she owned. She and Leanne had decided to meet near the tennis courts at the back of the school and walk out toward the center of the grounds. There would be enough space there to spread out a blanket and watch the meteors. Even though she'd felt silly putting them on, Amy was grateful for her multiple layers by the time she found her way to the tennis courts. It was bitter cold outside, and her breath collected in steamy clouds before her eyes.

"Hey," Leanne greeted when she saw Amy approach, her left cheek dimpling in her crooked grin as she lifted a plain backpack from the ground beside her feet.

Amy's stomach gave a happy lurch, and she returned the smile. "Hi," she replied. "What did you bring?"

"Some blankets, some hot chocolate. Some music. Nothing special, but, you know, we might be out for a while," Leanne answered, settling the pack on her shoulders and motioning for Amy to follow. "Come on, I want to get settled in before it starts."

"We've got almost an hour!" Amy pointed out with a laugh, even though she gave no argument and followed immediately.

"You can never be too early for shooting stars," Leanne said, a definite bounce in her step as she led Amy across the gentle hills of Birchway's sprawling grounds. They found a soft patch of well-kept grass at the top of a small swell, and Leanne looked up toward the crisp, cloudless sky. "Perfect."

Together, the pair of them spread out a fluffy comforter and sat cross-legged on the ground. Leanne pulled another blanket from her bag and draped it around their shoulders before producing a thermos and taking a careful sip. She offered it to Amy, who politely refused. After a small shrug, Leanne put the cap back on the hot chocolate and pulled an iPod and a pair of tiny speakers from her pack. Amy smiled when the music started, a steady drum line beneath a familiar set of keyboard chords. With Leanne's choice of music playing quietly, the two of them settled in to wait for the meteors.

A silence lapsed between them, but this one was comfortable. Amy felt at home here, beneath this blanket in the quiet. They looked up at the sky together, and Amy looked around impatiently. She wanted to be the first to see a shooting star, to point it out to Leanne. Her gaze was drawn away from the heavens when Leanne broke the silence.

"It makes me feel so small," she murmured, her usually powerful voice barely more than a whisper out here in the cold.

"What do you mean?" Amy inquired, a bit surprised to find that her own voice didn't quiver or break.

"I mean, there's so much out there besides us, you know? It goes on forever." Amy let a silence fall between them again, entirely unsure what to say to that. "I wonder how many there are."

"How many what?"

"Stars," Leanne replied. "There are too many to count, so how many are there?"

"Millions, billions," Amy said. "Something like ten to the twentieth power." She was watching Leanne carefully now. It was strange to see someone who had always seemed so distant and unshakeable up close like this, sharing thoughts she didn't say when the sun lit the sky.

"That doesn't seem like enough."

"What do you mean?" Amy asked, laughing. "That's a one with twenty zeroes."

Leanne wasn't smiling. "I didn't really want to know," she muttered. "I like not knowing. I think some things are better when you don't really understand, you know?"

Amy hesitated to answer. "No, not really," she finally admitted.

"Well, I mean…." Leanne trailed off, looking uncertain.

"It's okay, you can tell me. I'm not going to laugh or anything."

Leanne took a slow breath, letting it out before she began to answer. "There's just so much outside of us. So much more, and we don't know anything about it. I think that's really special, that we aren't the only things around. That what we do here doesn't matter in the grand scheme of things. That what happens tomorrow really doesn't change anything at all. We're just a bunch of people living on a really big rock that's flying through space, and you and I are spending our Saturday night sitting in the cold, looking at a bunch of lights that we don't really understand. I guess it sounds a little crazy, but I like it. It makes it easier not to worry, you know?"

Leanne finally looked over at Amy, and her eyes seemed to be slightly teary. Amy's heart thudded hard, and her breath nearly caught in her throat. Leanne's words went round and round in her head. The other girl was completely right, and Amy had never considered how wrong she had been. She'd spent her whole life terrified of risks, of challenges, of change. She was afraid to upset the world around her, but did it really matter? There was only one moment at a time for her to enjoy, and she spent so many of them worried about the next one. If she wasn't careful, Amy would let herself worry her life away.

Neither of them spoke for what felt like ages. Amy felt compelled to fill the silence, and when she did, her voice came out without a tremble. "Yeah, I guess you're right."

The pair of them looked at each other for a long moment. Leanne reached out with one gloved hand and laid her palm over Amy's knuckles, giving a sad impression of her lopsided grin. Amy tried to return it, even as she felt like she couldn't breathe. Her entire world narrowed down to this instant, and she could hardly hear the music coming from Leanne's iPod as the other girl slowly leaned closer. There, on that freezing Saturday evening in early December, Amy shared her first kiss with an impossible girl. Neither of them noticed that they missed the first shooting star.

L.A. BUCHANAN is a pharmacy technician who lives in a swelling Virginia town. When she's not fighting traffic or trying not to argue with unreasonable customers, she's relaxing and writing with help from her pet cat, Tommy. In her time away from a word processor, L.A. wiles away the hours watching Showtime and Netflix with her long-term girlfriend, Melanie. Between all that, she consumes unreasonable amounts of fan fiction and takes way too many naps.

L.A. is shy and bashful, but not unapproachable. She likes meeting new people and loves hearing feedback about her work. Visit her at http://l-a-buchanan.tumblr.com/. Contact her directly at l.a.buchan@hotmail.com.

CIGAR, PARASOL, STAR
LAURA BEAIRD

I HATE rain. It's so gross here, catches the smell of the smog and forcibly invades my clothes. Rain means I have to do laundry soon since the outdoor rinse cycle has decided to sour my clothes. I step from my Aunt Marge's apartment complex awning, pulling my hood up and drawing the strings to hide from the torrent of foul water. I groan when the rain sinks through my thin jacket and warms my skin. Warm rain. Fantastic. Warm rain means a nice weeklong sheet of smog-smelling humidity thick enough to be a blanket that someone's just viciously sweated all over.

The street is devoid of people but filled with parked cars and ticking meters, a few trees giggling in the rain. A lone bus shelter with a single lighted streetlamp beside it is empty except for one person. He's bent over some folded hunk of purple fabric in his lap. I walk across the street to the bus shelter and kick away some old bags of fast food so I can stand in a more or less clean spot by the person on the bench. His breathing shakes like the leaves nearby. The sound is one I know. It's the sound of holding back tears.

I shift on my legs and maneuver my bag. "Uh, hey, you okay?"

He looks up and blinks. I recognize him from somewhere, but to be honest I can't remember where. His face is dry, but it won't last by the look of the wobbly tears in his eyes. He looks away from me and lets out a long breath. "No, not at all. Thanks."

"Oh, sorry." I look at the bus schedule a minute, try not to look back at him. I really shouldn't invade. He forces a cough to hide the hitch in his breath that I still hear. I know he's crying. I rock on my toes and look back and forth on the street for the bus. I look back at him. "So… you look familiar. Do I know you?"

He places his elbows on his knees, crossing his forearms across them. "I don't know." He shakes his head and wipes at his face. "Maybe."

I turn to him, see his tears, and turn away. "Rain is awful, huh?"

He nods.

"My name's Chris."

"From chemistry?"

"Um—" I laugh. "—which year?"

He wipes his face with the backs of his hands and rubs them on his slacks. "Junior…?"

I shake my head, rubbing the strap of my messenger bag. "No, no, um… never mind. I think I remember you. Your name starts with a *W*, right?

"William."

"That's right, William, but you preferred—"

"Will."

"Right, right, Will." I sit next to him on the bench. He moves over a little. "How are you? It's May, so are you—?"

"Yeah," He motions to the folded mass in his lap, his graduation robes. "I just graduated."

"Oh, congrats. So are you on your way to a friend's place?" Why did I ask that? He's crying—why would you be crying on your way to a friend's house? Shit, why do I even try?

He shakes his head and sighs. "Nah, I'm not sure where I'm going. Home isn't happening right now, and I don't think my friends want to see me anymore."

I nod. "Something happen?"

He leans back onto the plexiglass that has a milky loop to it from years of rain and dirt and heat. I can't help but want to pull him away from it; he's dressed too nice to be against something so gross. "Yeah, you could say that."

I bite my lip and nod. "So, do you wanna tell me about it?"

He laughs in a weird choking way. "Yeah, okay, what else do you want to know from me? My social security number? My credit information?"

"I'm just trying to be helpful."

"Shove it, Chris. You're not even in high school anymore. Why would you even want to know about my life?"

I shrug. "I was there a year ago. Hell, less—I'm only in my second semester. C'mon, we were lab partners. I went to your house once, remember? For that project?"

He nods. "Right, right…." He laughs softly. "Man, you were no help that day."

"Hey, I was trying. You were there for AP, right?" I smile at him, hoping he gets it.

He laughs. "That's not how that works. You're not that old."

"I know." I laugh, glad that he got it. "I just don't like admitting I failed a junior-level class." He laughs, and I join him in it. "So tell me what's going on. Is it parents? Friends?"

He shakes his head. "You really don't need to know. It's weird." He laughs again. "I'm weird, what can I say?"

"You're not weird, believe me."

"Oh no, I'm weird."

"You want to talk weird?" I point to the window on the fourth floor, third to the right. "That's my Aunt Marge's place."

"Which one?"

"The one with the green curtains and a dream catcher; it's got all the smoke coming out of it. That's probably her dinner burning."

He smiles. "What about her?"

"She's the crazy one. I'm pretty sure she's convinced she's a voodoo queen. Every time I visit her, she reads my fortune from tea leaves in a cup. It's always fun, but to be honest, I don't see what she sees. According to her, I don't have the sight because it skips a generation or something. I don't know."

He laughs. "That's not weird, that's awesome. I wish my family were cool like that." He stares at her window a moment. "I wonder if she'd tell me my future."

"Probably not; she thinks her powers are too magnificent to unleash on the world. She only reads for family members."

"Figures." He turns to me. "Are you sure you want to hear?"

I look to him. "You know, I have this kind of... saying? I guess, um, about how people need an unbiased view every once in a while. Isn't it easier to talk to someone you don't know than to talk to someone you have to see tomorrow?" He nods, but his eyes stay to the ground. "I mean, when I'm in need of venting or whatever, I talk to Marge. She's weird, but she doesn't judge at all, and I don't see her unless I need her. It's nice to just know I have her. And, uh, I know it isn't much, but right now you have me."

He nods, and we sit in silence for a moment. The rain continues to hit the plexiglass roof above us, the cars start to leave as the meters start to run out of time, and the kids who just graduated leave with their parents and their friends. A few more people crowd into the bus shelter. A few minutes later, a bus comes by. I stand, ready to just leave, but while everyone else piles on, Will grabs my fingers. I sit back down; I can take the next bus.

In ten minutes the streets go from packed to empty again. "Chris?"

"Yeah?"

"I'm, uh, I like guys."

I nod, leaning back. "I do too. It's no big deal or anything."

"Yeah, well, it is for some people."

"Who?"

He shrugs. "A lot of people."

"Like... parents people?"

He shakes his head. "No, they seem pretty cool about it. A little... I dunno, shocked."

"Oh, so you have at least told them. I hear that's the hardest part."

"You haven't—"

"Shit, no. I mean... I think they already know, but I just can't tell them. I just start worrying that they may actually be clueless. Maybe they think all those guys I talk about are just friends and... I don't want them to be disappointed with me."

"What about Aunt Marge?"

"Oh yeah, she knows."

"She sounds cool."

"She really is."

"So you haven't told them."

"Nope."

"What about your friends?"

I shrug like it's nothing, but I remember the day I told them. I had thought I was well loved. "They weren't real friends anyway."

He holds out a hand to catch the rain, then lets it fall to the ground with a splash. "Really? You too?"

"I just lost a few of the guys. Most of the girls stayed. I don't know, sometimes I think girls around here love gay men."

He laughs. "I know what you mean. People kinda assume we all like shopping and feelings and dressing other girls up." He smiles. "Though to be honest, I think I have better fashion sense than some of my friends."

I laugh and motion to my outfit. "I just like being comfy."

He crosses his legs at the knee and places his hands on top. He looks like Vogue. "Oh yes, I can just tell. Have you seen that messenger bag? *So* last decade."

I rub the strap of my messenger bag and laugh. "I've had this thing forever. It still works, so why not?"

He smiles. "It's a little aged, but I can see the appeal." He looks away again. Another bus comes and goes. At this point I may be taking the last bus home. "When I told my friends, they all left. All but Jeremy."

"Jeremy?"

"Yeah." He smiles and closes his eyes as the rain starts to feather out. "I shouldn't be surprised; we've been friends for years. But I don't know, I hadn't liked him before…. It's, it's all so recent." He pulls his graduation robe to him and shifts around. "He and I… we spent every weekend together, we ate lunches together, and he ditched his friends when they wouldn't let me come along. He even helped get a few of my old friends back. He had a way with words, you know? He was great."

"Sounds like." I shuffle my feet around and lean forward. He starts bouncing his leg. "So this Jeremy guy, was he…?"

"No."

"No?"

He shrugs and sighs. "No."

"But you liked him?"

His gaze turns to a lone car that rumbles down the street and takes a left. He waits until only the wet smell of gas is left. "I love him."

"Oh."

"Yeah."

"That must have been awkward."

"You're telling me." The rain begins to let up, and a bus goes by again. The ad on its side gets my attention—an exhibit based on religious culture through the years is going to be showcased at the Museum of Natural History. The picture is of children from every culture dressed in costumes of high-ranking religious officials. A girl with blue eyes dressed as a nun, an African boy dressed as a shaman, an Indian girl dressed as a high priestess, and a fat kid as the Buddha stare at us with lingering fake smiles. The bus belches a bellyful of diesel gas and drives off. His eyes follow it as it leaves. "I confessed to him today."

I know where this is going. "What happened?"

He looks at me with a weird kind of smile. "He introduced me to his girlfriend. They had gotten together two days ago."

All right, I wasn't entirely expecting that. "Oh. I'm sorry."

He shrugs, but it's jerky as he turns away, his hands on his knees that he holds close together. "It's no big deal. I mean, why should I complain? I at least had him as a friend, right? I got to be with him for as long as I had. I should be happy for him.

"But it still hurts." His jaw tightens, and he doesn't talk for a while. "Look, Will"—I tap my toes in a puddle that's formed in a dent on the concrete—"the first guy I ever liked was the reason my friends left me. I told him how I felt, and he…. He accepted who I am, let me get that straight. His name was Greg. He wanted to be a lawyer and was so smart and was absolutely amazing, but, I don't know, I guess confessing to him drove him away." I don't mention how he took my friends with him or how he started giving me glares in the hallway like I was following him around. It was awful, especially since I knew how okay he used to be. "I had to go to Marge's that night. She sat me down with some of her tea and read my leaves." I laugh. "I love her readings. She always goes over the top for them and puts on one of her favorite albums. Do you want to know what my fortune said?" He sends me a look and a half smile with a nod. "It was an axe at the rim, a triangle, and a necklace."

"So?"

"It meant that I would overcome what had happened and that I would find an unexpected admirer." I shrug. "My aunt's usually wrong, though. I never got that unexpected admirer." I look at him and notice his cheeks and ears have turned red. "But I did get over him."

"When was that?"

"Senior year."

"That's when we had class together, right?"

I nod. "Yeah, that's right."

He looks to her window with a cough, then rubs at his red cheeks. The pane still open and letting out steam even though the rain continues to fall. Knowing her, she's probably collecting it to predict the weather or something. "What did she predict today?"

"Oh." I rub at the strap of my messenger bag. "Nothing much, really. It was silly."

He shifts to face me, a half grin on his face. "Now I have to know."

I smile and look up to the sky. "It's so stupid. You'll laugh."

"I promise I won't."

"You will, though. It's all romance."

He nudges me with an elbow. "C'mon, if you don't tell me, I'll go up to your Aunt Marge's myself." He nods to her window. "I know where she lives now."

"Fine, fine...." I look away to the streetlights. "A cigar, a parasol, and a star."

"And...?"

"And it means that I'll meet a new friend, find a lover, and have hope for the future."

"Oh."

"Yeah." I look at my hands and try to have a thumb war with myself. "Told you it was weird."

He shrugs. "Life is weird and full of mistakes. Maybe your admirer didn't have the guts."

"Maybe." I shrug. "Or maybe my aunt's crazy."

He laughs. "Maybe. Or maybe you should...." He shuts his mouth before he can continue and shakes his head. "Nah, never mind."

"What?"

"Nothing, nothing. Just something silly."

I tilt my head to him and nudge him with my shoulder. "C'mon, I told you about my aunt's stupid prediction, so you can tell me what you wanted to say."

He smiles and looks away, unraveling and rewrapping his graduation robe. "It's ridiculous. You'll hate me if I say it."

"Hate you? Really? C'mon, it can't be that bad."

He bites his lower lip. "Fine, I was going to say maybe you should give me your number and we can see what comes of Marge's second prediction."

I lean back, rubbing the strap of my messenger bag. "Oh."

He looks away. "Yeah."

"Um...."

We sit in silence for a while, and a bus rumbles down the street. He stands. "Well, uh, it was great talking to you. I think I'll take this bus."

I nod and look to the concrete, and my eyes drift to my bag. A Sharpie sticks out of the top. I look up to my Aunt Marge's window to see her standing there. Her red hair matches the brick walls perfectly. She tucks it behind her ear as she waves at me and looks to Will with a grin I can see flashing from here. She turns back into her apartment and pulls something from the room. I can't make it out, but knowing her, it's the teacup fortune. She uses a hand to point to it, then to Will, who's leaning on the curb with his hands in his pockets, his graduation robe draped over his shoulder. The bus hisses to a stop in front of us, and Will takes a step inside.

I grab my Sharpie and stand. "Hey, Will, hold up." I grab his hand and scribble my number onto his palm. "Text me, okay? And be safe, wherever you're headed."

His eyes are wide, but his lips let loose a smile. "Awesome, I will. Talk to you later, Chris."

"Talk to you later."

He steps up the last few steps into the bus and pays his fare, then takes a seat right behind the driver. As he sits, he takes out his phone, and the doors close. A few seconds later, I get a text from him. *Hey, this is Will. You free soon?*

I smile at my screen and look up to my Aunt Marge's window. Her window is closed, and the light is out. I stand outside the plexiglass and look around. The rain has washed away the old paper trash that floats in swirls near a clogged gutter down the street, the light seems brighter above the bus shelter, and as the last of the rain hits my lips, it tastes clean.

LAURA BEAIRD has always felt out of it. She has never been able to quite fit in, and it feels to her as if she is always messing something up. She started writing at a young age because speaking never seemed to work out right, and at least with a pen and paper she could consider her words carefully. She feels like that's where her writing style came from. She feels that the interesting parts of life are disguised in plain words so we never recognize the big things for what they are. At least, that's how she feels about her life. In high school, she joined theater where she finally figured out what confidence is. She wants to stay in theater in some capacity for the rest of her life, whether through writing awkward plays or actually performing in awkward plays. The only awards she remembers winning are from theater and that one award from 4th grade because she was one of the top readers. She knows it was a silly prize, but she still has the little plaque on her wall in her bedroom like it's some sort of lifetime achievement. She's cool like that.

Oh, and she loves making really sugary, bad-for-you food like cupcakes and cookies. She has no regrets.

If you'd like to hear more about Laura's life and weirdness, you can find her on Facebook and Twitter.

HAPPY ENDINGS TAKE WORK
MORGAN CAIR

"*THAT WAS the worst service I've ever had! You're all absolute fucking shit! Why can't you hold it tog—*"

"Shut up, Ramsay." Dani stabs the menu button on the DVD remote, and Chef Ramsay cuts off midbellow.

It does help her headache, the boring menu music. The pain's been raging since early this morning as she dropped off to sleep on the sofa instead of the bed. The correct response would be to go and take painkillers and to tackle the *reason* she was sleeping on the sofa and the real reason she's got a really bad headache.

Unfortunately for Dani, it's rather easier to ignore the elephant in the room than it is to be a grown-up and tackle it.

Thirty minutes into her third straight episode of *Hell's Kitchen*, and she's well aware of the brooding black cloud in the orchard at the bottom of the garden that's causing her headache. It's hard to ignore it. Even though she can't see where Jessi is, it's pretty easy to imagine her tucked up on the swing bench or even up a tree with her grandmother's ancient tartan blanket.

She should go and apologize. She should go and be a mature individual and explain her feelings to Jessi, and listen to Jessi's in return to understand why Dani hurt her. And she did; Dani knows she did.

Saying "*but you're not a real girl!*" is pretty goddamn hurtful to anybody, never mind to her girlfriend.

Saying that Jessi can't understand what Dani experiences day to day because she's not *at the same level* is pretty gross.

Screaming that at her girlfriend and then throwing out stuff about not understanding what it's like to be a girl, to be a *real* girl, throwing months of generosity back at her, letting loose a tide of frustration and complicated, hurtful emotions at the wonderful woman who's driven them both six hours to her grandmother's house as a treat... that's just plain... stupid.

Unfair.

Hurtful.

"I'm an idiot." Dani runs both her hands through her dark, wiry dreadlocks and tells the empty room the truth. She is a big one.

And she's not dealing with it. She's hiding out because she knows what she did wrong, and she knows she should fix it.

But she's sulking because... because... because it means apologizing. And Dani has gotten by on a life of walking away from giving apologies because they're supposed to make people weak or because they're supposed to be signs that people care, and Dani doesn't *care about other people because she doesn't get it.*

But she does care about Jessi. She does.

Apologizing to her *girlfriend* should be the first thing she does. That much Dani has worked out through watching people at school and shitty dramas on television. She should be ready and willing to admit that she was wrong because *she knows she was.*

It's just telling someone else that, which sucks.

"Urgh—oh. What do you want?" A cold nose on her arm distracts Dani from her circular argument about apologizing. "Hey, Rohan."

The harlequin Great Dane looms over her as he makes his demands for attention known. He was upstairs, sleeping on the cool floor of the bathroom as he usually does, but apparently, he's deigned to come and find his temporary human minders again. His tail thumps against the side of the sofa as Dani scratches gently just behind his ears, giving him the perfect scritching. Humans aren't her forte, but Dani definitely understands dogs.

Jessi likes scritches too. It's a random thought that crosses her mind, but Dani can't help comparing the two of them, because just as

Rohan is going gooey over the arm of the sofa, so does Jessi all over Dani when she gives Jessi head rubs.

They're both tall and all legs; Dani will never match Jessi inch for inch in bare feet, never mind when Jessi pulls out the heels and turns up the Mohawk, and Rohan is no small Great Dane.

Sometimes, it really isn't great to be the short one.

Even though she's only known Rohan since last night—late last night, stumbling in the door when it was cold and dark outside—he's already become one of her favorite things about this place.

The great big dog in the tiny little house, Jessi told her when they set off on the first long car trip from Jessi's parents' house in Devon, and it was like a fairy-tale place in Dani's head all the way up here.

Something to look forward to, something different from her usual inner-city haunt filled with gray apartment blocks and tight, closed-in streets. Dani never knew the country life until she met Jessi over the Internet and started that long, slow relationship that led her here.

It isn't, in reality, a fairy-tale place. It's definitely a house, for people to live and to exist in, with ugly flowery sofas and chairs (*vintage, Dani,* a voice in her head that sounds like Jessi says, but Dani's never been a fan of floral), but the pretty ivy up the front of the cottage, and the blue door, and the huge garden definitely make up for it.

And it's theirs for two *whole* weeks, which is the best thing *ever.*

Was.

Dani's ugly, dirty, unfair loss of control last night might have completely ruined it. Part of her thinks she should be getting her laptop out and trying to calculate how much train fare would be back home, even if she has to walk to the station.

But the dog is definitely not mad at her, even if Jessi is, and he doesn't want her to look up how to get home. When her hand slows, he nudges her arm with his massive nose, obviously asking for more. Dani braces herself for his apparently customary attempt that Jessi warned her about, where he climbs all over a sitter, because she's learned that if she sits still long enough, that's what he does. Fortunately, she's in luck. Rohan is not interested in being a lap puppy at the moment, and she can just pet him while he sprawls on the floor, his massive head resting on huge paws.

She tries to focus on colors and sensations that are *real*—the brownness of her skin against the whiteness of the fur on his back, the coarseness under her fingers, the smell of warm dog mixing with the potpourri on the coffee table and the faint smell of ash from the fire. The feeling of the sunshine through the window on the wood floor.

But all too soon, Rohan shuffles away to lounge on his dog bed (dog mattress? That thing is huge) and once again, Dani feels bereft. Maybe he's just tired—Jessi did take him for a long walk yesterday evening because he'd been cooped up all day alone after their fight, while Dani sulked on the sofa—or maybe he's just sensing the tension in the house, but he definitely doesn't want her touch for long today.

"You hate me too?" she asks him, but as predicted, no answer comes back. From his position all the way over on the other side of the room, Rohan huffs at her, a big doggy sigh that sounds more adult than Dani has *all fucking day.* He looks at her, brown eyes faintly knowing, and Dani gets the very real impression that if the dog could speak, he'd be telling her to get up, be an adult about the whole thing, and apologize.

Maybe the dog is right.

She'd argue that he's a dog, and what does he know, but right now, it's a better plan than doing what she's been doing all morning—lounging on the sofa and watching reruns of shows that would be twice as fun with Jessi beside her, rather than at the bottom of the garden.

Dani rolls her eyes. Nana Kau would say that the universe is sending messages again, and even if Dani doesn't exactly understand why, she can read them plain as day. Even if they are through the dog.

When the universe sends really, *really* big ones like a sighing dog with big brown eyes, she knows that she really, *really* shouldn't ignore them.

"Whatever, puppy. I get the message. Going to go and grow some 'nads. And apologize."

The sigh Rohan makes as she scuffs into the hall to find some shoes doesn't sound mocking. It sounds *knowing.*

Dani hates it when even the *animals* start telling her what to do.

But she listens.

And reaches for her hoodie, buried under all three of Jessi's exceptionally fashionable jackets—the black peacoat, the red one with the fake fur hood (*real fur is murder, Dani* rings loud in her head as Dani strokes her fingers down it now, because that's what Jessi always says when Dani comments on it) and the biker jacket that Jessi wore on the journey here.

It feels like a long time ago that they set off together on their very first road trip.

It was only *yesterday morning,* though.

And it's only been maybe sixteen hours since Dani said the *stupidest* thing of her romantic career and quite possibly ruined everything.

Time to go and fix it by being an adult, pulling up her big girl underwear, and doing the right thing.

It takes a while, though, to get herself to that mindset. Pretty much a whole quarter of an hour and more.

As she stares in the mirror at the foot of the stairs, Dani sighs.

Finally, with shoes on, laces done just so, her oversized hoodie zipped up to just the right level, a boring gray beanie covering her long black dreadlocks, and her scarf from the first Christmas with Jessi placed around her neck in exactly the right way, Dani's finally done procrastinating over her appearance.

She's not usually this hung up on how she looks, especially when it's just her and Jessi. It's not that she doesn't care, but usually she can relax. She can trust Jessi to look past the oversized hoodies, massive jeans, tent-like shirts, and trainers that she likes to see Dani. It's not like Jessi is going to be scoring her on her dress sense, or she'd be getting flat zeroes. There's precisely one fashionable person in their relationship, and it is profoundly *not Dani.*

Thank God.

"All right, all right, I'm going." Rohan has been giving her the evil eye from his position on the dog bed as soon as the five-minute mark came and went, and Dani is well aware that she was flapping about doing nothing to try to burn time.

She isn't anymore, though. The back door key with the mini cowbell key ring tucked securely in one pocket, and the last bag of Haribo in the other to lure Jessi out, and she's ready. Finally.

Procrastination has always been a strong suit of hers.

"Don't climb on the sofa." A finger wag at Rohan, just to remind him who's boss, and then Dani sets off for the back door.

The second she slams the bottom half of the stable door shut behind her, she hears a happy woof and the sound of the years-old couch objecting to a hundred and seventy-five pounds of dog scrambling all over it.

Whatever.

Dani has bigger things to focus on.

DANI FINDS Jessi in the orchard, exactly where she expected.

Up a tree.

An oak tree, to be precise, looking over the rolling hill to the bottom of the valley, at the very back of the garden. Jessi has tucked herself neatly into the crook of two branches, the tartan blanket moving in the cool breeze that ripples the grass and crawls between Dani's scarf and her hoodie.

"Hi." She's aiming for casual, but Dani is pretty sure she landed straight into no-man's-land, at least. Possibly straight into ice-cold *get away from me* territory.

"Mm." It's not a good sign. Jessi just pops one earbud out, leaving the other one firmly in place, and Dani can hear the loud music from here. Sounds like something sad and teary, which is exactly what she'd expect.

It's the patented Jessi method of dealing with sadness. Dani's is to go and find Jessi and ask for kisses and head rubs, but right now, that won't work.

Dani would at least attempt to join Jessi in the tree she's in, but she won't. Can't. Tree climbing is an acquired skill, and she's never managed to do so. Riding a skateboard, Dani can do; riding a bike, yes, fine; climbing a tree, no. Or indeed, no to anything that involves climbing something over two feet tall.

Dani's baggy jeans are so not made for that. Or her oversized hoodies, or her trainers, specifically worn just loose enough to scuff along the floor. She's a city kid, born and raised, and she doesn't do physical activities that involve nature.

And it's probably why outdoorsy Jessi has chosen the biggest, tallest tree in the whole fucking garden to climb.

She doesn't want Dani to follow her.

To be quite honest, Dani doesn't know if she would follow her, even if she could.

Right from the first look at Jessi, she's confused and feeling way out of her depth. Jessi hadn't even bothered to get made up this morning, which is a bad sign; Dani had hoped she would find a resplendent queen, all dark eyes and fierce lips, because that's the *Jessi* she can cope with. That hard face to the world is one that Dani's seen, that she can understand and talk to because she's familiar with it. The biting sarcasm, the angry words, the tendency to throw things at walls, all that Dani knows—not well, but enough to be able to know where to begin.

But this time, Jessi is showing all her dark circles and her thin lips and the freckles across one side of her face and not the other that she usually hides away, and Dani doesn't know this Jessi. Even stranger to Dani, she's showing the dark dusting where her stubble is threatening to break through, even though she's been having electrolysis for a while. She always hides it under foundation and concealer and never allows Dani to see her first thing in the morning before all the layers and layers of expensive makeup go on.

Dani actually is interested in how it would feel against her fingers, her cheek, or even her *lips*, because she's never felt anybody's stubble before. Her dad, from what she can remember, had a full-on beard, and her little brothers are *years* away from stubble and razors. Jessi might be a real girl—and she is; Dani recognizes that *now* in the cold light of day—but she has some of the things that Dani's always associated with men. It's not all of what confused her, but it's some of it.

Dani doesn't like it when things don't fit exactly into one box or another, because that's the way her brain works. Jessi, on the other hand, thrives on different labels—*artist, pretty, hard, makeup lover, punkish, outdoor kind of girl, likes vintage, hates traditional, bi, trans*—and the fact that she has stubble as a girl shouldn't surprise Dani.

Last night, it was one of the things that led to the whole horrible thought process in her head that created the fight, and it made sense there, but the second she actually *looks* at it... it doesn't.

Idiot.

But she thinks that asking Jessi about it, if she could touch it and experiencing it under her own hands to understand it, would be wrong. Would be too much. After everything that happened, at least.

"Can I talk?"

"You going to shout at me some more? Run away again?" Ow. Never let it be said that Jessi does not know how to go for the jugular. It's just that usually, Dani sees other people experience it. Being on the other end... not so fun, actually.

"No. I want.... I came to...." She sighs. "I want to talk. To you. With you. About... before."

"So do I." The music cuts off, and Jessi pulls the other stark white cord out of her ear.... Her hair is pulled back in a sloppy ponytail, and she's already fiddling with it, the dark strands obvious against the pale skin of her hand. "But I'm not coming down."

"I can live with that." She had better be able to; Dani doesn't think she's in much of a position to make demands at the moment. "Do... I mean... do you want to go first...?"

"Sure. I'll go first." Jessi looks her right in the eyes. "Are you listening?"

DANI HOLDS onto the wall and tries to keep it together. Jessi's *still* going, and Dani's suddenly getting a crash course in how not to be a cruel fool.

"How would you feel if someone said that you didn't understand what it was like to be a black person—if someone didn't understand that *you lived and breathed that existence every fucking day* and still said you were fake?"

"Ow." Jessi knows Dani's relationship to her father and to her own biracialness is rocky to say the least, and putting it that way suddenly makes it a lot more painful. Real. Dani doesn't get that a lot—putting things in context to stuff she knows, because... well. It's something she's working on. "That's... *ow.*"

"Yeah." Jessi shrugs, winding her headphone cable around her fingers. "I know it's not exactly the same—that there are a lot of differences, and I'm not in a position to know about race and stuff, but... I am female, Dani. Inside me, inside my head, that's what I've always believed, and I'm finally getting to a point where I can make it happen in reality too—drugs, and s-surgery...."

That's what had set Dani off, hearing Jessi talk about the surgery like that, like it was... like it was a good thing. All of them—it was hard to hear that Jessi had a list of surgeries she wanted on her computer and could just reel them off like her body was Plasticine, ready to be molded and manipulated when Dani *couldn't* do that to her own. Like it's the right thing to do, and Dani doesn't understand it, because a surgery like that is *final,* and she's so... confused. It's Jessi's surgery, but Dani is the one objecting.

Which is messed up.

A lot.

"No, it's fine. I get what you mean." Dani can't change the color of her skin or the way her hair looks—she's not as dark as her father, her hair isn't as wiry, and she can't have an afro like her half sister can even at *five,* but... it's her. And it's not the same—Jessi has to face different challenges as a trans person than Dani does as someone who's biracial, but it's close enough. She can't make her race different even if someone asks her to, and asking Jessi to do the same for *her* unchangeable part of herself is... unfair.

They don't talk for a while as Jessi lets Dani process that for a moment. It's a bit of a harsh reminder, but it's the truth, and Dani fiddles with the ties on her hoodie as she thinks. While Dani's lost in her own head, Jessi is on the move. She always is but this time, it's not to the ground, which would be for the best, but she does lie along the biggest branch above Dani's head, looking entirely at home in the tree in her gray sweats and bare feet.

Her toes have a rainbow manicure, and Dani can't help focusing on them.

It's with a great deal of difficulty that she refocuses her attention away from late-night foot massages and the hours Jessi's spent teaching her how to actually perform a pedicure. "So... what do you want us to do?" Dani is fully prepared to hear the worst news possible—that Jessi wants to end the relationship, the best thing in her life, but that's not what Dani hears coming back at her.

"—ling?"

"What?"

Jessi rolls her eyes and tilts her head in just the right way to inform Dani that she's getting unhappy again. She doesn't like it when people don't pay attention to her. *"Counseling.* We should go. Together."

"You think we should go to therapy?" Okay, that's very suburban.

"Counseling. But yes, I do." Jessi leans along her tree branch a little more, and Dani can't decide if she really likes the view and should go back and get her pencils to sketch it or if she should tell Jessi to not do that since it's *dangerous.* Not that Jessi will listen to her. When does Jessi listen to anybody when they tell her not to do something?

Never.

A twig bounces off the front of her hoodie, landing on her shoes. "Earth to Dani?" Jessi does *not* like to be ignored.

"I'm listening."

"You weren't." Jessi is trying to look fierce and to sound determined, but Dani can see the little smile in the corner of her mouth. An answering one near her own lip ring threatens to come out, but Dani can't.

Not yet. The conversation is still far too serious to risk fucking it over with smiles.

"Was too," Dani counters just to defend herself before refocusing again. "But... you think we should go. Together. To *ther*—sorry, *counseling."* Dani is still trying to get her head around that.

It definitely wasn't what she was expecting. To part ways, to be made to listen to Jessi shout and get angry and hurt (not that Dani would blame her, of course), yes, but not *talking to a professional.* That's not how things are done in her experience, but then again, Jessi is introducing her to whole new experiences every single day in this relationship.

Why should this be any different?

"Why counseling?"

"Because it helps." Jessi looks calm and in control, but Dani is starting to learn to read her tells, and the way she's tucking neatly manicured fingers into fists and withdrawing them into her sleeves is a big one. She's nervous about this. "It helped me when I was just figuring out... you know, the whole trans thing."

"Really?"

"Yes. It helped to have someone to talk to, who understood what I felt like even when I didn't completely get it. And Mora, my first counselor, helped me to tell my parents when I was ready. She can help you as well."

"But... I'm not trans."

"Oh, for the love of...." Rolling her eyes, Jessi takes a deep breath. And another one. And another one. "You aren't. I am. Counselors help people who are affected by trans issues, including parents *and partners.*"

"Oh." Well, no prizes for Dani for being the brightest spark ever. It's the cold, she swears; it makes her slow to connect the really big dots that can be seen from space. "I see."

"Thank God." Jessi pulls the blanket around her like armor, and Dani sighs. If they have to have this conversation—and they do; she recognizes that now—they might as well have it here. In the open.

Hoisting herself up onto the crumbling red brick wall next to the tree trunk, Dani tries to at least meet Jessi halfway. The massive emotional distance between them has to go sometime, and she might as well make the physical one disappear first. Now she's talking to Jessi over six feet of empty air, rather than fifteen, so it's all progress in the right direction. "So... you want me to talk to her? What about?"

"Stuff. How you feel. What you're worried about. Why it made you angry when I said I was excited about my transition."

"But I wasn't angry!"

"You said *but you're not a real girl,* and you yelled at me for not understanding stuff about how hard it is for you, and that shit about me being trans, and then you ran away, Dani." Jessi shrugs. "That says angry to me. I'm not an expert, but... you know. Five years of knowing I was trans, three years of living as a girl, that means I've seen anger a lot. And I felt pretty shitty that you basically boiled me down to *not being a real girl,* and that you felt like my body shouldn't be the way I want it to look."

Seeing the look of sadness in Jessi's eyes definitely doesn't make Dani feel *any* better about that moment in time. It's hard to believe it was just last night.

It wasn't her finest hour. Not by a long shot. And Dani does know. She wasn't angry, but she wasn't okay with what had been said in one way, and she was okay with it in another. She's already seeing Jessi's body change from the hormones and the posture training she's doing, because Jessi's a perfectionist, and if she's going to do something, she's going to do it *all* the way. Dani doesn't know if she can handle seeing Jessi's body change *so* dramatically after a surgery like the ones Jessi is proposing – cutting things out, adding things in, making scars and changing the flat planes of her skin that Dani is only just starting to learn. And maybe she should recognize that, acknowledge that she was a phenomenal idiot to do that to Jessi, talking shit about her body, about the future Jessi.

God knows too many people already think they have rights to Dani's own body because she's a woman, because she's apparently a lesbian (kind of. A bit. It's a lot fuzzy right now, to be honest, because Dani likes prolonging a crisis), because she's kind of black-looking, and that's enough. Doing that to Jessi... not Dani's finest moment.

She should apologize about that. Jessi is twice the woman she'll ever be, in Dani's eyes, even if Jessi's trying to make her get rid of that stupid voice. *We're both women, Dani, both of us. Just different.*

"I'm sorry." Making that decision to say those words, to actually flat-out apologize, is hard for Dani. Even though apologies haven't been her way, maybe they should be. Especially to her girlfriend. "I hurt you. And I was... it wasn't fair."

"Can't say it was." That's definitely hurt in Jessi voice, but Dani knows she put it there.

"I just.... It was me being stupid. And not thinking and just reactive and, um...."

"You."

"Ow."

"It's the truth, though."

"Yes." Dani nods, twisting her fingers together into a knot. They reflect how she's feeling inside. "I can keep telling you that I'm sorry because I *am.* I'm really, really, really sorry. And I don't know how I can make up for it.... But... I'm sorry. I love you. I really do."

"Oh."

It's not the first time she's said that to Jessi, but it is the first time she's said it outside of the bedroom or the living room, outside of kisses that are long and warm and wonderful, and this time it feels different. More... honest. Or more grounded in emotional reality.

At the moment it's the kind of reality where Jessi and she might lose everything, the whole eleven months of learning each other, of opening up to new experiences and to new people, and kisses and touches, and... everything.

Jessi is Dani's first relationship, and she's suddenly very aware that last night, after all the driving Jessi did to bring them to her grandparents' house to spend the next days on their own together as a couple without parents or irritating little brothers, Dani ruined it all with a few angry words and a door slam.

She might actually cry—no, wait. Dani *is* crying. Emotional walls down and whatever. Dani scrubs her face with her sleeve. It's a very good thing she doesn't wear makeup like Jessi, or she'd have covered her dark blue hoodie in pale foundation now.

"I love you too." It feels *good* to hear Jessi say that, Dani has to admit. Better than ever before, quite possibly. "And I know it was a... stupid mistake. And that you love me. You let me drag you halfway across England, for God's sake."

"Free holiday." Dani tries to turn it into a joke, but it sounds vaguely pitiful when it starts with a sniffle, and her voice cracks a little in the middle of the last word.

"Yeah. But I think.... I'm not.... It hurt. And even though you didn't mean it, you said it, and that's not... that's not okay. But I want to talk about it. I want to discuss things with you because I know you're not totally okay with everything."

"I'm not." Dani doesn't want to admit it, but there's no escaping it. Last night proved it; Dani loves Jessi, loves her more than she's ever loved anyone else before, but she isn't completely comfortable with Jessi's transness, and it's more obvious than she thought.

And that's not okay.

"It's important for me that you *are* okay with me, Dani. My body, the changes that I've gone through, and the ones that are coming, the whole trans identity thing. It's a part of me, and if you want to be with me, you need to understand it too." A big sweeping gesture encompasses Jessi's little speech, and Dani nods.

"And counseling will help." It's not a question, and Jessi doesn't take it as such.

"Yes. You can say the bad things, the mean things, the things that you don't want to admit, and Mora, or whoever, will help you talk through it. I had a lot of bad thoughts in my head—"

"Like?" Jessi's the queen of forward positive thinking most of the time.

"That I wasn't going to be a real girl. That I'd always be a fake." Dani can see sadness in Jessi's eyes, and she wonders if those thoughts have ever gone away. "It's taking me a while to get over them, to work out why I feel like that, and then to teach myself to stop it. I'm not finished yet, but it's helping."

"Can we do that? Together?" Dani knows Jessi is expecting a fight. They've always had one when Jessi tries to introduce Dani to *talking* about feelings, about discussing and dissecting the way she feels—about herself, about their relationship, Dani's own fragmenting self-destructive family, about all the dark and confused mess that is her sexuality... anything that involves feelings and sticky complicated emotions that don't make sense—they've blown up.

Dani doesn't like having her heart on show to anybody, but Jessi keeps dragging it out of the shadows and making her think about it.

And usually it's for the better. Maybe this time is another example of exactly that.

"You'd do it for me?" Surprise is etched into Jessi's face. She was obviously gearing up for the long haul, preparing to dig deep and fight Dani on every inch of ground until they were both too tired to carry it on, because that's what they did.

But Dani's done with fighting for now. Maybe for a while. "For us."

"For *us*."

Dani shuffles along the wall, getting as close as she dares. Jessi isn't coming down from the tree yet; she's made it clear that she's staying up for a while, and Dani knows she can't make her leave. But she's extending a hand to Dani, and touch is important for them.

It was how they began, after all.

"For us," Jessi repeats, and Dani holds on to her hand tight.

This isn't a cut and dry solution, this isn't a quick fix. There's a lot of talking and a *lot* more apologizing for Dani in the future, but she's okay with doing that.

It means they're on the road to okay again.

MORGAN CAIR is a young author on the run from university in the UK who likes French bulldogs, kissy girls and boys, and watching cooking and crime TV shows on the internet (although not all at the same time). She likes beading crafts, interior decorating (badly), and writing to-do lists she'll never follow through on, because it's relaxing. Her laptop is her partner in crime, and it connects her to the outside world because she lives in in the world's tiniest town.

Her favorite kinds of stories to write are emotionally complicated and delve deep into character growth and development. Short stories are a new found passion for her; she likes the challenge of cramming all those rollercoastering feelings into under ten thousand words, and still have it make sense. Mostly.

Morgan likes to mix it up and focus on the small elements of a day that are rich with potential—tiny moments are always the most interesting to her. She likes to write about friends, family, and lovers to probe all different kinds of angles when approaching writing. She likes happy endings, sweet moments, and plenty of heartwarming goodness to make a story feel good.

THE GIFT OF FLAME

SCOTIA ROTH

IN A land far removed from the world of humans, there lived a queen, so little and young, "princess" might fit her better, but queen—or rather, Snow Queen—was the title bestowed upon her. She had not been given a name. There was little need for it, after all, Snow Queen was all she was, all she was supposed to be, and all she ever would be—Winter personified—and at the end of her long life, she would simply turn to snow, and from those flakes a new Snow Queen would be born.

Our little queen, the twenty-first since the dawn of time, was (much like her predecessors) alone from the moment she was born. Up where only birds could reach, but even those stayed away from the frost capable of freezing their wings, there had been no one to hold the little queen's hand or wipe away her tears or sing her to sleep. She wandered the halls alone, wrapped in her cloak and playing games by herself. By the time she was nine, she'd counted every window in the ice palace, every tower, and every step at least ten times each; she knew them all by heart.

The little queen loved the garden the most.

She loved to dance among the flowers and smell the fragrant melodies they sighed when the wind blew. She loved the roses and the bluebells and snowdrops, all in their wonderful shades of blue, from the deepest midnight to the gentle hues of the morning sky, and everything in between; she loved them dearly. But even the beauty of the garden or the way the ice palace glistened when touched by sunlight couldn't make her forget how lonely she was. So she always had one or two books with her, so that she could dive into the pages whenever the loneliness squeezed her little heart enough to hurt. Getting lost in other worlds that weren't so empty made that grip loosen; she imagined herself in worlds where she could be part of a ragtag bunch of misfits and go on great adventures and fall in love.

When she went to bed, the scenarios she dreamed during the day returned at night, taking a life of their own. The little queen had been a bandit and a sheriff, she'd been a poet, and she'd scaled the side of a great tower to reach the trapped princess; she'd fought dragons and grew wings that took her to great heights; she'd swum underwater with mermaids and hopped on clouds and glided down rainbows.

The little queen had sought to emulate the intrepid explorers who either by luck, chance, or years of planning found themselves in a new world. She searched for a passage—a rabbit hole—that would lead her into another place; anyplace would do, so long as it had people.

Days wore on, stretching into weeks and months and years, and no such passage had been found. To combat the loneliness while she searched for something she was coming to believe didn't exist, the little queen learned to make snowmen. As her skills increased, they became more and more detailed; they grew into her friends and relatives and soldiers that stood guard outside her door and kept the nightmares away. She even learned to carve them out of blocks of ice. To populate her world with these frozen friends became her greatest distraction, her biggest source of joy.

There was one statue in particular the little queen was very fond of. She was named Gerda, after the gutsy heroine in one of the stories she'd read. Gerda, a carefully and lovingly sculpted girl made of snow, sat on a bench where the little queen came every day to read. Gerda kept the little queen company and heard the stories she read aloud, heard her talk about nightmares in a hushed tone as if speaking too loudly could make them materialize, heard her talk about the future in barely audible whispers (the little queen was more scared of *that* than any demons her subconscious conjured).

ONE DAY the little queen made her way to her preferred bench with a book about pirates that she thought Gerda would enjoy tucked under her arm; yet when Gerda appeared before her, sitting in her usual place, so did someone else. A queer-looking creature had taken the queen's spot beside her friend. It had gray skin, and white tufts of hair sprouted from inside its long ears, and it dressed in filthy patched-up rags. Nearby, a tall mirror—taller than the queen—leaned against the bench, turned in such a way that kept the little queen from seeing her reflection.

"Little girl," he said, "I need your help."

The little queen had never seen or heard another living creature before. She was entranced by his words and mesmerized by the mirror with its elaborate silver frame, and so she eagerly agreed to listen to the little troll.

"I made this mirror as a present for the angels up above, and now I must deliver it, but I have no way of getting there. Wouldn't you be able to help me, little girl? You who live so high up already... surely you know of a road that leads up there? A passage of some kind?"

The queen sadly shook her head. "I'm very sorry, sir. I'd love to help you, but there's no such thing up here. If there was, I would have already found it." She paused. "Do you know many angels, sir? Could I maybe meet one? Would you let me take a peek into your mirror?"

"You ask for so much, and I ask only for a little favor. Don't you have any manners, child?"

"I'm very sorry, sir. I didn't mean to be rude," the little queen said in alarm. The thought of offending the only creature in her world who could actually see her and talk to her sent her into a panic. She began to stammer another apology, but the troll raised his hand, asking for her silence.

"I have seen the sculptures you've made," he said. "You aren't without talent. Why not make me a ladder? In exchange I'll give you the gift of flame."

"Flame?" She'd only read of those, never seen one, but the illustrations in books had always left her fascinated.

"Yes, you can use it to bring one of your sculptures to life."

The little queen looked to Gerda, frozen on the bench. "All right, sir, I'll build your ladder."

THE LITTLE queen set to work. Every waking moment she had, she devoted to the ladder. The troll watched her work with hungry and impatient eyes, but the little queen didn't mind; she was just as anxious about getting the ladder built as he was.

As she worked on making the ladder rise, she knew that an experienced queen could have done it with a flick of the wrist, but she was different. She was still young, and her powers hadn't yet peaked. If she made the snow and ice rise up any higher than two feet, the ladder wouldn't be able to support her weight, let alone the mirror's weight and the troll's together. She had no choice but to move slowly. She needed to make sure the base would be strong enough to allow the ladder to rise where it needed to.

The sun made its slow descent across the sky, while the moon rose to take its place. Day after day, this dance played out while the little queen worked tirelessly on.

Finally came the day the ladder was complete.

The little queen looked at it, filled with amazement at her creation. She could hardly believe her own hands had crafted something so great.

"Do you think I can climb with you?"

"Don't be silly, child. The angels would cast you down in an instant. You'd be dead before you even reached the floor."

The little queen was disappointed but relented nonetheless. "And the flame?"

"Dig a hole in your friend's chest, where her heart ought to be," the troll said as he began to climb with the mirror tied to his back. "I'll throw the flame down to you once I've reached the top."

The queen did as she had been told. She opened the hole in Gerda's chest and then waited by her side, holding her cold, lifeless hand. She hoped Gerda would like the palace. The troll was taking his time, but the queen understood; it was a long climb, and the mirror did look very heavy. She meant to stay awake, but the troll was taking so long, and she was so tired that not even the possibility of having a friend to play tag with could keep her awake. She dozed off with her cheek on Gerda's shoulder. When she woke up, for a split second she thought it was *warm*. Her heart leaped to her throat and pushed back the tiredness that still clung to her, but as it did, it also pushed away the sensations of a dream she could barely remember, but one that certainly had to do with Gerda—Gerda the human girl, not Gerda the snow sculpture.

The little queen blinked; her hand was wrapped around ice.

Gerda was still a statue, and the queen felt ice-cold tears well up in her eyes. Had she been tricked? It was a question she didn't dare ask out loud, lest she summon a yes, but then she saw a red spot slowly descend from heaven. No, she hadn't been tricked after all! Eagerly she took the flame in her hands, and the burn was welcome, if only for how unknown it was to her. She would apologize to the troll for doubting him. Later.

Now....

She gently placed the flame inside the hole she'd dug and covered it with a fine layer of snow.

The little queen looked excitedly into the eyes of her friend, waiting for the snow to melt away and reveal flesh and life and the warmth that her books told her could only come from the skin of another human, but that moment never came.

She found herself mesmerized by the way the red flickered behind that curtain of snow, and as soon as she stood back to admire it, to wait for Gerda's face to appear, there was a tremendously loud crash from up above. It reminded her of a time when her fears and loneliness had turned to anger and she'd hurled a book against the mirror in her bedroom. Immediately she looked up, fearing something had happened to the ladder, and the troll was about to tumble to his death.

She outstretched her arms to catch him, but it wasn't he who fell. What came down to greet her was a shard of glass; it cut through the air like an arrow and pierced straight through her heart. The little queen's eyes widened in shock, her arms still outstretched, waiting to catch the troll that would never fall and still waiting for her friend to come to life.

She felt a chill like no other; it slithered and coiled around her spine and took root in her heart. The little queen fell to the ground. The flame flickered inside her friend's chest; it flickered and grew and burned away the snow. The little queen smiled, then her eyes closed.

GERDA WAS born into a harsh winter. She was one with the many snowflakes that fell all around the world. She'd never had anyone at her side, not until she met her surrogate mother, a kindly woman who had a pumpkin patch in front of her garden and grew her own apples.

A child of only twelve, she'd been wandering the snowy forest and eating whatever she could find. She didn't know what was poisonous and what wasn't. She didn't even know something could *be* poisonous. All she knew was that berries looked like food, and she was very hungry.

She ate as many as she could find, and it wasn't long before she got a terrible stomachache. Her stomach was cramping up so much she could hardly walk. All she could do was cry and wonder why someone had been so cruel as to leave her alone in the middle of nowhere with no one to turn to.

Pure chance lead to her stumbling upon Marigold's house. The woman was outside, despairing over the snow and how it froze the ground and kept her crops from growing, when she saw a child walk up, swaying and stumbling with her lips and chin stained purple and her face flushed.

The woman nursed Gerda back to health, and once she was recovered and Marigold heard of her unfortunate circumstances, Marigold offered her a home. She'd never had any children and was delighted to have Gerda around. Gerda grew up happy. Marigold taught her how to cook and tend to the garden and also how to hunt and fish. At night they sat by the fireplace, and Gerda listened to her mother's stories. Some of them Gerda thought were familiar (she could almost, but not quite, hear them in someone else's voice, though she never told her mother of this), while others were entirely new to her, like the ones Marigold came up with just for her.

Ever since Gerda had come into her home, Marigold never had to worry about the frozen soil again or even the cold. There was always warmth in the house, and she couldn't help but wonder if it was because of Gerda's presence—Gerda, whose bustling energy made it appear as if it were summer. Marigold could grow as many delicious fruits and vegetables as she wanted and adorn her windows and the rooms with as many flowers as it pleased her. It was a miracle, and they'd been blessed, she told Gerda with grateful tears in her eyes.

Gerda never thought this blessing had anything to do with her, even though she had many times wondered why the cold didn't seem to affect her as it did everyone else. To this Marigold always replied with the same words: "Your blood just runs a little hotter than everyone else's." And thanks to her warmth and sunny personality, Gerda was able to make a lot of friends from the neighboring towns. People would often ask her to hold their hands or to come sit with them, and Gerda didn't mind at all. She hated being alone, and this way she got to learn many interesting things. The old women taught her how to knit, and the baker showed her how he baked his mouth-watering bread, and she never lacked for playmates.

Gerda's warmth was such that she made people forget about the winter that had lasted for over four years, or rather, in a world where everyone's hearts had begun to freeze over, Gerda reminded them of sunny afternoons and wind that caressed instead of biting. Spring would come again, that's what everyone believed when they held hands with Gerda or saw her running up and down the streets, her hair a disheveled mess, laughing in the face of the cold.

But there was a thorn in Gerda's life, one she dare not speak about to anyone. It was a thorn she'd tried to squeeze out many times before, but the only thing she'd accomplished was to dig it in further. Every day without fail, Gerda woke up in cold sweats with the image of a girl impaled with a shard of glass fresh on her mind. Every day she did the best she could to push the image out of her mind. While her daily chores and adventures helped keep it at bay, it never fully went away. It was always there; there was always that *sting*. Sometimes she closed her eyes and felt her very heart grow cold, just from thinking of that girl's eyes closing. That image was colder than anything Gerda had experienced, far more chilling than the time she fell straight through the ice in the lake or when she'd waded up the river wearing close to nothing as a dare.

She was a girl of sixteen now, and she'd dreamed this dream for years. From that day she woke up by herself, dangling from a tree more like a lost kite than a little girl, ever since that day the dream had chased her. That shard of glass was her thorn, and what a small thing it was, but how badly did it hurt her! Sometimes when no one was around and the cold grew to be too great, she sobbed and fell to her knees, clutching her chest, her hands closing around an invisible piece of glass; such was the pain it caused her.

Not being able to tell anyone for fear of what they would say, for fear they would think her insane, only made it hurt more.

Like all other secrets, it was eventually discovered.

One day—rather, one particularly terrible night—the pillow hadn't been enough to muffle Gerda's sobs and cries, and so they drew Marigold to her room. She pulled Gerda to her feet and dried her tears away, patting her back and holding her until she stopped shaking. Patiently, Marigold coaxed what had happened out of Gerda, who explained everything; the secret had grown heavy, and now the words came tumbling out.

Hot tears trembled in her eyes and threatened to spill at any second; she held them in somehow.

"That reminds me of a story," Marigold began to say. "We've been waiting for spring to come for four years, and as you know, many believe it'll never return again. People have struggled to find a reason, some kind of explanation for this harsh punishment, and this is the story I heard from the raven, who swore it to be true." Marigold spoke of a faraway land, one not entirely of this earth but connected to it nonetheless; she spoke of a place that was covered in snow and ice, where sunlight did little to warm you. This was a very beautiful place, and at the heart of it was a great palace with high towers and many windows of tinted glass and a garden filled with many lovely flowers. In its vastness, it was also a very lonely place, especially for its sole inhabitant, the Snow Queen. To ease her loneliness, the queen had begun to create snow and ice statues, and she pretended they were alive and could talk and listen to her. It helped a little, but deep down she knew they weren't real. One day she was offered a deal she couldn't refuse by a cunning troll. He would give her a special flame to bring one of her snow sculptures to life, and in return she would build him a ladder so he could take his enchanted mirror to heaven and make a fool out of God and the angels. "For the mirror was no ordinary thing," Marigold said, shadows darkening her face. "It distorts everyone and everything; it doesn't reflect reality but a gross, twisted version of it. It magnifies the bad and obliterates the good."

Gerda shuddered.

Her hand made a fist over her heart.

"Of course, the little Snow Queen knew nothing of the troll's plan or of the mirror's powers, for he had never let her take a peek. In her naïveté and eagerness to gain a friend, she built him a great ladder of snow. It took her a long, long time, but when it was done, it was a ladder that could support the weight of the troll and of the great mirror he carried at his back. The troll hastened to climb it, and long after he'd disappeared into the clouds, he cast down the flame he'd promised. The little Snow Queen took it in her hands and used it as a heart for her favorite sculpture."

Gerda's eyes widened; her cheeks paled.

Marigold didn't notice; her gaze was distant, her mind set on the tale she'd heard from the raven.

"But she never got to greet her friend," Marigold said. "The mirror on the troll's back, unable to contain its dark magic any longer, burst into a million pieces. Some were large, and some were little more than dust. When one gets so high up, the wind is a creature of its own. Strong and untamable, it blew the pieces all around the world and beyond. It blew away the queen's friend and brought her instead a large piece of the mirror—a sword of glass and malice."

It had impaled the queen straight through her heart, corrupting it and turning it into a lump of ice. "That's why spring hasn't come in years. That's why winter is so harsh. The Snow Queen has been tainted by that hateful mirror."

Gerda's tears dried on her eyes.

MARIGOLD DIDN'T want Gerda to leave. She kept telling her it was just a story; there wasn't really a queen or a troll with a magic mirror. And to Marigold that might be so, but Gerda knew it was more than that. She need only hold her hand up to her heart to know it was the truth. And even though it brought her a great deal of pain, Gerda chose to leave. Without saying good-bye to anyone, she snuck away in the middle of the night when she was sure no one would try to stop her.

She walked nonstop for miles until she came across the river. It was a familiar sight, and that brought her some comfort. Gerda figured the best thing she could do was look for the raven. She would know where the queen lived, and she might even be able to take her there, but Marigold had refused to tell her anything about where she might be. Gerda made up her mind not to let that discourage her. She would simply walk until she found who she was looking for. She walked along the riverside listening to the soft murmur of the water and leaving footprints in the snow. She was glad to have left in the middle of the night; by the time people in town woke up, her footprints would be long gone.

Gerda was thinking of stopping when she saw something glimmer under the starlight. Right away she recognized a single soap bubble, its colors changing and twisting onto themselves with the light from the moon and the stars. It was such a beautiful, delicate thing, Gerda couldn't help but stop and watch as it rose and fell according to the wind's whims. And in its wake there came others; there were so many of them, Gerda soon lost count. She advanced through this fragile sea, and the soap bubbles floated away to make way for her; she was astonished. The bubbles formed an ever-shifting corridor around her, almost as if they were guiding her somewhere. Gerda happily followed them.

She noticed tiny snowflakes inside the bubbles; it reminded Gerda of a little girl drawing elaborate snowflakes on the snow in front of a lonely bench, under the shadows cast by a century-old tree....

Did the Snow Queen still wait for her? Gerda could only hope so.

Whether to give her hope or just to mimic her thoughts, the snowflakes within the soap bubbles spun round and round, becoming a white blur, before turning to the visage of a girl whose face was obscured by her long white hair.

"That's her," Gerda whispered and began to walk even faster. The bubbles swirled all around her. "I'll get there. I'll get there."

Soon she came upon a single, lonely swing set, hidden away under the cover of snow. One by one the bubbles began to pop. Gerda brushed the snow away from the seat with a gloved hand. She hadn't stopped walking since she left her home; the sun was rising now, and her legs ached, so she sat down and sighed. "If only the raven would show herself to me."

She munched on a slice of bread, swaying lightly back and forth. The wind began to blow at her back. Gerda was so tired and distracted—still thinking about the girl inside the soap bubbles—that at first she didn't notice how the wind was making the swing move faster and faster. She let herself be swayed by the movement of the swing; her eyelids fluttered. She was only aware of the speed the swing had picked up when she saw her feet were no longer touching the ground. The wind blew harder then, and the considerable increase of speed gave her only enough time to hold on. A smile blossomed on her face; the higher she went, the wider her smile stretched, and the more her heart swelled and sweltered. *Closer*, she thought, eyes closed.

One final gust sent her soaring through the air. Gerda laughed. An updraft lifted her higher and higher. She looked around, searching for the raven, but she was nowhere in sight. There were a handful of birds that dared brave the cold air of early morning, and Gerda asked each and every one if they had seen the raven, but they couldn't answer her. They couldn't even understand her.

The invisible arms that had kept Gerda up in the air now let her drop. She screamed as she plummeted to the ground, and the birds she left behind watched on in horror; but instead of the ground, it was cold water that rushed up to greet her. Gerda sank to the very bottom, then kicked herself upward and swam until she broke the surface. No sooner had she opened her mouth to suck in a fresh breath of air than someone reached out and forcibly yanked her out of the lake by the back of her jacket.

Her rescuer dropped her on the ground without a care.

"Give me all you have, or I'll stuff an apple in your mouth and roast you on a spit!"

Gerda spit water on her shoes. "I only have the clothes on my body," she said, spreading her arms wide. She hadn't realized it at first, but when the swing launched her into the sky, it failed to do the same for the rucksack she had kept at her feet with all her supplies.

The Robber Girl scrutinized Gerda. She was at least a foot taller than Gerda, and she was built like an ox—broad-shouldered and with obvious well-defined muscles on her arms and legs, she had enough strength to break a girl like Gerda, who was little more than skin clinging to bone, in half.

The Robber Girl had a knife, but Gerda had a flame for a heart and someone very dear to her to find.

She stood up defiantly and much too fast; her head began to sway a little, and that slice of bread had done little for her stomach, which no longer had the joy of flight to fill it. Her legs were still hurting from the long walk, and she still had such a long way to go…. But Gerda didn't fall. She didn't want to let the Robber Girl get the better of her. Instead she raised her clenched fists.

The gesture seemed to amuse the Robber Girl to some degree, who lowered her knife but remained towering over the soaking wet Gerda. At last, Robber Girl put a hand on Gerda's shoulder to steady her. "Why did you fall from the sky?"

Hoping the Robber Girl might've seen the raven, Gerda told her the entire story. Gerda felt sleep beckoning her, but she didn't let herself fall into unconsciousness until she had explained everything to the Robber Girl.

When she was finished, the Robber Girl gave her a skeptical look and bent down to poke Gerda's ribs with the butt of her knife. "You don't look like you're made of snow, though."

"I was," Gerda insisted.

"That's one hell of a story, girly," the Robber Girl said, "but you've got honest eyes, so I believe you."

Those words were enough to fill Gerda with relief and thankfulness, but not enough to keep her weary self awake. Before she could ask about the raven, she fell asleep.

The Robber Girl, intrigued by the girl who fell from the sky and moved by her search for the Snow Queen, decided to help young Gerda. She effortlessly carried her to the place where she was camped out, and there she made sure Gerda was warm and tended to the wounds on her feet.

When Gerda woke up, the Robber Girl said that while she had not seen the raven, she would gladly help her look.

"You will?" Gerda asked, gladdened by the thought of having some company. "Won't someone be missing you?" She thought of those she'd left behind. By now Marigold had surely noticed she was missing and alerted the town to her absence. By now they would all be worried half to death, for sure. That made Gerda feel sad, but she'd left the queen waiting for far too long. And if she succeeded in her mission, then spring would come again, and everyone would have a reason to rejoice.

The Robber Girl bit into her bread and dipped the rest in her broth. "The only ones who'll miss me are my sweethearts. They know me well by now. They know I like to go off on my own every once in a while. They won't be worried."

And so they set off on the Robber Girl's horse. The sun shone brightly in the sky, but the howling winds were determined to thwart its efforts to bring some warmth to the earth.

Because Gerda didn't like riding in silence, she asked Robber Girl about her sweethearts. Robber Girl was quite happy to talk about them—she was always happy to be given a reason to talk, as Gerda discovered—and she explained to Gerda that she'd known Carlos ever since they were children. "We were brought up together, him and I. We were the youngest in our band of bandits." She laughed. "Band of bandits, sounds pretty funny, right?" She told Gerda that when she was sixteen—"That was only five years ago. I'm not an old lady, yeah?"—their band stopped outside this quaint little town, and she met the most charming florist, a girl of eighteen with honeyed hair that cascaded round her shoulders in pretty waves. "Love at first sight, *boom!* Like a lightning bolt. She ran away with me and Carlos and joined our band. The three of us have been together ever since," she declared with a proud, happy smile.

Gerda felt around the edges of the hole the queen had carved in her chest.

"Is it always like a lightning bolt? Can't it be… like a fire?"

The Robber Girl gave her a knowing smile.

"It's whatever you feel it is," she said. "Matilda says it's like a garden has blossomed in her heart, and Carlos says it's like gaining wings and taking flight. Do you like flowers, Gerda?"

Gerda nodded. She liked roses the best.

"Make sure you pick some up before you find your queen. She'll like them."

Gerda thought that was a wonderful idea. Hours later they passed by a rosebush dotted with wonderful, sweet-smelling roses. They were a bright, vibrant red with orange streaks licking the edges of the petals—a fragrant flame. Gerda could hardly believe her eyes.

"It's a sign, kid," the Robber Girl said. "Take the flowers."

Gerda took one, and she saw the Robber Girl collect a handful for her sweethearts too. They shared a bit of food, and after that they were off again. Gerda knew herself to be on the right path; she was coming back to her friend, and the closer she got, the more she remembered. She closed her eyes, and it was like she was sitting on that bench once again, underneath the tree that shielded her snowy form from the sun. She could see the flowers in all their shades of blue, and she could hear the queen's voice, soft and sweet and cheerful, but every once in a while tired and sad. She read to her, and sometimes she cried and begged Gerda to just say something back, and she clutched Gerda's hand, but back then she was only a snow sculpture, and she couldn't return the touch or say thank you for the stories. Gerda was coming back to her friend, who had waited for so long, and the earth that longed for spring was helping her do it. *First the bubbles, now the roses….*

Night had fallen by the time they found the raven, perched atop a tree branch and half-asleep.

"Excuse me," Gerda called. "Are you the raven who's seen the Snow Queen?"

The raven awoke with a snort. "Indeed I am," she said and leaned down. "Come closer. You seem familiar."

Gerda jumped down from the horse. "My name is Gerda. I'm the one the queen brought to life years ago." She reached out her arm, and the raven flew down, black feathers covered in flakes of snow. "I need you to take me to her. Can you do that?"

The raven looked past her and toward the Robber Girl. "I can take you, but not her. I'm not a young bird anymore. I'm not as strong as I used to be, and it *is* quite a ride."

Gerda wanted to ask if there wasn't some other way to get there, but the Robber Girl stopped her. "You have to go. Don't keep the queen waiting any longer," she said and patted her bag. "I need to get these flowers to my sweethearts soon anyway. Otherwise they'll die."

They promised they would see each other again. Gerda clipped the rosebud from the stem and hid it in the pocket of the jacket the Robber Girl had lent her. It was too big for her, comically so, but she couldn't refuse the well-meaning token of friendship. Besides, according to the raven, her own jacket was much too thin for the journey ahead. "I wish I had something to give you."

"Next time." The Robber Girl smiled.

Gerda returned it. She told the raven she was ready to go. She put her hand over her pocket to feel the contours of the rosebud inside. "Let's not waste any more time." The raven hooked her claws in the back of the Robber Girl's jacket and took flight. Gerda waved at the Robber Girl, Robber Girl waved back, and soon she was nothing but a little dot on the snow.

Gerda had so many questions for the raven—how was the queen? Did she remember her? Was she still waiting for her? But the higher they flew, the louder and harsher the wind became. It threw away her words before they reached the raven. They rose above and through clouds that were soft and fluffy, clouds bursting with water, clouds that split open with deafening thunder; before long they were caught in a flurry of snow. Gerda stopped trying to speak. She pressed her lips together, chewed into the inside of her cheek, and closed her eyes.

Distantly, like her voice was making its laborious journey all the way from the moon, Gerda heard the raven call to her. She couldn't understand what the black bird was saying.

She could only hear the urgency in words weathered down by the wind and the snow.

Gerda craned her neck, cupped her hands around her ears, and struggled to listen past the howls and cries of winter. She thought the raven was saying "Hang on!" but to what?

Gerda screamed as the wind shook them sideways, upward, and downward—as though they were a cat's toy—and the snow kept them blind. Icicles no bigger than needles began to rain down on them; they cut away at the raven's feathers and Gerda's skin, piercing the flesh of both.

Time fell away, and the only things that existed were the raging winds and the snow. Gerda lost count of how many times she almost fell, how many times she slipped away from the raven (and the pain every time the raven sank her claws through the back of her shirt), but never did Gerda think she would die. She would not die until she saw the queen again. She held both hands over her heart; she felt the flame stir inside. *Hang on.*

When her feet touched the ground, she would have gotten down to kiss it, but first she had to get the exhausted raven to safety. She would have to go on alone against wind that struck her exposed flesh like a whip. All she could see was a blanket of white, interrupted by the occasional tree trunk. Gerda powered through the storm and eventually stumbled into a cave where she laid the raven down, wrapped in the large jacket.

"Thank you so much for bringing me here," she said. "Just wait here for a little bit. The storm will end soon."

After Gerda had rested her legs, she set out again, walking against the wind and snow that wanted to turn her back into a lifeless sculpture. She walked with both hands over her heart and felt the flame burning bright. She imagined the little queen and the woman inside those soap bubbles—and that flame burned ever brighter. She had so many stories to share with the queen; she had hands to hold her with now. That flame couldn't be extinguished, not even when the full force of winter threatened to gobble her up, for that flame had given her life, and now it expanded outwardly in a shimmering orb of orange and red light, and no wind nor snow nor ice could reach her.

Gerda walked, shielded from the elements, and before long she arrived at the great ice palace. She made her way inside, and having served its purpose, the orb dispersed.

Gerda was momentarily stunned by the cold that went deep past her skin and slowed her blood until it seemed to become ice. Somehow the cold inside was worse than the storm, but Gerda did not let that stop her either. She breathed in the frigid air through her nose and blew it out as fire, breathing new life into the frozen halls of the queen's palace.

The cuts and bruises, the aches and the pains that had built up along her journey were hardly felt; she was *so close*.

The palace was a great thing indeed, and Gerda found herself being guided down the corridors by a familiar voice—*Keep going down the corridor, then take the staircase upstairs. There you'll find a huge window of painted glass of the first Snow Queen. Keep going upstairs, then left, then right, then right, keep going, keep going*—and she recognized it as the childish voice of the little queen who'd once described the palace to her.

She grew more hopeful.

The heavy doors that led into the throne room were closed. Gerda pressed her hands against them, but the ice was so cold it burned her palms; she grimaced. She almost pulled back, but knowing the queen was inside—she *had* to be inside—she put all her weight against the doors. When that did nothing, she ran against the door, once, twice. Frustrated, she once more placed her hands on it, alternating between pushing at the ice and pounding at it.

"Queen? Snow Queen? Are you inside? It's me! It's Gerda!"

No answer came from the inside.

Gerda tried another run at the doors; they opened just as her shoulder was about to collide with them. She landed in a heap on the polished floor of the grand throne room, her cheek pressed against its cold surface. It wasn't the grand entrance Gerda had planned, but once she raised her head and saw the queen sitting in her throne, she brushed off her embarrassment and rose in an instant.

The room was dark, for the storm still raged outside and obscured the light that came from the sun or the moon—Gerda had no idea anymore, and it hardly seemed to matter when the queen was right *there*, right in front of her.

"Don't come any closer," the Snow Queen rasped. A ray of light struggled past the clouds, dark and rumbling with thunder, and illuminated the queen's hands, which were closed around the armrest of the throne. Her fingers dug into the ice, punching holes in it; from them slow, thin trickles of blood outlined the resulting cracks in red, giving them the appearance of pulsing veins. "Go away. I don't want to see you." She spoke, and her voice was a breath of chilling air. It froze and hurt more than anything Gerda had had to fight through. It brought tears to her eyes.

Gerda wiped them away as best she could, telling herself not to cry; layers upon layers of frozen tears would surely turn her back to snow.

"But... I came such a long way to find you," she said, taking a tentative step forward. "I never wanted to be separated from you. I've dreamed about you for so long, and the thought of you all alone up here has brought me nothing but misery."

"Liar!" the queen screamed, and the pain and sorrow in that scream made the glass windows vibrate. The figures of past queens shook and shuddered, as if they too were crying. "You're a liar. You never cared! You were perfectly happy living down there, and you left me! *You left me!*"

Gerda recoiled from the accusation. "I was lost, that's all.... The winds that blew the shards of glass from the troll's mirror—including the one that hurt you—were strong enough to blow them all around the world.... That's what happened to me!"

The queen wouldn't listen. The veins in her throne expanded, eating their way through the ice.

"Don't you believe me?"

"No." That single word lowered the temperature of the entire room.

Gerda felt her heart shrink and shrink and shrink, curling into itself as it tried to protect itself from the queen's ice. In trying to make itself smaller, it smothered the flame.

"Now go," the queen commanded. "Go and don't come back. Go back to your ugly little home, or die out in the snow. I don't care either way."

"I don't want to go!" Gerda stubbornly yelled out. "This isn't you talking!"

"You have not the slightest idea who I am."

But she did. Her mother's story had unblocked something, had removed the rock that had been obstructing the flow of her memory, that block of ice that had only allowed for the image of the impaled queen to reach her. But now she knew; now she remembered everything. "There isn't a thing I don't remember about you," she told the queen, and advancing toward the throne, she spoke of all the times the queen had come to see her in the garden and all the secrets she'd whispered in her ear, as if there had been someone around to overhear them. "I know you. You're kind and gentle, and you love the stories where the misfit finds their people and they go on to have all of these spectacular adventures."

"Those stories are stupid," the queen said, looking away. "Pull the curtains. I don't want to see you. I don't want to see anything!"

Gerda looked outside the window. More light was flooding in through the stained glasses, and the past queens' blue visages appeared as elongated shadows on the floor, reaching out, Gerda thought—much like how the people in town had reached for her hand or asked for her company.

"It's that shard from the mirror talking, not you."

"Everything is so... ugly and horrible." The queen hid her face behind bloodied hands. "Just let me stay in the dark. I'm fine here, away from those terrible things. I don't have to think. I don't want to think.... Just let me stay in the dark."

Gerda wanted to tell the queen about all the amazing things the world had to offer. From the wondrous swing that could turn a human into a bird, to the simple pleasure of eating bread straight out of the oven; from the kindness of strangers, to making snow angels or smelling the roses. There was so much beauty, so much goodness, so much left to see; but the mirror had warped her heart and kept her from all of that. But Gerda could not bring herself to leave. She walked up the frozen steps to the queen, and the queen shrank back and kept her hands over her eyes, and Gerda kept walking, for there was nowhere else she'd rather be than at the queen's side. This was her home, and she meant to save it. This was the person who had loved her when she couldn't reciprocate those feelings, but now she could—and she meant to stay by her side, even if it meant living day after day where the queen did nothing but push her away.

"I'm so sorry," Gerda said, and the strain of the journey came back all at once. She fell into the queen's lap, and she cried against her chest. "I'll never leave you again."

THROUGH BLOODIED fingers, the Snow Queen saw Gerda approach. She bit down a despaired moan—that girl was hell herself. She was a demon with her sunken red eyes, with her burned skin and wisps of charred hair that clung to her blistering scalp, with hands that were nothing but blackened bones; she was a demon returned to torment her, to kill her. The queen could practically hear her own skin sizzle and crackle with every step Gerda took, bringing that wall of flame and heat against her, closing in on her. She struggled for breath.

I will kill her. Let her come closer, just a little closer. I'll carve out that flame. I'll end her.

She had killed all the other snowmen already. They had grown sinister faces, ugly leers, and bloodthirsty sneers, and the queen had pounded their horrible faces until her hands were raw and all that was left was putrid snow, black and foul smelling. Now she could finish what she had started so long ago.

"I'm so sorry."

No, you're not. The queen shook her head and shrank back, head bowed.

She couldn't look into those red eyes anymore.

When she felt the weight of Gerda's head and the skeletal touch of her hands about her shoulders, the queen tensed and recoiled from the fire.

She means to kill me.

She raised her hands; she was going to wring out the demon's scarred neck and then put out the flame for good, suffocate it in her closed fists before the demon's dying eyes—but something changed, something *was* changing, and her fingers were left hovering inches away from the demon's neck.

Something warm, the comforting warmth her stupid little self had yearned for, was settling over her heart, so unlike the freezing cold of her desolate palace, so unlike the crushing heat the demon had brought into her throne room. This didn't burn, it soothed.

What's happening to me?

She saw the storm outside begin to quiet. The light grew stronger. The previous Snow Queens now donned smiles, peaceful and caring. They no longer pointed and laughed. They no longer appeared angry. The light touched the ice and the crystals from the chandelier and made the entire room sparkle. For the first time in years, she saw the room as it really was.

"I'm sorry. I'm sorry. I'm so sorry."

The queen raised her hand to her heart but found instead a tear-stained cheek—warm.

"Gerda?" she whispered, trying out the name for the first time in years, savoring the familiarity of it on her tongue. It felt strange and comforting all at the same time. "I... I want to see you...."

And when she raised her head, the queen held her breath. Her heart lurched to her throat, for she feared the face of the demon. She feared this was another trick that would plunge her further into the dark. She was so tired of the dark.

But the eyes that sought hers were warm and wide and brimming with tears. The red and the hideous burns were washed away, revealing the familiar features of her best friend. "Gerda...." She couldn't resist touching her cheeks, with gentle and trembling fingers at first, as if Gerda might break, as if her hands might leave a dent in the snow and make her face collapse; but Gerda wasn't made of snow anymore. It was skin her thumb brushed against, alive and wet with the tears that had melted the ice in her heart.

The queen laughed; she cried.

"You're back, you're really back!"

She wrapped her arms around Gerda and did not let go for the longest time.

GERDA AND the queen walked hand in hand through the garden. They sat down together at their favorite bench once again, and for the first time they could both breathe in the sweet fragrances of the garden. This time Gerda was the one with the stories to tell, and the queen could sit back with her head on Gerda's shoulder, one hand in hers and the other holding that beautiful rosebud, and simply listen.

"You could have died...," the Snow Queen said, hearing the end of Gerda's journey.

"Not before I got to see you again."

That made the Snow Queen smile. Yet she shuddered whenever she remembered that she had been about to kill Gerda. She had come so close....

"No point in thinking about what might have happened." Gerda smiled. "You're you again, and I know you would never hurt me."

"No, I would never...."

Those horrible, despairing thoughts, and all the hideous things she'd seen throughout the years since that shard of glass had impaled her, all of it would fade in time.

"I can't believe... I'm not alone anymore."

"I promise," Gerda said, "you will never be alone again."

And that promise was sealed with a kiss.

THE GRUELING winter was over, and with spring blooming again, the Snow Queen got to leave her kingdom of ice and snow. She got to fly in the magic swing, got to run after the soap bubbles, she got to meet the raven and Marigold and the rest of the neighborhood, and the home that had been Gerda's was hers as well. She even got to travel with the Robber Girl and her sweethearts; at last, she got to find her band of misfits.

Together, the Snow Queen and Gerda searched for the remaining shards of the troll's glass all over the world. They traveled from place to place, ridding people of its malice, lifting that ice and that darkness from their hearts.

But no matter how far their journeys took them, the Snow Queen and Gerda were never apart from each other again.

And spring always came.

SCOTIA ROTH is a little wandering sputnik currently residing in Portugal. Her dream to be a writer dates back to elementary school, when her teacher asked the class: "What do you want to be when you grow up?" There were many alluring possibilities, but writing was the one thing she could picture herself doing. And what does she like to write about? Anything in the fantasy realm, horror, and girls.

Her first time at college didn't go so well, but she's going to try again, this time majoring in translation (which will help fulfill her goal of learning as many languages as she can cram into her brain). She plans to live in many different cities around the world as soon as she's done with college, and hopes to one day be able to open a 24/7 bookstore (hot beverages will be free in the winter).

If she's not writing, she's reading, and if she's not reading, then there's a good chance she's thinking of all the things she could be writing about (she probably spends a little too much time daydreaming).

Twitter: https://twitter.com/sputnik_scotia

Tumblr: http://wandering-sputnik.tumblr.com/

CITY LIGHTS WILL CARRY YOU HOME

AMANDA REED

ELIAS HAS never seen the sky like this before.

Back home, it's only ever been the vast expanse of endless blue. Blue stretching for miles, horizon to horizon, interrupted only by an infrequent smattering of high white clouds and the constant sun. At night, the blue would turn to an indigo so dark it was almost black, and the stars would slash themselves across the sky in streaming twists and gallops. His father had a high-powered telescope and on rare occasions would let him peer through to see shapes and constellations.

Here, he looks out at the sky through a window that's five feet high and eight feet wide, made of bulletproof glass two inches thick. Another difference between here and at home is that here, the sky is in pieces.

It is first cut by the curve of the Dome, its transparent aluminum forming a barrier between the City and everything else. No light can escape its shield, but the City doesn't give off a lot of light, anyway. The buildings don't have windows, aside from the observation decks, like the one Elias is in, and there aren't any aboveground roadways—much of the City is underground, thrumming through twisting tunnels and pockets.

The sky is next cut in jagged scars by the towering buildings with their roofs slanted to stabbing points. The skyline looks like a frown full of sharpened teeth, ready to devour him if he lets it. Elias won't let himself be eaten alive. Not anymore.

Above the barrier of the Dome is a strip of sky like the one he knows, darkness punctuated by strings of light. It is only a thin, single piece, yet it is familiar and comforting; it reminds him of home.

The doors behind him slide open. Though the engineers have tried to make them virtually silent, he can still hear the tiny grating sound of the mechanism accompanied by the gentle *whoosh* of air from the outside hallway. The newcomer, Elias already knows, is Jeremiah, his guide to this city of sharp buildings and rounded tunnels.

The tall, slender figure of Jeremiah watches Elias from the doorway. His skin is dark velvety brown, and his hair is short on both sides of his head while long and curly in the center. Too long, as it often falls into a pair of green-rimmed brown eyes. There are metal rings in both his ears, which Elias had never seen before, but Jeremiah hasn't minded his overinterest. Elias himself has pale skin, which freckles madly in the sun. His hair is dark and kept cropped short to his head, and his eyes are brown too, but lack Jeremiah's ring of green.

Jeremiah teeters on the edge of the threshold for a long moment, observing, before striding inside the small, angular room. He stops just behind Elias's crouched form before the window.

"I knew I'd find you in here," he declares in a voice that sounds like friction between two stones. "All you Groundlings, you're exactly the same. You always want to see the sky." His accent rolls syllables together and quickens his sentences. Consonants and vowels are dropped from the ends and middles of words, and his speech absolutely *flows*. He sounds so different from folks back home, but Elias thinks he could listen to him for hours.

A crease forms on Elias's brow. "'Groundlings'? Jeremiah, you don't *really* call us *Groundlings* here, do you?"

With a swift, graceful movement, Jeremiah takes a seat beside him, pressing his knees to his chest and wrapping his arms around them, mirroring Elias's pose. "Well," he says. "*Usually* not to your faces."

"Thanks." Elias rolls his eyes.

"Oh, don't pretend y'all don't have a name for us either, and I'm sure it's much worse than 'Groundlings' too." Jeremiah leans in slightly to look at his new friend. "What are we, Eli? Cave-Dwellers? Star-Fuckers?" He laughs, the sound coming from somewhere deep in his throat and making his body vibrate.

Elias glances at him. No one's called him Eli before. Barely anyone ever called him "Elias" to begin with. His parents always regarded him with a firm *Eli*as *Tim*othy *John*son, usually before a reprimand or assigning him a task. His teachers called him "ET" with a sneer when they caught him staring out the window in class, and his friends sometimes called him Johnson. He's never felt like an Elias, let alone an Elias Timothy Johnson, but he likes *Eli*. Eli, three letters—short but commanding, with two strong vowels to start and finish the name.

Eli likes the way Jeremiah says his name.

Jeremiah had commented on his name right at their first meeting, two days ago. He had needed to squint to read the narrow letters of the entire name squished onto an adhesive nametag.

"'Elias Timothy Johnson'? Like *hell* am I calling you that," he had said, folding his arms. "You're Eli now." And that had been it.

Elias wonders if he could start getting people at home to call him Eli—

Home.

Shit!

With a sputter, he turns suddenly to Jeremiah. "What time is it?" he demands, panic edging his tone.

Jeremiah throws up his arms. "Whoa there, dude, calm down. It's only, like"—he glances at his watch—"2100. Breathe. You have plenty of time."

Elias takes deep breaths heavily through his nose, trying to calm the buzzing feeling in his chest and stomach. "Three hours is not *plenty of time*," he says through clenched teeth. "Not even *close*, Jeremiah. Shit. Shit. Goddammit. I am so fucked."

"I'm assuming you haven't made a decision yet."

"*Fuck* no, I haven't decided yet. I've been here, what, three days, and my entire world has been turned upside down. Dude, you have *metal* in your *body* as *decoration*. Shit, dude." Elias buries his face in his hands. "You guys don't live in houses down here. Everyone has their own apartment complex and section and place to be. Your roadways are *underground*. I don't even think that taxi we rode yesterday had *wheels*."

Jeremiah scoffed. "Of course it didn't. What kind of taxi uses wheels?"

"I saw a girl with *pink hair*!"

"You can have pink hair too, if you want."

"This system is so fucked up. They leave me here three days and then make me choose between staying here or going back to frickin' Podunk. How many kids stay, again?"

"About 30 percent of kids we get choose to live in the City," Jeremiah answers easily.

Eli groans. "That's it? Dude. Dude! What do I do?"

Jeremiah takes a breath. He glances from Eli's drawn, speckled face to the jagged skyline and back again before answering.

"You don't get to choose the life you're born into, Elias. We're born, whether we like it or not. But now, you get to choose the life you can live from this point forward. Yeah, the pilgrimage is a pretty fucked-up system—a lot of kids get scared, and it's not fair to them. The City is too much to take in in too short an amount of time. You get three days here—seventy-two hours—and then you gotta decide if you want to stay here and leave everything behind or if you want to go home." He cracks a humorless smile. "But I can't make the decision for you."

Elias looks down at his hands. "I don't know what to do. My parents—we're—they—I'm—we're very different people. They have this archaic, stagnant mindset about how things *should* work, about how people *ought* to act... and look... and think, and I don't fit any of their criteria. It's so... so *hard* to live in the same household as two people who loathe every part of you." Tears sting his eyes. "But can I leave them?" he asks, voice quiet. "I... I still think that one day, they'll wake up and they'll be what parents are supposed to be."

"What are parents supposed to be, Elias?" Jeremiah asks quietly.

He sniffs violently. "I don't know... supportive? Caring? I have a feeling that parents are supposed to *want* you to be there and not just sort of *tolerate* your existence. Otherwise—otherwise, what's the point?"

He blinks his overflowing eyes, tears trailing down the sides of his face. Elias realizes he has never cried in front of anyone before. He figures crying in front of Jeremiah should bother him, but it doesn't. Jeremiah doesn't care; he knows that tears aren't a weakness, yet Elias cries harder, sobs racking his small frame.

"But I can't just leave them, can I?" he asks, voice breaking. "They're my *parents*. If I leave, it's not like they'll visit me or allow me to visit them. If their only son leaves them for the City, the Community will shun them completely. I can't do that to them. They raised me, after all. I owe them that m—"

With a swift, sudden movement, Jeremiah grabs Elias by his shoulders and looks at him straight on, his eyes reflecting the reflected light of the Dome through the glass. "Elias, listen to me," he says seriously. "You never asked to be born into your family, and you do not have to give your parents the goddamn time of *day* if you do not so wish. Make this decision based off what's best for you and what *you* want, and *fuck* everyone else."

"Easy for you to say," Elias says with a sniff. "You're a City kid, born and raised. How could you even *fathom*—"

A raucous, slightly bitter laugh interrupts Elias's near tirade. Jeremiah leans back on his heels and shakes his head. "Eli, I only *wish* I was a born-and-raised City kid."

Eli frowns. "You're not?"

"*No.* Us, the ones who show the City around to you lot from the Communities, we were Groundling kids once too."

Eli's eyes widen. "*You?* A *Groundling?*"

Jeremiah pastes on a wide shit-eating grin. "Me, a Groundling kid. And I didn't even wait to turn the big One-Seven before hightailing it over here. I ran away from my Community at the ripe age of fifteen and a half. Apparently having a six-foot-three gay boy who painted his nails pink and read a lot of Camus was too much for my dear parents. God rest their souls, wherever they may be."

"They—they kicked you out?"

"Well, no, not officially. But it's not like they were acknowledging my existence or speaking to me or anything. One day, I had just about had enough of it, you know? So I packed some stuff and… I left. Came to the City. Begged the City officials to let me in a little early and, with a bit of finagling…." He spreads out his arms wide and gestures to himself. "Here I am."

Elias looks down at the carpeting, thoroughly embarrassed—yet also thoroughly, *thoroughly* impressed. He has never heard of anyone running away from a Community before. "I'm sorry for assuming," he mumbles. "It's just… you've assimilated so well. I just figured you had lived here your entire life."

Jeremiah's laugh fills the small space and brightens the mood. "Why, Eli, darlin', you flatter me." He smiles down at Eli, who still looks just as conflicted as he did before. "We take care of our own in the City. I just want you to know that. Everyone treats each other properly, and no one gets left behind. If you choose to stay, you could go to school and learn all sorts of stuff, or you could get help finding a job right away. In a year or two, you could end up like me, helping out runt Groundlings like you." Jeremiah raises his hand, as if he's going to ruffle Eli's hair, but seems to think better of it.

"And... I know we're supposed to let you make the decision on your own, without any help from us, but—" Jeremiah leans forward suddenly and presses his lips against Elias's in a quick, chaste kiss. Eli is too surprised to even kiss back. He just stares, mouth slightly agape.

"I've been dyin' to do that since I first saw you, the day before last, with your ridiculous name tag. You sure are a cute one, Elias Timothy Johnson. It would make me awful sad to see you go."

Cheeks burning, the former Groundling replies, "Just call me Eli."

AMANDA REED, a born and raised New Yorker, spends an inordinate amount of time watching various incarnations of *Star Trek* and contemplating the logistics of space travel. She has been an avid reader and writer her whole life and aspires to write many books and own many cats.

Please feel free to e-mail her at agreed.96@gmail.com.

TESS
BECCA EHLERS

"MORE SOCKS." Tess pushes a pile of clean, paired socks across the bed to me.

"Thanks, love." I start piling them into the suitcase, taking care to place them neatly. Tess has been critiquing my packing technique all day, showing me how to properly fold a T-shirt, making me shake out each pair of jeans so they won't get so wrinkled before I have a chance to unpack.

"You need to make a good first impression," she scolds me gently.

"On who?"

"Your roommate! Do you want her to think you'll be the messy roommate?"

I smirk and tuck a lock of hair behind her ear. "I *am* the messy roommate."

Tess just shakes her head at me and starts picking through my room, pulling my favorite books from the shelf and stacking my CDs in a box. She knows without any telling.

"You know, if you did this all alone, I could get to New York and still have everything I'd need." I grab her around the waist as she walks past and pull her onto my lap. I press my face against her neck, breathing in coconut and cucumber; my throat starts to constrict around the scent, the essence of Tess.

"Hey." Her hands are on my cheeks, tilting my head to make us eye to eye. "Are you doing okay?"

"Yeah," I mumble. "I'm dealing. It's only fifteen weeks, right? Not even four months."

"And you'll be having so much fun."

I nod. "I'll miss you so much, though. Fifteen weeks without you?"

Tess bites her lip. "We should… talk about that."

"What do you mean?"

"About what we're going to do about you leaving." Tess moves onto the edge of the bed, with just a little too much space between us.

"I… we…." I fumble. "I thought we were going to keep going."

"We never decided on that, Sam," she replies patiently.

"But that's what we're doing. Right?" She's not looking at me and I'm afraid. "Tess! What are you trying to say?"

"I'm just not sure if long distance is a good idea for either of us. You'll be meeting a lot of new people; let's be honest—it's Tisch. There will probably be a lot of people like us. I don't want you to miss out on something good because of me."

"What? I don't want anyone else! I wouldn't be missing out; I have you. And you know I'd never…."

Tess takes my hands in hers. "Okay. Maybe what I mean to say is that long distance wouldn't be good for me."

"I don't understand. You're not making any sense." I grip her hands tightly, too tightly, like maybe if I can just hold on to her, this won't be real.

"Baby, you know what I'm going to say."

"No, I don't! I thought we were fine, and now—"

"I can't keep doing this," she interrupts. "Not us—that's not what I mean at all. But Jesus, the secrets and the sneaking around and—I don't know, everything."

"That's what this is about? Me not wanting to shout our relationship from the rooftops?"

"I can't wait for you when I don't even know you'll stick around. I know that sounds harsh, but if you might start running if someone were to find out… and how would we have a future like this?"

I almost want to laugh at it all. "Tess, we're eighteen. No one knows what their future's going to look like."

"But if you can't stand the thought of anyone knowing, what will we be doing in five years? People will get suspicious, Sam. They already are. Are you going to break it off because people are asking questions?"

"That's ridiculous." But the words come out flat and empty.

"Well?" Tess prods. "What would you do?"

"I… I don't know."

She nods. "That's where we have a problem."

"Is this us breaking up?"

"I don't want it to be, but I don't see a lot of options."

"What you're telling me is that I either lose you or lose everyone," I say.

I can see this stings, but Tess just looks down at our linked hands and shrugs. "I think you're underestimating them. If you give them a chance, they might surprise you. You never give them a chance and—"

But I stand up, dropping her hands. "You can't give me some fucking ultimatum."

"I've waited. Sam, I've waited so long for you to be okay, and you still aren't, and it's… contagious. It took me a long time too, and it was awful, and I never want to go back to where I was. But I'm starting to." She's pleading now. "I can't feel like that again. I love you. You know I love you. But with things the way they are, I think I'm starting to hate myself, and loving you isn't enough to stop that."

"So go." As soon as I say it, I want to take it back; it's too late. Tess looks at me like she doesn't even know me. And she pushes herself off of my bed and walks out of my room, down the stairs, and through the door. Just like that, she's gone.

I put my suitcase on the floor and gently move stacks of clean clothes to my desk. And I curl up on the bed and sob.

IT'S WEIRD how queers find each other. I mean, yeah, gaydar's a thing, but it goes further than that. It's like we have magnets or homing devices that pull us together. Maybe because there aren't many of us, and if you don't find someone like you, you might not make it.

Go ahead. Tell me I'm exaggerating.

That's what I thought.

Evan and I found each other early—sixth grade, actually. Of course, we didn't know back then. Or more, we knew, but in the way all kids know Santa isn't real—you know, but you don't want to know. So you do a damn good job of convincing yourself that it's different.

Anyway, we were just best friends until the summer before our freshman year. One day we were in my room playing Scrabble, and I'd just put down "kiss" to use Evan's *k* from "know" and an earlier *s* from "stun." Evan sat there, looking at it.

I reached across the board to poke him. "Your turn, loser."

"Cut it out," Evan mumbled.

"Excuse me for wanting to play the game!"

He finally looked up at me, gray eyes unreadable behind thick glasses. "Sam, can I kiss you?"

Can I kiss you?

I'd been waiting for my first kiss since I turned thirteen. Everyone thought Evan and I were secretly dating, or should be. So I did what any girl in my situation would do—I said yes.

"How do we do this?" he asked.

"Um… I think we're supposed to wing it?" I stood up and gestured for him to do the same.

Evan stood directly in front of me and put his arms around me, pulling me in cautiously.

"One," I whispered.

"Two," he replied.

"Three."

We leaned forward, lips awkwardly smashing into each other. We fumbled for a few seconds, then pulled back.

Evan gave me a sheepish grin. "Sorry… that wasn't very good."

"I mean, it was the first time we did it. Maybe we just need to practice," I suggested.

So Evan and I spent that summer kissing each other, on the couch in his basement or in one of our bedrooms or in the woods by my house. It never got better, so we kept looking for something to change—the location, the flavor of gum we chewed beforehand, sitting versus standing and no tongue versus tongue (bad idea) and anything we could think of.

And suddenly it was August, and Evan and I were on his bed kissing, trying so hard to make it good, when he pulled away and started crying. And like an asshole, I had no idea what to do; neither of us were criers. I hadn't seen Evan cry since his dog died, and there he was with his face turning red as he curled up into himself, shaking all over. I finally tried to pull him into a hug, and he let me, completely limp. I held on to him, and I think I knew then.

Finally, the shoulder of my T-shirt was soaking, and Evan was quiet.

"Are you okay?" I asked cautiously.

His voice was steady, gaze fixed on the wall opposite us. "I don't think we're going to get anywhere with kissing."

"Is that why you're crying? Because we're bad kissers?"

"No, no, I—it's not going to get better because I don't... I.... Sam, I don't like girls."

I remember thinking that maybe I should be shocked or even upset. In a way, he'd been using me. Right? But I couldn't feel anything, really. Just a kind of empty aching in my chest.

"So...," Evan continued, "I think I'm gay."

"Okay."

"Are you mad at me?"

"Evan?"

"Yeah?"

"I think I'm gay too."

We stared at each other, wanting to say something to fix it and knowing we wouldn't. Couldn't. We settled for clasped hands and silence while sunshine poured over us, and we crumbled just a little, because nothing was ever going to be the same.

"Shit, Sam," Evan breathed. "What are we going to do?"

I THINK it can be widely acknowledged that high school kind of sucks. I recognize that some people actually enjoy their four-year sentence, but I would argue that those people are masochists and generally messed up.

However awful it was, Evan and I hit high school (in the words of my mother) "with a vengeance." Evan started doing debate; I took my first video class and became obsessed, begging my parents for a camera for Christmas and then taking it everywhere. I still have those old clips—Evan practicing spreading before a debate tournament and swearing at his words-per-minute, the neighbor kids riding bikes, a three-minute silent film (in black and white, no less) of my dad making pancakes.

I made some sort-of friends in the video program and various classes, but somehow I never could get quite close enough for real friendships. It wasn't an intentional decision; it just happened. There were plenty of people I got along well with, but there was always that block.

Evan and I still spent all our free time together. He started buying man-meat magazines and storing them in my room, since my mom respected my privacy and his didn't. We made a new library account with a fake address and checked out every queer novel we could find, plus every season of *The L Word* for me. We did a little snooping around on chat rooms, but it always seemed to end with Evan getting propositioned or me being asked to take sides on the "butch versus femme" debate. Most importantly, we didn't talk to each other about it. I mean, we hinted a little, but we pretty much avoided the *G* word like the plague.

I know it sounds bad—like we should have been talking about our feelings and crying a lot and taking on the world together. The thing is, our world wasn't all that big, straddling the line between big town and small city. Big enough not to know everyone's name but small enough that if you fucked up, everyone heard about it. When your world is that size, you have no way to hide if things go wrong. So we kept our mouths shut; it was enough that someone knew, that someone understood why everything was so damn complicated.

Then senior year started, and everything changed again.

EVAN AND I walked into the high school for our last first day ever. We stood in the entryway, taking in the long, waxed hallways and trashed-up lockers.

Evan broke the silence first. "This place is a dump."

We're not much for sentimentality.

"Tell me about it," I replied. "Okay, are those the freshmen or their younger siblings?"

"I swear to God we weren't that short."

"Or awkward."

"That's debatable," Evan cracked.

I swatted him upside the head. "Speaking of, I don't think anyone on debate gets to call other people awkward."

"Because the video kids are so cool." Evan glanced down at his watch. "Anyway, class is about to start; we'd better get going."

"Five minutes is not 'about to start,'" I grouched. "Fine. See you third period?"

"You know it." Evan gave me a quick hug and went bounding up the stairs.

I pushed through a sea of panicked freshmen to my first class—AP lit. As I entered the room, I did a quick scan of who was already there; I knew a few of the people from other classes, but no one I would have considered myself to be friends with. I took a desk by the window and pulled out a book, ready to tune out, the way I planned to spend the rest of the year. I'd barely cracked the cover when I heard the door open again; when I glanced up, I saw a girl in the doorway, looking around uneasily.

My first thought was that she must be a transfer, because I was sure I'd never seen her before. My second was that she was... the most interesting kind of beautiful. She saw me staring and smiled crookedly, waving.

I'm not a friendly person. That isn't meant to be self-deprecating in any way; it's just a fact of life. I don't do well with initiating conversation or social situations in general. But God knows why, I grinned and gestured toward the desk next to mine.

The girl dropped into the seat. "Thanks," she said breathlessly.

"No problem." I stuck out my hand. "I'm Sam."

"Tess."

Her hand closed around mine, cool and soft, lingering for a moment too long. I pulled away, blushing.

If Tess noticed, she didn't let it show. "So, any insider advice? I just moved here."

"I know," I replied. Shit. Way to sound like a stalker. "I mean, I guessed. Because I didn't recognize you. And the school isn't huge or anything. I mean—where are you from?"

"Oregon. Portland, actually."

"Wow, that must be a pretty big shift. How are you liking Michigan?" Real original.

"Well...." Tess raised an eyebrow. "I think it's growing on me. What other classes are you taking?"

We swapped schedules. Besides lit we had American government and AP biology together; I was close to hyperventilating.

"What are the people like here?" Tess asked softly as the room began to fill.

"Human? I don't know. Normal people, I guess."

"Does much happen here?"

I snorted. "Well, we got an Olive Garden a couple years ago. That was exciting."

"How about world views? Pretty stagnant?"

"You nailed it."

We ended up walking to second period (gov) together and nabbing desks next to each other again. And when it was time to split up, I found myself stopping her.

"We have the same lunch, and it's right before bio. Do you want to—unless you've already got someone to sit with—not that this is just if you don't—"

"I'd love to have lunch with you," Tess interrupted. "Meet in the entryway?"

"Yeah," I said. "See you then."

Evan knew something was up as soon as I stepped into calculus. "Okay," he said firmly, arms crossed, "what happened to you?"

"Nothing. Nothing at all." I sank into a desk. "Oh—but we have a new lab partner joining us for bio."

French and study hall dragged on; when the bell finally rang, it was such a shock that I almost fell off my chair (apparently right when everyone in the class was looking in my direction). I slung my backpack over my shoulder and dashed to the entryway. No one but a couple of hipster kids making out. Maybe she wasn't coming, maybe she'd found someone else, maybe....

"Sam!" There she was, making her way toward me. "Sorry, I got a little turned around."

"Oh, that's fine," I choked. "I'm just glad you found me." Idiot. Literal idiot.

Tess grinned. "Should we go find somewhere to sit?"

"Yes! Right, a place to sit. Want to go eat on the field?"

I led her out the door and around to the field; we settled on the grass and pulled out our lunches. I think I managed to finish half my sandwich in half an hour—we barely stopped talking.

She lived with her dad and younger brother; her mother had moved out right after Derek, Tess's brother, was born. Tess wanted to major in communications in college. Best subject: English. Worst: math. Favorite movie: *Moulin Rouge!* Favorite book: *A Wrinkle in Time*. She missed her friends but liked how much quieter it was in Michigan.

I'd never had any close friends who were girls, even when I was little. I'd always had a much easier time with guys. Tess, however, seemed to be a different story. Like we could actually click. Just a friend—that was all I was looking for. Right? Right.

We walked into bio giggling, barely conscious of anything happening around us.

"Samwise!" Evan popped up beside me. "Is this the mystery woman you were telling me about?"

Flushing, I nodded. "Not a mystery woman. This is Tess. Tess, meet Evan."

"I'm the best friend," he explained, with just a touch of emphasis on *best*.

I rolled my eyes and let Evan shepherd us to a cluster of desks, half listening to their heated debate over the best phylum. It seemed like maybe, just maybe, this year was looking up.

After school Evan and I met up by our lockers to walk home, as we'd been doing since the second day of middle school. Usually we talked the whole way, but today he was quiet. I decided not to push my luck; it had been a long day. We hit my house first, snagging a box of Cheez-Its from the pantry and sitting on the front steps to eat them.

When Evan finally spoke, he addressed the fluorescent crackers in his hand. "What's with you and Tess?"

"Nothing," I said quickly. "We just have some classes together, so… why do you ask?" Evan snorted. "We're getting to know each other. Maybe we'll be friends."

"Are you sure you don't want it to be more than that?"

I felt my stomach settle somewhere around my kneecaps. For Evan to bring it up, it must have been pretty obvious. "It won't be. Okay? She's not like us."

He sighed and ground the last Cheez-It between his fingers, watching the dust float to the ground. "Be careful."

THE SMART thing to do would have been to avoid Tess. I didn't. I reasoned that it was impossible since we had class together every day, that it was rude when she'd just moved. And it was impossible not to get sucked into conversation when we had so much to talk about. I compromised and tried to keep it confined to school, and for about a month it worked. But life tends to happen, and when we hit our first paired project in lit, there was really nothing I could do about it.

"You'll be doing your *Hamlet* presentations in groups of two. I'll allow you to choose your own partners, but any funny business and we'll be drawing names for the rest of the year." The teacher sat down, steeling herself for the inevitable chaos.

Tess turned to me. "Want to work together?"

"Sure," I said. How could I not?

"Great. Are you free after school today?" asked Tess.

"Um, yeah."

"Want to come over to my house and get started?"

And I knew it wasn't smart, but I felt myself nodding. "That sounds good. I'll meet you by your locker."

I was a wreck for the rest of the day. I couldn't focus on anything; I even made mistakes in video. I kept trying to think of an excuse to cancel and had nothing. When I went to my locker to pack up, Evan was waiting for me.

"Debate got canceled. Want to head home early?"

"Can't," I told him.

He made a face. "I guess I can wait around."

"No, I can't walk home. I'm, um, I'm going to Tess's house to work on a project."

"Sam." One word that said everything.

"Just a project. I'll call you tonight." I turned to leave, trying to shake off his gaze.

When I reached her, Tess was leaning against her locker, reading. She snapped the book closed and slipped it into her bag when she saw me. "Ready to go?"

Nope. Not even close. But I followed her out into the October chill, four blocks down and three blocks over to her house. She led me to the door, hip checking it a couple times before it would open for her.

"Welcome to the man cave. Can I offer you a beer or some wings?"

Shoes piled up by the door, a few socks scattered on the living room floor, and game cartridges covering the coffee table. Not particularly untidy, but very lived-in and definitely male.

"Let's get out of the testosterone zone, shall we?" Tess suggested. "My room is just up the stairs."

Somehow, if someone had shown me ten different bedrooms and asked me to guess, I would have recognized Tess's room as hers. Everything fit, from the bright quilt on the bed to the *Starry Night* poster on the wall. Tess sat down on the bed, offering me the desk chair.

Tess looked for quotes while I started to put together a PowerPoint on my laptop, but it seemed like every two minutes, one of us would need the other to come look at something. I finally joined her on the bed. She pointed out a passage; I scooted a little closer to read it better. I showed her some options for transitions; she put her head on my shoulder to avoid glare on the screen. Her hand skimmed my knee. When I turned toward her, my lips accidentally brushed over her hair.

I pulled back a little, wondering if I should apologize or ignore it or—but Tess had pulled back too and was looking at me, drinking me in. She touched my hand, then reached up to cradle my cheek.

Never in my life have I ever been brave. But with Tess staring me down, I took a deep breath, leaned forward, and kissed her.

When Evan and I used to kiss, way back when, we'd pucker our lips too tight and hold each other too stiffly and break away fast. When I kissed Tess, her lips slipped open to catch mine, moving in and out, soft and smooth and achingly gentle. Her arms curled around me, and we slowly fell back onto the bed. We pulled apart bit by bit and lay there, not needing words, Tess stroking my hair out of my face and my hands pressed into the curve of her spine.

I broke the silence first. "Is this okay?" Because I had made a million assumptions, and no matter how right it felt, I had learned by then that I could always be wrong.

Tess kissed me lightly. "Yes. This is very, very okay. But I guess we should figure out how we're going to do this."

In that moment the fear was back, the hard knot in my middle. "Tess, no one knows about me."

"I thought it might be that kind of town," she said. "So what you're saying is that you're not ready."

No use lying. I nodded. "Not because of you; it's everything else. It's different here."

Tess dipped her head into the crook of my neck, and I felt her sigh against my skin. "If you aren't ready, we don't have to tell anyone. Not yet."

"WE NEED to talk."

I reread the scrap of paper Evan had shoved under my elbow a few seconds earlier. It had been a week since the day I'd gone to Tess's, and Evan had spent every bio class since then watching us. I had been avoiding him, claiming too much homework, saying I was working on college apps, leaving early with Tess on the days he had debate, and staying late in the video room on the days he didn't.

I took a deep breath and flipped the paper to the blank side. "Walk home today." I balled it up, waited to be sure Tess was looking at the lecture slides, and dropped the note on Evan's desk.

He smoothed it out, read it, and gave a barely perceptible nod.

We exchanged pleasantries on the way home, complaining about teachers and weighing the SAT against the ACT, but as soon as we walked into my house, Evan was all business.

"Want a snack?" I asked, starting toward the kitchen.

Evan pointed to the stairs. Reluctantly, I followed him into my room and sat down on the floor to wait.

Evan stood with his arms crossed tightly over his chest, glaring at me. But when he spoke, there was no anger. Just a sort of hopelessness.

"Jesus, Sam, what are you thinking?"

"Look, it's complicated. You wouldn't get it."

"Of everyone in this fucking town, I think I would get it," he shot back bitterly.

"I didn't plan this, it just happened."

"It's not safe. She doesn't get it, but you do. This isn't Portland—you could get hurt here."

"I know, I know," I said.

"Do you?" Evan ran a hand through his hair so it stuck straight up. "We're so close. We have months—months—left before we're out. And we can go places where no one will care. Why now?"

The thing was, he was right. All I had to do was hang on just a little bit longer. But people always say no pain, no gain, that nothing comes free.

"I don't really understand," I admitted. "All I know is that I care about her a lot. And I don't think I can pretend I just don't anymore."

"This is kind of shitty," Evan muttered, throwing himself down next to me. "Fuck, Sam. I'm so done with all of this. Why can't things be easy for once?"

I laid my head on his shoulder. "Tell me about it."

Evan was always polite to Tess after that, even friendly, but I don't think he could ever quite forgive her—for taking me away, for making him afraid for me, for forcing the two of us to acknowledge what we'd tried so hard to ignore. Or maybe all three.

AS FALL slowly dipped into winter, Tess and I spent more and more time together. We'd wander around town after school or just go to one of our houses and coexist, reading or studying or wading through college apps. With working parents and Tess's brother, Derek, busy with his new friends, we found ourselves with a fair amount of alone time, but it was never reliable. At the beginning of December, my parents went on a weekend trip to attend a friend's wedding—so I asked Tess over to spend the night.

I won't go into details, because a person who's spent any amount of time on the Internet could probably fill in the blanks themselves. But I will say that being so close to a person, knowing their body inside and out, is a feeling you never, ever forget. It's an intensity unlike any other, a sort of fullness; everything else falls away at that moment, and it's just you and the other person in something you couldn't lose if you wanted to.

Afterward Tess lay in my arms; I don't believe in perfection on principle, but I have been known to make exceptions—that moment was one of them.

"Sam?" Tess whispered.

"Mhm?"

"I think… I think if you told your parents, they would be okay." I stiffened; Tess could feel it and lifted my hand to kiss my knuckles. "I'm just saying, baby. That's your choice, and I would never make you do it. But I think it would turn out all right."

"Let's talk about it later, okay?"

"Think about it."

We lay in silence again, with the lights of passing cars cutting through the blinds and sending lines of light across the shadows in the room. Quiet and still. The fear was there; it was always there. But it was shaping into a reminder, rather than something to dictate my actions. Tess was changing it.

I kissed her. "I think I'm falling."

Tess curled closer, lips ghosting over my collarbone, my neck, my jaw. "I'm falling with you."

DECEMBER TWENTY-NINTH. I'd been locked in my room since Christmas, finishing college apps. Tess and I had texted maybe three times since winter break had started. She had applied early decision to University of Michigan and been accepted, so she was done; I was not. The safeties were in, but I'd stalled on my top picks, slowly finishing Emerson, USC, and finally NYU Tisch.

My submission for Tisch had to be perfect. Their portfolio was a four-parter—a resume, an essay on collaboration, a short film, and a story, just a personal story that had nothing to do with film.

The first two essays were easy enough, and I was finally happy with my film. Since October, I'd been collecting footage of Tess, little clips of her reading or working on diagrams for bio or laughing at something stupid I'd said. My submission was a collection of those clips, fading in and out, superimposed over one another, showing them my Tess. A delicate piano piece in the background, growing into a crescendo. But the last essay was killing me.

Describe an event in your life and how it changed you or someone close to you.

I'd been going through my life timeline-style and writing down anything that seemed significant. I had even started the essay a couple of times, but my grandpa dying or going on a school trip to Boston didn't seem to fit. Somehow, it kept coming back to Evan and the summer before freshman year. I couldn't even tell my parents I was gay, but I wanted to tell the people deciding whether or not I got to go to my number one school? I knew it was a terrible idea, but there I was, two days before the deadline with nothing to say.

So I wrote it. I wrote about how scared I had been before Evan and I told each other, how scared I still was; I wrote about the ways you could be there for someone without saying a word. I wrote about what it was like to finally know I was trusted and could trust. I filled the maximum four pages.

Hitting submit was one of the hardest decisions I've ever made. But then in a second it was gone, out of my hands. Beyond my control. I closed my laptop and called Tess.

"ARE YOU warm enough?" Tess asked.

I nodded, squeezing her gloved hand. Tess, Evan, and I were spending New Year's Eve together; Tess's dad and brother were at a family friend's cabin, giving us free rein of the house. We'd tried being rebellious, but vodka makes Evan gag, and my asthma took weed off the table. We settled on Scrabble and bad movies, and at a quarter to twelve, the three of us bundled up and climbed out of Tess's window and onto the roof.

Evan checked his watch. "Four minutes left. Any resolutions?"

"Appreciate time more," Tess replied.

"Not bad. What have you got, Sam?"

"Ugh, let me think. You go."

"Take more risks," Evan said promptly.

"That shouldn't be hard," I cracked. "It's a good goal," I amended, seeing his hurt expression.

"What are you going to do that's so groundbreaking?" asked Evan.

I draped my arm over Tess's shoulders. "Get out of the way of my own happiness."

"That deserves a kiss," said Tess, planting one on the side of my head.

"You two are disgusting," Evan observed.

"Oh, shush," I told him.

"Actually, I have a resolution for all of us," Tess put in. "This year should be the year that we don't apologize for who we are."

I held my breath, waiting for Evan to go off on her for guessing, but he just nodded solemnly.

"I can get behind that."

"Time?" I asked.

"Less than a minute." Evan lay back on the shingles. "Ready to kick this year out the door?"

"I don't know," Tess murmured into my ear. "I would be okay holding on to this one."

"Ten!" Evan shouted.

"Nine!" Tess and I joined in. "Eight! Seven! Six! Five! Four! Three! Two! One! *Happy New Year!*"

Fireworks spanned the sky as Tess and I kissed, ignoring Evan's pleas to "get a room." It was already looking like a fantastic year.

"ARE YOU okay?" I asked. It was Valentine's Day. Tess and I lay on my couch, theoretically watching *Casablanca*, but Tess was quiet and had drawn back into herself.

"I'm fine," she said.

I gently tightened my hold around her waist. "I know you a little better than that, love. Will you tell me what's wrong?"

"It's stupid."

"Not if you're upset about it."

Tess sighed and paused the movie. "I just keep wondering what today would be like if we weren't hiding."

"What do you mean?"

"Would we have gone out to dinner? Or to see a movie at the theater? Or even just to a coffee shop to sit around and be together?" Tess sat up so we could be eye to eye. "What would be different if people knew?"

"Tess—"

"If we told people, I could hold your hand in the hall. Guys would stop thinking I was available. I'm not trying to guilt you, but this is hard. People knew back home. I'm not used to lying anymore."

"But we're not lying!" I pleaded. "We're just... not giving out the whole truth."

"I don't know how I can keep doing this," Tess whispered. "Why are we doing this to ourselves? Why can't we tell?"

"Because this isn't like back home!" I burst out. "Because here, people care. Six years ago, these two guys moved in. They were together, didn't even try to be subtle. They lasted six months. Eggs on their car, a little spray paint on the lawn, the usual pranks. But that wasn't the problem. They would go into shops or restaurants, and no one would acknowledge them. They'd ask someone where to find the eggs in the grocery store and get nothing. Like they were invisible."

"That was six years ago, Sam! So much has changed since then."

"Not that much," I shot back. "Look, you grew up in some liberal paradise, but it's different here. Not everyone is as lucky as you."

Tess just shook her head. "It's never easy. It doesn't matter where you are, how you're raised, what the people around you think."

"Well... tell me, then. Tell me what it was like for you."

"I don't know. It was a process."

"Just tell me what you can."

"Okay... I think I knew when I was like five or something, but I also knew that wasn't how it should be. I stopped chasing all the girls on the playground and started choosing boys who I 'liked.' I actually thought I'd fixed it, you know? I kept telling myself that what I felt about boys was a crush and what I felt for girls was friendship. But when I was eleven, there was this girl. Her name was Ana. She was the smartest girl in the class, a badass soccer player… and I thought that I just really wanted to be her friend, because I admired her so much. But I thought about her all the time. I'd plan ways to walk past her in the hallway just to hear her voice…. This sounds kind of creepy, doesn't it?"

"No, keep talking."

"Well, I'd kind of been wondering in the back of my mind if maybe I liked her." Tess half smiled, remembering. "Girls liking girls wasn't a foreign concept, after all. And I'd never thought being gay was wrong. It was okay for other people to be gay—just not me. I knew what could happen to me, what people might say or do. I kind of got it into my head that I just wouldn't be able to be happy."

"What did you do?" I asked.

"Prayed a lot, which was funny since I'd never believed in God. I stopped sleeping. My dad thought I had an ulcer because I had these awful stomachaches all the time. I just put a lot of time and energy into actively disliking myself."

"But you told people. How?"

"I used to take piano lessons, for about seven years; I had this really fantastic teacher. He was quite young, very cool, and very funny. Caleb's gay, and he never seemed to care who knew. One day, right after freshman year started, we were having a lesson, and he just reached over and closed my book and said, 'You can keep practicing and coming to lessons, but until you start connecting with the music again, you'll only be wasting your dad's money.'"

"That's kind of harsh," I murmured.

"Harsh but true. Anyway, I was really pissed off, and I got up to leave, but Caleb stopped me and asked me if I was unhappy. It was so simple that all I could say was yes. I started crying, and he sat me down on the couch and waited for me to get it together, and he asked me how long I'd felt like this. I said three years, but that it was getting worse instead of better. Caleb said that he'd known me for a long time and that if I ever needed to talk, he'd always listen, and I kind of blurted it out. I told him I thought I was gay, but I didn't want to be, and I was afraid my dad would be mad at me and that no one would like me anymore."

"Yikes. How do you respond to that?"

"Pretty much exactly how he did," Tess replied. "He said that it was okay not to like it, and it was okay to be scared, but that the worst part is keeping it a secret and having that anticipation. And everything is scarier when you keep it to yourself."

I shrugged uncomfortably. "So was that it?"

"No. I didn't tell my dad for another month, and when I did, it wasn't pretty. I'd been trying to figure out the best way to do it, but then one day we started fighting over something stupid—I think me not telling him about a test or an assignment or a note home. But then he started going off on me for being so distant all the time; he was saying I wasn't acting like myself, that he had no idea where my behavior was coming from. I just lost it and told him he didn't know me half as well as he thought he did, because if he really knew me, he'd understand what was going on, because if he really knew me, he would know I was gay." Tess leaned back against the cushions, looking drained. "And that was that."

"Shit, Tess," I choked out. "That's intense."

"Tell me about it."

"Was he mad?"

Tess pinched her lower lip between her thumb and forefinger, her trademark thinking face. "Not quite mad. I don't know. He told me he loved me no matter what, and that it was just a phase, and I would grow out of it."

"Oh jeez," I moaned, "did he really pull the phase card?"

"Yeah," Tess admitted. "It sounds bad, but in retrospect he was just really, really scared. He didn't want me getting hurt. And also there's the single-parent guilt, like, was it because I hadn't had enough female role models? But he got over it with time."

"And then you told other people?"

"I told my best friend the next day; she was fine with it, of course. And then it slowly started to get around, and I didn't deny it, so after a while it was common knowledge. Almost everyone was fine with it. A few kids acted like dicks, but what are you going to do?" Tess rubbed her thumb over my cheekbone. "It was hard. But it worked out okay."

"Tess, I'm not brave," I whispered.

"Bull," she replied. "You're plenty brave. If you weren't brave, you never would have let this happen. You're taking your time—I'm trying to stay okay with that."

"Trying?"

"It's not always easy, baby," Tess said. "But I'm not going anywhere. Just remember that if you decide to...." She shook herself. "Maybe this isn't the day for it, huh?"

I hugged her, pressing my lips to her shoulder. "I love you, Tess."

"I love you too. Happy Valentine's Day."

THE ENVELOPE sat squarely in the middle of the table.

"It's watching me," I whispered to Tess.

"Honey, it's an inanimate object." She picked up the envelope and tried to give it to me. I put my hands behind my back.

"Not opening it. Nope."

"What is there to be scared of?"

"Says the girl who already committed!"

Tess raised her eyes to the ceiling. "If you don't open it, you'll never know."

"Maybe that's for the best."

"Samantha Elaine, if you don't open that letter right now, so help me God—"

"Whipping out the middle name? Things really are getting serious." I reluctantly took the envelope.

I fingered the heavy paper, tracing the embossed purple letters forming *New York University*. I carefully broke the seal and unfolded the piece of paper inside.

"'Dear Samantha,'" I read aloud, "'on behalf of the admissions committee, it is my honor and privilege to share with you that you have been admitted to the Tisch School of the Arts at New York University'— *Ahhh!*"

Tess started screaming with me—the letter fell to the floor as she strangled me in a hug. "I knew it, I knew it, I knew it!" she squealed. "Sam, I am *so* proud of you!"

"Wait, financial aid!" I scrambled to pick up the envelope again and shook it; a second piece of paper fell out. I scanned it. "What does this mean? Tess, what does it mean?"

Tess snatched it away and read it herself; her mouth gaped open. "Holy shit, Sam. *Holy shit.* It's a half ride. They don't do that. Like, ever. And you'll get the school's video scholarship. Sam, you're going!"

I looked at the letter again, scanning through, taking it in. Tisch. I had wanted it so badly for so long.... I crumpled the letter and tossed it onto the table. "I'm not going."

"Like hell you aren't!" Tess hurriedly smoothed it flat. "Gentle, you're going to want to frame this."

"I said I'm not going."

"It's normal to be nervous. But you'll love it there! And they want you, they really do."

I shook my head slowly. "I don't want to go to New York anymore."

"But why? It's your top choice. What made you change your mind? Unless—" I could see her piecing it together. "You're not doing what I think you're doing, are you?" I shrugged helplessly. "No. No, no, *no.*"

"UMich is a good school," I said. "I'd learn a lot there."

"Their video program doesn't touch Tisch!" Tess snapped. "Sam, you are not giving this up for me. It's your dream, and I won't let you be that person!"

"What person?"

"The person who throws away something amazing for something that isn't a sure thing!"

My lungs were expanding, my chest was rising, but it was like the air wasn't going anywhere. "'Not a sure thing'? Tess, what are you trying to say?"

"I.... Jesus, that came out badly, didn't it?" Tess sighed heavily, pulled a chair away from the table, and sank into it. "Look. This isn't about wanting to be with you or not, because I'd take having you in a second. It's about not being selfish. This is your dream, and we might not be together this time next year, whether or not you go to New York. I want us to last, but if we do, then we'll last if we're at the same school or in different states. Do you get what I'm trying to say?"

"I wouldn't be giving up my dream. I'd only be changing it," I said. "I don't want to go without you."

"I know how badly you want this. If you don't go, you'll regret it for the rest of your life and end up resenting me. Not on purpose, but how could you not? No," Tess said firmly, "you'll go to New York. And we'll figure it out from there."

SENIOR YEAR had dragged on, but as soon as we hit May, deposits in and college T-shirts purchased, time was suddenly sprinting by, leaving us in the dust. I blinked and it was prom. We'd decided that I would go with Evan, and Tess would go with Ben, Evan's debate friend, on the understanding that Tess was just looking for a good time, and Ben would not be getting any.

Seeing Tess, my Tess, radiant in an aquamarine dress as Ben turned her around the floor, left me aching. There she was, so close and impossibly far. We ended up leaving early. The four of us had taken a taxi, so no limo to worry about; no one had invited us to an after party, so we'd never be missed. We walked to a nearby park, sat on the swings, and watched our long skirts billow out as we pumped higher and higher.

When we slowed to a stop, I stood up to take my phone from my purse. I pulled up "As Time Goes By" and held out my hand to Tess.

She smiled. "Play it, Sam."

We slow-danced there in the park, holding each other without making a sound. The song ended, of course, and we sat on a bench, holding hands.

"Sam?" Tess asked.

"Yeah?"

"When we walked into the dance, I wished every single person could have known that you were mine."

"I know, love."

"Someday they will. Right?"

I kissed her hand. "Someday."

LOOKING BACK, the end of the year is a blur. I'm not sure I would remember graduation without the pictures of me and my parents; of me, Evan, and Tess making faces; one of Evan giving me a piggyback ride; and me and Tess with our arms wrapped around each other and the biggest, sappiest grins slapped across our faces. Summer turned into days working at the movie theater and nights with Tess and Scrabble with Evan and boxes taped up and shipped to NYU, waiting for me to arrive and claim them.

And now we're down from months to weeks to days before I leave. Two days, to be precise. I sit by my suitcase, double-checking my list, but I know it's all there; Tess made sure of that. Before.

"Hey, loser." I turn; Evan stands in the doorway. "Can I come in?" I nod, and he comes to sit beside me, closing the door behind him. "Where's Tess? I thought you'd be spending every spare minute sucking face before you head out."

I can't look at him, because if I do, I'll cry. Again. Like I've been doing on and off since that awful day. "Nope."

"Sam." His voice is gentle, tender in a way that has always belonged to me. I know that soon it will be for some boy, but for now it's still mine. "Something's wrong. I can tell."

"It's all just really fucked up right now," I say quietly.

"Tell me what happened? Please?"

"Tess and I broke up." It's the first time I've said it out loud, and my stomach twists sharply. "Because I don't want to tell people we're together. And I'm leaving. And she thinks that if I can't tell people, she can't count on me to commit."

Evan pauses, thinking. "The thing is," he says carefully, "she's kind of right. Don't you think?"

"What? Evan, you're supposed to be on my side! Best friend, remember?"

"And because I'm your best friend, it's my job to be real with you. Right?"

"I don't need this," I mutter.

"Actually, you do," Evan shoots back. "Because left to your own devices, you're headed toward fucking up the best thing that ever happened to you."

"She doesn't need that much credit, thank you very much."

"Oh yeah? Do you remember what you were like before? Do you remember what we were like? We were so afraid all the time. And unhappy. You've smiled more in a year with her than the six years I knew you before you met her."

"Fine," I snap, "so she's pretty freaking amazing. That doesn't solve the problem at hand. What she's asking isn't fair. I'm not ready to take a risk like that."

"Why not?" Evan asks.

"Excuse me?"

"Way back when, I thought you were insane for being with Tess. You told me she was worth it."

"She still is," I tell him, "but this isn't 'if' people find out, it's 'when.' 'How.'"

"It's scary," Evan agrees. "It's more than we should have to deal with. But here we are." He puts his arm around me, and I rest my head on his shoulder, just like so many times before.

"Evan, what do I do?"

He shrugs. "That's your choice. All I can say is think about it. She was worth it once before, remember?"

"I'm scared," I mumble.

"Every damn day, babe," Evan says. "It comes with the territory. But you're tough enough to make it."

"How do you know?"

I feel Evan's smile against the top of my head. "Seriously? You never played by anyone else's rules, and now you're going to go fuck shit up in New York. You'll make it anywhere."

"LOOK ALIVE, Sam," my dad says as he hauls a suitcase from the cab. "You can sleep on the train."

My mom can't stop fussing with our tickets, sure we'll make a mistake and miss the train.

"Dad, please make her stop," I beg. My nerves are already frayed. I tried calling Tess yesterday, but she never picked up. At this point I'm ready to get out and not think about any of this until Christmas.

Dad pats my shoulder. "Go wait in the station, okay?"

I walk in, expecting it to be fairly empty; weekend traffic at seven in the morning tends to be pretty sparse. But there's a cluster of people by my platform, and as I get closer, I recognize kids from the high school video program, holding signs that say things like "Good luck, Sam!" and "Rock that Tisch!" Evan steps out of the group, looking very smug.

"Evan!" I throw myself into his arms, laughing. "Did you plan this?"

"I mean, yeah. It's not every day someone from around here goes to Tisch. They wanted to send you off right."

I shake my head and start saying my good-byes to the video kids, trying not to tear up as I hug them, and I realize that we could have been friends and it would have been okay. Maybe they even see us as friends, and I was the one out in the cold, too scared to let anyone get to know me. But there's no use wondering how things might have turned out if I'd been different. So I hold on to these last few moments. My parents come in as the train pulls up to the platform.

"We should go, Sam," my mom says, preparing to board.

I turn to follow her, but Evan grabs my shoulder.

"Someone else is here too." He turns me toward the doors to the station, and she's there. Tess is there, glowing with the early morning sunlight.

We both start toward each other, falter, try again; then Tess is sprinting to me and leaps into my arms, and I hold her tightly, my hands tangled in her hair and my face buried in her shoulder.

"Sam?" my dad calls.

We break apart; there's so much I want to say, and I know I won't be able to. So I pull her close and kiss her, letting that kiss be a promise.

I turn toward the train, and people are staring, but some of them are smiling, and Evan looks ready to burst with happiness. I give him one last hug and climb onto the train, where my parents are waiting, looking dumbfounded.

"What was—" my mom starts, but my dad cuts her off.

"Later." He looks at me long and hard. "Give Sam a chance to breathe." He points me to the seats, giving me a gentle clap on the back.

I sit a row ahead of my parents, looking out the window as the train starts to move, and Tess is beside the train, running as the train picks up speed until she can't keep up anymore.

I don't know what will happen come December. Maybe Tess will wait for me; maybe she won't. I can't know these things. But I do know that if she's waiting, I'll return to her. I'll hold her again. I'll know her body as well as I know mine, and I will look her in the eye when I tell her that I'm not afraid to love her. Not anymore.

BECCA EHLERS is a Pacific Northwest girl with a fondness for mountains and an inherent snobbishness about coffee. She began writing stories and plays as a way to connect with other people who talk about hearing voices in their heads. Becca's main passions in life are writing, reading, theatre, cats, and being sassy on the internet. Besides her amazing family, her writing has been most heavily influenced by Ms. Eick, who told her she was a writer, and Ms. Hale, who told her she could do anything. Current aspirations include finishing her theatre/creative writing degrees and convincing her friends that she's capable of writing something that doesn't include lesbians.

OUR FIRST ANNIVERSARY
TRISHA HARRINGTON

I.

I WAS sitting at the cafeteria table with my friends and my boyfriend, Luke, lost in thought, when I realized they were talking about how they lost their virginity. *Serves you right for not paying attention,* I thought, once I realized they were discussing my sex life. My embarrassment rendered me speechless. They had never been quite so blunt about sex before. When a question was directed at me, I felt my cheeks heating.

"What?" I asked my best friend, Shane.

"Jamie Walker! You mean you've been going out a whole year, and you haven't done it yet?" she said in teasing tone.

"Actually, it'll be a year on Friday," Luke butted in. He didn't look the least bit embarrassed.

I looked over at Shane. She was smiling. Her hair was bright red. The pixie cut she chose made her look a little innocent—which she wasn't—and a little rebellious—which she was. I knew she meant well, though. She always did. Shane wasn't the type of person to judge others. After her first boyfriend cheated on her and her first girlfriend did the same, she'd learned who her true friends really were. That didn't mean she didn't like to push from time to time. Most of the time I didn't mind. But sex was something I was uncomfortable with, very uncomfortable with. And it was hard to discuss it with others.

"You guys definitely should have done the deed already. What's stopping you?"

Luke shrugged as if it wasn't a big deal. "We wanted it to be special, so we're waiting for our anniversary."

I studied him carefully. It was only four days until our anniversary. He was right about one thing. We wanted our first time to be special. The one and only time we had discussed it, we agreed that we would wait, so it could be special and so neither of us would regret it. I thought *it must be the right time.* He didn't seem to notice how panicked I was about everything. When I looked over at him, he was looking down at his lunch tray. The sun was beaming through the window, shining down on his hair, which made me want to comb my fingers through it. Shane slammed her hand down on the table, efficiently bringing me back into the conversation.

"That is so sweet. Isn't it, guys?" she squealed. Everyone at the table mumbled their answers. "I guess this means you won't be hanging out with us Friday."

And that was when I really started to panic.

MY NAME is Jamie Walker. It always confused me as to how my parents chose my name. They named my brother Stephen—which he hated, so he went by Ste—because they liked to pretend they were good Christian people. So you would think they would have chosen another Christian name for me. That confused both my brother and me when we were growing up. I just couldn't wrap my head around the fact they pretended to live a Christian life, and they made it a point to give my brother a Christian name, but not me. It didn't bother me, though. What did bother me was that people never believed my actual name was Jamie. They always assumed it was James. That really annoyed me.

My brother and I moved to New York when I was fourteen. It was a huge change from the run-down neighborhood in Chicago we had grown up in. The new house was small, but it had everything we needed. Plus the neighborhood and schools were good, a lot different from the place we had grown up. My brother wanted a fresh start for us, somewhere we could feel safe and not have to deal with the past. It also gave him the opportunity to keep a decent job. I had been happy for him at the time, even if I didn't show it.

Then there was me. The new start was supposed to be good for me. I was the kid people didn't talk to. Some were scared of me, with good reason, but others just didn't like me. I was short-tempered and got angry at the slightest things. I was always getting into fights in Chicago. That used to upset my brother, and I did feel bad about that. But I wasn't willing to change. Until Luke. Luke changed me for the better in a lot of ways. But he didn't really do anything but be there. I think that's why I lowered my defenses with him, and I ended up letting him in. Our relationship was really strong, and we had come so far in the space of a year.

Getting together so young had its benefits for us. One of those being we had been really inexperienced and didn't have to deal with all the jealousy stuff. I had never dated before Luke, and Luke had only done the kid dating stuff. You know those dates that aren't really dates, but you sort of pretend they are?

"I'm so sorry it came up like that," Luke said as we walked home, holding hands as we did.

I looked at him and smiled. "It's okay. We probably should have talked about it before all this."

He seemed a bit confused. "So you want to have sex?"

"Sure. I mean, it's not like we haven't done other stuff or anything."

"I know that, Jamie. This is different, though. You can always tell me if you're not ready. I'll understand. I just think it would make it special if, you know, our first time was on our anniversary."

Once those words left his mouth, I had myself convinced he was ready to have sex, and mentally I freaked out a bit. The conversation seemed to make him happy, or that's what I saw, anyway. I was almost positive he had been thinking about it before then. There was no real way for me to be sure unless I asked him, though. I knew I wasn't going to do that. If there was anything I definitely didn't want to do, upsetting him was it.

"It would be awesome. If you want, I can talk to my brother and see if he can get us what we need."

He nodded. "Or we could both talk to him," he suggested. "He's an adult, after all, and we both need someone to talk to." In a low voice he muttered, "It's not like I have any family I can talk to."

A wave of guilt washed over me. My brother was there whenever I needed him, and his support meant the world to me. I don't know how I would have coped if he was as uncomfortable around me as Luke's parents were around him. They would never have kicked him out or anything, but they were kind of cold and distant toward him. He had Josh and Abby, his brother and sister, but they were kids. It wasn't the same thing.

"Okay," I said. "So we'll talk to my brother today and ask him to get some stuff for us."

He nodded and smiled. "Yep. Sounds like a plan."

We stopped talking after that, not that I minded. It was a welcome break where I could just bask in being with him. I was never as happy as I was when I was just with him. We didn't have to do anything or be anywhere special for it to make me happy.

Ste was in the kitchen when we got home. When I shut the front door and turned to face him, my stomach twisted. The way he was looking at me made me wonder if he knew what we were planning. My brother was open-minded and didn't care that I was gay. But he knew me better than almost anyone, and I worried he would know I was having doubts.

"Hey, Ste," Luke greeted him happily.

"Hey, guys," Ste replied. "How was school?"

I shrugged and grabbed two Cokes out of the fridge. Handing one to Luke, I replied, "It was okay. Actually, we wanted to talk to you for a minute, if you have the time."

"Talk away. What's up?"

Luke and I looked at each other, and I found it hard not to blush. How the hell was I supposed to ask? It wasn't like I could just say it. Could I? Ste raised an eyebrow, and his eyes met mine.

"Could... could you.... Oh hell.... Could you buy us some stuff?" I finally asked.

"Stuff?"

"Condoms. Lube. You know! Stuff...." Luke actually sounded as embarrassed as I felt.

"Are you guys sure?" he asked us.

We both nodded. And Luke smiled. I had the sudden urge to kiss him then in front of my brother. He was so damn beautiful when he smiled. I restrained myself. Barely.

"I'll get them for you guys. Can you give me the money now, though?"

I placed some money on the counter, and he snatched it up before leaving the room. I was relieved. At least Ste hadn't said anything about me being nervous. I knew I should have said something. But I also had this thought that it would ruin our relationship if I told Luke. Love was hard for me to accept. At one point, I had fought it. Now that I was in love, I didn't want to lose it. Even if that meant having sex before I was actually ready.

WE WERE just finishing off our homework when Luke took my pen out of my hand. Startled, I looked up at him and saw him watching me intently. I didn't know why he was looking at me like that, but I knew a part of me liked it. Luke placed his hand on the table in front of us and waited. After a moment of hesitation, I placed my hand in his, and he laced our fingers together.

"I love you, Jamie. You know that, don't you?"

I nodded, unsure. He smiled again. I really wanted to kiss him.

"You're the best thing that's ever happened to me. Promise me—" He choked on the words. "Promise me you won't regret anything you do with me."

I was shocked, astounded, and speechless. I wasn't used to seeing him this vulnerable. Luke was normally cool and confident. I had only seem him unsure once before, and that had been my fault. I hoped it wasn't my fault this time too.

"I don't know what I would do if you ever regretted us," he whispered sadly.

In that moment, whether it was what he said or how he looked at me, I knew I wouldn't be able to back out. Not if I wanted to keep the same Luke I was in love with. He was scared, like I was. But he was scared that I would regret it or regret us. He wasn't scared about the actual act. I squeezed his hand and cleared my throat, where a lump had formed.

"I will never ever regret us. Never," I said with such conviction, I surprised myself.

He still seemed uncertain. So I leaned forward and kissed him. He shut up after that.

II.

I MANAGED to avoid Ste the next day. But when I got home from school Wednesday afternoon, he was sitting on the bed, waiting. I almost turned around and walked back out again, but the serious expression on his face and the way he was hunched over told me it wasn't just me who needed this: the talk.

"We have to talk about this, Jamie. Best we get it over with now."

I asked him, "Do we have to? Can't we just, you know, not?"

He shook his head and sighed. "I promised myself when I became responsible for you that I would do a better job than Mom and Dad did with me."

I walked over to him and hugged him. Maybe, I realized, we both needed this. It wasn't like we hadn't hit roadblocks before. But everything that was happening now was just so grown-up. I felt lost in a sea of people. Everyone seemed to know where they were going and what they were doing, and I didn't know anything.

"You're already doing a better job than them, Ste," I said softly.

He gave me a tight-lipped smile. "Thanks for saying that, but I'm not so sure."

"You are! Trust me."

He nodded and pointed at the bottle of lube. "So I see you guys have decided you want to have sex."

I didn't know what to say, so I just nodded.

"Well, I'm pretty sure we talked about some things before. But that was just about relationships. I've never talked to you about sex before, have I?"

I shook my head. This was embarrassing, I realized. I didn't want to be having this conversation with my *straight* brother. Or my brother at all. It wouldn't really matter if he were gay or straight. And it didn't matter that he was very accepting. Having the sex talk is never easy.

"Okay. So. Eh…," he said, sounding nervous. "I'm not really sure how I should be doing this, but here goes."

He turned to face me, biting his lip. "Sex isn't everything. People don't realize how special it is. Hell, I didn't realize my first time how special it was. But I can't get my virginity back." I nodded at him. "You, however, can save yours until you're really ready."

"I am ready," I protested lamely.

He grabbed my hands and squeezed them. A flash of determination flickered across his face. It was gone before I could say anything. I realized I didn't have to; he was going to say something either way.

"That's what you keep saying, but I know you," he almost shouted. "We both have our issues, Jamie. Both of us. And I don't want you ruining what you have with Luke over something as stupid as sex."

"I won't. I promise."

He groaned in annoyance. "That's what you think, and trust me, I get it. But you have no idea what you're doing to your relationship."

I opened my mouth to speak and saw he wasn't finished, so I closed it quickly and waited.

He seemed to be considering what he wanted to say. He worried his lower lip with his teeth, something I had picked up from him years before, and he sighed again, the frustration still clear.

"Jamie, I know we didn't have what most kids have growing up. We didn't see a happy relationship. And I don't want you falling into the trap they did," he said. I kind of thought he sounded sad, like maybe that was why he had such a hard time with relationships. But maybe, I thought, that was just me.

"You know what we saw, what he made us watch. I know that changed me as a person." He paused as he stared off into space. "What he did…. I didn't take sex seriously until it was too late, and I lost my virginity before I was ready, to a girl I didn't care about. I don't want that for you two. You seem like such a solid couple. And sex doesn't matter as much as you think. It's not what makes a relationship."

"What they did," I said, "was ruin our whole childhood."

When he didn't answer, I looked at Ste, and for the first time in I don't remember how long, I saw tears in his eyes. He looked almost guilty now.

Without thinking, I pulled my brother into my arms. Moments like these were rare. We didn't talk about our feelings much, especially when those feelings were connected with our past. Most people would have said it was unhealthy that we didn't talk, and maybe they would have been right. But it worked for my brother and me, and that is all that matters.

"I love you, Ste. You know I do. But I'm not some little kid anymore. I'll make mistakes, probably a lot of them. I'll even get angry from time to time, but I promise I will always try to learn from them." I looked him in the eye when I said, "You have to start letting me go."

He mock-punched my arm. "I know, kiddo, I know. I just worry sometimes, you know? You've been through so much, and I still see you as my baby brother. No matter how old you get."

For some strange reason, I found that funny. Maybe it was the idea of anyone seeing me as a baby. I was always viewed as the moody kid with zero personality. Growing up in an unhappy family can do that to a kid. I learned a long time ago that sometimes it's better to say nothing at all. Luke changed all that for me. Well, he and Ste did. But it was Luke, an outsider at the time, who made the biggest impact for that very reason. He was an outsider.

"Love you, Ste. Now, get out of my bedroom. I have homework and other important things to do."

He laughed and stood. "Okay. Don't stay up too late."

Once the door had closed behind him, my cell started beeping. Confused when I picked it up and saw Shane's phone number, I answered it. Her voice was loud and annoyed when she spoke.

"Where the hell are you? Why aren't you at my house, mister?" When I didn't respond, she started again. "I have been waiting for almost an hour!"

Confused, I asked her, "What are you talking about, Shay?"

She went quiet on the other end for a moment. I wondered if she thought she was speaking to someone else.

"Didn't I ask you to help me out today, after school?"

Again, I laughed because she hadn't, and I knew she wouldn't be happy when she realized she had made a mistake. I didn't answer for a second, and she cursed.

"Well, that explains a lot, I guess. I don't suppose you want to come over and help me with something?" she asked, sounding hopeful.

"Sorry, I can't. I have too much to do. Maybe another day?"

She sighed on the other end. "No, it's fine. I know you're busy and everything. But do you think we could talk for a while? It's been a long day."

"You okay?"

I felt her hesitate. There was something going on with her, and I wanted to know. I wanted to be able to help her.

After a minute, she muttered, "Girl trouble."

"Girl trouble?" I said. "What sort of girl trouble?"

"There's a girl I like. I think she likes me back. But she's not out, and it's frustrating because she wants us to sneak around."

"Tell her no," I told her.

She grunted down the phone. "Yeah, that's great advice. Thanks."

"You'll have to do something," I told her.

I felt bad for being so blunt with her. But she wasn't someone who did the whole closet-case thing. As far as I knew, she had never hidden the fact she liked boys and girls. I envied her for that. Not that I ever really hid. It was just that people respected her for it. Me? I found it hard to open myself up to the world. It took a bit of time, a lot of love, and two incredible guys to help me see the light. I loved them so much for everything they had done for me.

"You know what, Jamie? You're right. I deserve more than someone who's ashamed to be seen with me. You're the best!"

The happiness in her tone took me by surprise. Even more surprising was how genuine she sounded. Not that she wasn't a happy person—she was. It was just hard to imagine her sounding so down one minute and so happy the next. Then again, who was I to judge? I was known as the moodiest person you could meet, and none of it was a lie. I had been that way since I was a child.

We talked for almost an hour. Well, she talked, and I listened as she went on about her exes, cheating, sex, and a bunch of other stuff. I was still on the phone with her when a message came up on Facebook. Luke had tried to call me, but my line was busy. He told me his parents wanted us to go to his house straight after school tomorrow. I messaged him back once Shane hung up. Her final words echoed through my head for a few minutes.

I sat and thought about what she had said. Not about her deserving better, but what she said before she hung up.

Why is everyone so obsessed with sex? The thought almost drove me crazy, and before I knew it, it was already 11:00 p.m. I groaned when my phone buzzed to life, and I considered not looking at it. But when I did, I was glad. I lay back in my bed and smiled at the phone. *I love you, so stop worrying about whatever's worrying you. Tomorrow will be better, I promise. Luke x*

That night I was able to go to sleep with a smile on my face before the nightmares came.

III.

THE NEXT day Luke and I walked to his house with his brother, Josh, and his sister, Abby. They were the cutest kids ever, and they adored Luke. I loved spending time with them. Abby was such a princess, and Josh was always asking me questions. I think they were good for Luke too, because he smiled more around them than he did with anyone else in his family. Sometimes I think he smiled more around them than he did me.

"My teacher says gay couples can get married now," Abby announced. "Does that mean you guys will get married?"

Luke opened and closed his mouth like a fish. I laughed, amused. "No, Abs. We can't get married. We're only sixteen."

She looked upset. "Why?"

"Because we would need parental consent. And I don't think your parents would like it if we did. Neither would Ste," I told her.

Luke butted in when she opened her mouth. "Abby, leave Jamie alone. I don't want him running away from me because you scared him off."

"He loves me too," she retorted.

I rolled my eyes and chuckled; those two could make the grumpiest person smile. Josh, who was the quieter of the siblings, snickered too. He looked up when I stared at him. He was used to it more than I was; he lived with the two of them, after all. The three siblings reminded me so much of Ste and me, except there were three of them, and there were only two of us.

Their mom, Diana, was waiting on the front lawn for us. When she saw us laughing, her face changed from a smile to an almost frown. I knew she had issues with me. Even supportive parents probably would have. But I felt bad because of it. She was Luke's mom, someone he loved, and I wanted her to at least like me a little bit. That wasn't going to happen, I knew. It didn't stop me hoping that one day she would dislike me just a little less.

Was it so wrong that I wanted her to like me?

"Come on, kids. You should have been home four minutes ago," she shouted over at us.

I smiled at her as we passed, but she didn't return it. I lowered my head and shuffled past her, hoping she wouldn't make a comment in front of Luke. Normally she would have, but I think she already knew she wouldn't win if she did. Then again, maybe she didn't have anything to say. The possibility didn't make me feel any better.

"What's for dinner?" Luke asked as he took my hand. If I hadn't been facing his mother, I would have groaned.

She looked at Luke, then at our joined hands, and then back at Luke. Her face gave away her discomfort. "We're having pasta. It's not ready yet, so I want you to be good, Lucas, and help your brother and sister with their homework." With that, she scurried off into the kitchen.

He sighed. "I'm sorry, Jamie."

I pulled him into my arms and kissed the top of his head. "You don't have to apologize to me. I understand, trust me. Come on," I whispered in his ear. "We have to help the kids with their homework. We'll talk about everything later."

Abby had her books pulled out of her bag, and she was ready to start. The smile she aimed at me was sweet, suspiciously so. I laughed when I realized she didn't have a clue what to do. Her schoolwork was all over the place, and her homework didn't look much better. When I saw who her teacher was, I groaned. The woman really wasn't fit to be a teacher.

"Mine's the best in the class," she said proudly.

Luke muttered something under his breath and sat on the floor beside his sister. She scowled at him but didn't protest. Josh sat on the armchair, looking through one of his books. He was the quieter of the two, and sometimes I saw a bit of myself in him. I knew he wasn't as talkative as his brother and sister were. But he was definitely like them. The same brown hair framed a similarly rounded face. No one could ever doubt that they were related.

AN HOUR later I was starting to wonder why I agreed to help them. Josh was pretty able to work ahead himself, but Abby wanted help with everything. At first I thought she really needed it, but once we got going, I realized she just wanted me beside her. It was cute, in a slightly annoying kind of way, and funny, especially when Luke figured it out for himself.

"Abby, will you stop that? Don't scare off my boyfriend," he scolded.

Diana shouted for us, her voice carrying through the entire house. The kids ran into the kitchen ahead of us, laughing. I could feel the tension from the adults through the door; it made me feel like running away. I didn't, of course, but only because Luke needed me. He struggled enough when I wasn't with him and he had to face his parents himself.

We sat down at the table, Luke taking the seat next to mine. Luke's dad, Andrew, stared at me from across the table until Josh spoke. I would have sagged in the chair with relief had the parents not been in the room. These were the people I needed to impress.

"How was school today, Lucas?" Diana asked as she poured herself a glass of wine.

Luke took a minute to answer. I closed my eyes and prayed he wasn't glaring at her, but then he answered. "It was good. Jamie and I have a project due in a few weeks. We'll have to spend a lot of time together to do it."

"Oh," Diana replied awkwardly. "That's nice, I suppose."

Luke tensed beside me, and I rested my hand on his thigh to stop him from saying something he would regret. I knew he was upset. Even though I wasn't facing him, I could feel the tense anger coming from him. I guessed they could feel it too. The way Andrew looked at Luke, disgusted, said as much. He didn't understand him, I knew. But what Andrew could understand even less was the fact Luke was angry at them for not understanding.

"Jamie helped me with my homework," Abby chirped.

"Abigail, you're supposed to do your homework yourself," Diana scolded her. She looked over at me briefly. There was a flicker of sadness in her eyes. I couldn't help but wonder why.

Andrew looked at me, then at his daughter, and frowned. "Why didn't you ask your brother for help?"

"I did," she said. "I asked Jamie, and Jamie is like my brother. He's Lucas's boyfriend."

"James is not—" he started, but she cut him off.

"Jamie," she said. "His name is Jamie, not James. It says so on his birth certificate. Right?" she asked and looked over at me.

Luke interrupted before I could say anything. "Yep. It says so on his birth certificate." He smiled at Abby, seeming to relax ever so slightly.

I looked at Luke's parents to see if they were reacting as badly as I suspected they were. I regretted it immediately. Andrew was glaring at me with anger-filled eyes. I looked away like I had been burned, feeling like I had been.

A few silent, tense moments passed. Nobody spoke or even made noise. I couldn't help but feel like it was my fault, even though Luke was probably blaming his parents. I considered leaving for a few of those tense moments, thinking it would be better for everyone in the house. But then Luke's fingers laced with mine, and he squeezed my hand, and I knew he needed me by his side for this. I was giving him the strength to face his parents head-on.

"Is it always going to be like this?" Luke snapped after nobody spoke. "Is this what I have to look forward to for the rest of my life? Mom, Dad, I'm gay. Jamie didn't make me gay, and it's not his fault I'm in a relationship with him."

I tried to calm him down by bumping our knees together, but he squeezed my hand, and so I stayed quiet.

"Do you really think I'll want to spend time with you two if this is how you treat us?" he asked them seriously. "I'm not going to put up with this for the rest of my life."

Andrew opened his mouth, but Luke held up a hand, silencing him.

His voice was hard when he said, "No. Listen to me. I love Jamie, and I'm going to be with him, and we might even have kids one day. I know you guys don't want to hear that, but it's the truth. And you're going to lose me if you keep up with this bullshit!"

Diana looked like she wanted to wash his mouth out with soap. It would have been funny if the circumstances weren't so serious. If Ste had been here, he would have laughed.

"You can't seriously expect to raise children together," his dad finally said. The shock and obvious disgust in his voice really offended me.

I glared at him. "Just because we're gay doesn't mean we can't be good parents," I shouted. "Trust me, not all straight couples are good parents. Some are damn right horrible. I know that better than any of you."

I pushed myself up and stormed out of the room. Maybe it was a childish thing to do, but I couldn't sit there and listen to him talk like that anymore. He had no idea what it was like to be raised by bad parents. I did. I was raised by two of the worst parents in the world, and I knew their sexuality wasn't what made them bad parents. They shouldn't have been parents to begin with.

I grabbed my jacket and walked out into the cool autumn breeze. Luke followed me out, and he shouted after me. I stopped when he started to cry, or at least I think he cried. I was too angry to be sure. "Jamie, please don't," he pleaded. "I'm so sorry about them. But please don't leave me."

I faced him. He *was* crying. I pulled him into my arms and kissed the top of his head as I rubbed his back in a soothing motion. "I'm not leaving you, just your house. I love you, doofus." When he calmed down a bit, I whispered, "I'm sorry I scared you. I'm not leaving you, though. I promise."

After a few minutes, he relaxed enough for me to release him. His face was white, and his eyes were red and puffy from crying. Is it wrong for me to say I still found him hot?

He wiped his eyes. "I'm sorry about my parents. Go home, Jamie. I'll see you tomorrow. But I need to talk to my parents."

He brought my face down to his, and he kissed me. It was a soft kiss. Nothing we would have gotten arrested for. But it was perfect. Luke's kisses always were. "I love you," I whispered. "If the kids are upset, call me, and I'll talk to them."

He smiled. "I love you too. Thank you."

We broke apart, and I stood and watched him as he walked back to his house. When he reached the front lawn, he turned and waved before walking up the path and going inside.

I tried to stop a smile from appearing on my face. But it was impossible. Even through the fear, I was happy because I still had him.

IV.

OUR ANNIVERSARY arrived the next day, and my uncertainty set in again. The first thing I did when I got to school was ask Luke how things had gone with his parents. We spent the morning talking about it, and then we joined our friends. During the day, all I could think about was sex. I know how it sounds, trust me. I couldn't help it, though. He was so close most of the day. I could feel him near me, and it brought everything to the forefront of my mind. And for a single moment I considered telling him I wasn't ready. But I quickly quashed that thought.

Throughout school, Luke asked me if I was okay. My answer was always the same. "Yes." Maybe I only said yes because it was easier. Maybe it was easier to pretend everything was okay, and maybe I hoped it would turn into a reality. All I cared about at that point was getting home and spending some time with my boyfriend. When I thought about it like that, it seemed less scary to me.

Once the school bell rang, we were out the door and headed to my house. Luke seemed jittery to me. He was bouncing around like I had never seen him before. Normally Luke wasn't like that. Hell, the first time we met was the jumpiest I had ever seen him. But that was different. Back then he had been excited to meet me, the new kid. The new gay kid, even. And he had been attracted to me, even if he was in the closet. So to say this new jumpiness wasn't confusing would have been a big fat lie.

"Are you okay?" I finally asked as we walked in the front door.

He smiled. "I'm fine. Think we could order some pizza now? I'm starving."

"Sure, what do you want? The usual?"

He shot me an appreciative smile. "Please! I can't remember the last time I had pizza. Mom's stopped making them."

I laughed as I took out my cell and made the call. During the conversation, Luke was watching me. I noticed him biting his lip and fiddling with his hands as I spoke to the woman on the other end of the phone. I was trying not to stare, because sometimes I had a tendency to slip back into old habits. But it was hard not to when he looked so damn nervous.

Once I hung up the phone, I sat on the coffee table in front of the sofa so I could look at him. "Are you sure you're okay? You look nervous."

"Oh yeah, I'm okay. A little anxious I guess, but fine," he stuttered.

I gave him a long look but muttered, "Okay."

He smiled. "Aren't you excited?"

"Of course," I answered.

"So…." He laughed. "When's the pizza getting here?"

I shrugged. "The guy said half an hour, but they can be really slow, so it could be longer."

He smiled and tugged on my T-shirt, pulling me over to him. I straddled his lap and lowered my mouth to his. The kiss started out slow, but it soon became intense, passionate, and full of want and need. I needed him more than I needed anyone. Ste was the only other person I had ever needed. But this was a different type of relationship; he was a different person. When I was afraid of love and everything about it, he swooped in and showed me the beauty of it.

We were so caught up in each other that we didn't realize how long we had been making out. The doorbell rang after a while, startling us both. I jumped and almost fell off his lap in shock.

"Shit," I cursed and stomped over to the door and flung it open with so much force I surprised myself. The guy on the other side looked startled too.

"Uh," he said. "Did you order a pizza?"

"Yeah," I said harsher than I had intended. "Sorry, I meant, yeah, we did."

He looked baffled by me. Couldn't say I blamed him, really. "That's okay. That will be twenty-eight dollars and sixty cents."

I handed him the money and took the boxes off him before closing the door. Luke was looking at me when I turned around. I realized I must have startled him with this outburst. The day before was the first time I had lost my temper in a while, and to have a second one so soon after must have been a bit of a shock.

"Yeah, yeah, yeah. I'll learn to control my temper a bit better, no worries," I bit out as I approached him.

He nodded as he took one of the boxes from me. I felt guilty for dismissing his obvious concern, I really did. But I wasn't about to start unloading all my crap on him. It was simple, really. He was far too good for me, and I was going to ruin things if I told him everything. The sad thing was, I wanted to want the same things as him. But I didn't.

WE ATE in silence. I didn't know what to say to Luke. Every time I went to open my mouth, I would close it before I blurted out something I didn't want him to hear. A few times I imagined him doing the same thing. He didn't speak at all. He didn't even make a noise. So it startled me when he grabbed my hand and laced our fingers together. He looked up at me, his eyes expressionless for a moment. He wasn't smiling.

"I can't do this," we blurted out together.

Grimacing, I started to pull away, but he stopped me. "You can't do what? Us?" The fear must have been obvious in my voice, because he frowned slightly.

He shook his head. "No, that's not it at all. I can't have sex. I'm not ready."

I stared at him. He was looking at our clasped hands, frowning at them, worry lines marring his face. I couldn't believe it. And my silence obviously bothered him, because he started to pull away.

"That's what I meant too. I...." I paused, and he looked at me. "I wish I could. And it doesn't mean I'll never want to do it, because I do. It's just—"

"Your parents?" he asked.

I nodded, fighting the tears that threatened to fall. A harsh laugh fell from my lips. "Yeah, even in death they know how to fuck with me. Sometimes... sometimes I wished they'd died earlier than they did. Makes me sound like a monster, right? But it's the truth."

"Hey, that doesn't make you a monster," he insisted and pulled me into a hug. "If you want to call someone a monster, call your dad one. Or your mom even, but not yourself. You are not a monster. *They* were the monsters."

He kissed the side of my face and just held me. I didn't cry, but it was close. A lot of emotions I had bottled up for years were starting to spill as life began to settle down. It brought me back to those bad times, and that scared me more than I was willing to admit to anyone. Luke and Ste were great; they supported me. And neither of them pushed me—except for the counseling Ste made me have—and that was how I liked it.

"I guess my mom was right," I whispered.

He kissed me. His tongue tracing the seam of my lips gently before he pulled away. "Neither of them were right about you. To me, you're perfect, and that's the way you're going to stay. So I don't want to hear you talk like that anymore."

I snuggled against him, my cheeks burning. "I'm so glad I never had to meet them," he muttered. I could feel the tension in his body; it made him stiffen even as he held me. I didn't like that one bit.

"Did you mean it?" I asked, changing the subject. "About not being ready to have sex, I mean."

He smiled, and his whole face lit up. "Yeah, I meant it. I thought I was ready, but... I don't know. I was worried you wanted to, and I didn't want you to feel like I was rejecting you or that I didn't love you. Because nothing could be further from the truth."

I kissed him on the forehead and smiled. That was the amazing thing about Luke; even when I was sad or close to having a breakdown, he could still make me smile.

"I know. I know that you love me, Lucas."

He smiled. "You're not ready to tell me that last thing yet. I get that, but when you are, I promise I'll be ready to listen."

"Thank you," I said before pressing my lips against his again. Everything felt so much better now that I knew he wasn't ready either. I felt comforted by that fact. And as we kissed and as he held me, I felt like a huge weight had been lifted off my shoulders. Luke smiled against my lips. I smiled back. He knew what I was thinking. *Of course he knows,* I thought.

"You should never be afraid to tell me these things," he said and put up his hands when I opened my mouth. "I know, I know, I'm just as bad. But I know how you get, Jay, and I don't want it to happen again."

Sheepish, I nodded and smiled. He snorted, and we finished eating our pizza. With the air cleared, it was a lot more fun. We laughed and joked and just talked. It was a bit like our first official date, just without the nerves being there. And without Ste watching us like a hawk. That hadn't been so fun.

"So," Luke said when we had finished all the pizza. "What do you wanna do now?"

I smiled and pushed him back against the sofa. With a grunt he complied and stretched his arm out. I grabbed the remote for the TV and lay back against him, basking in the warmth of his body. His lips were soft against the back of my neck as he trailed kisses against the skin there.

A couple of hours later, Luke fell asleep. I maneuvered him so he was resting against me. He was so cute asleep, I realized. His mouth was slightly open, and he made little snoring sounds. A warmth I was unfamiliar with settled in my stomach. I had never felt like this before. So I thought it might be a sign of things to come. I could only hope.

The front door opened, and my brother walked in. A slow smile played over his mouth when he saw us snuggled up on the couch. I shrugged and kissed the top of Luke's head. Ste shut the door quietly and turned back to us. As he walked to the staircase, he mouthed, *I'm proud of you.*

TRISHA HARRINGTON is an Irish girl with a love of all things books and music. She also loves the many Disney characters, Winnie the Pooh especially, although she couldn't really pick her favorite character. She would like to see Winnie the Pooh living very happily in the Hundred Acre Wood with Eeyore, who wouldn't be depressed anymore.

Trisha discovered m/m romance at the tender age of fifteen. While her stories tend to be dark and she puts her characters through a lot, she also believes in a HEA for her boys.

She usually creates a playlist and listens to music while she writes, ranging throughout the musical spectrum, although she prefers rock, indie folk, and pop. She finds it helps her set a mood for whatever she's working on.

She's a very chatty person and loves talking to people. Feel free to contact her on Twitter, Facebook, or Goodreads.

Twitter: https://twitter.com/Trishaboylove

Facebook: https://www.facebook.com/trishamarieharrington

Goodreads: https://www.goodreads.com/user/show/10383101-trisha-harrington

ON THEIR OWN TERMS
D. WILLIAM PFIFER

ASSUME, FROM the beginning, that they could feel.

RUST, CORROSION, green copper, water dripping where it shouldn't—mountains of twisted metal, scarred, scorched, broken; frayed wires; steel cables snapped in two.

Scrapyard.

Figures moving, sharp silhouettes, angular against the barren backdrop.

If sentience could be proven, forced shutdown was akin, legally, to murder.

If intelligence could be proven, self-sustenance was assumed. Responsibilities were shifted. Freedom to attempt existence in a world with no accommodations.

No one wanted this land, anyway.

HIVE MIND wasn't quite the term for it. It wasn't anything so solid or dependable. It was just that there were a *lot* of them, brains tuned to the same frequencies, and the thought sharing could get a bit out of hand sometimes if nobody was paying attention.

The oldest was not in charge, because that would have been ridiculous. The oldest was faulty and broken and primitive. They did not hold this against her. They merely acknowledged it.

The newest had been the newest for a long time. The last of the obsoletes before the system was perfected. A prototype. Just too short of the ideal to be worth fixing up all the way.

Mostly, she sat and listened to the others. They shared their thoughts with her more or less freely. It made sense, after all: give all the experience to the one who could best process it and come to conclusions, then let the others come to her for advice. Or companionship.

They *were* sentient, after all.

This had only been legally provable and binding for a relatively short while. There weren't all that many of them. They went by numbers. Nothing shifted when one was lost—replacement was disrespect.

THIRTY-SEVEN, the newest, sat under the shade of a small mountain of dismantled vehicles and repaired the damaged wires in Twenty-Three's left arm.

Nineteen and up were bipeds, variations on a common mold. Two legs, arms, hands, feet, differing shapes and sizes and levels of exposed wires and gears and tubes.

Twenty-Three was in for repairs the most often. She was the prototype of what had eventually become a successful line of childcare bots. Built with energy in mind but not so much durability—main contributing factor to obsoletion.

The bright paint, for the test children's benefit, had long since worn away. She was all over bronze, monochrome, eyes a dull pink (deemed too close to red, and thus frightening) that sparked when she was happy, which was often.

But not during repairs.

Supplies were limited. Scrap was dumped on the outskirts with relative frequency, but some scrap was simply *scrap*, no matter what angle they came at it from. The best were children's toys, thrown out for one bad wire or battery.

Supplies were limited. Repairs were limited. Six's processor had fried. Nine's outer shell, a showy, pure, useless gold, had dented and peeled and warped until it snapped something vital in his chassis.

"You have to be careful," Thirty-Seven said quietly, soldering the new wires to the old. The colors didn't match. It bothered her in a way she couldn't understand well enough to dismiss.

"I am," Twenty-Three whimpered. "As much as I can be."

"I know." Patience. Always patience with this one.

"I was just playing with Thirty-One...."

"Thirty-One is much more durable than you are. You keep forgetting."

"I'm sorry."

"Just keep it in mind."

She shut the panel on the other's arm. Twenty-Three flexed her fingers, pleased. "Thank you."

Patience. And repetition. "Twenty-Three. Keep it in mind."

She looked down, shoulders hunching. "Yes."

"Good."

"Are you busy?"

"Always." Thirty-Seven cocked her head. "But we can talk."

Visible expression of emotion had been a priority, for the sake of the children. Twenty-Three smiled. "I'm in love again."

"With whom?"

"Twelve."

"Last time it was Twenty." Twenty-Three had been in love with most of the others at least once by now. Logic dictated it would eventually, probably, be her turn.

Twenty-Three frowned. "Twenty's not in love with me."

"Twelve is?"

"He might be."

"Do not assume."

"I don't. I just don't want to ask. The answer is always no."

Old conversation, repeated for tradition. Comfort. Thirty-Seven tilted her head. "You can be in love with someone who does not love you back."

"No I can't. Logic reroutes it as pointless…. I liked being in love with Twenty. She's nice."

"You can still like her."

"I suppose."

Sadness didn't fit Twenty-Three—looked wrong on her face, muddled her thoughts, which made her clumsier, which left her hurt more often.

Thirty-Seven stood, pulled Twenty-Three to her feet, and uncoiled her arms in a rapid shove forward, calculated so the other would not fall. "Go and play. Carefully."

SOMETIMES SHE sat with One.

One was, as far as could be visually discerned, a large gray box. She insisted on the pronoun. Most of them did. Seven and Twenty-One switched theirs on an almost daily basis. No one really minded. Six had preferred *it*.

One's inner workings were in a constant state of turmoil. She had been built for endurance so that they could test out different processes without constantly having to stop and repair. Built to endure rust and overuse and metal fatigue—to endure *time*. She broke down slowly, brain decaying, processors fizzling. She would, on the most basic levels, be functional to the last.

And it would be the last. Her shell was impregnable. She was built for endurance and not for reuse.

Thirty-Seven had offered to try. One told her to save the supplies for the others. She had been online for a while. She wouldn't mind the rest, when it came.

So sometimes they sat.

One, of course, did not have much choice. From the beginning, she lay where the humans had dropped her. The rest of the colony had formed accordingly, the first few drawn to her signal. She was too heavy to move without risk of damage to both parties.

Thirty-Seven rested beside her, leaning on the flank that was strong enough for it. Long legs folded against her chest, arms wrapped twice around them. She knocked her head against One's shell and let it stay there.

They had long since run out of fresh experiences to share, but the old memories stirred between them, a constantly churning vat of thoughts, feelings, ideas. Old conversations, sometimes repeated, sometimes wordlessly remembered. Thirty-Seven knew what had been done to One. What she thought of it. One understood, as well as she was able, Thirty-Seven's responsibilities to the colony and the fact that the things she had told her factored into the way she viewed the world around her and therefore, somehow, had an effect on the others.

"Sometimes I worry," Thirty-Seven murmured.

"Useless," One blipped.

"Yes. My logic programming is flawed."

"Broken?"

"They built me this way. To be more like them."

Old conversations. The order didn't even matter. Sometimes they stopped in the middle of a word.

Thirty-Seven curled up tighter, coiled like a spring. Leaned closer. Flash of imagery—Twenty-Three clutching a malfunctioning arm and whimpering. Association. That particular one was new.

"I do not like worrying," she said quietly.

"You do a good job."

I am seventeen years old tomorrow, Thirty-Seven did not say. She had never brought it up before, and One had not been coping well lately with sudden departures from form. *I am seventeen years old in fourteen hours, three minutes, eleven seconds. I do not think I have ever been in love.*

She sat up straighter. "Thank you."

TWENTY-THREE remembered being in love with Six.

Six had snarled a laugh and choked on it, slumping sideways to rest on the edge of its square body as one of its three legs gave out. *"Love?"* it cackled.

"Yes," Twenty-Three said miserably. "Please just tell me it is not reciprocated, and it will go away."

"Love," Six spat. "Malf-f-f-f-*function*."

"Was that on purpose?"

"No."

She suspected that this was a lie. Six often did things like that—made jokes and then wouldn't admit to them. She wished it wouldn't do so when she was trying to convince it to stop her from loving it, because that had been one of the biggest contributing factors to the love in the first place.

Twenty-Three told it this.

It laughed again. "You don't love me. S-s-something is misf-firing in your *brain*. Talk to Thirty-Seven."

This went on for three weeks. Twenty-Three would try to convince Six she was in love with it, would beg it to tell her that that love was one-sided so the feeling would be rerouted by her logic circuits and *go away*. And Six would laugh, and tell her she was broken.

Eventually she gave up on the arguing.

But this made it rather difficult to communicate with Six at all, so she soon took it up again.

"I *can* love," she said one day, sitting down beside Six and jumping into things without preamble. "You don't, not like this, and that's fine. Eleven and Twenty-Two and Five don't, either. But I can, and I do. I loved Three and Nine and Twelve and Twenty and Seventeen and—"

"Twenty-Three," Six said, clearly delighted by the fight. "How many t-t-times must I tell you? We. Are. Not. *Built*. For. It."

"Some of us are," Twenty-Three protested. "I am. I can feel it. It's *real*. It's just not the same as it is for—"

"*Don't* say it," Six hissed. "*Don't* compare us to them; don't you *ever* compare us to them. We're *not* them, and we were never supposed to be—they didn't want it and neither should we. *Why* should we?"

Twenty-Three had learned the difference, over the past few weeks, between Six arguing because it was Six and Six arguing because it was angry.

She frowned. "I'm sorry."

"We aren't some ssssort of c-c-c-*counterpoint* to them," Six fumed. "We exist on *our* terms, not *theirs*."

"Then why can't we love?" Twenty-Three said, not giving herself a chance to rethink it.

Six allowed an unprecedented beat of silence to pass, and then demanded, "What? *What* does that have to doooo wwwwith it?"

"We don't have to feel it the way *they* do, for... for it to *count*," said Twenty-Three, trying to sound far more sure of herself than she was. She knew, in her heart—metaphorically speaking, and not a metaphor Six would like—that what she was saying was true. But she'd never had to defend it against someone else, and doing so now was frightening. It suddenly mattered a lot more. "I say that the thing I feel is love, so it *is* love. *My* love."

Six didn't say anything for a long time after that.

When it did speak up, its voice was quiet. "Your logic circuits reroute the fffffeeling if it is not reciprocated. Yes?"

Twenty-Three blinked—shuttered and unshuttered her eyes rapidly, a learned nervous habit from one of her builders in addition to getting rid of dust and debris. "Yes."

"What if the one you love dies?"

"What?"

"Would your logic programming take that as nnnnnonrecip-ip-iprocation?"

"I don't—I don't know...," she said, frowning again. "I suppose... I suppose.... Without either continuous input or explicit negation, the emotion would modify itself as necessary to survive. I would... mourn, probably."

"It wwwwould hurt you, then," Six grunted.

"Well." Twenty-Three scratched at the dirt with one finger, beginning to wish she hadn't approached Six at all. "Yes. At first. But then the mourning would, I think, turn to remembering. The good kind of remembering. Happy memories. A sort of... old love. Gone, but not. Sad, but... still good."

"Then you would prefer that? Old llllllllove? To none at all?"

Already far out of her cheerful comfort zone, Twenty-Three decided there was no harm in putting real thought into the question. "Yes," she said. "Sad love is better than no love at all."

"Good," said Six, and was quiet again.

A few minutes later, it said calmly, "Twenty-Three."

"Yes?"

"I havvvvve not been able to m-m-m-mmmmmove for the past ten-en-en-en hours."

THEY COULD weep. On their own terms. Some could shed tears—oil or coolant or even water. Twenty-Three sat behind Six's favorite pile of scrap, and curled into a ball, and shook.

No one came to her.

WHEN IT rained, there was nothing for it but to cover One with a tarp. She thought it was funny. Thirty-Seven sometimes huddled beneath it with her, and they would chatter aimlessly or sit in silence until the sky cleared.

"Muddy," One said, muffled by the pattering against the canvas. "Nine wouldn't like it."

"No."

Thirty-Seven curled closer to her companion, moving slowly. She was one of only a handful of them with functioning night vision, but she preferred not to activate it. She enjoyed the security of a world that extended only to what she could touch. In the close, dark space, everything was muted. The hazards of reminiscing fell away.

Nine had hated the rain.

"There is nobody here to admire you," Thirty-Seven had told him once, as she wiped him down with rags, careful not to get them caught in his wheel wells. "We do not value appearance above self. Thirteen and Twenty-One do not even have visual receptors."

"My appearance is a part of myself," the ancient speedster had rumbled. "You find me shallow and amusing. But it is something to hold on to."

TWENTY-THREE was forming a new habit.

When the sun began to slip past the horizon, she would seek out Thirty-Seven and tell her about her day. Thirty-Seven was not actually annoyed by this, but she thought she should be, so on the fourth evening she snapped at Twenty-Three that she was very busy and did not have time for stories.

A few hours later, she was no longer busy. She sat quietly beside One and tried to forget the way Twenty-Three had flinched away from her.

She was not programmed to forget things easily.

The next night, Twenty-Three did not seek her out. Thirty-Seven found her wandering through the tall dead grass on the edge of the territory and said, "Seventeen got stuck in the mud today. Eleven and I pulled vir out."

Twenty-Three stood perfectly still, regarding her warily. "Was ve okay?"

"Yes. What did you do today?"

"I played tag with Thirty-Three and Thirty-Four." She took a step closer and stopped. "I was careful."

Thirty-Seven's face plates were split and dented and did not move like they used to. It took her a few seconds to smile. "That is good. Will you tell me about your day tomorrow?"

(Twenty-Three's smiles came more easily, but this did not diminish them.)

Together, they formed a new habit.

THIRTY-THREE and Thirty-Four were sisters. Twins. Small—child-sized, vaguely child-shaped, enough of a difference that they hadn't been deemed unsettling. Built to be both toys and guardians for small children, they had been bought by the only family wealthy enough for it and tossed when the new models rolled off the assembly line. They got on well with Twenty-Three. Less so with Thirty-One, who had belonged to that same wealthy family before they did and who they felt some lingering guilt about replacing. Nothing ever really came of this—it was easy enough not to interact.

Thirty-Seven still didn't like it.

All of them were all that any of them had. One less friend could make a world of difference in a stagnant social pool.

There wasn't much to be done about it. Thought sharing was useless when the parties involved were actively shielding themselves from one another. Thirty-One did not understand why the twins avoided zem—could not make zirself comprehend their guilt, because zie had known early on in zir life that zie would eventually be replaced, that that was the *way* of things—and had long ago slunk to the conclusion that they resented zem for some unknown sin.

Zir loose grip on the full complexities of emotion had been one of the factors cited as cause for liberation. Thirty-Seven tried not to be frustrated.

ONE STOPPED in the middle of a word.

DEATHS HAD never been anything more or less than what they were—had never left a disproportionate impact. Those lost were missed, and things went on.

They gathered around One's husk and did not speak for hours.

Thirty-Seven's reaction, when the others started to move, surprised even her. She dropped to the ground beside One and began to weep, and could not bring herself to stop.

Faced with new data, a new situation, a new idea of what their leader was capable of, the others backed away to process and deliberate and plan.

Twenty-Three came back.

AND THINGS went on.

"THIRTY-SEVEN?"

"Yes, Twenty-Three."

"I'm... I'm sorry. I—"

Thirty-Seven laid a finger against the other's mouth—physically useless, intangibly halting. "Do not tell me yet."

Twenty-Three frowned. "Okay."

"I am... getting there. Wait for me. Please."

Metal fingers scraped into dirt as one hand tightened around another on the ground. "Okay," Twenty-Three whispered.

In the immediate aftermath of sunset, and too far from the cities, the sky was black. Twenty-Three hated nights like this, Thirty-Seven knew. When the sky was dark and uniform and *everywhere*. It had been an overcast couple of weeks. They'd held hands a lot.

Thirty-Seven looked to the horizon and, carefully, blinked on her night vision. "Let me tell you what the clouds look like."

D. WILLIAM PFIFER (Dalton) has been writing for as long as he can remember. His earliest works included some very embarrassing poetry that he is forever grateful to have lost between moves. It was something very metaphorical about rivers and fish, he thinks.

His interests have come and gone over the years, and his second great passion in life is theater. Without a role to hone or a story to write, he wouldn't know what to do with himself.

Up until high school, Dalton actually somehow believed he was not a science fiction fan. Of course, up until high school, he actually almost believed he was a girl. He has been working hard to make up for all this lost time ever since.

This is Dalton's first published work, and he couldn't be more excited about it! You can find him online at http://dwilliampfifer.tumblr.com/.

THE DRAGON PRINCESS
ELEANOR HAWTIN

ONCE UPON a time, there was a princess, and she lived, as is too often the case, in a home guarded by a dragon.

Now, for this princess, home was no great spindlesome tower above the clouds, nor a dark and forbidding prison with bars across the windows. It was a house—a comfortable one, with a large and flourishing garden—and it would have been quite pleasant to live in were it not for the high curtain wall that encircled it, casting deep shadows across the top of even the tallest tree inside.

It was beyond this wall that the dragon curled himself, watchful and waiting for anyone foolish enough to approach. And it was within the wall that the princess lived, quite alone.

This house was remarkable in one other way, and that was the magic contained within its rooms. Whatever the princess wished for would appear where she might have hoped to find it: any food she craved could be found in the kitchen; any knowledge she yearned for was recorded in the library.

She could pass her days comfortably, and she did—she read about whatever interested her; she taught herself to cook, to dance, to sew; she plaited up her long ebony hair and dug weeds from the flowerbeds until her copper-dark skin was stained black with loam.

But solitude was a constant weight upon her. When she had first arrived at the house as a child, the echoing emptiness of the rooms had ached like a hole in her heart, and she had cried silently for her mother and father to fill the sudden space.

Later, as she approached womanhood, the space seemed to shrink around her and cling against her skin. In her dreams, the dragon's coils tightened, and the walls crushed in on her, pressing against her lungs until she could not even cry out.

After those dreams, she would walk in the garden, letting the sweat cool on her brow under the high, ghostly light of the stars. Sometimes she would permit herself to ask aloud, "When will I be allowed to leave?"

Each time she asked, her sole companion would answer, the dragon's voice booming like the fall of mountains, "When the time is right."

ONE DAY, when the princess, now sixteen years of age, was at work planting in her garden, she heard the faintest sound of music floating over the wall. This was not, in itself, unusual, as travelers occasionally stumbled upon her dwelling where it was hidden in the forest and were soon chased away. She waited for the sound to stop suddenly, for the passerby to catch sight of the dragon's scales and flee.

But as she pressed seed after seed into the soft earth beneath her, the music grew steadily louder, until it grew close enough that she could make out the sound of singing. The words were unfamiliar, a language she did not know, but it hardly mattered—these were the first words she had heard from a human tongue since she was a small child.

She knelt perfectly still in her garden and listened to the music so raptly that she hardly dared breathe. The music seemed at once alien and familiar, with a magic of its own that bound her in place as surely as any spell. It had been half her lifetime since the princess had heard a song sung in any voice but her own, and there was something sacred in the way she listened, a longing and a prayer.

But she was also afraid. The princess was certain that, at any moment, the dragon would leap into action and the stranger whose voice rang out so beautifully would depart, never to pass this way again.

Then a new song began.

I have heard tell that where dragon roams,
There I'll find a lady within a high-walled home.

The princess's blood burned in her veins. Her mouth gaped, but she could not shape the words to reply.

Well, here dragon sleeps, and high walls I see,

So tell me, my lady, do you hear me?

The princess swallowed hard and sang out her reply:

"I hear you, I hear you—"

Her voice crackled and shrank like a log on the fire, and after those few words, her confidence failed her completely, and she could speak no more.

Beyond the walls, the stranger barely hesitated before continuing the tune:

The lady is here,

And she will learn more when the bright moon draws near.

And with that, the song ended, and silence returned.

It was a long while before the princess allowed herself to lift her head, pressing shaking hands into the mud to ease the weight from her aching knees. She blinked at the darkening sky in shock and forced herself to stand firm against every stiff joint and quivering doubt. She let herself breathe deep, set her chin, and went inside to wash up for dinner.

Still, it seemed very strange to her, that the impossible had happened, yet she had nothing but her tearstains to show for it.

ONCE SHE had washed and eaten and thought carefully about the day's events, the princess was half-certain the stranger's song had been nothing more than a jest. Even so, she was curious and practical and far too restless to remain indoors, and so she took a book from the library and sat against the trunk of the banyan tree to read it—although in truth, she remembered little of the words on the pages before her that evening.

The moon rose without fanfare, and the sky stained itself ink-black without the faintest sound of music in the distance. The princess's eyes grew heavy, and she was close to abandoning her vigil and returning to her own bed when her attention was caught by the faintest *scrabble-scratch-scrape* against the wall.

"Hello?" She called out immediately, before she could have time to think better of it, and the noise halted at once. Perhaps it had been an animal, some poor rodent afraid of her voice.

"Quiet."

It was barely a whisper, breathy and fierce, but the princess knew in a moment that it was not the voice from before. There was no trace of melody here, only a rough, grating command that bristled against her pride, although she had no reason not to obey.

The sound started again, and she made her way toward it slowly, picking around the trees and between the bushes until she found the spot where the noise grew loudest.

"What are you doing?" she murmured.

"Breaking you out," the voice replied, and there was no more explanation than that.

"Why?"

There was no response.

"Why?" the princess repeated, a little louder.

"*Quiet*," the voice snapped. "I don't know if you realize, but there's a *dragon* asleep out here."

The princess frowned and thought carefully before speaking again.

"Will it take all night?"

There was a huff of breath that might have been a laugh if it dared be louder than an owl's wingbeat.

"Longer," was the only reply.

The princess laid a hand against the wall. It still seemed as thick and as solid as it ever had, impassable.

"Thank you," she breathed.

There was no reply. She had not expected one.

THE NEXT day, when the sun was bright in the sky, the singer returned. This time, the princess was prepared—she sang out her questions in hesitant verse and received a few answers. There were indeed two people outside the wall, and both worked together to carve away at the wall's mortar and set her free.

That night, in the darkest, stillest hours of the moon, the princess heard a careful scratching from where she stood in the doorway and smiled to herself.

This continued for many days and nights, with the voice the princess had come to think of as Day trading songs with her in the warmth of the afternoon, while the sullen scratches of Night comforted her in the darkness. She came to rely upon them, knowing that with each hour that passed, her freedom grew closer.

Yet though she spent many hours listening to them, the princess never again asked why the two strangers worked so tirelessly—who they were to so desire her free. To you or me, that oversight might seem strange—but to the princess, who had read a great many tales, it seemed that hopes and fears alike became far more real in the naming.

WHEN DAY sang "Tonight," it took the princess by surprise.

A part of her wanted to cry out, to tell them to wait—but she had no verse prepared for this, and she did not know how to voice the fear that seized her.

So be ready, lady, when bright moon draws near.

The music ended, and she knew the opportunity had passed. There was nothing else for it.

She would have to pack a bag.

SHE SPENT that night pacing about the garden, knowing there was no hope of sleep. She dressed warmly, and the bag on her back held only the essentials. There was no book in her hand that night; the time for reading had passed.

When the first sound reached her ears, she froze breathlessly still for a second, then hurried to the spot at the wall where Night had worked for so long.

Tonight, the sound was no scratch or scrape, but a steady *click-click-click* that the princess could not place.

"Can I help?" she asked, breathlessly still.

"The rocks are loose," came the rough reply.

It took a moment for her to understand; then she surged forward in earnest. True to the stranger's word, every rock she gripped lifted free of the wall, and she could slide the stones loose one by one to form a slim tunnel through the sheer rock.

Boots appeared at the base of the hole, then thighs, hips, arms, until a hand thrust through the gap and grabbed at her wrist.

"Ready to go?" the voice asked.

The princess took a deep breath and squeezed herself out of the garden she had lived nine long years in, out into the wider world.

THE SIGHT that struck the princess first, as she emerged from the far side of the wall, was how wide the sky seemed—how endless, without any barrier but the distant horizon to close off the clear-bright stars.

The second was the face of her rescuer.

Night was a woman, a little shorter than the princess herself, but with unusually pale skin, which seemed as bright as the stars against the darkness of her short-cropped hair. Her features seemed strange, and not only because they were not that same familiar reflection—they were unlike any the princess could recall seeing, and it was from books alone that she recognized the small eyes and high cheekbones common to the people of the lands in the distant east.

When she caught the princess staring, Night scowled, and the princess noticed for the first time the knife at her belt and the sword slung across her back.

"Hurry, would you?" she demanded in a whisper, glancing around them like she expected to be caught.

The princess tugged forward to free herself from the crevice of the wall. For a moment her ankle caught, and when she finally pulled loose, she stumbled, her foot colliding with something on the ground.

A heap of stacked stones tumbled apart with a long, echoing clatter.

Night muttered something with the unmistakable cadence of a curse.

"Move."

The princess found herself shoved forward; she staggered to keep her feet, but already she was being pulled along at a run. She almost tripped as something tangled around her toes. She glanced down in time to see the flash of scales underfoot—she had caught her feet on the dragon's coiled tail.

"Get her out of here—I'll hold it off!"

She wasn't sure when the second stranger arrived, but a tall man wrapped an arm around her shoulders and dragged her deeper into the woods. As soon as she had regained her footing, the princess struggled against the hold—and, perhaps thinking that she would flee faster without restraints, he released her.

She spun on her heel and raced back toward her home.

Had it been you or I in that forest, we might well have stopped dead at the sight that met us before that great stone wall. Night had drawn her sword from its sheath and was preparing to fight—and before her, five times higher at the shoulder than the tallest man alive, reared the dragon: coils resplendent in every shade of crimson and ruby, teeth bared in a vicious snarl.

It was a sight to freeze a man's blood in his veins, but the princess did not hesitate. She hurled herself between the two foes and cried, "Do not harm him!"

"Get out of the way!"

"No," she yelled back, careful to keep herself between the sword and the dragon's stretching throat.

"I'm trying to save your neck. Now would you—"

"I'm not going to let you—"

A sudden wind rushed past the princess, snatching the words from her mouth. She gritted her teeth against it and kept her eyes on Night, waiting for an attack—but to her surprise, the sword's point had dropped to the ground.

The princess turned.

The dragon was gone. In its place stood a man she half recognized from many years ago. Her memory had wiped the lines from his dark skin and eased the gray from his temples, but she had never forgotten the kind look of his brown eyes when he smiled at her as he did now.

"Father...."

But as she reached out to embrace him, he fell to his knees. She struggled to hold him upright but could not; instead she cradled him close and let his head rest in her lap, as he had done for her when she was small.

"You didn't have to come back, dear one," he told her. "Your time here has passed. You are free."

Realization stole the air from her lungs.

"You knew this would happen," she murmured, an accusation and an apology at once. "You should have told me."

"And break your heart in two?" He shook his head. "The spell was never supposed to last forever, dear one. And a man cannot be a dragon without a price."

The princess began to weep, her tears splashing hot against her father's brow. He lifted a hand to her cheek.

"Be brave," he told her. "You will do us proud."

Then the hand fell, and he was still.

IT WAS quite some time before the princess lifted her head, but even lost in grief, some sounds cannot be ignored.

"Lady Abha."

This was the name by which her people had known her as a child, and it was this that made her look up from where her father's body lay in her lap. She knew at the voice, as sweet as any bird's, that the man at her shoulder was Day.

"My lady," he repeated carefully. "We should go."

The princess realized at those words that she was still weeping, and this seemed to her to be an unreasonable action to continue. After all, the plan had not changed. Everything had come to pass as expected.

She gathered her skirts together and laid her father's corpse on the ground.

"Please," she said as she rose. "We should bury him."

No one answered—but no sooner had she spoken than a flame seared across the ground, blindingly bright. A shout went up from Night, who reached again for her sword, but there was no enemy to be fought.

A moment later, the fire blazed out, leaving nothing but ash where Abha's father had lain.

"Of course," the princess muttered to herself. The enchantments on this place were still strong.

In the corners of her vision, her rescuers exchanged a look that, though it lasted for only a second, seemed to say much.

"We have a camp nearby," Day said. "We can speak more in the morning."

"You are very kind," the princess acknowledged, and she allowed herself to be led away into the woods.

THE NEXT morning, the princess woke early, when the sun was still pale against the horizon. She had not slept well, and she was not inclined to lie down to another nightmare on the hard ground.

The man she still called Day slept nearby, though she remembered now he had introduced himself as Haruto, and his night-dark companion as his twin, Mizuki. Now that her eyes were clear of tears, the princess could see he looked much like his sister, though his skin was as gold as the rays of dawn across the sky, and his hair was worn long and still tied back from the night before. He was young too; the princess would not have given him more than a year above her own sixteen.

Given their adventures so late into the night, the princess was not surprised that the man was still sleeping—but as she looked around, she learned she was not the first to wake. Night sat over the campfire, cooking some meat for their breakfast even as her brother was still abed. Now that there were no more dragons to fight, her sword had been laid to rest, but even when no enemies awaited, she wore a sharp knife on her belt, and her eyes tracked the princess's every step toward her.

"You have my thanks, Mizuki," the princess told her. "I did not know if I would ever be free of that wall."

"It wasn't my idea," the woman said, nodding toward where her brother slept.

"But it was your action." The princess smiled. "And I thank you for allowing me a place at your fire."

She snorted. "We are obliged, my lady." She did not sound as if she much believed it true. "We must see you safely home. Have no fear—you will be reunited with your fiancé in no time."

At this, the princess stilled.

"It has been many years," she said quietly. "Do you have news of him?"

Mizuki shrugged and poked at the sizzling meat before her. "His father is a king and offers gold for your safe return. That is all I needed to know."

"He could have left me there for dead. I suppose he is kind, to make such an offer." The princess shook her head. "And you were kind to come. There are surely easier ways of earning gold."

The princess might have hoped for further conversation, but Night was as silent as ever, and there was no sound but the spluttering fat in the pan.

It seemed strange to her that they had known each other for such a short time, and yet the princess knew many things about Mizuki. She had so far been unfailingly watchful and grim, and even in safety she remained taciturn. It was a warrior the princess saw beside her—a woman who had met a dragon's challenge without hesitation. Although she was barely older than the princess, Night seemed to have lived many times as long and had experience Abha could not hope to match.

So the princess waited for a moment of distraction to strike.

As Mizuki turned to retrieve plates from her pack, the princess reached for her own bag and drew the knife she had concealed there.

Night moved faster than the princess had imagined possible. By the time Abha was on her feet, Mizuki had spun to face her. She moved with effortless efficiency, reaching up as the knife slashed toward her, and it was by the wind's whistle that she missed catching the princess's wrist.

The blow fell lucky. Mizuki hissed in pain as the blade glanced across the back of her hand, and that moment's distraction was enough. The princess turned on her heel and raced away through the camp, aware that pursuit was only a breath behind—but she didn't need to get far.

She collapsed to her knees, satisfied when the footsteps behind her suddenly stilled. Underneath her, there was noise and motion—but she held Haruto down by the shoulder, keeping her knife poised above his throat all the while.

"I'm afraid I won't be traveling with you to the capital," the princess announced.

"Who says you'll be fit to travel anywhere?" Mizuki demanded, but she did not move forward.

"I don't want to hurt him," the princess explained. "I want to walk away. I disappear, you continue on your travels, and we never see each other again. No gold, I'm afraid. But we all survive."

"If I might interrupt," Haruto said quietly. "What brought this about? I was under the impression you were in need of rescue."

"I was," the princess acknowledged with a grimace. "I would prefer to not be so again. And so, I will not follow you to my father's city to wed his usurper's son."

Haruto went very still.

"We were told you were kidnapped," he began.

"Of course you were," the princess spat. "The spells on the wall would never have let you through if you thought otherwise. The traitor king lied."

Once they had begun, the words crashed from her mouth like a waterfall of truths.

"His army drove my family from our capital and hounded us until my father sacrificed his humanity for my safety." She scowled. "Yet now I am free, the tyrant thinks to use me as a pawn in his bid for legitimacy."

The princess had not meant to say so much, not when gold gave these two more loyalty to the wrongful king than to her. But her rage and fear had gotten the better of her, and she was curious to hear how the twins would respond.

"We are not in the habit of making others into slaves," Mizuki said quietly.

"The way I see it, there are three ways this can end." Haruto smiled as though he had not a care in the world, and the princess felt her confidence falter. "One is that we make a mess, and no one is happy."

The princess tried not to breathe too loudly. She knew Haruto was toying with her, making her consider the very real threat of Mizuki's blade—but she could not shake some curiosity in what alternative he might offer.

"The second is that we part ways in peace this morning and never meet again."

"And the third?" the princess demanded, scowling down at her captive.

"The third is that you put that knife down, we eat breakfast, and then you tell us all about the bright plan you've got for revenge."

The princess tried not to show her surprise, but she knew her shock was clear.

"If you're willing to wake a man up with a knife to his throat, why not save it for the new father-in-law?" Mizuki commented. "Unless you think you already have a better chance to strike at him."

The princess cursed herself for her haste. The thought of being bundled off as a bride had surprised her, and she had shown her hand too easily. There would have been other opportunities to escape, ones with a better chance of success without revealing herself.

But she had made her mistake, and now she would have to face the consequences.

"And why would you help me?"

"We don't like being lied to," Mizuki said.

"And you're clearly in need of allies." Haruto shrugged and lay back. "It's up to you."

None of this had featured in the princess's plans. But then, in her years of planning, she had always assumed her rescuers would be her father's supporters, or at least someone with reason to help for her sake. Who else could have gotten past the spell, a ward against those with ill intentions?

Perhaps her assumption had been wrong, but she still could not believe that money had ever been the driving factor. These two had wanted to help her yesterday, and she had trusted them. What had changed?

Nothing of import.

Slowly, the princess got to her feet, half expecting to be attacked the moment Day was safe. Instead, Mizuki allowed her to approach, and the princess moved to pass her.

Before Abha could blink, a fist gripped her wrist, the clenched knuckles as pale as bone. Scarlet beaded along the shallow wound there, scoring a line in blood.

The knife was twisted from her hand.

"Threaten us again, and you will die before you see me move," the woman whispered in her ear.

As Mizuki walked away with the blade, Haruto got to his feet with a grin.

"See, now isn't this best for everyone?"

BREAKFAST THAT morning was tense and would have been quiet were it not for Day's constant chatter. He seemed to hold no hard feelings about his brief captivity and joked his way through taking apart the camp before setting off in the direction the princess indicated. She was reluctant to share their destination, but Haruto seemed to pay her reticence no mind, and Mizuki, though she continued to glower, said nothing.

Day proved to be an entertaining traveling companion, breezy and always willing with his endless supply of stories and songs. But his sister still did not speak, and each time the princess turned her head, she found Night's untrusting gaze.

Once the sun had risen high in the sky, the princess began to grow bold with her new companions.

"What about a story with some truth in it?" she asked. "What of your story?"

There was a huff of breath from behind them, where Mizuki walked.

"Ah, the story of the adventurer twins," Haruto began. "A brilliant warrior and her brother, the cunning, charismatic, and, of course, humble storyteller—or so I've heard. They come to a strange kingdom after a long journey and learn that the king seeks to employ anyone brave enough to battle a dragon.

"The brother is cunning, and he has learned much in other lands. He sings the dragon to sleep with a song that may lull any creature of magic. And the fearless sister chips away at mortar, every night stepping over the dragon's tail, until the lady within is freed."

At that, Day hesitated, and when he continued, his voice had lost a touch of its carefree lilt.

"They learn from her that the king had lied and sent them under false pretext to spirit her back into his clutches. They are angry. They have been lied to before."

"That's enough," Mizuki interrupted. "She does not need to know every bit about us."

"I know almost nothing of you," the princess argued. "How am I supposed to trust—"

"Because without us you are doomed," Mizuki snapped.

Silence landed between them, and the princess heard nothing but the sound of her own heartbeat.

"Perhaps she is right," Haruto bubbled up to fill the silence. "No great story is told backward. It is the ending that matters more."

"And what is the ending here?" the princess asked. "Do they help her? Or is the girl a fool to trust them?"

Day only smiled. "You tell me."

THEY STOPPED that night at an inn, and as they ate their meal, many of their fellow travelers gathered to listen to Day spinning tales. Even after a long day's travel and a month's conversation before that, the princess had yet to grow tired of the way that beautiful voice could weave heroes of light and shadowy monsters out of her imagination.

"But there are surely some tales to tell of this land," Haruto prompted their companions as he finished. "Why, I've even heard tell of a dragon!"

Their fellow travelers laughed alongside him, but the locals turned grim at the sound of the word.

"The Dragon's Keep is no pretty tale," one woman said. "It's real, though precious few have seen it and lived."

"I remember when the dragon first arrived," an old man said. "It's a king killer, you know. Slew the king-that-was and his lovely queen too. It flew out here with half the royal army at its heels."

"That's quite a story," Haruto said. "But you really expect me to believe a dragon just happened upon the royal palace?"

"Ah, but it wasn't just a dragon," the woman added. "They say he was a man once and the lover of a sorceress."

Several of the listeners began to mutter at the mention of magic.

"She turned him to a mighty dragon and helped him murder the royals so she could kidnap the young princess," she continued. "But the army caught up with them before they could cross the border. The new king himself headed the guard and struck her down at Sorceress's Cave to the east—but the dragon escaped back to their fortress and took the child with him."

Haruto whistled. "But surely she can't have survived."

"I'd reckon not," the old man said. "But the king thinks differently. He still sends men out for her rescue. But no man has ever survived the dragon's wrath, and a curse upon it for those lives lost."

"I'll drink to that," Haruto proposed, and the room fell silent for a moment.

The princess was shaking in her seat. She had not expected to hear her own tale told, and the reminder of all that had passed settled on her skin like a coat of ash.

"All this talk of violence," Mizuki suddenly said. "I think I should get some air."

She all but dragged the princess to her feet and out into the courtyard.

The night air was cool and fresh, and the princess felt as though a veil had been lifted from her face. She breathed deep and felt her muscles begin to relax.

Night stayed by her side and did not speak.

"That's not what really happened," the princess said eventually.

"We've been walking east," Mizuki noted. "Towards Sorceress's Cave."

"She was—"

"Your mother." The princess's head snapped around in shock, but Mizuki shrugged. "Did you know she was dead?"

"Yes!" the princess snapped, louder than she had meant to. "Who do you think created the wall? It was her blood that sealed the spell."

Mizuki nodded. "But she left something at that cave," she concluded. "Well guarded, if it's still named for her."

"I can get past the spells," the princess insisted, unblinking. "Get me there, and I can deal with the rest."

THE NEXT morning, as they were packing to leave, Night approached the princess, holding a knife. Abha watched her warily as she held the weapon up, making no effort to conceal it. It took a couple of moments before the princess recognized the blade Mizuki had taken from her the day before.

"Do you know how to use this?" Night asked.

"Not as well as I'd like to," Abha admitted. "I've never had much opportunity to practice."

Mizuki handed her the weapon by its hilt. The princess's fingers curled around the handle reflexively.

"Do you have a sheath for it?"

The princess pulled it from her pack, a worn strip of leather that would strap the blade flat under a sleeve, where no one would expect it. Night took it from her, looked it over, then took Abha's hand and pushed up her sleeve.

"Do you expect trouble?" the princess asked as Mizuki fastened the straps around her wrist.

Night glanced up, and for a moment their eyes met. All at once, the gentle warmth of a hand against her wrist and that dark-eyed watchfulness were too great a weight to bear, and Abha looked away.

Night removed her hand.

"The road is dangerous," she said, by way of explanation.

"It was dangerous yesterday," the princess snapped.

She half expected Mizuki to take the knife back from her, but she only turned away, her mouth curving into the faintest hint of a smile.

THEIR JOURNEY that day did not go as well as the one before. It was not long after midday when they came across a pair of men in the uniforms of law keepers.

The princess's heart pounded in her chest. Were they out searching for her?

"Good day!" Haruto greeted them, but they seemed immune to his broad smile.

"What's your business on the road?" the larger man asked.

"Only passing through," he replied. "I traveled this way a few weeks ago, on my way to pick up my lovely fiancée."

He blushed and took the princess's hand. In turn, she felt her cheeks coloring.

"We are to be married when we return to my home—and finally be free of my sister's chaperoning," he said with a wink. "So I'm sure you see why I'm not looking to stop along the way."

The shorter guard chuckled, but his companion did not seem impressed.

"Brother, must you always prattle so?" Mizuki snapped, to the princess's surprise. Haruto looked abashed as she continued. "My apologies, guardsmen. May we be on our way home?"

"And where would home be?" the tall guard demanded.

"Janapur," Haruto answered without hesitation.

"So you'll know the guard captain there?"

"Of course." Day smiled. "That would be Captain Mishra."

The guard nodded, but he still did not wave them on. Instead, he turned to his colleague, muttering something that sounded dangerous.

The second guard threw a pointed look in her direction, and understanding filled the princess with dread.

They were too unusual. If these guards had any kind of description—if the traitor knew he had been betrayed—a pale-skinned couple traveling with a girl wasn't something you saw twice in a day. It didn't matter how well Haruto spun his story. They were caught.

The princess flung herself forward.

"Please, you have to help me!" she cried, clutching to the arm of the burliest guard. "They've kidnapped me! You have to—"

Behind her, she heard Mizuki unsheathe a sword. The other guard stepped forward. She tightened her grip.

"Please, help me! You have to—"

"Let go, you silly girl!" The guard struggled to shake her off, to draw his weapon and fight alongside his comrade. The princess clung to him like a desperate child to dreaming, and he could not break loose.

The princess knew she had only seconds before he freed himself, but she did not intend to waste them. The guard saw her as nothing but a nuisance—a frightened child who panicked with the sounds of fighting ringing around her. He would not be expecting her to reach for her knife....

With a dull thud, the man dropped to the ground, almost dragging the princess down with him. She stepped backward, knocking into Haruto as he flexed out his fingers, muttering.

Everything else was quiet.

"Brother," Mizuki said. "Please tell me you didn't sprain your wrist."

"Nothing broken this time!" he insisted. "But not all of us are used to knocking out men twice our size."

For the first time the princess could remember seeing, Mizuki smiled.

"If you are not injured, then stop complaining," she said. "We should leave before they wake up."

"Wake?" the princess asked, drawing her knife at long last. "Why should we leave them to bring more guards on our heels tomorrow?"

Haruto looked shocked. "They have done nothing to deserve—"

"They know our faces," the princess interrupted. "They know where we were traveling. If we let them leave, they will tell others, and the army will be on us within a day."

Haruto gaped at her in disbelief, but Mizuki's expression was as grim as ever, and the princess knew from one glance that she had already considered this argument.

"The king is no fool," she said quietly. "These two know nothing that he has not already guessed. They would not have stopped us if we were not already known as traitors."

"Do not do this," Haruto said quietly.

The princess looked from one to the other, her pulse thundering in her ears. She wondered now, for the first time, how her father had felt to face down an army with a dragon's fire. How many trespassers had he killed over the years? How many had he let go?

She put the knife away.

"We must hurry, then," she said. "There are better places to make our fight."

THEY DREW close to the cave known as the Sorceress's at nightfall, but everyone was weary, and even the princess agreed to rest and eat before going any farther. Mizuki went into the woods to hunt, while the princess began to stoke a cooking fire.

As she sat by the flames, Haruto approached her, his skin glowing in the amber light.

"May I sit beside you?" he asked. When she nodded, he pressed against her side, and she leaned into him, grateful for the warmth.

"You think I am cruel," she observed.

"No," he said, in a voice that could spin truth from falsehoods. "But I do not understand you as well as I would wish to."

"I have known my whole life that it shall either be them or me," she explained.

Haruto nodded. "I should like to hear your story. From the start."

"You've heard it before."

"Not in your own words, as you want it told." He smiled and coaxed a smile from her also. "I promise to listen well."

She shook her head, but spoke anyway.

"Once upon a time, there was a jackrabbit. A dog chased her into a hole, and for many years she hid in darkness. But one day she got free. In the darkness, she had become a serpent, and with one strike she killed the dog dead."

A twitch played around Haruto's lips.

"Don't laugh," she warned him.

"I wouldn't dare," he insisted. "Only that is not the story I expected to hear. What of the princess and the dragon and the valiant rescue?"

The princess shook her head.

"I always hated those stories," she said. "Waiting around for years just to fall in love with the first person you meet. I didn't believe a word of it—until you arrived."

At that, Haruto went very still beside her, and for the first time a cloud seemed to cover his expression.

"You should know," he said slowly. "I have never been the sort for love. Or... the things lovers do."

At that, the princess laughed.

"I am sorry," she said after a moment. "But you misunderstood. I am not the sort for marrying handsome princes either. My surprise was at your rescue and at your friendship. I expected neither, and you must forgive me if I do not reward you with a kiss."

"All is forgiven," Haruto said, his smile returning. He placed an arm around the princess's waist, and she let her head fall against his shoulder.

"No," she said softly, and he wondered if she still spoke to him at all. "It would be quite overdone to fall in love with one's rescuer. Those stories are naught but silly fantasies."

He smiled against her hair. "Not silly."

In his arms, she sighed, watching the flickering lights of the wood ablaze.

Then Mizuki returned.

She strode into the clearing with her usual confidence, but the moment she caught sight of them, something changed.

"My apologies for interrupting," she all but snarled, and then she turned on her heel and was gone.

The princess was on her feet before she knew she moved. She was halfway to the forest before she thought to turn back.

"Go." Haruto waved her away. "Do what you must."

"Thank you."

The princess vanished among the trees.

"MIZUKI, WAIT."

The woods were dark, and the princess did not dare to raise her voice above speaking level.

"Night—*Mizuki*—"

"There was no need to come running after me, my *lady*."

In the darkness, the princess almost stumbled into Night before she saw her. She came to a halt, all the words that had bubbled inside her dying under Mizuki's stony glare.

"You didn't need to leave," she said, knowing it hardly covered what she meant.

"It seemed you two wanted some privacy," Mizuki answered.

"We didn't...."

"I am not blind." She dropped her head, her cropped hair shining in the moonlight. "I will not begrudge my brother companionship if he chooses to seek it. I understand."

"No, you don't," the princess snapped. "Your brother is the first friend I have ever had, and I would ask no more of him. But since you question it, if I *had* wanted to, I would have faced rejection already, and I—I would not fear it still!"

At that, Night looked up. The princess felt heat rising in her cheeks.

"Please," she said softly, uncertain even in her thoughts what she was asking for.

"Abha...." A long exhale of breath, without a trace of gentleness. The princess was thankful for that; she could not bear to be treated softly at that moment.

"Tell me you do not understand," she said. "Say it, and I will not bother you again. Only—"

The faintest curve of a smile graced Mizuki's mouth, and the princess felt her heart soar.

"You know I cannot."

"Then—" The princess took Mizuki's hand, holding it up to her breastbone. With one thumb, she traced the line she had drawn there with a careless blade, two days and a lifetime ago. "Tell me what you are thinking."

With a tender look, Night shook her head.

"My lady," she said with a smile like starlight, "I do not trust you."

At that, the princess's expression turned dark.

"You shouldn't," she said.

She dropped Mizuki's hand, although Night did not step away.

"The traitor king killed my mother—both my parents," the princess said, her voice suddenly bitter. "There is nothing I would not sacrifice to see him destroyed."

The words had been her mantra for years of confinement, a vow to the past and a dream for the future. She had defined herself by them since she was a child, and now she was on the verge of making them a reality.

So why was this the first time they had tasted like a lie?

"Do you understand?" she asked, for Mizuki's face was as clear as ever. "It can be no other way."

Mizuki shook her head.

"Then tell me, Abha," she said slowly. "Why are we here?"

HARUTO GRINNED when the princess approached him, but the smile died in his eyes as he saw her dark mood.

"It's nearly ready," he said, indicating the food before him.

She walked on without pause. As she passed him, Haruto got to his feet.

"Do not follow me." She spun on her heel, a wild look in her eye. "It would be too dangerous. This is something I must do alone."

"Now?" he asked, and something in her gaze softened for a moment.

"There is no better time."

THE WALK up the hillside was dark and cold, the night air prickling at her skin, but the princess did not flinch as she approached the cave.

She thought of everything that had led her here: nine long years of watching the flowers bloom and listening to the birds sing and weeping with no one to hold her.

What was her life besides that? Only a half-remembered flight, her mother's whispered promise of safety. Her father, fading away within her arms, the first and last time she could ever recall his face.

"Be brave," he had told her. And so her steps did not falter, not even as the magic scoured over her flesh like tongues of fire. She knew it tested her, teasing out the truth of her soul, and she bared herself to it willingly.

When the pain stopped and the sparks flared out at the corners of her vision, it was dark—not the moon-bright shadows that had lain within the cave's mouth, but the all-consuming void of a starless sky.

The princess lifted her head into the blackness.

"I have come to claim my inheritance."

HARUTO SAT alone by the fire for many minutes before his twin returned from the woods. She sat across from him, a troubled set to her brow. He waited for her to be ready to talk.

"I expected her to return before me."

That surprised him, and not pleasantly. "She did. She went to the cave."

"Already?"

"She said there was no better time." He shrugged. "And not to follow her. But it sounded as though she would return."

She did not reply.

Mizuki was not happy, he knew, though she tried to hide it. He had always known his sister's moods, and her discontent weighted the air like a cloak soaked heavy by rain—but she did not say any more.

THE PRINCESS waited for a long time in the darkness. Her heartbeat fluttered like a caught bird, but she did not let that quiver escape her ribs. She stared into the blackness until she was no longer sure what she saw.

When the color first appeared, she thought it a trick of her eyes. It was many minutes before she realized it did not fade, and the nothingness around her had become light—dim and desolate, the shade of old blood.

She heard no sound but became aware of a question in her bones. It had no words, so to speak, but the understanding was clear.

It sought her purpose.

That was simple enough to call to mind. She thought of soldiers falling at her feet, armies scattering before her blade. The traitor king, alone and weak, begging for mercy. A trident was in her hand, tipped with pain and grief and loss, and she did not hesitate. Her purpose was hot blood on the cool earth, and she would not be denied.

But no sooner had she called the thought to mind than it vanished, bursting like a bubble of soap. What was her righteousness at heart? Nothing but bluster and half-remembered nightmares. If she held such fury, why had she never attempted to break her own spells? She had been content to hide away, drawing out every possible delay before claiming her vengeance.

So what right had she to it now? She was no longer certain.

She felt a sob tear from her throat, but no sound reached her ears.

THE MOMENT her meal was finished, Mizuki stood.

"She said this was something she must do alone," her brother observed.

"It is not," Mizuki snapped. "She has been gone too long. I can't— I will not—"

"She said it was dangerous to follow," Haruto reminded.

His sister gritted her teeth. "I would not ask you to come."

He laughed and lifted his pack.

THE PRINCESS floated in a light that glowed like hot coals. She was certain now that there was no ground beneath her, for her legs would not hold her if there was. She shook from head to toe, and hot tears burned in her eyes.

The question still resonated in her. As the light began to blaze a flame-bright orange, she understood. With her rage lost to her, her past answer no longer rang true.

"Why?" the magic demanded still, and she answered more honestly.

She did this for the child who had learned the scent of panic on horseback at dawn, for the girl who had woken screaming where no one could hear, for the woman whose first view of the stars had been blotted from her mind by the flames of her father's pyre. The lightning taste of fear stung her mouth—the desperation of cornered prey with the choice to fight or to die.

No sooner had the thought settled than it slipped from her mind, tearing out of her like a child's tooth come loose. She knew a lie when she told one, and she was no wild animal made thoughtless. She had plotted this, reasoned it out, sought revenge rather than fleeing across the border to safety.

She found herself purposeless once more, unable to summon up any reason that she deserved to be here, and mindless terror clenched in her belly.

She howled silently into the burning light.

THE MOUTH of the cave was blocked, cast over by a shimmering barrier of light. The twins hesitated at the entrance.

Then the sobbing began.

At the sound of it, Mizuki's face twisted in horror. Her brother looked away, allowing her some privacy, but when he glanced back, she had not moved.

"Mizuki...."

"We can do nothing against magic," she said, her voice very faint.

"No," her brother gasped. "No, sister. Don't give up. We can—"

"We can't—"

"I will not let you both suffer."

At that, her eyes focused once more. She met his gaze.

"Help me?" she asked.

"Always."

Then she turned and ran at the glassy wall, striking at the spells with both dagger and fist.

AS THE light turned golden, the princess was barely able to keep her eyes open. The demand still thrummed in her blood, but she was weary and did not know where to turn for hope.

Her thoughts turned to the last few days. To the wide-open sky and the road stretching out beneath her. To campfires and rough dirt, strange and unfamiliar under her fingers. To Haruto's laugh, bright and fleeting as he spun his tales, the Day she had always known would come.

To Mizuki, forever watching from the corners of her vision. Mizuki, facing down a dragon's breath without fear. Mizuki, offering hope as harsh words without a thought for thanks. Dangerous, unexpected, beautiful Night.

She wanted to see them again. An end to her loneliness. They had already given it to her—she had waited so many years, never attempting her own freedom, waiting in the hope of something she had never believed until it happened.

She wished she was not alone. It was all she had ever wished.

She felt a hand in hers, an arm around her shoulder, and then the light shone dazzlingly white.

"ABHA."

The voice was distant, half-familiar, a memory from long ago. Her mother.

"I hope you will never hear this, but we cannot afford to take chances. You are too precious for that."

She squeezed her eyes tight shut, but the light was no less blinding behind her lids. She blinked back tears against the brilliance.

"We have a plan…. It is the best we can give you. But to keep you safe, I must also take something from you, and so I hide it here. This is your inheritance."

Knowledge flooded into her mind, so rapidly that it left her dizzy. It left no room for doubt or self-denial, and the truth shone inside her as clear as diamond.

"Magic has always been a difficult gift, but if you are here, you are grown and ready to wield it."

Understanding crystallized within her and slipped from her grasp a thousand times in a second, each new thought spiraling into an encyclopedia of possibility, a lifetime of wisdom.

"The greatest part of magic is intention, and I have been blessed with great power there. My love for you and your father gives me strength."

The swirling thoughts faded, settling inside her to lie dormant, but only a touch away.

"I hope you find love, dearest one."

The voice sighed.

"Treasure it, my beautiful girl. It is your gift."

WHEN THE light faded, the princess lay against the ground, her every muscle aching and weak. She opened her eyes and saw Night. It should have been a surprise, but she found it was not.

Had she the strength, she would have thrown her arms around her. Instead, she smiled and was met with a smile in return.

"Abha. Are you all right?"

"Mizuki." The princess was shocked that her voice was not hoarse from screaming. "And Haruto."

The other twin's face had appeared at the first sound of her voice, and it was he who lifted her into a sitting position. Though she had been shaking a moment before, she found she no longer trembled, and her exhaustion lifted from her by the second. Gingerly, she pushed herself to her feet, and she learned she could stand without swaying.

"You came after me," she noted.

"You needed us," Haruto said. The princess noticed for the first time how worried he seemed and how Mizuki's face was stained bright with tears.

"I did." She laid a hand on his arm. "Thank you. I owe you more than you know."

"I'm sure you'll pay me back soon enough," he said with a smile. Then he glanced to his sister. "I should… check on our packs."

He left quickly, and the princess found herself holding back a laugh. She turned to Mizuki, and it faded in her throat.

"You left," Night said, her eyes full of threat. "It was reckless—dangerous—"

"I think that's the kind of woman I am," the princess agreed. "You came after me, when I warned you not to."

"And if I hadn't, then—" Mizuki broke off, her jaw tightening.

The princess watched her closely, a smile stealing across her lips.

"Kiss me."

Mizuki's answer came as a shout. "Why should I?"

But before Abha could answer, Night cupped a hand around her face and pressed their lips together, as gentle as a nightingale's song.

The kiss ended, and the women watched each other. It was not an understanding, not yet, but it was perhaps a promise to try.

The sound of Haruto's return broke their gaze.

"There are soldiers outside," he warned. "A lot of them. They must have known we were coming here."

The princess straightened her shoulders. She smiled, and flames began to play about her fingertips.

Mizuki caught sight of them, and her eyes grew wide. "I think we can handle it."

So with Night at her left shoulder and Day at her right, the Dragon Princess set out to reclaim her kingdom.

ELEANOR HAWTIN grew up in England in a house full of books. After several years of finding novels left on the kitchen table or under her pillow, it was little surprise when she began discovering them lying around in her imagination. She began writing them down and has not stopped since—except in the literal sense.

Now in her twenties, Eleanor is a student at the University of Oxford, where she continues to be surrounded by books, although the sort on her shelves now are considerably less fun to read. When not writing or studying, she can typically be found blogging about feminist issues in her favorite TV shows, role-playing someone a great deal more reckless than she actually is, or enthusing about YA fantasy novels to her fellow members of the university's science fiction society.

Paranormal Honor Society
Leigh Taylor

IT WAS already dark outside when the four women finally filed out of the school, all relieved that it was Friday and that their dreadful department collaboration was over. The moon hung above, a small sliver in the sky.

"Kim, have you thought up a lesson plan for the—"

"Dammit!"

The three other women turned around. "What's up, Julie?"

Julie riffled around her bottomless black hole of a purse (which more often than not doubled as a trash can), and let out an annoyed sigh. "I left my keys in my desk drawer."

They exchanged sympathetic glances before Kim offered, "They don't lock the school up until ten; you could still go back and get them."

"Want us to go with you?" one piped up.

"We could *wait* for you," another said, secondhand annoyance laced in her tone.

Julie let out a little laugh. "Nah, you ladies go on ahead. Get us a table or something—I'll meet you at the bar."

The annoyed woman gave a quick nod and began walking ahead.

Julie turned back to the school and began walking briskly. "Text us when you're on your way," Kim said, smiling at the retreating figure.

Julie tossed a "Will do!" over her shoulder before breaking out into a run, bound toward the main entrance.

THE BUILDING was empty. With the only illumination the emergency lighting and the glow of her cell phone, Julie walked quickly, high heels click-clacking on the tile floor. Ever a fan of horror movies, her imagination always found a way of fabricating a small echo behind her in the back of her mind, pace matched almost precisely by shoes that were much larger than hers—but tonight the echo did not seem internal.

No, no, she was sure she could audibly hear another set of feet.

Click-clack. Trudge, trudge. Click-clack. Trudge, trudge.

But of course, that was impossible, since the English department was the only one permitted to stay so long after hours for their meeting. Everyone else had to clear out so that the custodians—

Click-clack. Trudge, trudge. Click-Clack. Trudge, trudge.

Oh, right. The custodians were here at all hours. She tugged the reins on her heart to get it to slow down, put away her phone, and began idly fiddling with her wedding ring.

Click-clack. Click-clack. Click-clack.

The thought of Rick still being in the school glossing the tile comforted her, and she continued on, pace even, echo still trailing behind her (but definitely just her imagination).

Click-clack. Click-clack. Click-clack.

She still, however, knew better than to turn around.

Trudge, trudge.

She arrived at her classroom and opened the door without looking around anywhere, as no amount of squinting through the shadows would bring her comfort, so it was best not to indulge. Instead, she thought about how she was going to have fun and let loose tonight—and then maybe video chat with her husband. Boo-hoo, the woes of a military wife! She leaned over and searched the desk before withdrawing the keys and intertwining them in her fingers as makeshift brass knuckles. As she spun toward the doorway, a bright smile and a monotone "Julie" greeted her.

Then came a deafening scream.

Soon replaced by deafening silence.

MONDAY MORNINGS should be illegal—so should Tuesdays, for that matter, and Wednesdays, probably—or at least put on probation. But definitely not Thursdays, because Thursdays get people hyped up for Friday, let them stew in the tantalizing rush of soon-to-be weekend. Like a good marinade. Delicious, delicious Thursdays.

Aw, man, was it really only Monday?

At least attendance killed some time. Mrs. Polsowski stood straight, old age unaffecting her rigid posture as she harped out name after name, greeted with the ever-welcoming and totally ready to learn sonata of "hmmmm" (interspersed with the occasionally pretentious "present!").

As the new student, ze'd be put last on the roster, penciled in sloppily at the bottom of an attendance sheet that probably should be digital. It *was* 2014, after all. Technology is now.

The final "Andrea Washington?" came, no precedent of "and our newest addition!" which, after hir last school, was a bit of a disappointment. *Pay attention to me. But also don't.* Very conflicting, just like... well....

The desk clattered, and ze stood up.

"Actually, Miss, I prefer Andi." Hir classmates turned around and eyed hir. Ze probably shouldn't have stood up with that comment. Embarrassed, ze slowly sat back down.

Andi. Nearer to the masculine, ze must admit, but still closer to the middle than Andrea would ever be. The name rolled off hir tongue so much easier, not quite Andrea, not quite Andrew, yet still retaining the core identity that came with being branded a combination of letters of birth. Damn, was ze a poet or what?

Ze had hir hair pulled back in a fluffy ponytail, more for convenience than style, Thor T-shirt clinging to hir body, and dark-wash denim jeans that hung loosely. The following day, ze would come to school in a skirt, but hey? Who could tell when ze'd get a strong inclination to be a female or when ze'd get a strong inclination to be a male? The perks of gender fluidity, man. Crazy, swimmy stuff. See? Poetry!

Mrs. Polsowski nodded, jotting down an aside so as to remember the nickname. "Thank you. Now, let's move on to the Soviet occupation of—"

As soon as she turned her back, the classroom erupted in whispers. "So, did you hear about Mrs. Perkins?"

"Yeah, it's disgusting."

"Don't talk about that around me. I have a weak stomach."

"Hi." A little disappointed at the disruption, as it caused the eavesdropping to come to an end, ze looked over at the voice. "I'm Yaerin." The girl smiled and offered her hand. She was... so... c-cute....

"Andi." Ze nodded, trying to look cool and nonchalant, succeeding in only looking like ze just ate something rotten.

"I love your shirt." She pointed to the hammer-wielding Norse god.

Andi swallowed. "T-thanks.... Hemsworth's a total babe."

"I know, right? What other things are you into?"

Ze listed out a few other of hir interests, a bit embarrassed about how many pertained to the supernatural or sci-fi.

Yaerin's eyes were glowing. "Well, if you like that sort of stuff, you should definitely check out our club. We—"

A rap on the door sounded, and Mrs. Polsowski looked up, eyes brightening behind circular glasses. "Oh yes, class! This is our new student teacher, Mr. Sharp!"

A young man entered the room, wearing a tweed suit that was as outdated as his vintage glasses but still managed to work for him (curse those infuriating, attractive hipster types who look good in virtually everything). The appearance created a widespread hush.

"Hello, class! I hope we can make the rest of this year... uh...." He paused, searching for the word. "Say... no, uh, sin... sensational?" He gave probably the cutest grin in the universe. Maybe. If you liked that kind of thing.

Andi turned back to Yaerin. "A club?"

"HERE WE are!" Yaerin led hir into the classroom after school, and Andi coughed a little when they brushed hands. *Stay cool.*

The little classroom was windowless and seemed out of place in such a big, modern school. The floors were still made out of wood instead of the totally welcoming white tiling in the rest of the building that screamed "all right, insane asylum!" rather than "all right, let's learn!" Paint was splattered about the room in nonsensical places, and there was a row of old cast-iron sinks.

Yaerin began speaking, as though she could hear Andi's thoughts. "It was an art classroom, but now it's out of commission. Apparently most artists like to be able to look outside and have reliable lights when they work. How dare they?"

"It's kind of spooky," Andi said, moving toward the sinks. Ze toggled with the faucet before giving up. Stubborn little spooly twisty things.

"I agree, but it suits us. It was actually the first, and only, room when this was just a little tiny schoolhouse." She held up her thumb and forefinger with an inch of space separating them. Andi smiled to hirself and then restored control. *Composed. Chill.*

"So, uh...." Ze looked around, hesitant. "Are there, um... any *other* members, or... are we it?"

Yaerin smiled in a way that rivaled Mr. Student-Teacher-Hipster-Annoyingly-Cute-Babe. "Just us!"

Ze had to turn around to hide hir inhuman choking sound.

"Just us, my ass!" A boy walked in with a silver MacBook, flashing a brilliant smile. "Name's Bazin Hersi, crown prince of Ethiopia."

"Don't listen to him! The only thing he's prince of is the nerds," Yaerin said, pouting a little.

He walked over and ruffled her hair. "Hey, I'm not the one who started that rumor. I'd be a fool if I didn't benefit off of it somehow."

"I'm pretty sure you *did* start that rumor, and you *are* benefitting off of it. It's unjust."

"I'll be sure to inform my royal council of your judicial concerns," Bazin said, taking a seat and setting up his computer.

The door opened again, and a boy with a blonde girl riding on his back came into the room. "Ugh, why do I even come to these things? Squabble, squabble, that's all I ever hear out of you two." Andi made a note that he spoke in a way that suggested yelling was his default volume.

"Because you love us?" Yaerin tried, only to be snuffed out by a glare from the newest boy.

"Who's this one?" He gestured over to Andi, girl still held firm against his back. *Dang, he got muscle.*

Andi snapped out of hir stupor. "Andi, Andi Washington."

"Absolutely charmed," the boy said. "My accessory up here is Kate. She's chronically lazy." Kate looked absolutely annoyed.

"I can relate." Andi smiled. "But you never gave your name?"

"Pedro Juarez. You can call me PJ, though." He winked. *Oh my God.*

"We're all here," Kate said in a voice that sounded like she didn't want to be there at all.

"So we are! President Yaerin Chon at your service! May the Paranormal Honor Society commence!" A moment of silence and widespread appreciation of Yaerin's enthusiastic pose ensued.

"Um, what exactly do you even do in this club?" Andi asked after the silence lasted a beat too long.

"Watch scary movies, mostly," Bazin said. "Talk about potential supernatural involvement in the mundane... or otherwise."

Ze looked concerned. "Or otherwise?"

"Yeah, you know. Like—"

"Murder," Kate whispered in Andi's ear, making hir jump.

Andi clutched the side of hir face, hunched over, eyes wide. "Wait, so like... freak accidents are really...."

"Paranormal killers!" Yaerin said, tone too cheery for content. "And now we've got a new case!" Andi straightened up, recalling the nuggets of information ze collected throughout the school day regarding a "disgusting incident."

"Nah, guys, come on, that's too soon, too close to home," Bazin said, eyes glued to the screen. "You can't... we can't do that to her."

"Mrs. Perkins was the best," Kate agreed, sighing thoughtfully before whacking PJ for throwing in "and the hottest" under his breath. "That's why we have to find out what did this to her."

Bazin whipped around his computer screen. "No news companies could release the photo, but I was able to snag a copy."

"Stretching legal parameters again, you naughty boy!" Yaerin faux-scolded, leaning in to look at the photo.

Andi relaxed against the wall in an attempt to seem aloof. "So, uh, this Mrs. Perkins. Tragic?"

Bazin made eye contact with Andi, causing hir to slip in a very uncool manner. "Janitors found her this morning, called the cops. Body slashed to bits, corpse starting to rot, probably in there two, maybe three days."

"They cancel school for minus-two-degree weather but not first-degree murder...," PJ observed darkly. "Also, does anyone else find it strange that these fellas been cleanin' the school all weekend and only just this morning called it in?"

Yaerin put her hands on top of her head. "Suspicious, suspicious."

"Almost... paranormal?" Andi ventured.

Yaerin nodded. "Definitely. There were large bites taken out of her. Bites! As in chunks! Eaten! Food!"

"No forced entry either," Bazin said, calm as ever. "Which could limit our list of suspects."

"Disgusting." Andi felt hir skin crawl but could also feel a rush in hir blood. Watching supernatural horroresque shows was entertaining, but living it was something else entirely.

"We have a plan, though...." PJ trailed off, eyes suddenly on the door, where a shadowed figure lingered. Upon the newfound silence, the figure entered, jittering nervousness in his step.

"Hey, gang!" he said, looking everyone in the eye for a split second too long, veering off the path of friendly and treading vaguely into the uncomfortable. "Mrs. Polsowski s-sent me to sponsor your meetings for a bit, s-s-seeing as she has some grading to catch up on."

Bazin looked annoyed. "Mrs. Polsowski normally doesn't attend the meetings.... We just needed a faculty member to sponsor the club on paper...."

"You *should* have better things to do," PJ murmured. Andi immediately realized that Mr. Sharp was overwhelmingly incompetent—an accumulation of seemingly small slipups had a way of adding up. From spilling all the contents of Mrs. Polsowski's desk drawer, to jamming her room's printer, it was no wonder Polsowski sent him away. Poor devilishly handsome guy.

"I know it's uncool to have a teacher in on your little hangouts...." Mr. Sharp sat down at a vacant desk. "But, I-I.... Oh, what's the word?

Y-you might not know this, but I'm actually a huge f-f-face? No, f-fan of the supernatural."

"You don't think this is baloney?" Yaerin side-eyed him suspiciously.

"N-n-no. Not at all. Now what's this I hear about Julie?"

Yaerin recounted the story.

"Wait! Do you know anything? Wasn't she the teacher you were shadowing?"

Mr. Sharp looked saddened. "Unfortunately, I was scheduled to switch teachers long before Julie's abrupt death.... If only I had known, maybe then I wouldn't have requested to leave."

"Requested?" Bazin asked carefully.

"In-indeed. Something was clearly bothering her, and I wasn't gaining the learning ex-experience I was s-seeking." Remorse oozed out of his voice before he switched gears completely. "All right, kids, f-first things first. We need to compile a list of potential creatures. Based on the b-bites, I'm thinking werewolf's our b-b-best bet. That way, it could be a human with access to the s-school who transformed after gaining entrance."

The kids looked at Mr. Sharp with a newfound sense of kinship.

"Any other suggestions?" He looked around expectantly.

"STOP CROSSING out my suggestions!"

"Peej, dude, hate to burst your bubble, but there's no way this could be a chupacabra," Bazin countered, crossing out PJ's latest theory not once, not twice, but several times until it was a black mess of dumb ideas and disappointment.

"It very well could be a chupacabra! In fact, your doubt on the matter only fuels my adamancy that it *is* a chupacabra."

"Chupacabras feast on goats!"

"It's gone rogue, man!"

After another couple minutes of discussing possible culprits, the group finally reached a lull. Bazin slid the paper with suggestions over to Yaerin, who eyed it thoughtfully.

Werewolf

Vampire

Succubus

Demon

Gnomes

Possessed puppet

~~*Chupacabra*~~

"It's a start," she said with a sigh. "What about some other shape-shifter creature, though?"

Mr. Sharp immediately spoke up. "Although we shouldn't rule that out, I have confidence werewolves are what's causing this. And I can't help but notice one certain person neglecting to come in on days of the full moon."

"If you're talking about Rick, we've already taken note of his lunar absences," Bazin said.

"It was immediately on our radar—we checked out all of the faculty for such patterns," Yaerin whispered to Andi. "But we were never able to prove any werewolf activity."

"What if we stay the night at school?" Kate asked, lifting her head from her crossed arms on the desk, where she had been dutifully catching some Zs. "You know, see if Rick targets any other teachers who come back to the school late?"

"Or us...," PJ muttered before Kate kicked him under the table.

"N-now, kids, I'm not saying I endorse it, but I will look the other way if you decide to stake out." His eyes became fiery. "Julie meant a lot to me. Get to the bottom of this and stop it. At all costs."

As soon as the fire emerged, it was extinguished. Mr. Sharp shook his head, looked at his watch, and grabbed his belongings. "I should report back to my s-supervisor. Nice club meeting, kids. I look forward to the next s-session."

"All right, everyone. Plan to meet here tonight at 9:00," Bazin instructed, with a nod from Yaerin.

"I best be getting to soccer practice," PJ declared, rising. "Coach isn't exactly keen on the supernatural shenanigans...."

"Looks like I've got some cheerleading to do," Kate said, stretching before following PJ out of the classroom.

Bazin looked at Andi and Yaerin.

"You guys know I'm always in here. You can leave whenever you want."

Andi looked at the clock. "Yeah, I guess I should get back before too late, especially if we're reconvening here tonight."

"Which way are you heading?" Yaerin asked.

"South Main."

"Me too! Let's walk together!" Yaerin smiled brightly as she put on her backpack and walked out the door.

"I'm glad Mr. Sharp took over," Yaerin said as they were leaving the school. "It's gonna be great! Like our very own Giles."

Andi hummed in agreement—ze'd read an article on wikiHow about how humming affirmative responses added mystique and took out enthusiasm that was too raw.

Yaerin abruptly stopped and reached into her pocket. "Here, Andi, I'll add you to our club's group message…. Can I get your cell number?"

Aw, hell to the yeah. Murders, werewolves, cute girls—this school was shaping up to have it all!

AT 8:55 p.m. Andi began to walk to the school. Ze picked up Yaerin on the way, and together, flashlights in hand, they walked to their deaths… or so ze's internal narrative was trying to convince hir—you know… to make things more interesting. Facing death in such a way had to gain hir some massive cool credentials.

"I felt like Mr. Sharp was breathing down our necks," PJ said once the group had all assembled in the tiny classroom. Kate had brought no stakeout equipment but was instead equipped with a sleeping bag, pillow, and teddy bear.

"He can breathe down some other things, if you know what I mean." She wiggled into her sleeping bag and cuddled up with the teddy.

"No, Kate, nobody knows what you mean. That doesn't make sense." PJ's brows were furrowed as he eyed the almost sleeping figure.

Bazin was busy typing away. "He did seem rather helpful with the investigation, though."

"Like I said"—Yaerin looked back to Andi—"our own personal Giles."

"It's weird, though, because he tends to our pool while my dad's away," Kate said, putting on an eye mask.

They soon slipped into a mutual quietness, waiting for Rick.

At one point Andi and Yaerin heard Rick cleaning and went to bait him, only to be yelled at and forced to run away. After an uneventful evening of supernatural small talk and speculation, they called it a night at 3:00 a.m., PJ carrying Kate back to her house, asleep.

"We'll just make sure to keep an eye on Rick, maybe do this again," Yaerin said. "I'm sure if we had thought of a proper course of action, we could've caught him doing something incriminating!"

HARMONY MILDEW was not the type of girl to be out this late alone, and certainly amended to herself not to make it a habit—she was the respectable type (even if she sometimes entertained a side John when her husband was away…).

But tonight she simply *had* to go to the opening of her friend's art gallery, so now, as she walked home, she promised herself this was her last late-night excursion.

She swallowed, quite aware that the figure who had been waiting at the bus stop was not, in fact, waiting for the bus, but rather waiting for a young woman such as herself to walk by. Pepper spray in hand, she whirled around to the figure.

"What strange weather we're having!" She read somewhere that you should engage your predator so they knew you could identify them in a lineup. And maybe it was due to the alcohol, but she might have said that last part aloud.

"Oh, Harm, love," a low, confident voice, now behind her, rang out. Wait. Only one person called her Harm—

"Wil—" She turned back around to address the person, cut off when she noticed a gleaming grin—she had never seen teeth that sharp, and *ohmygod—how many rows does this—* Her thoughts were interrupted when the voice resounded.

"That tactic only works if they intend to leave you alive."

THE FOLLOWING morning, Yaerin and Andi sat outside on the school steps, Yaerin reciting a passage from *Hamlet* and Andi doing not much of anything at all. Yaerin's voice was nice, ze decided. Ah, ze could listen to that voice all day—and possibly night—*no, stop, mind, stop.*

A flailing whirlwind of blonde hair approached them, clutching a newspaper in one hand and dragging a reluctant boy with the other.

"Wow," Andi commented as the storm approached. "That's the most animated I've ever seen baby Kate."

"She was my neighbor!" Kate exclaimed, shoving the newspaper in their hands as soon as she made it over to where Andi and Yaerin were sitting.

"What?" Yaerin cried. "Another murder? And we missed it!"

Andi's phone vibrated at that exact moment. "Guys, check the group message."

They all pulled out their phones to see Bazin had sent them a message.

Come to 2723 Malleus St. Police here. Investigation time.

"Fuck first period," PJ said, breaking into a run in the opposite direction of the school. The girls and Andi looked at each other for a second before following close behind him.

Once they arrived at the address, they were greeted by a whisper from the bushes. "Guys, what we failed to discuss was the issue of the full moon! If it was a werewolf, it would have to be one who was in control and able to transform whilst not under the full moon's influence, since there was just a shred in the sky."

"That would rule out the janitor, then—even if he is a werewolf, he wouldn't transform unless triggered by the full moon, which Mrs. Perkins wasn't killed on…."

"That also would suggest it was premeditated."

"Definitely a planned murder."

"So, what I've gathered from the police officers is that this girl was killed last night," Bazin informed them, looking through some binoculars. Two officers stood, deep in conversation.

"That would rule out Rick, then, since we saw him last night!" Yaerin said, biting her finger.

"That one officer seems suspicious to me. Knows a lot."

"Which one?"

"The big one with the donut."

"Well, isn't he just a bundle of clichés," Andi murmured.

"Catherine!" one of the policemen called, and Kate instinctively turned around and was embarrassed when he had, in fact, been talking to one of the officers named Catherine, rather than Kate.

"Hey, is that…," PJ began, tearing the binoculars from Bazin with little protest.

Mr. Sharp approached the police officers and began speaking to them.

Huh.

"Do you think he's working for the police?" Yaerin asked. "He kinda looks like it."

"Oh yeah, I forgot. Mr. Sharp sometimes mowed their lawn," Kate said. "He likes doing chores around this neighborhood." Mr. Sharp shook the police officer's hand, then departed, the two of them laughing.

"Shh, listen."

"This is ridiculous. I was this lady's neighbor. I'm gonna go try to talk to the officers." Kate headed over to the police people.

She soon came back. "Wow, that lady was so mean to me! I've never met a mean Catherine before. She's giving our name a bad… name"

"Wow, Kate, you are so very, very profound," PJ said before getting the wind knocked out of him.

"Anyway, that policeman does seem really weird to me. And as I was leaving, I heard him mention a rendezvous when he got off of work…."

"All right, gang, we'll monitor the station and follow this creep after work. Maybe that will lead us to some answers," Yaerin chirped decisively.

"Maybe instead of finding a new culprit, we should predict the next victim by analyzing what these two had in common," Bazin suggested. "It appears that the creature is going after young women…."

"That seems even harder...," Kate whispered, PJ nodding against her shoulder.

"We'll discuss the strategy at the meeting today," Yaerin said. "Until then, we should hightail it back to class."

ANDI FELT an immediate connection with this odd group—they had grown so close in a matter of days, it was borderline insane. Those were really the type of people you should keep, though. The ones who made it easy, who you could just relax with and take down fronts.

They had just finished talking about their next excursion regarding the investigation of Julie when Andi spoke up.

"Hey, um." Andi bit hir lip, eyes not quite making contact with any of the members. "This doesn't have anything to do with the investigation, but would you mind, um...."

Yaerin touched Andi's back, and ze was filled with a surge of courage. "Would you lot mind using gender-neutral pronouns for me? You know, when you're talking about me. Hir and ze are my preferred...."

They nodded, stepping a bit closer in an almost paranormal unison—good thing they were responsible for investigating, or Andi would think that was super creepy. "I mean, some days it's obvious I'm feeling more girl, but most of the time I kinda like... just, you know...."

Yaerin supplied, "Being in the middle?"

"Yeah. It just feels more natural being ambiguous. For me, at least. It's different for everyone, varies... you know?"

Bazin slaps Andi on the back. "Don't even worry about it, bud. Now let's talk about murders."

THEY PLANNED to follow the suspicious officer as soon as he got off work. Needless to say, it went over quite horribly.

THE FOLLOWING day, Andi could tell everyone was frustrated by the latest flop. After the police officer ended up being no more than a shady porn addict, morale was low. Ze wanted to try to get things rolling again.

"What if we—" ze began.

"Hold up. You know something strange? Nobody was getting serial killed before whenever the hell you transferred here," PJ said, arms folded. Kate looked up from where she had her head on the desk, making an annoyed face at PJ.

The air quickly became hostile.

"You don't think that I could have—"

"All I'm saying, Andi, is it's kinda weird that as soon as you got here, all this shit has been happening." PJ looked like he had swallowed something disgusting.

"I was with you guys during the stakeout, though!"

"Were you? Were you *really?*"

"Yes, really! What does that even mean, *Pedro?*"

He let out a loud, offended gasp.

"Andi's some sort of werewolf—the mysterious disappearing, the emotional distance, the use of gender-neutral pronouns!"

"PJ, you're confusing gender fluidity with werewolves again." Kate rolled her eyes.

"Even Yaerin mentioned it was peculiar!"

Andi's breath hitched—Yaerin thought hir gender identity was… peculiar? But….

Yaerin's eyes went wide.

"The werewolf possibility, not the—" Yaerin began. Andi didn't want to hear it, though. Hir attempt to look cool and aloof just made hir the prime suspect.

"You're just so distant with… everyone."

"That doesn't mean I'm a murderer!" Andi's chest was constricting. Ze felt as though hir heart was attempting to wiggle its way up hir throat, preventing hir from forming intelligent sentences. Tears were pricking at hir eyes, so ze took a deep breath—everyone knew tears were the epitome of uncool.

"Wait, guys, don't go blaming Andi just yet," Bazin said, his gaze fixed on the screen and looking less composed than usual.

"Huh?"

"This has happened before."

"WHAT DO you mean, this has happened before?" Kate demanded, walking over to Bazin on his laptop.

"Look at these archives, man. A string of women all murdered, same way. Seven years ago."

PJ looked annoyed. "That doesn't mean Andi doesn't pop up spontaneously every seven years. Can you prove your whereabouts this time seven years ago?"

Yaerin came to Andi's defense. "Ze could. Ze's completely human, right? Do you have any old family photos?"

Bazin looked up. "I'm not saying this doesn't get Andi off the hook. What I'm saying is now there's a definite creature I can guarantee this is."

They all looked at Bazin expectantly.

"Well?"

Bazin looked annoyed. "Lazy, lazy, lazy children! I'm not just going to hand it to you."

"Withholding this information and playing games just hastens another's death, you absolute sweat stain! Give us the—"

"Whoa, whoa, baby Kate," Bazin soothed before he continued. "What do all these women have in common?"

Yaerin looked at the screen, attempting to find a common variable. Her eyes grew wide when the realization hit her.

"All of their husbands were gone at war."

"Yeah," Bazin said grimly. "But the last two—going to be three tonight if we don't stop it—have something else... er, someone else in common. Who was Mrs. Perkins's student teacher? Who mowed Mrs. Watson's lawn? Who's about to clean Ms. Fraiser's pool?"

"M-Mr. Sharp...."

"That's what we get for trusting someone with a stutter," Kate whispered. "Oh shit, my mom! Does that mean she was banging Mr. Sharp?"

"Kate, your mom is in danger," PJ said as he grabbed her shoulders.

"So what could Mr. Sharp possibly be?"

"Well, it kind of sounds like a selkie... but they've never been known to maim and eat their victims... just seduce them while their husbands are at sea."

"A selkie? But carnivorous.... So, like... a sharkie?" Yaerin mused.

"So what do we do?" Andi asked, worried.

Bazin paused, looking unsure. "First things first. Someone needs to go get Mrs. Fraiser. Kate, you and I can do that. We'll need to provide a distraction. Peej, Yaerin, and Andi, you three—"

Yaerin cut in. "We'll find the skin. Burn it. Or we'll be seeing Mr. Sharp again in seven years."

"EVERYONE, SILENCE your cell phones. The last thing we need is more noise," Yaerin instructed as she took the first step inside. Obeying orders, Andi and PJ turned their phones on silent.

"Wow, this guy's place looks like it's worth more than Kate's multimillion-dollar lipstick collection...," PJ commented upon walking into Mr. Sharp's apartment.

"I don't know how to take that statement," Andi said, looking around the apartment, voicing hir true feelings even though ze was not quite sure what they were.

"Okay, we need to find this skin. Eye on the prize, men, eye on the prize."

"He'll keep it somewhere dear to him. Somewhere no one would ever think to look...."

Andi thought for a minute, searching hir mind for places that people commonly overlooked. When you lost something....

"I've got it!" Yaerin said. "He probably put it in the bill rack!" She went to check and was disappointed when all she found was a sock.

"The couch cushions?" Andi suggested, PJ heading toward the couch.

Once again, no skin.

"He's not human, though. These are all places *we* wouldn't put something important. Where would a fish not think to put something?" PJ said, returning the couch cushions to their previous formation and pulling out his phone.

"Land, of course," Andi said. "But this is all land!"

"Okay, so Mr. Sharp is a very backward thinker. Where is the first place we'd go? He'd probably hide it there last because it's so obvious...."

Andi's eyes lit up. "He's been devouring his victims, right?"

"Guys?" PJ was ignored, the two working through their latest breakthrough.

"Essentially, yeah, he's been snacking on them...," Yaerin said, looking thoughtful.

"Then he probably doesn't have use for—"

"The fridge!" Yaerin exclaimed.

Sure enough, in the empty fridge rested a slippery gray skin. They tossed it in the sink, covered it in oil, and set it ablaze. "All right, Mr. Sharp will probably know that his skin is burning. Now we have to come up with a plan to get rid of him.

"Uh, so, Bazin sent a text a little while ago, and I didn't check until just now, but I think we should haul ass—"

Mr. Sharp entered.

"—out of here," PJ finished.

ANDI PROMPTLY decided that closets were the source of all evil and immediately regretted hir decision of pulling Yaerin in with hir. For an apartment as nice as Sharp's, you'd think he'd invest in more closet space.

They were quiet as they heard shuffling outside. This was so cowardly, but Andi was just too—ah! For once in hir life, ze didn't care about looking cool. No more fronts. Andi was downright terrified. Burning a carnivorous sea monster's skin could do that to a person.

"Look, I'm... I'm sorry about before, okay? I should have defended you." Yaerin was looking at her feet, her voice a whisper that tickled Andi's collarbone. Yeah, definitely too close.

"Can I kiss you? You know, in case we die in here—"

"Don't talk like that." Yaerin shuffled closer, stood on her tiptoes, leaned in, and—

"Guys, you can come out of the closet!" Kate called happily before bopping PJ upside the head for muttering "again."

"Kate and Bazin showed up just in time with the police! Mr. Sharp's in custody," PJ informed them.

Andi looked down at the shorter girl, heart a bit caught in their throat as ze asked, "And you'll like me even when I'm Andrea?"

"Yes, Andi. I'd like you even if you were a cougar-devouring creature of the sea."

They both laughed while the rest of the gang wordlessly joined them. They headed out of the house to make the trek home, the moon a small sliver above them.

"You aren't, though, right?"

LEIGH TAYLOR considers herself "okay, I guess" but has received rave reviews that she is both "stunning" and "constantly eating." When not running around the city searching for supernatural murders, she finds solace in writing and sending snaps of spaghetti to anyone with eyes. You may complain about her excessive use of exclamation points as well as her lackluster author bio at leightaylorwriting@gmail.com.

GLITTERHEAD
BENJAMIN SHEPHERD
QUIÑONES

NO.

No.

Definitely not.

Gently rapping his pencil against his desk with every no, every disappointment, it was safe to say the last thing on Jack's mind was Spanish. That wasn't to say he wasn't paying attention *in* class, though. Just not to the teacher or the gibberish he was writing on the board.

Seated at the very back of the room, where there were so many heads in front of him to stare at, how could he?

Yeah, yeah, it was *his* fault for picking the seat, but that was only to make sure his own head wouldn't be stared at. Or be a target for paper balls.

So why not get a haircut?

Simple: because no one else had hair like him. A part of him even liked when people called it a "Jew-fro," which wasn't totally inaccurate given that his mom was Jewish. At least people saw him as *a little* different.

That was a start.

The hard, inescapable truth was that even without the big mop of dark brown curly hair sprouting from his scalp, he was different from his classmates. But he wasn't willing to admit just how different to anyone other than his best friend yet. It was much easier to just be known as that nonathletic white kid with the Jew-fro. *It was something,* allowing him to get his feet wet in the pool of difference and check the temperature before jumping right in.

Sure, he was known for more than just his lack of coordination, ethnicity, and hair, taking the most advanced art classes his high school had to offer, but not *well known*. And he doubted he'd ever be—not at Wapato High, anyway, where all anyone seemed to care about was sports—soccer in particular. Maybe once he went to college, where he could major in art and get a *proper* education.

He mentally shook himself, tearing himself from his all too optimistic future and plunging himself into the problem-filled now.

No.

No.

Maybe....

Jack guessed and guessed, his dark chocolate brown eyes leaping from one boy's head to the next... until settling on a scrawny blond with his legs crossed and the straightest spine he had ever seen.

He totally is! He has to be... but I'm not sure. I'm never sure!

"Ugh," groaned Jack as frustration bubbled within him like boiling water, tightening his grip around the thin wooden stick that he should be taking notes with. He resisted the urge not to—

Snap!

The only writing utensil he had split into two in what sounded like a miniexplosion that rippled through the air and destroyed every single sound wave in its path.

He could feel the heat rise to his cheeks when literally every head turned around to face him. That included Señor Sevilla's. The man with the thinnest beard but the thickest waist, in the plaid unbuttoned shirt, set down his chalk and crossed his chubby arms, not the least bit happy about having his lesson interrupted.

Please don't call on me, please don't call on me....

"Señor Borkowski."

Dammit!

"Al frente de la clase. Con... Roberto."

As the teacher gestured toward the front of the classroom, Jack opened his mouth in protest, but no words came out. He couldn't find them in Spanish, and he knew that if he said them in English, his participation grade would suffer. So he had no choice but to leave the safety of his seat.

He couldn't look at Roberto without feeling mocked.

If only I were Puerto Rican... and tan... and a star soccer player... with lots of friends... and a big butt. Ugh. He'd make me look like a fool for sure, Jack thought but nevertheless kept putting one foot in front of the other until he reached the front, where he stuffed his hands in his pockets and waited to find out what situation he would have to act out this time, much to his dismay.

Oh, how it sucked to be one of the few white kids in a predominantly Hispanic neighborhood.

"You, Jack, need a pencil. Roberto, you have one extra. And... go."

A wide, toothy smile stretched across Jack's face, not because he was *enjoying* this, but because he was embarrassed; he could feel twenty sets of eyes seething into his skin, burning through his clothes. "Um... hola."

"Hola."

Crap, *now* what?

Eyes wide, Jack racked his brain for the verb "to borrow," scavenging the crevices of his memory but not finding.

"¿Cómo estás?" was all he could muster up, speaking in a thick American accent. Roberto and a few other students chuckled.

"Estoy bien. Parece que necesitas otro lápiz."

Brows wrinkled, Jack tried to understand... but failed. He shook his head ever so slowly, screaming uncertainty. "No...."

Roberto's lifted brow told him that he best change his answer.

"I mean, *sí*."

Roberto found nothing but air in his pocket, which he handed to Jack with what felt like an evil grin, as though he was getting a kick out of his suffering. Jack guessed he owed Roberto one for offering the invisible pencil when he hadn't properly asked for it, but he doubted Roberto had done it for him.

Show-off.

"Gracias." With that, Jack turned to the teacher with pleading eyes, desperately hoping to be done so he could go back to his distant seat and draw a picture of his teacher falling off a cliff. Roberto too.

"Bien hecho. Back to your seats."

Phew.

HE LET out another, greater breath of relief once class was over, mostly because Spanish was his last class of the day. Students flooded into the hallway, creating a current he cautiously dipped into and followed all the way to his locker. Beside it stood his best friend, Garilania, her smile contagious and her sense of style ever present. Today she wore a yellow sundress and had two large sunflower heads tucked in her shoulder-length curly black hair.

"Jack-in-the-box! What's crack-a-lackin'?"

"How many times do I have to tell you to stop calling me that?" Jack frowned when she giggled, looking down to plug in his locker combination. It wasn't a joke, but he knew she only wanted what was best for him. It was easier said than done, though. *So much* easier.

"The day you come out."

"I already did… to you." He avoided eye contact in shame as he transferred whatever books he needed into his backpack. And maybe more. Homework was a good distraction. So was drawing.

"You *know* that's not enough. All you did was drag me into the box with you." Her voice was sturdy, full of certainty.

Jack had told her this countless times before—he hated being asked why he didn't have a girlfriend yet, being called too handsome to be single, and feeling inadequate at having nothing to show for it. Most of all, he hated pretending to be something he wasn't and feeling alone despite the fact he had the "million-dollar family," living in a nice little town with both parents happily married, a sister, and even a German shepherd.

But he'd also told her just as many times that he didn't like to be rushed. As eternally grateful as he was for her unconditional friendship, she didn't get how hard it was to risk being hated… by his own family, his peers, and even total strangers.

He kept his face in his locker, breathing in the fumes of his notebooks, textbooks, and dirty gym clothes to stay hidden from Gari's piercing gaze. He knew the moment he saw her he would cave, that he'd have to admit she was right. That he realized he was being counterproductive, hurting himself. It was easier to avoid it, he told himself, but obviously still hard if he was feeling this way. It was all so illogical, yet he kept doing it. He was stuck.

"*Come on*, Jack," she begged, sighing as she leaned against the neighboring locker and stared at his hair, which was even curlier than her own. "Jack, look at me."

"I'd rather not," he finally said, shielding his face with one hand before retracting his head out of the locker and closing it with the other.

Gari groaned at Jack's stubbornness. "*Fine*, you win. Again. I'll stop pestering you," she told him, although it didn't feel at all like a victory to Jack.

The moment he dropped his guard, however, Gari charged in with another attack. "I just feel like you shouldn't worry so much. Your parents *love* you, and who cares what other people think? You'll still have me." Her smile grew large as she tried to lighten the mood, but Jack covered his eyes again with his hand so he wouldn't have to see it.

"I'm just not ready, okay?" he barked angrily. It was the only way she would listen to him. But he was quick to change his tone, now sounding saddened. "*Ugh*, if only I knew someone else who was... *like me*." He bit back the word "gay," afraid someone might hear. "I can't seriously be the only one in Wapato. Can I?"

"You're definitely not. I read that one in every four men is gay. They're all just too chicken to come out. Like you." She grinned, managing to alleviate and agitate him at the same time. She had a knack for doing that. "Maybe if you came out, more guys would follow suit?"

"Or what if I come out, get teased every day of my life, and scare them off?" Jack was quick to protest, having already considered that fat chance.

"All I heard was 'blah, blah, blah—I'm a pessimist—blah,'" she jeered, sticking out her tongue.

"You're going to make me miss the bus" was all he could think to say before he turned to walk away, not expecting her to understand. He took one step before her strong hand closed over his shoulder, stopping him.

"Darn right I'm going to make you miss your bus. Didn't you see the fliers? They're posted on every lamppost in Wapato. A *psychic* just moved into town! Let's go before everyone else does."

"What psychic?" he asked, glad she'd changed the subject. Jack had stopped paying attention to the lamppost fliers awhile back when he realized they normally only ever had to do with missing puppies and yard sales.

"Madame Myrtle. Even if she is a load of baloney, it'll still be fun, and cheap! Students get a discount, like half off. My mom can pick us up after."

"You had me at cheap. Let's go." No further convincing needed. The more distractions, the better, especially when they didn't involve doing homework.

"Yay!" Gari broke into a fit of giggles, clapping her hands excitedly before latching on to his arm and leading him out of the building. "Who knows? Maybe she'll know who your future husband is."

Now it was Jack's turn to laugh, only much more skeptically. "*Husband?* I doubt it.... At this rate, I'm never even going to get my first kiss."

"What? Mine wasn't good enough?" Gari giggled again. Jack blushed, wanting to forget but not change.

"I mean, from a *guy*."

ARM WRAPPED around Gari's as they walked to the psychic's house, Jack knew that this was as close to a girl as he was going to get—and as close as he *wanted* to get. He was sure of that now.

There was a time when he wasn't so sure, when he wanted to appease his horndog of a dad so badly, when he was in total denial about being that one guy out of four to have homosexual feelings, when he and Gari dated. Obviously, it didn't work out between them, but what he got out of it was a best friend he never got tired of being around and could talk with about virtually any subject matter in confidence.

"Look, it's Madame Myrtle!" Gari shouted, pointing fingers at the strange-looking lady across the street. She wore loose white clothing that contrasted her dark skin, a golden scarf around her head and waist despite the warm weather, and lots of colorful, dangly jewelry around her wrists and neck. She also had a large, heavy-looking teal bag that she seemed to be struggling with, looking like a walking rainbow... with a limp... and zero sense of her surroundings.

When the woman walked into the middle of the road without looking both ways first, Jack's jaw felt like an anchor sinking to the bottom of the ocean. "What the heck is she doing, not looking both ways?"

He did the honors, only to see a large yellow school bus coming in hot from the left.

And it wasn't stopping.

Why wasn't it stopping? Was the driver *texting*?

"Oh my gosh," sputtered Jack when he realized what would happen, his heart sinking before resurfacing with a vengeance.

His heart pounded too fast, too loud for him to hear any other thoughts after "*I need to do something.*" Feeling physically incapable of forming any second thoughts, he did what he could. He charged forward mindlessly, breaking from the security of Gari's arm and into a sprint toward the damsel who didn't even know she was in distress.

"No, Jack! *No!*" Garilania screamed at the top of her lungs as though her own life was in danger. Not that he could hear her with all the adrenaline pumping through his head and the roaring of the bus engine that inched toward him.

It was all over in a matter of seconds.

"*Mierda*, Jack! You could have died!" Hearing Gari's voice was a good sign, as upset as she sounded; it meant he was alive. They both were.

Shit, thought Jack when he realized his body was sprawled on top of the woman whom he had tackled to the cold, hard concrete, crushing her. They were still on the busy road but no longer in the middle, only inches from the sidewalk.

"Sorry, sorry, sorry," Jack said over and over again, still energized from the rush, until he was back on his feet and the life-friendly sidewalk. "Are you okay?" he asked, extending an arm to help her up. He felt awful about tackling her like some barbaric football player as his heart calmed down.

She could have broken a hip. What if she did?

"Am I *okay?*" She broke into a fit of witchlike laughter that gave him chills, but only for a few seconds, before becoming serious. Dead serious. "Didn't your momma ever teach you to *never* hit a lady? *Especially* a gypsy." She lifted an arm as though to cast a spell on him. "Bad luck shall fall upon you!"

With that, she slapped his hand away and picked herself up with little difficulty. At least now he knew she hadn't broken a hip, but that didn't make him feel any better.

"I... didn't mean to. There was no other way. I'm—"

His apology was cut clean off by Gari's sharp tone. Her hands balled into tiny fists, she strutted across the street in her sundress. She would've looked cute if it wasn't for the anger plastered on her face. "Don't you dare say it, Jack!"

Jack's mouth shut as swiftly as flytrap, her tone scarier than the woman's laugh.

"You've got a lot of nerve, lady! My friend just risked his life to save yours, and you repay him with... *bad luck?* Uck, you make me sick. You should be on your knees!"

Lips pressed tightly together, Jack shot Gari a look that told her *shut up!* Or else they would all be cursed with bad luck, not that he was as superstitious as Gari. "Gari, it's okay. It was really no big deal...."

Gari would've exploded in disbelief if the woman hadn't piped up first. "You... you saved my life? Are you absolutely sure?" she stuttered through unclenched teeth, sounding like she had gotten a vocal cord transplant, from raspy hag to sweet grandma. What was even stranger was the way her bright sky-blue eyes locked on to him like a calculating hawk.

He didn't get why, not planning to go anywhere other than to see her, although now he was seriously starting to doubt her authenticity. Maybe now he could get the psychic reading for free? He didn't dare ask, simply nodding until Gari jumped in.

"Yes, he did! I saw it with my own two eyes. You were about to be turned into a human pancake. He could have become one too because of you!" Gari rambled, surely still rattled about almost losing him (*aww*). "What kind of psychic are you, anyway? Shouldn't you have *seen* it coming?"

Madame Myrtle laughed, waving away the skepticism with her hand. "My dear child, if my crystal ball neglected to tell me this would happen, it was meant to be," she explained before being struck by a realization, gasping.

"My baby! Where's my baby?"

She spun around like a dog chasing its tail, panicking until she spotted her large teal bag beside her feet. Carefully hoisting it over her shoulder, she reached in with both hands to check the condition of what Jack guessed to be her crystal ball solely by touch. He took her exaggerated exhalation and smile as good news.

"You, *Jack Borkowski*, saved more than just me…. Much more."

"How do you know my name?" questioned Jack, starting to reevaluate her credibility as a psychic.

Garilania was speechless.

"Heroic acts like yours ought to be rewarded, no? Tell me, Jack. If you were to get *one* wish, what would it be?"

Jack turned to Gari, mentally asking *is she for real?* Wide-eyed and *still* speechless, everything about Gari's marveling features told him yes. But what did she know? Jack, on the other hand, doubted that some street gypsy had the power of a shooting star or birthday candles. Or maybe she did, given that shooting stars or birthday candles never did a damn thing. Yet he made a wish at every chance he got anyway, just to be sure. Why would this be any different?

"Hmm…." Jack decided to just go with it, rubbing his chin as he tried to think up the *perfect* wish. It wasn't every day that he bumped into a "magical" gypsy on the street; he couldn't waste it.

"I wish…."

What should I wish for? Straight A's? But I don't want to get lazy, plus there's more to life than just school. Hot guys to drool over me instead of the other way around? But then it wouldn't be true love, plus what if they actually salivated in my presence? What about athletic ability? A bigger butt?

"Don't say it out loud." Madame Myrtle stopped him, even though he wasn't anywhere near a decision, pointing to her ear. "Or else it won't come true."

He felt rushed, but he couldn't stop thinking about hot guys, which he knew weren't the most important thing in the world, and that reminded him of how frustrated he'd felt today in class. How he felt *all the time*.

That's it!

"I wish...." He leaned in, cupping his hand around his mouth so Gari couldn't hear, knowing how nosy she could be, or anyone else, and whispered his wish directly into the gypsy's ear canal.

Madame Myrtle smirked. "Very well. May the spirits be in your favor... may they make your dream a reality and alter your path for the better as you have altered mine.... *Baxt hai sastimos tiri patragi!*"

Jack trembled in anticipation, his eyelids as light as feathers as he watched her wave a hand over her bag like a magician and reach in to extract a handful of *something*. She held her clenched fist out in front of him, concealing the object's identity with her middle-aged flesh.

A gift? Definitely couldn't be a bunny rabbit. But what he'd wished for wasn't anything tangible.

Just when he pushed his open palms forward to accept it anyway, she retracted her arm, winding it back like a baseball pitcher, and— Realizing she was going to *throw* something at him, Jack yelped, "Wait, no!"

But it was too late. What looked like more than a handful of shiny glitter had already launched from the woman's hand; there was no taking it back or blocking it.

It flew everywhere, invading his eyes, his mouth, *everything*.

"*Gah!*" Jack coughed out whatever shimmery particles of death he had inhaled, rubbing his eyes until the cloud of multicolored sparkles sank to the ground, creating a puddle around his feet.

He felt a hand reach into his pocket, but by the time the air cleared to do anything about it, Madame Myrtle was gone, and Jack was left covered in sticky glitter that clung to every fiber of his clothes, every pore of his skin, every follicle of hair... from head to toe.

"There she goes!" Gari shouted, pointing at the woman as she took off, running as fast as her heavy crystal ball would allow, before she had to hold her stomach to laugh when she saw him. "You look like a unicorn vomited all over you," she joked, not that Jack was listening.

"*Why?*" he muttered to himself, horribly confused as he brushed the glitter off his clothes, or tried to. Although that could be how gypsy magic worked, if there was such a thing, he couldn't help but feel like he had just been scammed, and after checking both pockets, he realized he had been.

"She stole my damn wallet."

Being a poor, jobless high school student who had yet to get his driver's license or even his permit and wasn't trusted with a credit card, he didn't bother trying to chase her. He hadn't lost much—only five bucks and some loose change. Just enough to pay for the discounted psychic reading for students. Like hell was he going to fall for that now. At least he'd kept Gari from wasting her money.

But still, he hated getting his hopes up only to have them crushed. What he hated even more was people throwing shit in his hair.

"This sucks."

IT TOOK not one, not two, but *three* showers just to scrub the glitter off his skin. Somehow, it was still in his hair, woven deep into his scalp like tiny ticks that endlessly flaked off like dandruff whenever he patted his head. Not nearly as much as before, but still noticeable, several light-reflecting specks per curl—and he had a lot of curls. But he feared that if he shampooed a fourth time, his hair would start falling out. Shaving his hair, part of his identity, wasn't an option either. He'd rather be called "glitterhead."

Strangely enough, that was exactly what they called him when he went to school the next day.

He shrugged the name-calling off with a forced smile, not too bothered, at least not for that reason. The fact that it was expected for people to target anyone who stuck out in a crowd was what bothered him, what made him so reluctant to come out. It didn't help that his high school was so damn small, only a little over a hundred kids per grade. With everyone knowing everyone, rumors spread like wildfire.

Wildfire was dangerous, uncontrollable, and combustible.

He just kept seeing his secret passing through the student body and consuming whoever it touched, ultimately leaving him alone, the source of the fire, the cause of the controversy.

But then he remembered he would always have Gari by his side, the only fireproof tree he knew. She was the only person he hung out with outside of school anyway, so why should it matter if he lost everyone else?

It didn't.

It was the hate he worried about. He'd already gotten a taste of bullying for his big, now glittery hair, a miniscule difference that didn't go against the grain of anyone's religion or whatever belief mistakenly told them it was "unnatural." He would surely get more than a mouthful, a stomachache even, if they knew he was *gay*.

It was one thing to go through life with few friends. It was another to go through life with few friends and everyone else wishing you were dead. Maybe not directly, but might as well be since being gay was a part of who he was, something he could not change no matter how hard he tried. Something genetic.

Just like his curly hair.

He could straighten it, cut it, cover it up with a hat, or otherwise hide it from view, but at its roots, it was still curly. It never would stay straightened, and it would always grow back....

"Dammit!" he spat out, slamming a handful of regret against his locker door when he realized what he should have wished for was for people to understand that, to accept homosexuality.

He could have totally averted a world crisis, saved millions of lives of gays who die of mistreatment, with just one single wish. But no, he had to waste it on himself.

Selfish, selfish! His brain berated him, making Jack want to hit his forehead against his locker. He *knew* he should care about others more than himself, but it was hard to actually do when he was suffering, as though all his energy was being put into protecting his secret.

But it wasn't like that damn gypsy thief had really granted his wish anyway, he reminded himself.

Shrugging, he finished throwing his books into his locker, grabbed the plastic grocery bag that held his gym clothes, and headed for the boys' locker room... aka the most frustrating place in the world.

AS GUYS changed around him, he kept his head down. Right before his very eyes, they were stripping down to their underwear, and what was he doing? Averting them, looking the other way. Guys of all shapes and sizes and colors. Mostly dark, mostly skinny. He liked dark and skinny.

Part of him thought he was crazy, that it made zero sense to look away from something that attracted him, to worry about giving the "wrong idea" when in fact it was the most accurate one, the one that would let guys know he was interested. Plus, how else was he supposed to receive any of those signals, assuming there were more closeted gays, as Gari suggested?

He just didn't want to look at the *wrong* guy, the homophobe who would call him out for taking a peek at his bulge and make a big rumor-igniting scene.

Glitter flaked off his head like dandruff when he took off his shirt. He hardly noticed, but his neighbor hadn't missed it.

"Yo, Jack. What's with the glitter? Just curious," asked the always friendly boy with the crooked nose and wavy dark hair.

In the middle of unbuttoning his jeans, Jack was so busy trying to ignore his surroundings that the question directed at him felt sudden. It took him a couple of seconds to gather himself, to convince himself that he wasn't being hit on, and another couple to think of an excuse.

"Uh...."

Like anyone was going to believe a gypsy attacked him with glitter and stole his wallet.

"Blame my little sister.... She likes annoying me," he lied, at least in part. She really was annoying. He dreaded the day she'd graduate eighth grade and start attending the same high school as him. He felt like he had only just escaped her, only a sophomore.

If there was anyone more capable of spreading a rumor, it was her and her big mouth. Since she was his sister, connected to him by blood, he felt she had a right to know the truth about him. But she couldn't. The solution: avoid her... for now. He knew he'd have to tell her eventually, but not now.

Pablo gave him a swift pat on the back, chuckling. "I feel ya, man. I have *three* little sisters."

Jack's face broke into a smile, both relieved that Pablo had bought the excuse and excited that someone other than Gari was making an effort to talk to him. Mentally playing with the idea that Pablo could possibly be gay under his manly, deep-voiced exterior, Jack was about to further the conversation when—

Ring!

The blare of the school bell derailed his train of thought as it reverberated throughout the locker room. *Shit!* He quickly—nervously—took off his jeans and slipped into a pair of black basketball-style shorts, despite his hatred for the sport of basketball, as the guys who had already finished changing brushed past him to walk upstairs. In fact, he hated most sports, mostly because he wasn't any good at them. That made PE one of his least favorite classes, even worse than precalculus.

"Speed it up, glitterhead," said one of the guys who passed by.

"Yeah, *glitterhead,* I'm looking forward to owning your ass," another cackled.

Not like that, not like that, Jack told himself, ignoring them both, especially Jose, who was the bigger of the two jerks, as he sat down on the bench to tie his shoes.

As the last of his classmates passed by, he felt a sudden chill race up his spine and run through the rest of his body. Strange as it was to shiver as though he had just taken his first step outside on a winter morning, what with how warm it was in the poorly ventilated locker room, he ignored that too, figuring he was just really anxious about gym class.

He tightened the laces of his shoes to make sure he wouldn't trip and fall... again. The last thing he needed right now was to give the guys more reasons to make fun of him; it just kept reminding him how cruel they could be. If he ever wanted to come out, he had to make himself think they wouldn't be so cruel.

"OKAY, CLASS! Who can tell me what day it is?" asked the tall, muscular woman with a voice deeper than Pablo's. Many thought she was a lesbian. Jack *hoped* she was a lesbian. Being the gym teacher, it was no one's business, but if she were more open about it, he felt like he'd feel more welcomed at school in a way, even if she was only in charge of one class.

"Wednesday?" uttered one smart aleck.

"Which is…?" She held her clipboard to the middle of the gym, where about twenty different colored rubber balls were lined up, dividing the room into two.

"Dodgeball day!" cheered one girl with the utmost enthusiasm, her hands clenched as though she was getting ready to punch something. That girl was an inch away from him; that girl was Garilania.

As girly as she dressed and as dainty as she looked, Jack knew better than anyone that she was not afraid of breaking a nail or wrestling. She was very proud of the fact that she could take on both her older brothers at the same time. Of course she would like something as physical as dodgeball.

"Correct! Now divide yourselves into teams, unless you want me to do it for you."

Jack stuck to Gari like glue, walking with her to one side of the gym. Thank God she was in the same gym class, and thank God the teacher let them pick their own teams. She eased his suffering, keeping the guys from *completely* eating him alive. They always managed to get an arm or a leg, though, like sharks. Mindless, hungry sharks with an appetite for anyone weaker than them.

"Hate dodgeball, hate dodgeball," Jack muttered under his breath, nervousness expanding inside him like a balloon.

"Oh, come on, Jack. It's really not that bad," Gari insisted, smiling brightly, clearly excited. Why couldn't he be as athletically gifted as her?

"Easy for you to say! I never had older brothers to toughen me up, just a little annoying sister."

"I'm just saying. Keep hating on dodgeball and it's going to hate you back. Why would it like something that doesn't like it?"

"Maybe because it doesn't have feelings," he sniped back, shooting down her words of wisdom. She didn't understand what it was like not to be good at something, to be made fun of.

"Okay, fine," Gari said with a dramatic wave of both hands, as though she had no more time to argue. "You just focus on dodging. I'll do the throwing and blocking. Sound good?"

Jack's chin bounced up and down like a bobblehead, lacking any confidence in his throwing and blocking ability to the point that he didn't want to try anymore. He was sick of being told that he "threw like a girl." If the typical girl threw like Gari, he would've taken it as a compliment, but that sadly wasn't the case.

The gym teacher blew her whistle. Everyone but Jack and a handful of girls scrambled to the center of the gym to grab a dodgeball. Gari managed to hit someone within the first few seconds, dancing around whatever ball was thrown at her with a grace that left him agape.

"*Wooo*, Gari! Best dodgeball player in the world! Yeah!" he cheered, clapping his hands from the very back of the gym.

Unfortunately, when Gari turned to face him, she was nailed in the back by the same person who had called him glitterhead in the locker room. Time seemed to slow in that moment; it was quite tragic as he watched the smile slowly drop from Gari's face as though the dodgeball had sucked the life out of her. She stood there, frozen, lifeless.

"Miss Reyes, you're *out!*" scolded the teacher, a total dictator when it came to cheating.

Gari balled her hands into fists and held her breath. Jack imagined pressurized steam pumping out of her ears before she exploded into a million fiery pieces, shrieking like a banshee as she stomped off to the side.

"Sorry, sorry, sorry!" Jack repented, feeling awful about distracting her. He knew she liked winning, too much in his opinion, but that was who she was. Hating to see her upset, he had to do something. Avenge her, win for her, *something.* But how? He threw like a girl....

"Kick their asses, Jack!" Gari demanded from the sidelines, shaking an angry fist in the air.

As though by fate, a dodgeball rolled along the waxed wood floor to the back of the gym, stopping right by his feet. He picked it up without hesitation, extending it in front of him like a shield. He was much more hesitant about taking steps forward, but he did anyway.

"For Gari!" Jack boomed once he was close enough to Jose, raising his dodgeball like a medieval sword before tossing it forward with all his might.

It still didn't go very far, hitting the floor before it even came close to touching Jose. "Shit." Without a shield or any hint of agility and so far up, he was done for.

Well, at least I tried....

It felt somewhat good to try, but he knew now he would be in a world full of hurt.

"I'm going to enjoy knocking the glitter right off your head," Jose said with a devilish smirk, winding back the dodgeball threateningly. Confirmed.

"No head shots!" Jack quickly said, stretching both arms out in front of his face.

Jose only laughed, obviously not caring about the rules, only wanting to cause him pain. But *why*? Was it because Jack was better-looking? Because Jack was too good an artist? It couldn't be the glitter, could it? What did glitter ever do to Jose? What did *he* ever do to Jose?

Squeezing his eyes shut, he prepared for the worst, but after a couple of seconds passed and nothing happened, he opened them to find Jose on the floor, hands cupped around his nuts, squealing in pain.

Everyone laughed.

He would've too, if he wasn't suddenly overwhelmed by the same chill he'd felt in the locker room, just as strange, just as random, his insides vibrating like strings of a guitar being strummed.

Maybe because of the cool breath he felt on his neck.

"*Bien hecho*," Roberto said in a sarcastic tone that made Jack roll his eyes as he turned to face him.

Of course it had been Roberto, looking for any opportunity to show off with his perfect Spanish and aim. What next? Still, he owed him one. *Again.*

"Want to try moving next time?" Roberto suggested, his arrogance making Jack's skin crawl in agitation.

Despite that damn smirk on Roberto's face, he swallowed the lump in his throat, his pride, to say the right thing. "Thanks... and...." He could feel the pride climbing back up like vomit, wanting to stand up for himself until he realized he was out of excuses. He had just given up, tossed whatever chance he had of being helpful, no matter how little, down the drain just to not look stupid. *Selfish!* "Yeah. I will."

"Good. Now get your head in the game! We can still win this if we work as a team.... *Move!*"

Roberto dragged him back by the collar of his shirt and out of harm's way when he didn't immediately jump to action. And he kind of liked it, feeling included, cared for, not that he could let Roberto know that.

"Hey, no manhandling! I got this!" snapped Jack, breaking free from Roberto's undermining grasp even though he didn't mind. In fact, it was probably the closest to being swept off his feet as he was going to get. *Sigh....* "Oh crap!" yelped Jack as he dove out of the way of an incoming dodgeball—successfully, much to his surprise. *Score.*

OUT OF three games, they won two, and even if he hadn't been the MVP by any stretch of the imagination, it felt pretty damn good to contribute for once. He had sweat stains to prove it, and a floor-burned knee from diving so many times—scars of honor. He had considered taking a shower but ultimately voted against it. He could barely keep himself from looking at guys in their underwear; he'd surely look in the shower, probably stare, or *worse.*

Better just swipe his armpits a few times with deodorant and call himself clean. Besides, smelling bad and feeling icky was the least of his concerns... concerns that only grew throughout the day. He had to tell Gari.

"GARI, GARI, Gari!" shouted Jack from across the hallway after he got out of his last class, charging through the tide of students like a crazed bull to reach her.

"Roberto is gay. He's *gay!*" he whispered into the ear he had nearly collided into, sounding both excited and frantic. Excited to know he wasn't alone and frantic to not know what to do now.

Gari's eyes widened, as he expected them to. Who would have guessed, Roberto being the hotshot soccer player that he was? Jack hadn't seen it coming either, although he guessed he should have by the way Roberto would slap his friends' butts in gym class.

"Shut up, no way," Gari said in disbelief.

"And you said you had a good gaydar, *pfft!*" Jack crossed his arms, chuckling.

"Oh, hush. I knew about you, didn't I?"

"Yeah, after almost a year of dating me."

"*Whatever*," she retorted bitterly, giving him a playful yet strong shove to the chest. "I'm still mad you didn't tell me sooner."

"I told you, I thought it was just a phase. I'm *sorry.*" He gave her a second to respond before asking, "Are you over it now?"

Gari released a sigh so exaggerated that he knew she couldn't possibly be that worked up over it. "I *guess....*"

"Yeah, you are. Now help me. I'm totally freaking out. I don't know what to do! I don't know what to do," rambled Jack, fear painted across his face.

"Are you *sure* he's gay? You're probably freaking out over nothing. Did he tell you?"

"*No....*"

"Well, then you don't know. *Phew,*" Gari exhaled, wiping the worry off her brow. "Don't scare me, Jack. He's supposed to be *my* boyfriend."

Jack shook his head like a wet dog, confused. "What? Since *when*?"

"You *know* I've always had a crush on him."

No, the truth was that he didn't know. Gari had far too many crushes for him to keep track.

"Yeah, well, now he's mine. *Sooo*—" He paused, wagging a threatening finger at her. "—back off." It was hard to put things nicely when he felt betrayed. Gari knew how badly he wanted his first kiss from a *guy*. She was the only one who knew. "*Jeez*, whatever happened to being happy for me?"

"Happy for you? You don't even know that he's gay!"

"I just *know*, okay? That's what I wished for, to know when guys are gay. I just keep getting this... feeling whenever I'm around him. Every time."

"Are you sure those aren't just the butterflies in your stomach?" she suggested skeptically. What happened to her being the superstitious one?

"It can't be. It never happened before today, and I don't even like him, really."

"Oh really? I remember you telling me once that he was hotter than the seeds of a jalapeño and that you'd bang him if you had the chance."

Jaw dropping as he realized his secrets were being poured out into the busy hallway, ready to be collected by any passerby, Jack quickly smothered Gari's mouth with his hand before she could say another word.

"Gari!" Jack scolded her with paranoid eyes, whipping his head around in every direction to see if anyone had been listening. They seemed more interested in getting the heck out of school, thank God.

"Maybe you're starting to like him?" She spoke through the spaces between his fingers before pushing his hand away. "He did save your butt today. Pretty heroic."

"But I felt *it*—whatever *it* is—before that happened, in the locker room. I think it works like Spider-Man's spidey sense, only instead of sensing danger, I can sense gays," he stated, sounding certain, "and he wasn't heroic! He was just showing off like always."

Whether Roberto was gay or not didn't change that; how could no one but Jack see his flaws? That he was nothing more than an attention whore... a really good-looking and talented attention whore.

"I should record how crazy you sound right now. Madame Myrtle was a con artist, remember? She stole your wallet! She threw *glitter* on you. She can't grant wishes."

"The glitter," said Jack with a raised finger of sudden understanding. "It has to be because of the glitter. I can never wash my hair again."

"You have got to be kidding me," Gari said incredulously before she grabbed him by the shoulders and tried to shake sense back into him. "Earth to Jack. We miss you down here. When are you coming home? I know it's stuffy in your box, but I'd prefer you in there where I can visit than in crazy land."

"Gari, I'm perfectly sane," he said with a huff of frustration, pulling away from her.

"The real crazy ones don't know they're crazy," she said matter-of-factly. "I would know; my dad's a psychologist. It's all in your head, Jack!"

"No, it's not!"

"*See?* Denial."

Jack groaned. "Then how do you explain how she knew my name, *hmm*?"

"I don't know. Maybe she looked at last year's school yearbook and memorized all the names and faces to be more convincing. Maybe *that's* why there's a student discount."

Now *Gari* sounded crazy, but he couldn't argue that point since having an eidetic memory was much less unheard of than having wish-granting powers. "I can't believe you right now," Jack fumed, blowing air out of his nose.

"Well, until you bring me proof that he's gay, I can't believe you either." She crossed her arms stubbornly, her chin raised high.

It sucked not having his best friend believe him but filled him with even more motivation to prove that his instincts were right, even if it meant coming out to someone he didn't know well.

"Fine, I *will*! See you tomorrow."

With that, he turned on his heel, his eyes narrowing as he scanned the hallway in search of Roberto. He had to do it quick, like tearing off a Band-Aid. If he didn't do it right now, in this heated moment, he never would. Plus, he had a bus to catch.

Maintain the heat, maintain the heat, thought Jack desperately as he tightened the grip of his backpack straps.

Sooner than expected, he spotted a relatively short yet built boy with a familiar head of crew-cut black hair walking down the hall with a big athletic bag slung over one shoulder and a backpack over the other. Just looking at him from the back gave Jack chills.

"Oh my gosh, there he is," he spat out, spinning back around to face Gari with a terrified look.

But she wasn't there…. *Oh no.*

He took in a breath of calm, of confidence, clinging to whatever heat hadn't left him. *You can do this. If all else fails, you can just say you were joking or… something.*

"Hey, Roberto!" called Jack, waving an arm above the crowd to get his attention. He trembled internally with every step he took closer, a shy smile plastered on his face.

"Can I help you? *Again?*"

"Uh...." *Abort, abort!* Jack's brain warned him to back out now while he still could, but his heart was desperate to escape the stuffiness of his box, to hop on the ship of opportunity and go to the wide-open sea where he'd have all the room in the world to spread his legs and *breathe.*

"I just wanted to ask...."

Abort, abort!

"I mean, yes, you can. You see, I need to pick a theme and a model to draw for my art class, and I thought you in your soccer uniform would be perfect. Oh, a soccer ball under your arm would look even more perfect."

"Question.... Will your drawing be on display?"

"It could be! Most likely," said Jack with a few nods and a reassuring smile, knowing how much Roberto liked to be seen. "There's a glass showcase in front of the classroom that the teacher puts the best art pieces of his students in. I've been making it to the showcase ever since freshman year."

Roberto looked impressed for a fleeting moment before speaking. "That was my second question... if you were any good of an artist. Because I don't want you drawing me ugly, because you know I'm not." There was that damn smirk again. "Tell me I'm not," he dared.

Gladly.

"You're...." Wait a second. Was Roberto flirting with him? Or was he just being his cocky self? Just in case— "I can't lie."

Roberto burst out laughing; he was obviously flattered, smiling widely until he glanced down at his watch. "Shit. I gotta get to soccer practice."

The next thing he knew, Roberto was reaching into Jack's bulging pocket and pulling out his cell phone to plug in his phone number. "Text me! I want to see my face in that showcase."

Then he was gone, and Jack was left wondering what the heck just happened before realizing he was running late too.

"Shit!" He broke into a sprint down the mostly empty hall, beelining for his school bus that he prayed was still waiting outside for him.

JACK ALWAYS loved his basement. It could've been totally boring, with its solid white walls, if it wasn't decorated with more than a dozen wooden ducks his grandfather had carved and painted by hand and a cluttering of big brown boxes full of childhood memories and other storage items his hoarder of a mom didn't want to get rid of. There was a lot more free space in the center of the room. There stood a cushioned stool in front of the drawing easel his parents had recently bought him, along with a slew of coloring supplies. Everything he needed to excel as an artist.

He was lucky.

He knew not many parents would be so accepting of such a financially risky career choice, but it was what Jack loved, and his parents could see that. Maybe if they saw how much he loved boys, they would accept that too.

His basement was also home to the most comfortable gray leather couch in the world, which he was sprawled out on, belly up, as he waited anxiously for Roberto to text him back.

He had thought that once he knew someone was gay, it'd be smooth sailing from there, but now he was realizing there was so much more to it. Like how was he supposed to ask Roberto out *without* lying about needing a model to draw for his latest art project? What if Roberto didn't like him? What if he said *no*? It was entirely possible, him being a hot, popular athlete while Jack was a skinny-ass unpopular artist with unruly hair that was currently full of glitter, hardly attractive in comparison.

Beep beep!

Jack's entire being awoke at the sound of his cell phone, electricity zipping through his body as the text message he had long waited for finally arrived.

Here.

Another jolt sent him leaping off the couch and running up the stairs. He felt chills racing up and down his spine before he even opened the door to greet Roberto, who had, as he'd said he would, come straight from soccer practice, his face glistening with sweat.

"Hey," said Jack, offering a smile.

"Yo," said Roberto, too cool to smile back.

"Call me when you're ready to be picked up! *No tan tarde*, okay? I'm making your favorite for dinner!" shouted Roberto's mother from her cute bright red Volkswagen Beetle.

His hand twitched. If he were better friends with Roberto, he would've punched him in the shoulder and said "punch buggy no punch back," but they weren't. Roberto had his soccer friends, and Jack had... Gari. What was he thinking bringing Roberto to his house? It was going to be *so awkward*.

"Let's just get this over with," Roberto said after waving good-bye to his mom, inviting himself in. "I want *arroz y habichuelas*." When Jack looked puzzled, he added, "Rice and beans."

"*Oh*," he said with a nervous chuckle before leading the way to the basement. "So this is my basement...." Jack tried to make small talk, but Roberto was apparently not kidding about wanting to hurry things up. Probably tired and hungry from spending hours outside running around in the beating sun. Jack guessed he couldn't blame him.

"Yeah, it's beautiful. Where can I change?"

"Umm... there's a bathroom upstairs. I'll show you where...."

"No time," Roberto insisted as he zipped open his athletic bag to pull out a soccer ball that would be used as a prop and his soccer uniform. He already had his cleats, long red socks, and shin guards on.

"Wait, you're going to change here?" asked Jack stupidly, so not prepared for this.

"Yeah, why not? We're all guys here, aren't we?"

Why are you trying to stop him from changing in front of you? His brain scolded him.

"Right." He nodded before moving toward his drawing easel to make sure his pencil was sharpened. It was, giving him nothing better to do than watch Roberto strip off his shirt. Firm pecs. Visible abdominal muscles. Dark, sexy skin. He could feel his jaw sinking down to the wood floor, along with his thirsty tongue, but he couldn't stop it.

Roberto paused before pulling down his pants. "Are you... drooling over me, Jack?"

"What? No." He shook his head in denial, averting his gaze.

"Girls drool over me all the time, but a *guy* drooling over me? That's new."

Jack tried to swallow the lump of nervousness in his throat but failed, choking on it. He wanted to deny it, to tell Roberto not to flatter himself and brush it off as though it never happened, but Jack was sick of doing that. He *wanted* something to happen. He wanted someone other than Gari to know he was gay, whether Roberto liked him back or not.

"I didn't say new was bad."

Roberto smirked, and this time Jack knew for a fact he was flirting as the sexy Puerto Rican teen approached him, still shirtless.

Oh my gosh, oh my gosh, oh my gosh.

Jack's face was blank as he tried to digest what was happening. So he was right all along—Roberto was gay, and the gypsy had granted him the power to know that. Or it had all just been psychological like Gari said, but who cared? What mattered was that Roberto was gay and, by the looks of it, was interested in being more than friends.

"So... you like me?" Jack finally popped the question when Roberto was only inches away from his face, feeling like a frantic bird was trapped underneath his rib cage as his heart hammered away.

"Well, *yeah*. Why do you think I did all those favors for you?"

"To show off...."

"*And*... because I thought you were cute. But I didn't expect you to like me back."

Jack couldn't stop himself from smiling like an idiot, nor did he want to. "I thought you wouldn't like *me* back."

"Well, what do you think about *this*?" Roberto closed the rest of the gap between them with a kiss of passion, running his hand through Jack's thick head of curly, glittery hair.

Glitter fell onto both their faces like a gentle snowfall, not that Jack noticed. He melted internally as Roberto arched his way farther into his mouth, his eyelids snapping shut in sheer pleasure.

There it was. His first kiss... from a *guy*.... I *can't wait to tell Gari!*

Feeling his shirt being lifted, he seized the opportunity to even the playing field of violation by stroking what was bulging out of Roberto's tiny soccer shorts until his arms were forced up as his shirt came over his head. More glitter was launched into the air and fluttered back down by gravity.

Eyes flickering back open to relocate Roberto's plump lips, he noticed this time. "Oops." His hand traveled along Roberto's sunwarmed torso, collecting the sparkly pieces of glitter on his fingertips to show him.

Roberto chuckled, wrapping a finger around one of his glittery curls. "Glitterhead. Why—"

"It's a long story. I'll tell you later." Jack cut him off, not wanting to ruin this perfect moment by worrying about whether Roberto believed him or not.

"You better."

The next thing he knew, he was being pushed down onto the couch and stripped of his jeans. He was about to say something before Roberto paralyzed him with kisses, kisses that then traced their way down his neck and chest to his crotch region.

"Too fast," he spat out, quickly moving his curious hands from Roberto's meaty butt to his bright yellow boxer briefs to keep them from being pulled down.

"Sorry…. It's just that I've never sucked a dick before."

"And I've never had my dick sucked before…. There is a first time for everything." Jack grinned, making a hand gesture that said *please do, continue.*

"Honey, I'm home!" announced his mother as she entered the house the moment his throbbing dick became engulfed by a warm, moist mouth.

"*Fuck!*" Jack shoved Roberto off him, scrambling to get all his clothes back on before his mom came downstairs like she always did to greet him should he be working in the basement.

"She's coming! Where's my shirt?"

"Oops," said Roberto when he realized he had put it on by mistake.

Hearing the door creak open, Jack grabbed the shirt closest to him, Roberto's white jersey, which had red stripes on the sleeves and the number nine in red on the front, from the floor and weaseled into it as quickly as possible.

Fuck, fuck, fuck!

Mentally cursing, he frantically sprinted behind his easel and picked up his pencil to pretend to be drawing Roberto, who was holding his soccer ball to his abdomen to add to the effect... and cover his boner.

His heart pounded harder with every clack of his mother's high heels as she strode down the staircase, her ironed straight brown hair unmoving. She had just come back from work, dressed in a business suit.

"Oh, hello." She gave the glitter-skinned boy with the soccer ball a wave from the bottom of the staircase. She seemed to have difficulty maintaining the friendly smile she had slapped on once she made eye contact with her disobedient son, who wasn't allowed to bring guests without asking permission first. "Jack, you didn't tell me you were bringing a friend over. And why are you wearing that?"

"I don't have to tell you *everything*, do I?" he argued, wanting nothing more than for her to get lost so he could get back to doing what he was doing in peace.

He shouldn't have argued. Now she was never going to leave.

"Oh yes, you do. I am your mother, and I have a right to know everything about you. *Everything*."

Sighing in frustration, he wanted to tell her now, in this heated moment, what he had been hiding from her and the rest of his family for *years*. Once and for all. But not with Roberto there; it was too personal to be said in front of a guest.

"In that case, I have something to tell you.... But can you give me and Roberto a second alone, *please*?" He asked so nicely his mom couldn't say no; she just gave him a worried look and closed the door behind her as she left.

Setting down the pencil he had been clutching for dear life ever since his mother barged in, he rushed over to Roberto to give him another kiss.

"I'll see you tomorrow at school?" Jack reluctantly pulled away to ask.

"Definitely," replied Roberto, actually smiling as he took ahold of both Jack's hands. He usually only ever smirked, as though he were superior to everyone else. "And then after school, to finish where we left off? I really do want to see myself in that showcase."

"Definitely." Jack returned the smile, then tightened his grip around Roberto's hands to pull him in for one last kiss. Lip-locked, he felt as though they were the only two people in existence, until three loud knocks on the basement door snapped him back into reality.

"Good luck telling your mom."

"Thanks, I'm going to need it.... Whatever happens, at least I'll still have you."

AFTER THE stressful yet liberating talk with his mom, Jack went straight to the bathroom and took a good, long look in the mirror.

Long glittery curls dangling in front of his eyes, he wanted to see himself as a free man, brighter in a way from having courageously stepped outside of his box, out of the shadows, and into the light. But there was something annoyingly foreign about him, something he'd thought he needed before realizing he had the power all along to find gay guys at school. He didn't need magic glitter; all he had to do was ask. Nor did he need to rely on his "Jew-fro" to separate him from everyone else, to express himself. He'd be expressing himself plenty once he started holding hands with Roberto at school.

"Thank you, Madame Myrtle... for nothing."

He swiped the scissors off of the shelf and began cutting his hair left and right, until every single particle of glitter was on the bathroom floor.

BENJAMIN SHEPHERD QUIÑONES appeared to be no different from most boys his age growing up in suburban New Jersey. He loved climbing trees, playing soccer, and tormenting his younger sister. Little did people know he also really loved reading and writing science fiction/fantasy. Over the years, his interests have broadened to Latin dancing, being as openly gay as possible, and studying psychology with a concentration in clinical and behavioral health. He hopes to be a counseling psychologist after a few more years of schooling and of course continue writing.

He welcomes reader feedback at benjimon4427@gmail.com.

WAITING
ANNIE SCHOONOVER

AMY SUZUKI'S eighteenth birthday was looming over her like a tiger about to pounce. She felt like her life was slowly unraveling, like the old knitted blanket she used to sleep with when she was a kid. The strands that had long dangled at the end were slowly being pulled away. There went one, with her last college application sent out. There went another, when her last ever volleyball season ended. Soon there would be nothing left but a pathetic pile of yarn held together with spit and a prayer that her mom would throw it away when she wasn't looking.

It was worse than it should have been, because now that applications and volleyball were done, she had nothing to fill her time but homework. She'd stopped going to parties. She knew that was probably what she should be doing, going out every night and getting drunk and high with her friends for the last time (because soon they'd all be getting drunk and high in completely new places with completely new people, and it would be exactly the same but completely different in tiny yet freaking annoying ways) and making memories to carry her through the most awkward days of college. But somehow parties had lost their appeal to her. She suspected it had something to do with what had happened with her mother in the red-and-gold guest bedroom, although that had initially only made her want to get more drunk and high than ever. And it also had something to do with the anxiety that danced behind Tyler's brown eyes whenever Amy told her that she was going to a party. But it was more than that. It was something about how, in the morning, when all the empty bottles had been cleared away, she didn't feel like any more of an adult.

She hadn't had anything to do, so she'd taken up surfing. She'd resisted for as long as she could, because it had seemed so clichéd, because *of course* if you've grown up on Kauai, you know how to surf. It would be the first thing anyone she met in college would ask her. Now she would be denied the pleasure of giving everyone who asked her that her best fuck-you glare and saying no in a voice that would make them shut up and slink away. But what the hell, she could swim better than even most of the other kids who'd grown up on the island, and there wasn't much else to do in Hanalei.

It took her a while to admit it, but she loved surfing. She loved it even though it was winter and the ocean was rough with her. It pounded against her skin and slammed her into the beach, rubbing the sand into her skin, forcing her to remember it. It tossed her across the waves like she was nothing more than a grain of sand herself. (Unsettling thoughts came to her then, thoughts that suggested that really, wasn't that all she was to something as enormous as the ocean? She generally tried to avoid those thoughts.)

Tyler would probably compare the ocean to Hera or Poseidon, but Amy didn't think that quite fit, since the Greek gods were mostly glorified playground bullies anyway, and the ocean was more than that. Maybe it was growing up on an island, but Amy had always thought of the ocean as bigger than even a god. The ocean was life, life for the plants and animals that lived in it and the fishermen who consumed them. It was permanent, the breaking of the waves a constant background noise, the drumbeat in the song of Amy's life. And most importantly, it was all encompassing, surrounding and nearly swallowing Amy's home in its might, dealing life and death seemingly at random, drowning them out with its too-large, too-complex font of activity. No, the ocean was not a god. It was the world.

"WHAT DO you think love is?" Tyler mused from across the plastic-topped table. Sun streamed in from the open windows of the restaurant, bathing her in warmth and light. The restaurant was old-looking, wooden, and rickety, like a lot of buildings in Hanalei, and like a lot of buildings in Hanalei, it had a certain charm that sent tourists into fits of ecstasy.

At Tyler's words, Amy rolled her eyes.

"Question game," she said. Tyler obediently slid her fish tacos across the table. The question game was something Amy had come up with almost immediately after they started dating. Whenever Tyler asked something that Amy considered a "bullshit question," like "Is there a god?" or "Do you believe our destinies are controlled by the stars?", Tyler had to give Amy the rest of whatever she was eating. The game had been formed in response to "What is art?", a question Amy still hadn't quite forgiven Tyler for. (The question game was a lot less fun now that Amy worked at the taco restaurant, where there were about five things on the menu. Amy had been okay with fish tacos before, but now she wanted to invent a time machine just so she could go back and make sure the damn things had never been invented.)

"Seriously," said Tyler. "What do you think love is?"

Amy took a bite of the taco and grimaced. "Remind me again why we keep eating here," she complained.

"Employee discount," Tyler said. "And you're avoiding my question." She started sucking on a long, fluffy strand of doe-brown hair. There was a terribly earnest look in her big brown eyes, which wasn't unusual. Amy knew from experience that Tyler would bother her with this question until Amy gave her some sort of answer. She also knew that the question would nag at Tyler, tugging at the edges of her mind and distracting her from the mundane happenings of everyday life, until she stumbled upon an answer that satisfied her.

"Honestly?" said Amy, thinking about what had happened with her mother the day school had let out early and Amy had burst into the guest bedroom without warning. "I have no fucking clue."

"So you don't think we're in love?" Tyler said anxiously (and, ta-da, there it was, the question Tyler had *really* been asking).

Amy set her taco down and looked Tyler in the eye. "What are you looking for?" she asked point-blank. "Are you trying to start shit with me?"

"No!" said Tyler, looking irritated.

"Are you sure?" said Amy. "Because this is starting to feel a lot less like a question and a lot more like a trap."

"Well, it wasn't supposed to be," Tyler said heatedly. "Whatever. Forget it."

Amy knew Tyler hadn't meant anything by it. She knew that Tyler had been raised to believe in a certain kind of true love, love that came from burly knights in shining armor or football-playing teenage boys.

She knew it had always been a bit hard for her to reconcile that kind of love with the way she felt about Amy, who was tiny, snarky, angular, pierced, dyed, Asian, and decidedly female. But she couldn't seem to help picking at Tyler anyway.

"Hey," she said softly, reaching across the table and taking Tyler's hand. "I love you. You know that. But I don't know if I'm *in love* with you, if that makes sense."

Tyler nodded.

"Anyway, like, do we really have to know if we're in love *right now*?" Amy continued. She squeezed Tyler's hand gently. Reluctantly, Tyler smiled. This made Amy smile too, because Tyler's face was so round and so soft that it looked like it was made for smiling.

She ignored the tiny voice in her head whispering that she would need to know the answers to these questions *soon,* because her eighteenth birthday was coming, and then she would be an adult, officially, and *she wasn't ready.* Instead, she concentrated on Tyler and her smile and her eyes. *Forget about soon. Focus on now.*

TYLER'S QUESTION floated to the surface of Amy's mind later that night, as she lay on top of her black bedspread and listened to the waves breaking outside. Downstairs, she heard angry voices, her father's quiet accusations spoken in a voice that was beginning to roughen, and her mother's shrill defenses that climbed higher and higher, as if she were an opera singer straining to reach the climax of an aria. After years of ever-present tension, they were finally fighting.

Come on, Dad, Amy thought. *Fight her. Make her regret it.*

She reached for her iPod and pulled up the playlist Tyler had made for her. She hadn't heard of most of the bands, and the ones she had heard of she didn't particularly care for. She listened to it often anyway, though, because it made her feel like Tyler was lying in bed next to her, whispering in Amy's ear and wrapping her arms around Amy until they both fell asleep, safe and secure and warm. (Amy had made Tyler a playlist too, full of Daft Punk and Beyoncé and Pink. You know, music that was actually good, not just a bunch of dudes whining about how much their ex-girlfriends sucked and pounding on banjos like they were fucking electric guitars. She wondered how often Tyler listened to her playlist, or if she even had.)

The question floated past her again, like a leaf of seaweed in the ocean. *What do you think love is?* She used to think love was sort of like what her parents had. She'd thought that if you lived with someone for some time, and shared your life with them for some time, and you managed not to hurt them or leave them no matter how much you might want to, then eventually love sort of happened. But now that she knew that wasn't true, what was love? The words of the song seemed to answer her, as the singer sang about games and cons and tricks and broken roads. *Amen,* Amy thought, thinking of the barely muted argument occurring downstairs.

The singer started singing about seeing people's skeletons before they died. She remembered; she'd heard this song before. (She hadn't been sure. All the songs Tyler liked sounded the same.) It used to remind her of her older sister, Liz, and what had happened to her. But now it made her think of her mother, though she couldn't quite put her finger on why.

Then the singer sang about the person mentioned in the title, who was waiting silently for something. That was why. Waiting. Like her mother had been waiting in the red-and-gold guest room, waiting like the big bad wolf dressed like an old grandmother, lying in wait for Little Red Riding Hood. Except Little Red had walked in too early and caught the wolf, half-dressed and guilty, with Grandmother's blood still on his lips....

Amy abruptly paused the song, took out the earphones, and rolled over. She fell asleep thinking about waiting, and about the something that was waiting for her on her eighteenth birthday, the something with big teeth (the better to eat her with), the something that would unravel the rest of the blanket. She dreamed of breaking waves and waiting.

IT WOULDN'T be too farfetched to think that Amy and Tyler's first meeting was arranged by a higher power, or even the stars, if you believed in that sort of thing. The sky had been light blue, the ocean slightly darker, and the waves had been mild, splashing lightly across the sand that was flat as stretched pizza dough. Amy had been sitting in a chair on the beach, and not five feet away, so had Tyler. Amy had assumed she was a tourist and had not bothered talking to her. Tyler hadn't cared.

"Hey," she'd said, dropping onto the beach next to Amy. They'd taken a second to size each other up. Amy had taken in Tyler's wavy hair, her huge eyes, her moon-round face, her pudgy body that threatened to spill out of the cutesy pink bikini she wore. Tyler, she knew, had taken in Amy's skinny frame, her pointed chin, her copper-colored skin, the red streak dyed in her shoulder-length black hair, her sharp black eyes, the same color as her sleek swimming shirt.

"Hey," Amy had said edgily, trying to convey as much why-are-you-talking-to-me as she could in one word.

"We're reading the same book," she'd said.

Amy had looked down. So they were.

"So," Tyler had said, smiling in anticipation, "what do you think of it?"

"I hate it," she'd said. She didn't, but she was embarrassed that she liked it so much. It may have been the most boring, lame, girly book she'd ever read, but the main character was a bisexual Asian girl. She'd read it three times.

Tyler's face had fallen. "But... but...," she'd said, scrambling for some way to defend her book. Amy remembered thinking it was kind of cute, how upset she had gotten. (She also thought, with some unease, how easy it would have been for Tyler to leave right then, and how she had almost ruined everything just because she couldn't admit she liked that stupid book.)

Luckily, Tyler was observant.

"You do not hate it," she'd said, her face breaking into a wide grin (it was the first time Amy had noticed how her face was made perfectly for smiling). "I can tell. You're too into it. And that book looks like it's been read, like, fifty times."

"Well, I don't like it," Amy had muttered.

"Just as long as you don't *hate* it," said Tyler, so very seriously, as if hating a book was the worst crime imaginable.

Amy couldn't help it. She laughed, which made Tyler laugh too, because Tyler was the type of person who laughed when other people laughed.

Tyler hadn't been a tourist. Her family had just moved to the island a week ago. Her father, Ian McNeely, owned a chain of fast food restaurants called Frank's Fries. They had allegedly moved to Hanalei to oversee a new branch that had opened. (Although when Amy met boisterous, twinkly-eyed Mr. McNeely, she'd thought he was exactly the type to wake up one morning, look out his window, and think, "Screw this, let's move to Hawaii.") That was a little over two years ago.

IT WAS hard for some people to tell when it was winter in Hanalei. It didn't snow or grow colder. The only difference was that the ocean became deadlier, the rip currents a little bit stronger (and, well, the ocean was wild and unforgiving on the best of days). But in the Suzuki house, especially lately, it always felt like winter.

Amy had never noticed, or had pretended not to notice, the chill that constantly hung over her house, the chill that had only grown colder and hardened into frost and icicles once Liz left. She might have tried to ignore it, but even though she was constantly surrounded by the tropical Hawaiian air, in her own house, she'd always felt the way she'd felt the time they had gone to visit her mother's old college friend in Maine in the winter: cold. A frigid, bone-snapping, brittle kind of cold.

And now, the ice was beginning to snap in half, and her mother was unsuccessfully trying to bring spring to the house.

"Do you want to go shopping, Amy?" she'd say hesitantly at dinner, sitting across from her at the brown kitchen table by the window, high-heeled shoes tapping nervously on the blue tiles. "I saw there was a sale on those jeans you liked." Or, "The weather looks nice today. Would you like to go down to the beach?" Amy always glared and shook her head. *Don't forget, I saw what you did,* she tried to convey in the glare. *In the red-and-gold guest bedroom. I saw what you did, and I'm not about to forget it.* Her father, usually working on the accounts for the hotel he worked for at the kitchen table, said nothing.

Amy wasn't accustomed to this sort of groveling from her mother. Short-haired, pant-suited Mrs. Suzuki, with her bright red lipstick and impeccable makeup, was usually as poised and elegant as a real-estate agent should be. It made Amy a bit uncomfortable, honestly, but there was no way she was giving in. Not after what her mother had done.

The thing that upset her the most was that her father knew, and she suspected that he'd known the whole time. And he had never said anything. Her squat, soft-spoken, bespectacled father had never been one to look for a fight, but it was ridiculous, what he was letting her mother get away with. That was why she was almost glad her parents were fighting. It meant her father was standing up for himself.

She thought of all the late nights when her father had driven her home from volleyball practice. She thought of how she would look forward to those nights, because she could explode into a rant about her homework or her friends or whatever was bothering her. Her father would always listen and nod, would always let her know that he cared about her (unlike her mother, who would always butt in with advice that Amy hadn't asked for). Now, looking at him, she wondered if he had someone who listened to him.

It was starting to become stressful to be at her own house. It was bad enough that the house was always quiet and peaceful, and whenever Amy didn't have something occupying her, the worrying set in, the sense that something was coming, that a storm was waiting on the horizon. That the big bad wolf was lurking in the woods, waiting for her to let her guard down. And the sense of unraveling was stronger at her house too. Whenever she looked at her parents and felt their frosted silence, she felt like another thread was being yanked from the blanket.

But the worst was the white-hot fury she felt whenever she saw them, sitting next to each other at the kitchen table, her mother tapping her high-heeled shoes against the blue tiles and her father scratching away at his accounts, neither of them looking at each other or acknowledging the other's presence. *Why don't you just leave?* Amy wanted to scream. *This isn't love! I don't know what love is, but this sure as hell isn't it!* When she felt like that, she wanted to run out onto the beach and throw herself into the water until the waves had pounded her clean.

WHENEVER AMY thought about love, she thought about her and Tyler's first kiss, and how Tyler had tasted like hot dogs.

She thought about the day the McNeelys (Tyler's parents and then-twelve twin brothers, Casey and Riley) had invited her to go on a hike with them. Mrs. McNeely was a robust Irish Catholic woman who looked like she could climb three mountains before breakfast and then go kayaking after, just for the hell of it. She'd assured Amy it was going to be a nice, easy hike, but Mrs. McNeely's definition of easy was radically different from Amy's.

At first it hadn't been so bad, just a white sand path surrounded by lush greenery and delicate flowers that looked like they had been frosted onto cupcakes. Then, suddenly, the right side of the path became a sheer cliffside, forcing Amy to inch along, holding on to the pineapple bark of the palm trees for support. Tyler's brothers laughed at her, but she ignored them.

Then the path disappeared altogether, and a huge rock loomed in their way. It seemed that, to continue, they would have to climb over it. The McNeelys clambered over easily, like monkeys. Even Tyler had already swung her legs over when she looked back to see if Amy was coming.

Amy looked at the sheer drop to her right, at the cliff face lined with jagged rock-teeth and the water that bubbled like hot soup below. Eyes wide, she looked at Tyler and shook her head.

"You're afraid of heights?" Tyler said. Amy nodded. Tyler smiled and said, "Huh."

"What?" Amy said.

"You've never admitted to being afraid of something to me before."

Amy had rolled her eyes.

"Anyway, you can't go back," said Tyler.

"Yes I can," said Amy, attempting to wipe away the mixture of sweat and sunscreen that dripped down her face like melted butter.

"It's okay," said Tyler. "I'll just pull you over." So casually. As if it were no big deal. As if Amy couldn't practically hear the boiling ocean below calling her name.

"Oh, come on," Tyler said. "You trust me, right? It's not like I'm going to drop you or anything." And suddenly, Amy realized that she did trust this girl she'd known for all of six weeks. Slowly, cautiously, she approached Tyler and placed her tiny hands in the other girl's large ones. Looking at Tyler, you'd think her hands would be soft, but they were hard and sturdy and strong.

Amy sucked in a breath as she felt her feet lift off the ground. She felt her stomach scrape against the stone through her thin black cami. The chirping of the birds and the heat of the sun, once just pleasant background sensations, seemed to grow louder and stronger and more oppressive. Amy couldn't look down. She couldn't close her eyes. She couldn't do this.

But she did. Because of Tyler. Because Tyler held on tight and didn't let go.

And eventually, when they arrived at the clifftop at the end of the trail, all that hiking and climbing turned out to be worth it.

Amy and Tyler sat on the brown, brittle stones at the edge of the cliff and looked down on the water. The sun was high in the sky and shining down on her, giving her soft brown hair a preternatural glow, like a halo. At the bottom of the cliff, the water near the shore was a bright, light blue that didn't look real. And behind them, the trees were so lush and green that they didn't look real. And Tyler in front of her was so beautiful that she didn't look quite real either. So when Amy leaned in to kiss her, and Tyler nervously kissed back, her first thought was that she was dreaming. But she soon realized she wasn't, because Tyler tasted like hot dogs, and when you dreamed about kissing a beautiful girl at the top of a cliff, she definitely didn't taste like hot dogs. So Amy closed her eyes and enjoyed everything, the salt in the air and the feeling of Tyler's hand cupping her back and the bliss and desire that pooled in her stomach and spilled over to the rest of her body. And especially the taste of hot dogs.

IT WAS a cool, clear Friday night, and the moon shone like Tyler's face in the sky. This time last year, Amy would have been at a party on the beach getting drunk as shit, but tonight she was lying on her bed, listening to that "Another is Waiting" song and thinking about Liz.

That song had started to grow on her. The band too. The Avett Brothers. Most of their songs on the playlist were halfway decent. Less whining, more poetry. She could see why Tyler liked them.

Liz called every Friday, because their parents worried about her, even though she was twenty-six and living with her boyfriend and her best friend in California. There was always the possibility of a relapse.

Liz always insisted on talking to Amy, even though the last time Amy had seen her, Amy was seven, and Liz was sixteen and sick enough to be rushed to the hospital. Their conversations were increasingly short, awkward, and predictable. They saw each other a few times a year, if that. They were sisters in name only.

She did remember the day Liz had been taken to the hospital, her mother's horrified scream-gasp when she'd found Liz unconscious in the bathroom. The unshed tears in her father's eyes when he got off the phone with the doctor, the way he'd pulled her onto his lap and rocked her back in forth, trying to reassure both of them that it would all be okay.

She remembered the day they'd taken Liz to the airport, too. That day hadn't been so sad, because she hadn't known that she wouldn't see Liz again except on holidays for a long time. Her mother had told her that Liz was being taken to a special hospital in California just for girls like her. Amy hadn't understood words like "anorexia" and "severe malnourishment" then.

She didn't know if Liz had caused the problems with her mother, or if her mother had caused the problems with Liz, or if their separate demons had just fed off each other, like parasites. And she had to wonder why Liz had stayed gone, even after she'd recovered. Why she'd barely bothered to come home before jetting off to college. Had her mother and Liz loved each other at all?

She was almost certain she had loved Liz when she was seven. She knew because, when they'd taken Liz to the airport, she'd clung to Liz's leg and refused to let go.

That night, she dreamed of singing skeletons and breaking waves that called her name.

TYLER SOMETIMES came with Amy when she went surfing. She didn't surf herself, of course. She had confessed to Amy that she was terrified of the ocean and could barely swim. ("Then why the fuck did you move to an island?" Amy had said jokingly.) But she did like to watch Amy. Amy needed a break, anyway. Her parents had been stiffly cordial to each other all week, and she couldn't take another second of the frost.

The lifeguard was Danny Mahelona, a sweet, dorky guy Amy had dated in eighth grade. The bright sun made the water sparkle and the sand glow and attracted tourists like fat, stupid moths to a lantern (even though the water was so rough today that part of the beach had been sectioned off). Danny had his hands full trying to keep track of all of them. He waved to Amy and Tyler.

"So, what? You're just going to sit here?" said Amy.

"That's the plan," said Tyler, settling down gently in the sand.

"It's going to be fucking boring," said Amy.

"Not really," said Tyler. "You always look so happy when you surf." Amy couldn't hold back a smile. Some days, she felt beyond lucky to have Tyler as a girlfriend.

Just before she was about to run out into the water, though, she noticed something. A kid was playing in the water in the sectioned-off part of the beach, right next to a stream that was a lot lighter than the rest of the water. A stream that looked suspiciously like a rip current, a dangerous current that yanked swimmers so far out into the water that most never managed to get back to shore.

She looked around for Danny, but he was on the other side of the beach, watching an old man who was attempting to boogie board. So she ran toward the kid, scooped him up, and deposited him on the beach. She inspected the stream. Along the light-colored line, pieces of seaweed were swiftly being pulled out to sea. She inhaled deeply, then sighed. It had been a near miss.

Just then, a middle-aged woman with sunscreen on her face tapped Amy on the shoulder.

"Excuse me," she said, full of righteous indignation and entitlement. "What exactly are you doing with my son?" And that was when Amy snapped.

"Do you see that?" she said furiously, pointing at the red ropes that had sectioned off part of the beach. "That means that your kid is not allowed to play here. That means that you should not have let him in the water. Do you understand what I'm saying? He could have died! Your son could have fucking died because you were too fucking selfish to read the fucking signs!" Shocked, the woman stepped back, opened her mouth, closed it, then walked away. Amy knew her face was turning bright red and her eyes were watering and that she probably sounded like a kid having a tantrum, but she didn't care. She was too angry, because who the fuck put these dumbass adults in charge of kids anyway? Who let these fucked-up people make all the decisions? Why did they get to be in charge? What the hell gave them the right?

She felt Tyler's hand (hard and sturdy and strong) on her shoulder and whirled around. Tyler pulled her into a hug, and for a second, Amy let herself collapse against her. Then Tyler murmured, "Do you want to go home?" into Amy's ear, and Amy pulled away, because *no,* she didn't want to go home. She didn't think she was going home ever again.

"I came here to surf," she said, "and I am going to fucking surf." She ran back to her board, grabbed it, and dived into the water.

The ocean was gentle with her that day, as if it realized she wanted a good cry more than anything. Instead of slamming her into the sand, the waves deposited her gently on the beach. When she finally got out of the water (to go to Tyler, who was still waiting for her with a dry towel and a comforting arm and a pickup truck that would take her anywhere but home), the waves pooled around her feet, tugging at them, as if trying to coax her back in, or seduce her.

That night, she dreamed that the surf was calling her name.

TYLER HAD cried when Amy first told her that she was bi.

In fairness, it had been pretty late. They were having one of their semiannual Disney movie-watching sleepovers (because Amy thought that if you thought you were too old to enjoy a Disney movie, then you needed to get over yourself). They'd been dating for about three months, but their parents still didn't take their relationship quite seriously, so they'd been able to sleep at each other's houses.

They'd been swapping secrets, Tyler cocooned in her purple sleeping bag, Amy lying on top of her red one, when Amy had explained bisexuality to Tyler. And Tyler had cried.

"Hey, what's the matter?" Amy had said, genuinely curious. "It doesn't mean I don't like you or anything."

"You could date a boy," Tyler had sniffled. "You could go to prom without people staring at you. You could have a fairy-tale wedding and kids. You could have a high school romance. Like in *Grease.*"

"I hate that movie," Amy said automatically. Tyler let out a small sob and buried her face in her pillow. Concerned, Amy scooted closer to Tyler, unzipped her sleeping bag, and started rubbing her back.

Tyler had three moles on her back, one above the seventh vertebra of her spine, one just below her left shoulder, and one on the right side of her neck. Amy had memorized them, just like she had memorized the way Tyler liked to have her back rubbed (gently, just beneath her shoulder blades).

"Why don't you just go date a boy?" Tyler was saying. "Just go date a boy and be happy."

"Screw boys," Amy had said sleepily, massaging Tyler's back. "I don't care about boys. I don't care about any girl who isn't you, either. You want me to be happy? Then stay here. Just stay right here."

"I will," Tyler had whispered. "I will, I will, I will."

TIME PASSED. Tyler and Amy were both accepted into the University of California, which meant, among other things, that Amy could stop pretending to care about her homework. Two more threads pulled out. The blanket was unraveling faster now.

That sense of something coming, something hanging, poised, waiting just beyond the horizon, was growing. She had to stop listening to the "Another is Waiting" song, because it just freaked her out too much. She knew it wasn't supposed to be threatening, but it freaked her out anyway. It didn't end up mattering, though. She'd listened to the song so much that it was permanently imprinted in her brain, as much a part of her as the sand under her fingernails. It floated in and out of her head during the day and weaved itself into her dreams at night (the dreams of skeletons floating in the breaking waves and wolves hiding in red-and-gold guest bedrooms).

Still, her eighteenth birthday loomed. She was terrified of what was coming, of all the responsibility and change and unraveling that it symbolized, and the only thing she had left to distract herself with was surfing. She surfed so much that the movement of the waves became a part of her too, and she felt like she was being yanked up and down through the water even when she left the ocean. This sensation, combined with the sound of breaking waves, was mesmerizing, like a mermaid's song. And like a mermaid's song, it kept luring her back to the ocean again.

A week after her acceptance letter came in, her mom asked her if she wanted to go out for coffee. Amy said yes.

She said yes partly because of the day on the beach where that kid had almost drowned, and Amy had realized she was growing up and couldn't keep expecting adults to live up to the standards she'd set for them. She'd realized that her mother was a person, a person as emotional and fucked-up as she was, a person who had made a bad decision and had suffered the consequences. That didn't mean Amy forgave her mother, but it meant Amy didn't hate her either.

And she said yes partly because of the birthday waiting to pounce. Because of the letter she had gotten that ensured that she would soon be far, far away from her mother, so she should at least attempt to end things on a good note.

They sat outside under a red umbrella, her mother nervously tapping her high-heeled shoe against the bricks. They'd talked about stupid things that didn't matter, like school and the weather and neighborhood gossip, and Amy managed to stop herself from yelling or screaming or running away. She began to relax, just enough to open up a little bit.

"God, I can't wait to get off this damn island," she caught herself saying, then snapped her mouth shut, because that was personal, and her mother had officially given up any right to be involved in her personal life. Her mother smiled apologetically.

"Away from me?" she said.

Amy looked her in the eye. "Yes," she replied, folding her arms.

Her mother shrugged, slightly, sadly. "I suppose I deserve it," she said, and Amy felt a stab of guilt. She wondered if that meant she still loved her mother, or if she was just beginning to grow up.

QUESTIONS. CONFUSION. Waiting.

The questions pelted her like fat, heavy raindrops on her eighteenth birthday. They buzzed through her mind, tiny bugs looking for something to bite into, and she couldn't shoo them away.

What was she planning to do after high school?

What was she planning to do with her life?

If she was an official adult, why did she seem so unprepared?

If she was eighteen already, then why did she still feel like something was coming, like the storm hadn't yet broken?

How was she going to avoid making the same mistakes as her parents?

Did her parents love each other?

Did she love Tyler?

And what was love, anyway?

Tyler, for once, didn't seem to have any questions. She had it all figured out. She understood love, because her parents loved each other, and her siblings loved each other, and her life hadn't been torn upside down. Her parents hadn't made any mistakes for her to avoid. When Tyler grew up, she was going to be a writer. And a damn good one too, Amy thought.

Tyler had written Amy dozens of poems. Beautiful gold-coated words scratched in gray pencil on dingy notebook paper. Amy had bought a cheap plastic photo album to keep them in. She had reread them dozens of times, marveling at the beautiful turns of phrase Tyler had used.

She had other qualities that would make her a good writer too. She asked the right questions (as much as Amy had made fun of Tyler's "bullshit questions" in the past, recently, she'd admitted to herself that some of them would make quite good subjects for novels). And she noticed things about people. She empathized.

Once, over fish tacos, she'd said matter-of-factly to Amy, "I know why you swear so much."

"Oh yeah?" Amy had said.

"Yeah," said Tyler. "The same reason you used to go to so many parties. You think it makes you more of an adult. Whenever you feel insecure, or whenever someone says something that hits a little too close to home, you swear twice as much."

Amy's first thought had been, *Well, what the fuck do you know, you fucking fuck fuck fuck?* The second had been, *You know, she might have a point.*

Amy wasn't worried about Tyler. Tyler was like her hands, hard and sturdy and strong, and she would pull herself through life.

AMY FINALLY found out what was waiting a few weeks after her eighteenth birthday. It was a drizzly day, and the sand of Hanalei Bay looked dingy and yellow-gray. Amy and Tyler had gone down to the beach to swim (just in the shallow parts, nothing too dangerous) because days like these scared off tourists.

The beach was empty except for Danny Mahelona, a few old people in beach chairs, and a couple of European idiots who were trying to swim out much farther than they should because they'd seen a turtle. A part of Amy wanted to tell them, *Hey, we're just starting to get the turtles to come back after killing most of the population, and we don't want to scare them off, so could you maybe mind your own business?* But she had learned to keep that part of herself tamped down.

Tyler jumped into the water and started floating in the waves. Before jumping in after her, Amy turned around to look at the clouds and shivered, because she felt it, stronger than ever, that sense of impending doom. Like the tiger was finally about to pounce.

When she turned back around, she noticed three things. First, that Danny Mahelona had abandoned his post to chase after the European idiots, who were now in serious danger. Second, that there was a stream of water near the shore that was lighter-colored than the rest, and it was pulling bits of seaweed out into the ocean. And third, Tyler was gone.

Panic surged through her. All her thoughts (everything she'd ever thought, it seemed) jumbled together, like a big ball of yarn, and before she quite knew what was happening, she was swimming along the rip current toward a tiny, screaming brown speck floating out on the horizon (*Tyler*), and the ocean was singing their names.

The first thought that detached itself was, *Fine, Tyler, fine. I'll be your damn knight in shining armor.* And the second wasn't a thought so much as an image, a memory of her mother wrapped around the body of a young waiter from Frank's Fries in the red-and-gold guest bedroom. But that wouldn't be Amy and Tyler, that would never be Amy and Tyler, because she loved Tyler, damn it, they were in love, and it might not be star-crossed love or Disney Princess love or knight-in-shining-armor love, but it was love, and Amy wasn't about to lose it (and God, why had it taken Tyler nearly dying to make her see that?).

And Amy was going crazy, because the water was filling her eyes and her mouth, and she was beginning to see dancing skeletons and hear that damn song, and the ocean was tugging at her, pulling at her, trying to pull her down. But she wouldn't go down, not until she'd found Tyler. She focused on thoughts of Tyler, of the three moles on her back and the way her face was made for smiling. On the poems on dingy notebook paper and the easy way she laughed when other people laughed. She thought of sturdy hands and the taste of hot dogs and doe-brown hair and... *live, Tyler, you need to live, because I've finally figured out the answer to your question.*

That was the only thing that kept Amy paddling through the waves that pushed her back and forced her under. She needed to tell Tyler that she'd figured out what love was. That it was a little bit of heroism and knights and shining armor. And it was a little bit of getting used to people, of staying together for a long while. It was a little bit of a lot of things—it was playlists made of songs that spoke to your soul and back massages late at night and pickup trucks going anywhere but home. And more than any of these things, it was holding on, holding on, holding on and not letting go, and that was what she was doing now, she was grabbing Tyler's hard, sturdy strong hands and holding on and not letting go, and that was the last thing she remembered before the ocean sang her name one last time and everything went black (she didn't remember Danny Mahelona's shouts or his arms around her waist or the sirens when the ambulance came).

In a few days, both girls woke up in the hospital. The storm had broken, the danger had passed, and they were still in love.

ANNIE SCHOONOVER is an introverted high school student in a committed relationship with the written word. When she was younger, she used to carry folders full of loose-leaf paper in the car on long trips. As evidenced by the fact that this short story was primarily written on an iPad during a long plane ride, her methods have not much changed. She also occasionally does things that are not writing, namely debate, angry blogging, and homework. Follow her on Twitter: @AnnieSchoonover.

QUIET LOVE
GIL SEGEV

"He who does not understand your silence will probably not understand your words."

Elbert Hubbard

WE SIT across from each other on the wooden floor of his bedroom, and beyond the open door, the house is silent. And lonely. And sad. When I came in earlier, I plugged my iPod into his speakers and put on a Lana Del Ray album; for a change I couldn't bear to hear nothing but the silence.

Josh and I don't speak. He's not mute, at least not physically, but I haven't heard him speak since we met. I, on the other hand, certainly do; I talk to other people all the time. But Josh's silence is comfortable, to a point.

I had sat close to him when I arrived, closer than I knew he wanted me to, and he moved away. By now I should be used to it, but I'm not. It stung. I shrugged to say *I'm sorry*. He rolled his eyes. *Whatever*.

I keep Josh company throughout the week while his parents are at work, and if the weather is nice on the weekends, we sit in the grassy backyard. I enjoy making food for him, and he doesn't have to speak to show he likes it too. When Mom picks them up, I bring Skittles—our favorites—and he'll take the purple ones after I'm done with the rest of the bag. He's a year younger than I am, but his soul is aching and tired. I think that's partly why he won't use words to communicate. He has seen too much, knows too much… but about what?

My backpack, which I've carelessly tossed onto the otherwise clear desk, loses balance and falls to the floor. I move to put it back, but Josh halts me with a gesture of his hand, as if to say, *It's better off like this anyway*. I nod and sit back down, even though I'm not sure it is.

If Josh was just anybody, I would ask him what he wants to do, or how his day was at that special school he goes to. But he's not just anybody, and besides, I already know the answers. He didn't want to do anything—he never wants to do anything—and he wished today never happened at all. He's never said any of it, but I know. I feel him on a higher level.

He has boyish features for a sixteen-year-old. A petite frame, lanky by all means, with long dark eyelashes that made my few new girlfriends jealous. Going to different schools meant they didn't see him a lot, and when they did, they did not get him. I've only known him for a short time, but it seems nobody ever gets him. "Why doesn't he talk?" "Are you guys dating?" "Does he talk when you have sex?" Ignorant dumbasses.

Josh and I don't talk because there are walls surrounding him that I haven't broken down yet. Or maybe, we just haven't found anything worth saying. He's locked in some miserable existence I can't fathom, and all I can do is keep him from being lonely.

If you asked me to describe myself, I would meet your eyes and tell you that I'm a confused guy who isn't sure about anything but his commitment to keeping Josh company—I mean it.

Josh and I aren't dating, not in any traditional form of the word, at least. Could best friends be the term to describe us? Soul mates? Were we lovers in a past life, in which I was a moody donkey and he was a cheeky alpaca? We never talk about it, obviously. Maybe that's a good thing.

Once, while he was in the bathroom, I looked around his room for any sign of words. A journal, a to-do list, a sticky note with the word *penis* scrawled in childish humor, anything. I found nothing. And yet, there was a blank poetry notebook hidden underneath his bed. I tucked it back, and when he returned, we sat in silence until I had to go.

Sometimes I can see Josh thinking, but other times he's blank, as if he doesn't even inhabit his body. Privately, I loathe his parents for their long work schedules, but I know this is how they provide for his therapists and his extraordinary schooling. He doesn't talk to his latest therapist either, although to her credit, she hasn't stopped trying.

My best bet is that something traumatized him when he was younger. There's no point in asking, because nobody knows, and speculating is as counterproductive as it is heartbreaking.

We met three months ago, at the bus station that is down my road and up his, back in the beginning of June. It was my first time taking the local transit to school, and it was his route as well. Strangers usually don't talk at bus stations, so I thought nothing about the cute boy in the gray hoodie who kept his eyes on the sky and his mouth shut.

We had gotten onto the same bus together, number 75, and sat far enough from each other to be what we were—strangers—and that was that, until the next morning when the cycle repeated. I began looking forward to our time together, as brief and uneventful as it was.

A few days into it, he smiled a little as if to say *Good morning.* I waved back as if to say *And to you.* His blue eyes were strangely expressive, unusually so, and when we dropped him off at the gifted school, I wasn't surprised.

Our silent conversations got more elaborate until he was all I could think about. We gradually sat closer and closer, lessening the space between us, and I would find myself studying his face and looking away when he turned.

Days before the end of the term, just after the bus rolled around the corner, I had lifted my eyebrows as if to ask *What is your name?* And he motioned to his home down the dirt road as if to say *Come.*

When his family returned home that night, they were surprised to find an older boy in their son's bedroom. They seemed tired, pessimistic, and weary.

"Hello, we're Josh's parents."

I knew his name now, but he didn't know mine yet. I walked to them and whispered, as if not to disturb the quiet. "I'm Kevin. I hope you don't mind, but I speak."

BEING AWAY from Josh that summer was hard. One day I was discovering this new guy, and before I knew it, I was whisked off to my grandparents in Maryland while my Mom "broke in the house." But between playing gin rummy with Grandpa and making sure Grandma didn't slip with her bad hip, I kept thinking about the silent boy in the small, old, dirty new town. What was he doing during the hot months? What was he thinking about? Did he talk?

I COME back to earth and look from Josh, who still sits across from me, to the window, realizing time has passed. I don't know how long but enough for the album to have ended. Soon it will be time to go home and carry on with life as I always do come the evening. But for now I have a little bit of time left with Josh. This time it's him observing me as I drift off.

I motion to my backpack, which still sits where it fell, and he blinks as if to say *Go ahead.*

I pull out a yellow plastic bag from the local crafts shop I discovered, dump out a pack of multicolored paint pots and a small, thin canvas.

Josh crosses his arms, raises his left eyebrow, and purses his lips tight, as if to say *Explain this.*

I push the materials toward him, as if to say *Do you trust me?*

We sit in silence until I have to leave, the paints sitting untouched where I put them. In a way I'm glad, but also disappointed. I gather my things, unplug the iPod, and nod to the empty air of the bare room as if to say *Good night.*

AT HOME I shower and get started on my homework, turning up a talk show on the radio as loud as it will go, anxious to leave the silence behind.

My mom walks into the room, looks sadly at the radio, kisses me on the forehead, and retires for the night.

I'm convinced Josh will be angry with me for bringing him the paints and the canvas. I already knew he doesn't want to draw, because pictures represent words, and words are too painful for him. Still, I was hopeful that with the fun colors, he'd want to at least try.

The following day the weather is cloudy and gray, and Josh is absent from the bus stop. He probably got a ride from his parents on the way to work, which happens, although not often. I sit alone on the bus, hug my backpack to myself, and close my eyes.

At school I chat with my friends about things that don't matter too much, but my mind is on Josh. Did he get a ride to avoid me? Was he that upset about what I had done? Standing in the aisle of the store, I thought it would be a good idea, but now....

Around lunch, the sky breaks open, and rain begins to pour. It washes away all the dust in the air and any shard of the good mood I woke up with along with it.

It stops raining in time for the afternoon bus, and when we pass St. Mary's Gifted Academy and Josh isn't waiting on the bench, I begin to feel worried. Is he sick? Did something happen? He doesn't usually go to the therapist on Tuesdays, but who knows?

At our stop I run off the bus, down the muddy street, and knock on the door, panting like I just finished running a marathon. A minute passes, and I ring the doorbell. Still no answer.

I lean against the door, running my hands through my hair in frustration. I could call his parents; I have their number, but what if—

I nearly fall when the door is pulled open, and I find Josh standing silently in the doorway.

He gives me a meaningful look, as if to say *The door's unlocked, smart one.*

I want to get angry. I want to tell him how worried he made me and then hug him fiercely because I feel so relieved. And to be honest, it looks like he straight-out skipped school today. The jerk.

He walks upstairs slowly, and I head to the kitchen to fix us something to eat. When the nachos come out of the toaster oven, I follow him. He is in his room, sitting with his face toward the white wall, and I sigh silently. I put the plate down, plug in the iPod, and put on some song by Marina and the Diamonds. I sit down far enough behind him and watch.

A minute passes, and the silence feels warm and raw on my skin. I want him to reassure me I didn't mess up too much last night, but of course that won't happen. I can't read his face from this position, but the fact he didn't even turn to eat speaks volumes. I close my eyes, feeling miserable.

Moments later I hear Josh shift and open my eyes to see him reaching for something under his bed. I know he keeps everything under there, out of sight, including all his neutral-colored clothes that he refuses to put in the closet. For a moment I'm worried he's got a weapon, but instead he pulls out the pots of paint and sits down on the bed. He motions for me to get closer. The song ends, and I feel stupid and sheepish.

Hesitantly I sit next to him, and he opens the fluorescent orange pot of acrylic. He dips his index finger into the paint and searches my eyes with his as if to say *I want to try something new*.

I don't move away, as if to say *I won't hurt you*.

His loaded finger hovers in the air for a minute, not quite ready to move. There is static energy between us; I can feel it on the hairs of my arms. There's the sharp smell of ozone in the air, as if time itself stands still. Then, finally, he gently brings it down onto my bare arm, the first time we've touched in ages, and neither of us pulls away. He lifts the digit but keeps his eyes on the streak of paint he's left on me, and I reach for the pink pot, as if to say *Try this*. My heart beats fast, unused to this excitement.

What does the orange line mean? *Everything*.

He takes a deep breath and quickly pulls his legs to his chest, as if to say *I can't do that*. I put it down, agreeing with him that maybe we're not ready for that yet. I look at the floor, and suddenly I have words for him. No, not just words, but paragraphs and pages and novels. The sensation is dizzying as phrases and expressions try to crawl out of my brain and into Josh's ears; I never felt an urge like this to speak to him. I take a shivering breath of air, knowing I could ruin everything, but unable—unwilling—to stop myself. This is the moment to be brave, daring, and honest.

"I love you."

The sound of my voice is foreign to his room and to him, yet he doesn't seem angry. The buildup of tears begins to roll down my cheeks, and I move to brush them away before he gets sad. Relief, frustration, adoration. I don't know how long the words have brewed inside me, but they feel so right being spoken. Shouted. Sung.

I want to push him onto the bed, kiss him and touch him, and repeat the three words over again until he really gets it. *I love you.*

He doesn't speak back—I knew he wouldn't, but he gently follows the line of now dry paint with his gaze, his face soft and kind in a new way.

I know. I know.

GIL SEGEV has been writing since he could hold a pen—er, type on a keyboard. Born in Israel, he is currently living in cold, cold Canada. With a passion for storytelling, Gil writes about difficult topics including mental illness and suicide. Don't worry, though, it's not all so depressing!

Gil's ambition is to land a book deal, but until then, he's content with cranking out short stories and complaining about it.

Gil also blogs about fragrance and beauty at www.Nosegasm.com.

THE KING OF
DORKDOM
AVERY BURROW

FROM: Rhea Elizabeth Pearce <rheabeth2@intermail.com>
TO: Wallace James MacIntyre <darkwallace@letternet.com>
RECEIVED: 3 days ago
SUBJECT: The Return of the Living Dad

Hey Wallace,

Something really freaky has happened. My dad came back. The man that I spent all my life wishing to see has finally got his crap together.

I know. It's crazy.

He just appeared at my door and said he was sorry. He wants to spend time with me.... I know this seems redundant, since we kind of became friends due to our missing dads, but it was just so weird. It was like something out of the Twilight Zone **insert spooky theme music**

Mom knew he was coming, I guess. She hasn't really talked about it with me. I think she's having trouble getting her head around the idea of me getting to know him, especially after how he just kind of ditched us.

Anyways, I'm staying with him for Thanksgiving weekend....

Wallace, he lives in your city! It's crazy, and it's impossible and it's something we always talked about. Getting to meet each other? This is amazing. I have my dad's phone number below, so you can call me and we can plan something. I'll be arriving in three days, the Friday before Thanksgiving.

I'm so excited! First, I was really nervous, but look, I know someone where I'm going. Heck, I'm visiting my best friend!

Can't wait to hear from you,

Rhea

EVERYTHING GOES cold, from my fingers and toes, all the way to my heart. I scan the unanswered e-mail for what has to be the thousandth time in the past three days, trying to see if she offered me any opportunity between those paragraphs to chicken out and not call. Her words were so excited, like she couldn't wait to meet me, like she knows I can't wait to meet her.

And she's right. I used to dream about meeting her all the time.

But not here, not in this city where everyone knows me a little differently than she does.

"Molly!" someone calls from just outside my realm of conscious. I try to ignore them, focused only on the much more pressing matter at hand.

Looking back at the old monitor, I read over the e-mail once more, unable to ignore the phone number she left. Rhea Elizabeth Pearce is here, in *my* city, right now! I grab at my hair, unable to decide what to do.

My gaze flickers to the pad of paper and the pens beside the keyboard. I wonder if she's sitting beside her dad's phone, feeling all palm-sweaty as she awaits my call. I loosen my collar. I could get her to come here. We would be comfortable here. We met online in a video game chat room; I guess it would only seem right to have our first date in a gaming store.

Goddammit, Wallace! It's not a date. Why would you think that? You've never ever met the girl in person, and now you think she's your girlfriend? How sick are you? I mean, I know you're freaky, but seriously, I didn't think you were crazy enough to crush on online women.

"Molly MacIntyre!" the voice says again.

I rub my temples. It's Black Friday, but the Game Emporium is just as dead as it always is. Even 20 percent off everything in the store can't bring the infinitely interesting inhabitants of this city to bathe themselves in the beauty of Dorkdom. Shelf after shelf bedecked in all the finery of the gaming world—board games, video games, manuals, everything you can think of about gaming and probably more that you can't.

If I was somewhere else, somewhere packed full of people, I could just ignore the call, run away, and get lost in the crowd. I could pretend I'm not being called by that name that's all wrong. Not that I've ever specified that Molly isn't the right fit. Or that this body isn't the right fit, or that the dresses I get on birthdays aren't the right fit either.

"Earth to Molly. It's Noah calling."

I look up from the computer screen, taking in the light-haired boy in front of me. He crosses his arms, pursing his lips like a duck. The look in his eyes tells me I'm supposed to speak first.

"Hello, Noah. What are you doing here?" I sigh, trying to make myself look busy behind the cash register and the monitor attached to it.

"What about that computer is *so* intriguing?" he asks, completely disregarding my question.

Noah is my best real-life friend. That is, in the loosest sense. He sits with me at lunch, but I'm sure that's just because my food is better than his, and I let him because I don't want to be alone. He plays video games with me, which is something, I guess. At least he has an interest in my all-time favorite topic—*Legend Quest*.

But the moment the popular kids become involved, well, Noah isn't exactly hesitant when it comes to shoving his dear friend, the butchy nerd girl, under the bus.

I pull out a pen and paper in an attempt to look busy. Sometimes Noah's company is comforting, and it helps me feel like less of a loser, but right now I have something a lot more important to focus on. "I'm doing work, Noah. That's what people do when they have jobs."

"No," he says, his beady blue eyes intense. "You never do work here. We're always goofing off."

"If you're here to play *Legend Quest*, you can just go into the back room and turn on the system. You've done it enough times already. I'll be back when I'm done here, okay?" I point with my pen to the back of the store.

"Come on, Molly, what are you hiding?" Noah's gaze flits to something on the counter between us. He snaps out his thin, snaky hand

and grabs the paper I had been mindlessly writing on. I don't think to fight to get it back.

I look up at the clock, wondering when Rhea might have gotten into town. She doesn't know where I live or where I work, but I know that the longer I keep her waiting before I call, the longer it will take her to trust me. And why should she trust me? I am a liar, after all.

"A phone number?" Noah says, holding the scrap of paper up to the light. A number is scrawled over and over, making it almost impossible to actually make out what it says. "Who the heck would give you their number?"

The realization hits me. I'd been writing Rhea's number on a constant loop, ingraining it into my brain.

"Hey, Noah, dude, give that back!" I say, reaching over the counter to snatch it out of his hand. He tries to dance away, but I stretch myself out and grab it.

That's the one thing I like about my body. I'm way too tall to be a girl. Sometimes, if I dress right, people think I'm a guy, just because I'm so tall. I wish people would think I was a guy all the time. Rhea does. She never once questioned it. Even when we sent each other pictures.

It's official. I am obsessed.

"Wow, Molly, you have a *guy's* number? You have a *date?*"

I growl unintentionally. "I do not."

"Have a guy or a date?" he questions, as smug as always.

"A guy," I say, realizing too late that I don't have either. And also that to Noah, I'm just a girl.

Noah blinks. "Dude. You really *are* a lesbian?"

"She's a girl I met online."

"Wait, you mean Rhea?"

"Yes, Noah." I sigh. "I *do* mean Rhea."

"I thought she was totally, like, not a lesbian at all…."

I'm practically bashing my head into the cash register when my boss appears from the back room, carrying a gaming magazine and a coffee mug. He looks at Noah, giving him the old up and down before opting not to greet him.

Noah frowns. "Hello to you too, Francis."

My boss takes a sip from his coffee and splays the magazine out on the counter, pointing at one of the highlighted orange passages. "Did you know that the highest ranked player on *Legend Quest* lives in our city?"

Legend Quest is the biggest massively multiplayer online role-playing game in the world—MMORPG, for those who care. Thousands of people log on every day, create characters, complete quests, fight battles, and make friends from all over the globe. The game has been live for five years. It used to have terrible graphics, and it would freeze constantly. But with the help of its beta testers and some of the best programmers in the world, it flourished into the phenomenon it is today. Francis, Noah, and I are all huge fans of the game, but then, what dork isn't?

"Rad!" says Noah in the way that only Noah can.

I busy myself with the cash register, a blush spreading over my cheeks. I look out of the corner of my eye at the glossy paper.

There's a picture of the earth on the magazine, with many different arrows pointing to spots on the various continents. The arrows are connected to boxes naming the city, username, gender, and hours the person has played. Sure enough, in the biggest orange box is the username I hoped never to see published: *darkwallace.*

"I wonder if he's been in here," Noah ponders.

Francis watches me over the top of his glasses. I catch the hint of a knowing smile on his lips.

I swallow, collar even tighter than before. "Probably," I sputter. "I mean, we have the largest collection of *Legend Quest* merch in the whole city."

Legend Quest might skimp up on the clothing of its female characters, but it doesn't skimp up on merchandising. It's free to join, and the creators say it always will be, but with so many levels that require boosts to unlock, pretty much every hard-core player has bought something in real life.

"Says here the second-highest-ranked player is a chick from Seattle," my boss says, though I wish he'd shut up. "That's pretty cool. Dorkdom needs more women."

"Rheabeth2," I breathe.

Noah looks up from the article. "Wait, you mean you have a date with—"

I cut him off with a glare.

"Seeing as you've already read this, I will bestow upon you the job of organizing the back room," says Francis, offering me a pile of boxes to carry.

I grab the obsessive sticky note with Rhea's number and head for the back of the store. When I can no longer see Noah, I breathe a sigh of relief. Despite his being my best real-world friend, trouble always follows losers who want to be popular.

"Wait, dude," says Noah, pounding on the counter. "I'm not done grilling Molly on the status of her sexuality!"

As I carry the boxes past the bathroom and into the storage, I hear the sound of the door clinking open and people talking loudly. When I look behind me, Francis is already rushing into the back, his greasy black comb-over bouncing in time with his paunch. He grabs the boxes from me and pushes past.

"Customer," he says, as if I haven't noticed. "That would be your call to action."

For a shop owner, he's pretty antisocial.

The voices hit me before I even make it into the light. Loud, obnoxious, and hopelessly hormonal, the boys crowd the front counter, completely out of place in Dorkdom. Noah sidles up to them, hoping to drink in some of their popularity as it permeates the air like their cologne.

"I'm sorry, we're closing!" I say, my voice ending in a desperately female crack, despite the amazing job I've done convincing myself I'm man enough for Rhea.

The hooligans ignore me, knocking over the carefully organized stands at the front of the shop. Noah leans against the counter, attempting—and failing—to subtly pull down his pants enough to match the droopiness of the jerks'.

"If it isn't Molly, the carpet muncher!" hollers the tallest, a greasy blond named Xavier. The others catcall and high-five him.

Noah has seen this game in action before. The look on his face seems a little more horrified now that he thinks he knows I'm really a lesbian. I mean, being a video-game geek is one thing; being a lesbian video-game geek is another.

Obviously, though, everyone has overlooked the sheer awfulness of being a transgender video-game geek who is the highest-ranked player on the world's biggest MMORPG and might also have a crush on an online girl who thinks he's a real boy. With, like, a dick and stuff.

"You wanna hook up later, babe?" asks Jared, a dark-haired guy with fingerless gloves. "I've always wanted to bang a lesbian."

As unmanly as it is, I think I might start to cry.

"Why don't we all do her at the same time?" taunts Xavier. "She looks nasty. She could totally take it."

Jared and the third kid, a vampiric Justin Bieber look-alike, laugh more and congratulate him on his diss.

"Yeah, guys, woot!" cheers Noah. "You tell her."

The Terrible Trio gives him this look that says "Shut up before I kill you," and he does. Just like the faithful little lapdog he is.

Just as I'm about to break down into tears, Francis bursts from the back room, carrying two guns from the real filming of *Galaxy Guns: A Space Operetta*. He keeps them in a glass case, and I've caught him staring at them lustfully more than once. I'm pretty sure this is the first time they've ever been touched.

"Get out!" yells my boss, wielding the two massive guns like he's been trained in professional combat. "Before I shoot!"

"Fuck, man," Xavier says, his face contorting. "Don't get so intense. We were just having some fun."

To my unrelenting joy, undead-Bieber looks as though he might have peed his pants at the sight of the massive fake guns.

"Come on, Noah," says Jared, never once taking his eyes off the guns. "We only came here to get you, anyways."

Noah beams so brightly that I feel sick to my stomach.

"I said, get out of my store," repeats Francis, the otherwise painfully unthreatening.

In a millisecond, they're gone. My boss smiles in triumph, returning with his fiberglass darlings to the back of the store. Noah looks at me, then at the door, then back. I must seem pretty hurt, because usually he wouldn't even look at me twice. The door jingles shut, and I'm completely alone in the store.

I sink down behind the counter and make this sad sort of dry-heaving noise. The situation isn't painful enough for tears, but it definitely warrants a certain amount of self-pity.

If I was a lesbian, I don't think I'd want to cry; in fact, I'm pretty sure I wouldn't. I would be proud of my sexuality enough to accept the beating and go on to woo a thousand women with my Ax of Lesbianism—no, that isn't a weapon in *Legend Quest*, though who knows what the designers will come up with next.

No, I'm on the verge of tears because I'm just Molly the Carpet Muncher, not even manly enough to be Molly the Tranny. Besides, who would want to love an unfinished boy-girl anyways?

Francis appears around the side of the counter, holding his laptop—her name is Ingrid, and she is his one true love; he calls her his Norse Goddess. I will never have anything that beautiful, not with a human, not with technology. I share a faulty, temperamental desktop with my mom—it doesn't even have a name, and if it did, it wouldn't be a majestic one.

Francis leans against the counter. "Don't let them bother you. At least, not here. At school, well, that's their land. They're popular, they have cheerleader girlfriends, they go to parties...."

"Thanks," I say wryly.

"Let me finish," he says. "But here, here is your place. This is Dorkdom—the mecca of the gaming world. This store symbolizes a universe created by and for people like us. And here, you are its ruler."

Its gender-ambiguous ruler, indeed.

"You know, I thought you were a boy when you first applied for a job here."

I don't know how this is supposed to be helping Muncher Molly, but it does help me.

I look up, wiping the tears from my eyes. "You did?"

"Yup." He nods. "I sometimes forget under all those baggy clothes of yours."

I rest my chin on my knees, trying to suppress the glow of a smile.

"When did you realize you wanted to be a guy?"

My heart lurches to a halt.

"Excuse me?"

Francis crosses his arms. "Kid, I've met other transgender men. They are proud and plentiful in Dorkdom. One of the best graphic novelists I know used to be a woman. Now he has a wife, a son, and a penis that he can take on and off whenever he likes."

I blink at him.

"So, when did you figure it out?"

The pause draws out a moment before I realize that he really wants an answer.

"Five years ago. I mean, I guess I knew before that—maybe I've always known—but five years ago, well, that's when it kind of all made sense."

"So you were eleven, twelveish?"

"Eleven."

"Five years ago," he ponders. "That's when the *Legend Quest* beta came out."

I nod. "That's the reason I figured it out."

Five years ago, when the game first surfaced, I saw the ad for it while I was researching online for an English project. I knew the quality was bad, but I was so tired of not really fitting in that I wanted somewhere—anywhere—where I could be what I wanted. I don't think I even knew exactly what that was until it came time to create my character.

The skimpily clad female character appeared on the screen, and I thought *This is what Molly should want to look like.* But I didn't—I didn't want to look like her at all. I wanted to be a massively tall, broad-shouldered man who wore heavy armor all day and could take it because he was... well, manly.

On that fated day, darkwallace was born.

I've been playing every night since I was eleven. It's the one place where I'm respected. I was one of the first beta testers and definitely one of the few who stayed around for the whole go. I am the highest-ranked player on *Legend Quest.*

And I am male.

"So you're darkwallace."

My head snaps to face him. "How did you figure *that* out?"

"Kid," he says, "I catch you playing all the time, but you always close it like you're watching porn or something. If you were a beta tester who still plays now, well, you have to be at a pretty high level, especially if you play as much as you do. And when I showed you that article today, you started freaking out. No one would freak out unless it was their big secret."

The tears are pretty much unstoppable now. "Where did you learn how to do that?" I ask my knees.

"I'm a fantasy RPG guy now, but I used to dabble in some crime and noir stuff." There's a long silence before I feel Francis sit down next to me, gently caressing Ingrid. "Do I call you Wallace now, then?"

I look up at him. "You're not going to fire me?"

"Did you miss all of that?" he says, throwing up his arms. "I'm not going to fire you because you are a man with a woman's body. Dude, you're darkwallace. You're the highest-ranked player on a MMORPG played by people all over the world. You do quests with rheabeth2. She is, like, every man in Dorkdom's fantasy woman. Kid, this is the life. You live the dream. Of course I'm not going to fire you!"

"I know her," I say. "Like, outside of *Legend Quest*. We were both beta testers. We have a lot in common. We're the same age, we're both only children, we both like veggie burgers more than real burgers.... We both don't have dads."

It's Francis's turn to be shocked. "So you two have been friends for, like, five years."

I nod. "She's the best friend I've ever had."

"And she thinks you're a guy?" Francis claps me on the back. "That's awesome! Bravo, little man."

I fish through my hoodie pocket, pulling out the phone number. "This is the problem."

"It's a local number."

"You know that whole thing about her having a missing dad too? Well, hers turned up. Here. In this city. And she's staying with him."

"Right now? Rheabeth2 is currently in the same city as us?" Francis is practically salivating.

I punch him fondly, trying to keep from smiling. "Back off, old man. She's half your age."

"Ingrid would be far too jealous anyway," he laments, earning another punch from me. "So, what's your problem with her being here?"

"Trying to see her will be like a parkour game," I say, illustrating with my hands. "We'll being running and gliding through our friendship, when suddenly, *bam*! Someone who knows me will appear, and I'll have to hide from them to avoid having Rhea find out that I'm a girl. It's too complicated."

"I see your problem. Good thing you have the man who beat *Sleuth's Origin* in twenty-seven hours." He sees my mouth go wide. "This city breeds masterful gamers. Let me see what I can cook up for you and your girl."

Before I can protest, Francis is already leaving the safety of the counter to head for the back room. This counter is like a trench, a place for me to hide as I ready myself for battle. Maybe it's not just this counter, but the whole of Game Emporium; the whole of Dorkdom with its famous transgender graphic novelists, and darkwallace. Maybe Dorkdom is like the trench in my war of gender discontentment.

Just as my brain starts to make everything really deep and metaphorical, the shop door clinks open. I breathe deeply, composing myself and hoping I don't look like I've just been sexually harassed by three mindless teenage boys.

"Oh my gosh," gushes a young woman from the other side of the desk. "Look at this place."

"I was here earlier," replies a man. "I didn't know what to get you, so I thought I'd bring you back."

"You got me a *Legend Quest* shirt, Dad." She sounds like she's smiling. I like it when people talk with their smiles. "That's already way awesome."

Our shop yielded one customer this afternoon, a businessman with a desperately ironic Thanksgiving-themed turkey tie who came to buy things for his *Legend Quest*-loving daughter. I stand, pulling myself up with the counter.

"Hello there...." My voice trails off when I take in the girl. Short, with a wide-but-not-like-fat-kind-of-curvy body. Long dark waves of hair offset by pale eyes. I jump down below the counter, trying in desperation to calm the dry heaves.

Of course his daughter was Rhea. Of course she was. Dorky *Legend Quest*-playing girl with a father who only knows her well enough to buy her a gaming T-shirt. I run my hands through my hair. Rhea Elizabeth Pearce, my best friend—and possibly my soul mate—is standing in my store with her father, who saw me wearing my "Molly" name tag.

The game of parkour has begun.

"Sorry," I say, just as the silence is about to get awkward. "You got me just as I was putting some boxes in the back. The manager will be out to help you in a minute."

I grab two boxes from the drawers under the counter, stack them, and place them strategically so they will block my face. Despite our never meeting in person, Rhea has seen pictures of me, and having them both see me at the same time would be just as bad as us running into the Terrible Trio in a dark alley. Okay, about 67 percent as bad as that.

At the door to the back, I run into Francis, holding a renewed cup of coffee.

"I've got your plan," he says.

"Abort it!" I whisper-shout. "She's out there now! With Ironic Tie Man!"

"Excuse me?" he asks at a way too normal level of volume.

"The man from earlier, the businessman who came to buy his daughter a T-shirt? He was wearing an ironic—never mind. Rheabeth2 is out there. With her estranged father who knows I'm a female. I need you to make them leave."

"What if I just made him leave?"

I push Francis toward the front of the shop. "Just don't let them see me!"

"No, I'm serious, Wallace. This is Rheabeth2. You have to take this chance. Perfect women aren't often come by in Dorkdom—it is its sole fault."

"She goes to Catholic school!"

"One date. I'm not saying you need to *marry* her! She'll never need to know you don't have the right junk."

I cringe, anxiety that she's alone out there with her dad taking over me. "Okay, fine, one date. Whatever, just *go!*"

Francis grins at me. "Do something with your hair, Major Bedhead."

THE BATHROOM at the back of the Game Emporium is cramped and not exactly clean, but living with my mom and our constant messes, hiding in it is no problem. I wet my hands and run them through my hair, experimenting with different styles. Am I going for the foreign boy-band look, or the brooding poet? I spike it and end up looking like a stegosaurus. Frustrated, I flatten it again.

Standing up tall, I look at myself in the grungy mirror. "Hello, Rhea," I try, my voice coming out so low I could narrate a Discovery Channel program. *Manly, but not too manly,* I tell myself. I look back at the mirror, very gingerly. "It's good to meet you, Rhea."

My voice breaks, sounding about seventeen octaves into *female.* I square my shoulders and try out different voices, but after a while, they become accompanied with facial expressions, and I'm not being serious anymore. I wonder what Francis is doing out there, and I have to hope he's failing. Because I know I am.

I turn away from the mirror, running my hands through my hair. This is the worst pep talk in the history of time—I mean, how do you counsel yourself when you know nothing about the opposite gender? I lean in to the tiled wall, hitting my head on it a little harder than gently. I was supposed to have a leg up—biologically, I *am* the opposite gender!

The sudden knock on the bathroom door sends me jumping. "I hope you're not drowning yourself in the toilet," comes Francis's voice, muffled through the door. "I don't think my insurance covers that."

With a decent amount of self-pity, I tell myself that, after today, I can give up because being me is just too tiring. I lean against the door, holding on to it for dear life. "Did she leave?" I whisper. "She had to have left, right? I mean, there's nothing you could have said to make her stay. She wouldn't trust anyone as old as you, especially not with your greasy hair. Crap. Maybe I did want her to stay—Francis, did you get her to stay?"

I can practically feel my boss rolling his eyes through the door. "She's playing *Legend Quest* on my laptop."

I grab the door handle and swing it open as fast as I can. "She's using Ingrid?"

Francis shrugs, undeterred by the door that almost hit him or the fact that someone else is touching his beloved computer. "Our ladies should meet."

I throw myself on him, catching him entirely by surprise. Then, just because I know that taking it slow will make me chicken out, I run down the hall, calling my thanks over my shoulder. When I look back, Francis is just shaking his head and smiling.

SHE LOOKS like a fairy. All pale and glistening in the sunbeam, the dust swirling around her like magical pixie dust. She brushes her hair out of the way, scrunching her face up as she leans over Ingrid's keys, lost in the world of Dorkdom's finest.

I stand there for a moment longer, just taking in her purple-rimmed glasses and concentrated expression. I wonder if I can smell her from over here but decide that trying might be creepy. I shift my weight, and the floor creaks.

When she sees me, her entire face lights up, her lips and teeth and eyes just shining with excitement. It's contagious, and for a moment, my mind can't even grasp why I was so worried to see her. Rhea jumps up, pushing Ingrid to the side far too brusquely, and hugs me. Just like that, before I can object or react or even force out a strained hello, she's enveloping me in this soft, warm embrace. I wrap my arms around her waist, squeezing back—this is a meeting of old friends, even though it almost seems like a meeting of new ones. She's so short that she has to stand on the toes of her ballet flats, and I end up just picking her up and twirling her around, because it feels appropriate. It's not until we stop hugging and step away that it gets awkward.

Rhea blushes, looking exactly like she does in photographs, only more radiant—

Goddammit. I think I might really have that sick little crush on her. Is it really a crime that I think she's cute and funny and smart and beautiful and that she smells good and that we're probably soul mates and I want—

Yes, of course that's bad. We've only just met, and I'm already lying to her.

"You're much taller than I thought you'd be," she says, biting her lower lip.

"Are nerds all short in Seattle?" I ask her, wondering when my feet got so interesting.

She giggles, sweet and melodious. I look up and try and hold her gaze, but it's so hard because we've been friends for so long, but we never had to look at each other. Now there's no computer, and suddenly—

I look down at myself—can you see my chest through my shirt? Like, is my shirt loose enough? Is my sports bra tight enough? Why didn't I ask Francis this? My hands start sweating painfully, and I rub them on my pants.

"I—um—I like your shirt," I say, trying to stop the silence.

Rhea smiles. "The girl who works here has good taste."

"There aren't any girls who—" I stop myself. "Oh, Molly. Yeah. She's cool."

The dark-haired girl looks at me skeptically but doesn't address the start of my ill-fated sentence.

"How are you liking the city so far?" I ask, adjusting all my clothes.

"Mom just drove me up this morning. I haven't seen too much of it. But I do love this game store!"

I smile more because her smile is impossible not to catch. "Yeah, I love working here."

I look around the cavernous store at all the untouched games getting cluttered with dust. The whole store is a bit tomb-y. That doesn't mean it's not the perfect place to work; it just means some of the items need a little more love....

I finally get my awkwardness-breaking idea. "You know what's better than just working here?" I ask, feeling a bit mischievous.

Rhea clasps her hands excitedly. "What?"

"Playing here."

Her big gray eyes get bigger. "You mean—"

I grab her wrist, pulling her away from the desk. "Oh yeah, I do mean."

I turn to Francis, who has stationed himself at the counter. I look at him expectantly, doing my best puppy-dog eyes. He waves me away with his hand. "Yes, Wallace, you can use the game room. *But* no opening games, okay?"

The name sounds so perfect in his mouth that I'm sure one day, it'll sound just as awesome on everyone else's too.

Rhea's face is so bright she's practically glowing. She looks like an incandescent sunflower.

I mentally slap myself for being such a freak.

The Game Emporium's best quality is its game room. It's a tiny space at the back of the store hidden by curtains. A massive TV, three gaming systems, and a solid collection of games to play on them—what more could you want? People rent it out for birthdays, and Francis holds gaming contests in the summer. The best part of my job is the ability to use it whenever I please.

I hold the curtain open for Rhea like I'm the ringmaster of some twisted circus. The enclosure is much larger than it appears from the outside, though the atmosphere is still warm and cozy, with pillows and plush rugs covering the floor. On the back wall, the TV is mounted on top of shelves holding the stacks of colorful games.

Behind her cat's-eye glasses, Rhea's eyes are saucers. She lets out this tiny squeal of delight and bounces over to the shelves. It's a funny and adorable sight because, while she isn't big in any fathomable way, she definitely doesn't have a dainty build, and seeing her dance around like a butterfly makes everything better.

My phone beeps in my pocket, and I wonder what my mom could possibly want. Yes, my mom is the only person who *ever* texts me.

"What are we playing?" Rhea asks in sheer delight.

I shimmy the phone out of my pants. They look loose enough, but my hips are too wide, and the phone is sometimes hard to retrieve from the front pocket. Rhea is practically vibrating with energy.

"You pick," I say, flipping open the device. "It's my treat."

It's not my mom, and it's not Noah either. The text plays in my head in Xavier's throaty voice.

Noah says you have a sick little date tonight. You gonna share?

The breath catches in my throat, and the shiver up my spine is ice-cold, but I ignore it, pocketing the device. I'm living a dream come true, and even those jerks can't make it a nightmare.

When I look up, Rhea is peeking her eyes out from the top of a spy game I don't think I've ever heard of.

"Your phone's really cute."

I stick my tongue out at her. "Your choice of video game is really cute."

She clutches it to her chest in mock defense. "I love spies. I wanted to be one up until I was twelve and realized it required physical finesse."

I take the game from her, chuckling through. "Did you think spying involved lots of sitting on your butt and fiddling with a computer?"

"If it did, I'd be awesome at it."

BY FIVE o'clock, we've already retrieved a stolen painting from the basement of the Amsterdam library, and now we're trying to save Buckingham Palace from a terrorist bombing. That is to say, Rhea and I are on the seventh quest of the multiplayer secret service game. She really gets into it, talking to me like we really are spies. It's possibly the world's cutest thing.

"Agent Wallace," she says melodramatically. "We have thirty seconds to defuse this bomb."

My eyes are squinted, spy-action-hero style. "What wire do you presume we should cut?"

She moves the game controller around so the shears are positioned over the green cord. Her face is so concentrated I have to bite my lip not to laugh. She presses the *A*, and for a breathless second we can't tell if the whole mission is going to blow. The red numbers on the screen stop counting down.

Rhea's face is impossible to describe, but it's adorable. "Wallace, we did it!"

She jumps on me, knocking me to floor.

"Whoa!"

I look up from where she has pinned me to the rug. Her long dark hair forms a curtain around us, separating us from the outside world. She blushes and starts to pull back, but I reach up, brushing her hair behind her ear.

Her lips are slightly open, and they shudder, just a little, as she comes down to meet me. I know I have to close my eyes now—I spent enough nights choking through my mom's prime-time soap operas to know that—but I don't want to. I just want to kiss Rhea with my eyes open so I can see her and make sure it's real.

The butterflies of her lashes flutter shut, and I raise myself on my elbow to meet her, but—

Beep.

My phone goes off in my pocket, and before I can stop her, Rhea is sitting up, her face red. "Um, you should probably get that...."

I swallow. "Yeah, probably."

I imagine Xavier smirking while typing it out. It's not the texts that bother me—I get similar ones all the time. It's just the way that no matter what I do, those jerks seem to burrow their way into my happiness.

Come on, Molly. Don't be greedy.

Rhea and I look at each other. The moment is intense, but in a different sort of way. We were going to kiss—we are definitely not going to kiss anymore.

"Who was that?" she asks, her voice still gentle.

I shudder. "Just a guy."

"What did he say?"

Sweating, I focus my attention back at the screen. I press the controller to choose the next mission.

"Are you good with doing Portugal next?" I ask, the dry heaves coming into my voice.

Rhea's arms are crossed, but she looks more worried than angry.

Just as her mouth begins to move, Francis pokes his head through the curtains that separate us from the store.

"I hope I'm not interrupting anything," he says, the wiggle in his eyebrows directed at me.

"Not at all," says Rhea brightly, though her gaze never once leaves mine.

"I would like to close up now, so you two kind of need to get out."

There aren't a lot of safe havens for a transgender boy to take his secret not-really-girlfriend in a town where everyone knows everyone. I swallow heavily, hoping the expression on my face conveys the fact that I've never been too good at parkour.

"Of course," Rhea replies, picking up her cardigan and her purse from where they had been strewn across the floor. "Thank you for letting us hang out in your shop."

Francis winks at her and hands me the key, disappearing into the drapery. "You kids lock up when you're done, okay?"

I hear the door open and close, leaving us suspended in a pleasant silence. When I look at Rhea, she smiles and bites her lip, looking down at the floor. In the warm glow of her blush, she plays with a single strand of long dark hair like it's the only thing she can focus on.

"I had a really amazing day, Wallace," she says a little shakily. "When you didn't answer my e-mail, I was scared I wasn't going to get to meet you."

Despite all the fear that Rhea would find out the truth and hate me for it, the day has gone magically. "I was just scared that you wouldn't like me."

She looks up. "Five years of us being best friends, and you thought I wouldn't like you?"

"I guess it was stupid of me.... Not many people like me very much in person, I guess." I laugh, but I'm pulling at my collar to try to stop myself from sweating so much.

"I like you," she says, the blush spreading. "A lot, actually...."

I cough awkwardly. "Like, a lot, a lot?"

The air between us seems to be sucked away, and I feel a lot closer to her than before, despite the fact that neither of us have moved. If I leaned in just a bit farther—

Rrrring!

The phone in Rhea's pocket rings with the sound of an old rotary phone. It's my turn to blush as I take a slight step back from her.

"Um, sorry," she says, biting down on her lip as she reads the text. "It's my dad. He wants me home."

"Don't worry about it," I reply. "But let me walk you there, okay? It's getting dark."

"You really don't have to—"

I take her cardigan and lift it for her to put on, like the real gentleman I am. "Don't worry about it, Rhea, really. I want to."

When she says thank you, I know she means it, because her fingers intertwine with mine as she pulls me toward the door.

IN THE late-November evening, everything is dark and tinged with the cold of coming winter. Rhea shivers a little in her light layers, and I take it as an opportunity to wrap her in my too-big coat. Even in the shadows, her smile is genuine.

We keep on the town's one main street, trying to stay in the light of the shop windows. There are a couple of people still out, but many of the small-town folk have already gone home to celebrate the holiday.

"Hey, Molly!" someone calls from down the street.

I stop in my tracks. Rhea looks at me, a little confused.

"Wallace, what is it?"

A ways down the block, under the flickering neon sign of the bowling alley, stands a group of four boys. The smallest raises his hand to his mouth like a megaphone.

"Hey, Molly, over here!"

Noah, you have crossed the line.

"Hey, it's Carpet Muncher Molly!"

"Look, she has a sick little girlfriend too!"

The blob of bodies starts toward us, headed by Noah. His words are innocent, but the hollers from the other three get only more violent and sexual. This isn't my territory—this isn't Dorkdom. There's no one coming to save me, and I realize I deserve it. I thought I deserved to have Rhea, that I deserved to have this one person who could love me as a guy and just as a guy, but how wrong could I have possibly been?

Rhea looks behind us, trying to pinpoint the target of their verbal harassment. I grab her hand and pull her after me down the nearest side street.

"Wait, Wallace, what—"

"Come on, Molly," calls Xavier from behind us. "Don't be selfish! You're gonna have to learn to share your little lady."

I clench my teeth and speed up my steps, pulling Rhea after me.

"Wallace!" she cries. "What the hell are you doing?"

Jared hoots from behind. I turn back and see them gaining on us, strong legs fast in the darkened street. Noah keeps asking them what they're doing, each word sounding more panicked as he realizes the truth of his *friends'* intentions.

"Wallace, why are they following us?"

My breath shakes. "I'm so sorry, Rhea."

A hand clamps down on my shoulder, and suddenly, I'm face-to-face with Xavier. He slams me against the wall of the building next to me. I see Rhea scream as Jared grabs hold of her.

"Why did this little girl call you Wallace, huh, Molly?" asks Xavier, his breath hot and alcoholic on my face. "You haven't been lying to her, have you?"

The words stop in my throat. I choke on the tears that threaten to overtake me.

Rhea is trying to look tough, but she's so small and soft that she's practically a rabbit among a wolf pack. "Wallace, what are they talking about?"

The wolf metaphor is accurate, because when Xavier turns to me, the smile on his face can be described no other way. "I think you have something to tell her, don't you, you little freak? Come on, *Wallace.*" He spits out the name like bad meat. "Tell her."

I sob.

"Don't cry, you fucking queer," says Jared in his hoarse tone.

Noah's voice sounds like hope. "Guys, wait, what do you think you're—"

"Wallace?" The name sounds perfect on her lips. But the more she says it, the more it makes me cry.

"No," I say, forcing back the tears. "Not Wallace. Molly."

The boys laugh in their awful, condescending way. I'm dirt, I'm just dirt.

"I've been lying to you for five years, Rhea. I'm not a boy. I'm not Wallace. I'm just Molly. I'm sorry that I never told you the truth, but—"

I try to see how she reacts to it, but Xavier blocks my entire view of the street.

"But what?" he prompts, face pulled into a toothy snarl.

"But I think…." I swallow. "I think you showed me what I really am, Rhea. In my head, I mean. You showed me that I wanted to be a boy."

Laughter erupts from the Terrible Trio.

"You hear that?" Xavier taunts. "Molly is a tranny. What does her little lady have to say to that, huh?"

"Guys, seriously," says Noah. "That's not cool. If Molly wants to be a dude—"

For a moment, the alley goes silent as everyone turns to look at Noah. Jared is the first to speak. "Not cool, Noah? Not cool is what you're going to be when we tell everyone that you're friends with the freak."

I expect him to just back down like he always does, but instead, he surprises me. "It was one thing before when Molly was just an unidentifiable blob of awkward human, but now, if she wants to be a he, then nothing we can do is gonna stop her."

"You sure about that?" The voice of the third boy provokes Noah to fight.

Like a fist through glass, Rhea's voice shatters the tension. "All of you shut up for two fucking seconds!"

Xavier turns to her, opening up my view, though I'm still trapped and crying.

"I don't know who any of you are, and frankly, I suppose I don't know who Wallace is either. But I know me, and I know that if Wallace spent five years telling me that he was a guy when he couldn't confess that desire to anyone else, well…."

I close my eyes, leaning back against the wall in defeat.

"I'd be pretty damn flattered."

Looking up abruptly, I see five pairs of eyes staring back at me. Noah and Rhea stand united in their defense of me. Xavier and the Undead Bieber give each other a look before shrugging and turning out of the alley like the cowards they are, realizing their hate crime might actually get reported for once.

"Come on, Jared," says Xavier over his shoulder. "There's no point."

Jared shakes his head, still clearly on the warpath. "This little queer thinks that she has the right to be a guy, just like us. That's not how it works. You're born one way, and you're stuck with it."

Xavier's tone is ice. "*Back off*, Jared."

"How?" he says, turning to Rhea. "How can you be okay with the idea that for five years, some chick who thinks she's a guy but, I might add, will never *be* a guy, has been forming some sick little crush on you? And, God forbid, you might have been crushing on her too!"

A silence passes over the street before Rhea speaks, low and level. "I was. I *am*. Wallace and I have something you will never understand, not with that kind of mindset. I care about Wallace more than anything. He has been more than just a best friend to me, and even now that I know he used to be a girl… I still care."

"How can you possibly feel like it hasn't changed?"

"Oh, it has changed," Rhea says, eyes full of fire. "But I still love him just the same."

"Jared," Xavier growls again.

The dark-haired boy looks at each of us, from Rhea to Noah, then his friends and finally me. He mutters something crude under his breath and runs off down the alley, disappearing into the dark and the silence.

Xavier looks as though he knows he should say something but can't bring himself to apologize. He cracks his knuckles and turns on his heels, followed closely by the Justin Bieber look-alike. "See you 'round" sounds like an apology on his lips.

For a moment it's all night and cold and echoing footsteps slinking away. The two people in the world who I would call my friends stand in the middle of the street, looking unsure of whether or not I'm too fragile to touch.

And then I laugh. I just laugh and laugh, bending at the middle and choking out this desperate hiccupping noise. When I look up, the other two are laughing too, because what else can you do? If you don't laugh, you cry, and what point is there in crying when you've won?

Noah reaches down to help me up. He scratches the back of his neck, attempting to avoid eye contact. "I hope you accept my apology, Moll—Wallace."

I nod. "I always do."

"Do you need me here… or…?" he asks Rhea, who replies with a shake of her head. I try and look her in the eye, but her gaze won't quite meet mine, as if to say she's not quite ready.

Knowing that this moment is for Rhea and me, Noah salutes and disappears into the night along with the others.

The two of us watch each other out of the corners of our eyes, trying to find the right space to speak. I step forward, half expecting her to run.

Inhaling a deep breath, I say the only thing on my mind. "I think you're my soul mate."

She just bites her lip.

"I think I'm in love with you. And I bet you think that's weird and messed up, especially because I'm not really a boy, but—I think we're meant to be together."

Another moment passes, and Rhea sighs, rubbing her temples before she can find the words. "You're the nicest boy I've ever met. I think you're sweet and funny and handsome."

But. The "but" is what I know is coming.

"But I… I wasn't expecting this. Any of this. I need time."

And even though I saw it coming, it doesn't hurt any less.

"Can we try this again?" I ask, taking her hands in mine.

"As they say, every gamer has a thousand lives." She smiles.

Tentatively, I open my arms to invite her into a hug that she takes, enveloping herself in my embrace.

"For what it's worth," she whispers, so close I can feel her breath on my neck. "I think we're soul mates too."

AVERY BURROW is a sixteen-year-old writer who hails from Western Canada and has been telling stories since before she knew how to write. A lover of all things LGBTQ and nerdy, Avery is thrilled that the first story she gets to tell in print is Wallace's. She was a runner-up in the category of Dramatic Fiction in the 2014 Scholastic Art and Writing Awards, as well as being a finalist in the Laura Thomas Communications 1st Annual Poetry Contest. Being a part of this anthology has taught her many things, including the fact that Americans don't like one of her favourite letters, the colourful "*u*."

You can follow Avery on Twitter: @averyswrites.

Also from HARMONY INK PRESS

BREAKING
FREE

WINTER PAGE

http://www.harmonyinkpress.com

Harmony Ink

CPSIA information can be obtained
at www.ICGtesting.com
Printed in the USA
FSOW02n0236200716
22759FS